WIGTOWN PLOUGHMAN

WIGTOWN PLOUGHMAN

Part of His Life

John McNeillie

Introduced and Edited with Notes and Appendices
by

Andrew McNeillie

BIRLINN

This edition first published in 2012 by
Birlinn Limited
West Newington House
10 Newington Road
Edinburgh
EH9 1QS

www.birlinn.co.uk

Wigtown Ploughman: Part of his Life by John McNeillie;
'My Grandfather' by John McNeillie;
'Letters from North Clutag' copyright © The Estate of Ian Niall 2012
II. 'Introduction' and notes copyright © Andrew McNeillie 2012
Wigtown Ploughman: Part of his Life first published by
Putnam of London & New York 1939
'My Grandfather' first published in *The Countryman* July 1939
Appendix: 'Letters from North Clutag' first published in
Ian Niall: Part of his Life (Clutag Press, 2007) by Andrew McNeillie

ISBN: 978 1 78027 086 9

British Library Cataloguing-in-Publication Data
A catalogue record for this book is available from the British Library

Designed and typeset by Iolaire Typesetting, Newtonmore
Printed and bound by Clays Ltd, St Ives plc

In Memoriam

SHEILA MCNEILLIE (1920–2011)

Wigtown Ploughman's first reader

CONTENTS

LIST OF ILLUSTRATIONS

INTRODUCTION

Readers who do not wish to learn details of the plot might prefer to treat the Introduction as an Epilogue

John McNeillie's first novel enjoyed startling success, a *succès de scandale*. It divided its readers sharply into those who hated its raw violence and dramatic distortions, and those who admired its poetry and 'authenticity', its truth to life. Inevitably it was nowhere more passionately contested than on its home ground. Few novels are mapped as explicitly to their terrain as *Wigtown Ploughman*. Its end-papers bear a map of the county, naming actual places just as the novel does, not fictions, such as the 'Kinraddie' and environs you find mapped in Lewis Grassic Gibbon's inspirational *Sunset Song* (1932), where only the general location is indicated by 'The Grampian Mountains' or we see that a particular road leads to Stonehaven. This distinctive intimacy drew the people of Wig-townshire into what the Glasgow *Sunday Mail* ('Scotland's National Sunday Paper') declared to be 'The Most Widely Discussed Story for Years' and implicated them in what it had to say. There is some necessary disguise but the novel is more detailed than the map. You could still use it to follow the roads it travels to the places it names.

The *Sunday Mail* ran the book as a serial and so made sure it reached the widest possible readership in the district. The whole thing was so persuasive in its particulars that some believed Andy Walker, the ploughman at its centre, must have been drawn from the life, from a particular individual. One or two were proud or aggrieved to point the finger at themselves in this respect, even many years later. But of course he was a fiction. The farms where he worked – Drumlin, Balturk, Doonhall, Blackriggs – were fictions too, but others mentioned – High and Low Malzie, Clutag, Barness,

Sheep Park, Capenoch – were and are still real enough. A recently discovered report on the book (reprinted in the appendix here) shows the publisher's lawyer concerned at the potential for libel in such an explicit and specific approach. The author's prefatory note carries the standard disclaimer: 'No reference is made or intended to any living person.'

Much else apart, *Wigtown Ploughman* offered an account of the living conditions and lives of the agricultural labouring poor: the cothouse folk and the ill-maintained hovels they occupied. Quoted in hellfire excerpts from pulpits across the shire, it sparked a furore of condemnation, accusation and denial. As what else might they do, the 'unco guid' weighed in against it, deploring it and lamenting the sensationalism of 'Sunday serials'. But many another, like the author's grandfather, found the story of the 'harum scarum plough-man . . . only too true', though much about it, above all 'the swearing', gave him pause at first. (Another relation of the author threw it on the fire, in a dramatic gesture, in front of her children.)

In the wake of the novel, a committee was set up to enquire into the state of housing and living conditions affecting cothouse folk. It found a case to answer and urged new efforts at reform, to implement the terms of the Rural Workers Housing Act of 1938. (The latest version of the Agricultural Wages (Scotland) Act (1937) was also involved.) At one point the issue was aired in the House of Commons, through the good offices of Tom Johnston, Labour MP for Stirling. Of how many novels, first or otherwise, might such things be said?

John McNeillie admired Émile Zola, the great French exponent of 'naturalism', as well as the American realists, John Steinbeck, Sinclair Lewis and Upton Sinclair. His only published piece of literary criticism, devoted to Steinbeck and *The Grapes of Wrath* (1939), appeared in October 1939[1]. Naturalism is an approach to writing requiring deliberate documentary research, such as informs Zola's novel *La Terre* (1887) – 'The Earth' – and was famously

---

1 *The Countryman* Vol. xx, No. 1 Oct–Nov–Dec 1939: 'Rural Authors – 49. John Steinbeck by the author of *Wigtown Ploughman*'. See also *Ian Niall: Part of his Life* (2007) by Andrew McNeillie, pp. 43–4.

undertaken by Steinbeck. No such formal research stands behind McNeillie's book: it fell more by chance than design into a smouldering controversy. But he did fulfil other requirements of Zola's, particularly to write from 'what you know'. Like Zola, too, he had a farming grandfather in his life, in this case: a surrogate father, an acknowledged storyteller, and a down-to-earth hero in his grandson's eyes. Turn to Ian Niall's memoir *A Galloway Childhood* (1967) and the posthumously published *My Childhood* (2004) for accounts of old John McNeillie and life at North Clutag. You will also find in these books – as in others across the range of Ian Niall's writing – some incidents in the fields, and much of topographical interest, germane to *Wigtown Ploughman*.

The *Mail*'s serialisation ran for twelve weeks – a fair period of time in which to fuel and sustain a controversy. The episodes came complete with dramatic illustrations of the vivid life in the book's pages. It also added fuel to the fire by reporting reactions from readers, agricultural workers among them, as well as those engaged in civil and religious life. In this way, a three-hundred-and-sixty-plus-page novel was read very much more widely than it would otherwise have been (at 7s. 6d. – a significant part of a ploughman's weekly wage). Of course the abridgement tended to give preference to those parts of the novel most likely to shock and agitate.

The fanfare and fuss were acute in Scotland but as a first novel the book did not go neglected elsewhere. Its publisher – Putnam of London and New York – even had its delivery van go about the streets of London with 'By John McNeillie WIGTOWN PLOUGHMAN' blazoned on a sign across its roof. There were numerous reviews in the London national papers. So were there to the far ends of empire.

The young man who wrote this book was born not in Wigtownshire but in Old Kilpatrick, near Dalmuir, just outside Glasgow, on 7 November 1916. His father Robert, a native of Garlieston in the Machars of Wigtownshire, had been sent there at about fifteen to an engineering apprenticeship with the firm of Beardmore, on Clydeside. His mother Jean McDougall was born in Govan, and was a Munro on her mother's side. It was said that Nellie Munro was an aunt of the writer Neil Munro (*aka* Hugh Foulis, author of the *Para Handy* stories), though this is disputed by a genealogist retained by Neil Munro's descendants. At any rate Neil Munro and Nellie's husband John McDougall were bosom cronies, often drinking to excess together.

Trying domestic circumstances, around the illness and eventual tragic death from meningitis of his younger sister, led to the young John's being sent to stay with his paternal grandparents, John McNeillie and Elizabeth McGarva. They were tenants at North Clutag farm, a few miles west of the town of Wigtown, a place invisible from any road, in the wilds of the county. Old John McNeillie was born at Stoneykirk in the Rhinns of Galloway in 1865. He had been a blacksmith at smithies across the shire, gradually accumulating means to take on a tenancy. That of North Clutag came up, about 138 acres owned by the Vans-Agnew family of Barnbarroch (another place named in *Wigtown Ploughman*), and the McNeillies took it on.

★ ★ ★

The slow headlights of an occasional motor car might comb the otherwise empty country roads at night. First light might see a milk lorry rattle along carrying churns to the creamery. A donkey engine might serve to grind corn in the barn at North Clutag where not so long before there had been a walk-mill. But the internal combustion engine had many miles to go before it made a difference in the shire and farming was by no means automated. Indeed, the horse-drawn, oil-lamp-lit and candle-powered circumstances at North Clutag, the terms of tenancy too, even down to 1939, scarcely differed from those at Robert Burns's 'Mossgiel' in the 1780s, although at some point in 1938 or 1939 Old John McNeillie is known to have acquired a radio. He would say it 'maistly talks tae itsel' but it brought him news of Hitler and war to which he certainly attended. Encroachments of modernity aside, the McNeillies spoke a rich Scots no different from Burns's own, unless in the matter of occasional Gaelic derivatives not uncommon in west Galloway, or Little Ireland. Burns was their poet.

But the McNeillies were Irish in origin, as were the McGarvas or McGarveys, and *Wigtown Ploughman* plays with the Irishness of the Machars in interesting ways.

Young John was about three when in 1919 he arrived in what was then a time-warped world. Certainly by the age of eight he was back with his parents and younger siblings born in his absence at Dalmuir. The experience and its attendant shocks changed his life forever. Thereafter his driving passion was to visit his grandparents and aunts and spend his holidays at the farm. To him they were his first and dearest family. In 1926 Robert McNeillie lost his job. Times were hard and he ended up going south to look for work. When he found it, with Fairey Aviation, in Middlesex, his family followed, deeply unhappy to be uprooted from Scotland. John McNeillie, the author-to-be, was now twice removed from what he knew and what mattered to him. His brothers both became engineers but John wanted to be a writer. This was largely incomprehensible to his parents. For her part his mother cited the example of Neil Munro as, in her eyes, an alarmingly Bohemian one to follow. Like Munro, when he left school at seventeen, McNeillie joined a local paper, in this instance, the *West Middlesex Gazette*.

He proved a compulsive and compelling storyteller, following on the printed page the oral example of his grandfather at North Clutag, and at some point in his nineteenth year while at the *Gazette* he began work on what became *Wigtown Ploughman*, finishing its first three chapters before he turned twenty. A little more than three months later he had reached chapter eighteen, the nineteenth being undated, and the remainder of the otherwise carefully dated manuscript lost. Given his rate of production – about two chapters a month – it seems likely he would have finished in about May 1937. A typescript of the whole survives. There is almost no difference between it and the hand-written version, as far as the latter goes.

A contract newly come to light was signed with Putnam on 15 October 1938. It is surprising to find that it was for a work then called 'Poor Man Ploughman', a title as yet undiscovered anywhere else in the surviving documents. John McNeillie was twenty-two when *Wigtown Ploughman: Part of his Life* appeared, in March 1939.

It is surely worth saying that twenty-two is no age at all for such a confident achievement. In the copy he sent to old John McNeillie he wrote: 'Dear Grandfather – The book at last. May you read it, enjoy & understand it, and if at times, like Robbie Burns, I have taken liberties and shocked the modesty of those who open its pages to read it, I hope they will forgive me.' Burns enjoys a minor walk-on part in the novel, in the form of a drunkenly garbled recital of 'Tam o' Shanter'. His world might be said to haunt its pages, if not in the sober spirit of 'The Cotter's Saturday Night'. However, the book sounds a cautionary note, wary of 'the romantic who revels in the work of Robert Burns'. Indeed as one reviewer suggested *Wigtown Ploughman* may be described as 'a vigorous counterblast' to Burns's decorous poem. John McNeillie is sceptical and intends to give no comfort to romantics. Domestic harmony is not his theme. His prefatory note makes this plain: 'As for the harshness of this tale . . . there is no need to invent truth. Would you have me tell you a fairy story?' On the other hand he is not sceptical in the spirit of Stella Gibbons but writes with passionate commitment as if her *Cold Comfort Farm* (1932) had never been.

The story *Wigtown Ploughman* tells is of the growth to manhood of Andy Walker, named after his ploughman father. Its plotting is minimal, its trajectory sweeping and full of dark and light, earth and sky. The Walkers – Andy senior and Sarah – married in 'November 1907' – inhabit a run-down cothouse on the Alticry Road, the road to the shore. Their ignorance is palpable, highlighted by violence, underlit by extreme poverty. Sarah dallies with men off the road whom she takes in while Andy's away at his work at Drumlin. Calling home early one day, he discovers her in bed with a shepherd. The shepherd is beaten mercilessly and so is she and thrown out of doors for her trouble.

Later, the shepherd incident behind them, her sister Meg comes to stay (Meg's husband having enlisted with the Borderers) and Andy prefers to bed her. Protest as she might, there is nothing Sarah can do about it. The young Walker boys – Andy and his older brothers Jimmie and Wullie – witness all this and more. When in his turn young Andy marries Jean Cope the violence he visits on her

outdoes even his father's example. For a wild passage of the book in
which he means to murder her, he is regarded by the rest of the
world as 'aff his haid', a madman at large.

Andy senior next joins up with the Borderers and does not return
from the war. We never learn whether he has been killed, or has just
decided to start a new life. Tam Brock moves in with Sarah and a
slightly more benign atmosphere prevails in the cothouse, but with
Sarah ruling the roost with her own brand of irascibility. Young
Andy has been attending Malzie school for some time now. It's not
long before he proves delinquent. He resists the old school dame's
efforts to punish him with fierce kicking and struggling. He scares
his fellow pupils and is never remotely a popular boy. A figure of fun
in his 'faither's oul claithes', he fights for his pride and proves 'a
clever fighter', against all comers.

On leaving school – in 'the summer of about 1921' – young Andy
– 'a little over thirteen' – goes to a job at Drumlin, where his father
had been ploughman. (As suggested, this is very much a story of like
father like son, describing the inescapable trap that is social depriva-
tion and poverty.) His mother dies of a neglected broken leg. The
cothouse is abandoned. Tam Brock goes to Ayrshire and young
Andy, who got on well with him, never sees him again, pointing to
a theme of individual isolation that runs through the novel as a
whole.

The regime under old McKeown at Drumlin is brutal but Andy
works hard and gains the respect of his master. However violent and
unattractive Andy can be, he always earns the respect of his
employers. Whether they be tyrannical or lazy, he never proves
anything less than hardworking. *Wigtown Ploughman* is very much a
novel about work, about labour on the land and its meaningfulness
for the individual, exploitation and hardship notwithstanding. This
is the note on which it ends, in a kind of reconciliation, a possible
turning point. Aspects of old John McNeillie may be seen in the
character of McKeown, as for example in 'his uncanny ability to
foretell the weather'.[2] More pointedly, in his portrayal of McKeown's

---

2 See 'My Grandfather' in the Appendices.

son – 'the docken' – the author clearly chose to settle a score with his
father.

At Drumlin, Andy is eventually joined by Paddy O'Hare,
described as 'Every inch an Irishman, though he'd been born in
the "shire", and spoke its language.' The shire's language is spoken
by the novel too, in a phonetic approximation perfectly tuned to its
task. Paddy is wild and fearless. He laughs affably at McKeown's
ferocities. The old man can't intimidate him. No one can and in his
company Andy has new adventures on 'the lonely roads to the
Whaup, the Port, and Bladnoch, fighting, quarrelling, laughing'.
Paddy at last leaves under a cloud and lures Andy away to join him at
Balturk. There the master Aird is lax and lazy, over-fond of late-
night drinking at the pub in Whauphill or farther afield. This
provides Paddy with ample opportunity to seduce Aird's lonely
wife. Andy gets an inkling of what's going on and extorts money
from her as the price for his silence. She eventually dies in childbirth,
the stillborn infant surely Paddy's.

Both now look to move on, but they fall out and this time Andy
goes his own way, to work for Craig at Doonhall. 'Strangely
enough,' we're told, 'as in the case of his brothers and Tam, Andy
never saw Paddy again.' Craig takes to Andy and brings him on to
work at the plough, so that on his eighteenth birthday Andy Walker
is no longer the boy who milks the kye but a ploughman in his own
right, as was his father before him. He fathers a child – his 'first wean'
– on one Molly Docherty but refuses to wed her. Her father seeks
revenge and there follow episodes of extraordinary feudal violence
from which Andy is lucky to escape with his life and which cost the
Docherty tribe their cothouse.

Craig stands firmly by Andy and clearly cares about him. There is
undeniably something of old John McNeillie to him too. But soon a
court order, brought for the maintenance of Jean Cope and her
brood, takes the greater part of Andy's pay. He turns to poaching on
a commercial scale to recoup his loss. The poaching scenes were
singled out by some reviewers as among the best in the book. In the
end Andy falls foul of the laird's keepers. It takes a peppering of
shotgun pellets in the legs to halt his escape. The court sends him

down for six months. On being released he goes to Doonhall to collect his few belongings only to find Jean has been there before him, presenting Craig with the court order as authority. As a tenant Craig can't re-employ a convicted poacher. Andy must move on. He does so but in a crazed state of mind, determined to kill Jean.

There is much incident. He's caught by the police at last but soon manages to escape. Ever resourceful, he takes to the country and shakes off his pursuers under cover of darkness. The manhunt loses its impetus. Andy encounters a policeman on the road. He talks his way round him, giving his name as M'Courtney. The officer is from Glasgow, knows nothing of local families, and lets him go. So our hero reaches Kirkcowan, a good way to the north west of Wigtown. He sees a job in the *Galloway Gazette* for a ploughman, advertised by 'Yates of Blackrigs'. There he's taken on calling himself Pat Hanlon. As he explains to Yates: 'ma fether wus Irish, bit A wus born up by Stranraer. Ma mither wus a M'Guigan'. His cover story of recent employment at places beyond local rumour in Kirkcudbright, at New Galloway, and then at Creetown, goes unchallenged.

It's not long before things revert to kind, involving a woman and a pregnancy, and Andy's dismissal. He exits towards Glenluce whistling 'The Wearin' o' the Green' – his signature tune throughout the novel, the tune with which the novel ends – with forty pounds stolen from the farmer Yates in his pocket. He enters the boxing booth at a fairground, acquits himself well against the 'Battling Tinsmith' and is offered work as a boxer for twice what he'd earn at the plough. He accepts but then the counsel of an older man prevails and he slips away, back into the country to look for work, once again as Andy Walker. Something in the lyricism of the old man's account of life on the land captures Andy's thought and memory of 'things he had noticed as a boy'. It is the nearest the novel comes to transformation.

The old man put his hand on his arm. 'There's nae finer place, boy, than working in the fiels. There's jist you an' the Lord God and the green grass. Nocht metters. Folks in the toons haes tae work bi' the clock, but in the fiels there's nae clock bit the sun.

There's aye anither day tae work; there's the hills and the dykes lik' they wur whun yer granfether wus a boy. Bit ye gang tae the toon an' ye're aye wonnerin' whut time o' day it is. Every man is lik' the next. Everybody eats an' sleeps at the same time. They ken nocht aboot the fiels an' the wee birds, the snigger o' a horse, whaur fairy tatties grow or whaur the hare beds in the holla.'

The sentiments here were never far from John McNeillie's mind. Nor should we forget the quieter pastoral interludes in the novel itself. These range from entire chapters (VI and VII deal with farm work) to briefer episodes, at the plough, or such as those in which young Andy walks the moss for 'whaup eggs', and crosses ploughings for those of the peewit. He fishes the burn. In springtime he haunts hedgerows for birds' nests, and in autumn gathers mushrooms or picks blackberries. There is much that might be fairly construed as autobiographical here. John McNeillie attended Malzie school. The two books Andy Walker takes an interest in at school, *Robinson Crusoe* and *Swiss Family Robinson* were boyhood passions of the author. Young John McNeillie roamed the country: here, there and everywhere. He later became the bane of the Barnbarroch gamekeeper William McGowan's life (McGowan a relation by marriage to the McNeillies). There is also the prefatory note to the book to weigh in which McNeillie asserts that 'Only those who live near the soil can see true beauty when it is before their eyes. I make no ambitious attempt to give a conception of hidden beauty, but offer a humble story of the things that the eyes of thousands have seen in the country, and, I fear, their minds have forgotten.' In some respects such 'humble' stories would become the author's life work.

Violence apart, there is much in his future writings that is earthed to this first book. But it was a book he would soon come to scorn and to reject as crude and an embarrassment. If he ever intended to write a sequel as might be implied by its subtitle he quickly abandoned the idea. Not that he abandoned violence on the page. It is the mainspring of several of his subsequent fictions, from John McNeillie's *Glasgow Keelie* (1940) to Ian Niall's *No Resting Place* (1948). At least one reviewer considered him a 'specialist in violence'.

No Resting Place was the first book to appear under his pen name. (Few if any beyond the family and his new publisher Heinemann connected Ian Niall with John McNeillie. It was as if the latter had been a casualty of war.) The next work of special note was the classic *The Poacher's Handbook* (1950). Both books are significantly of the Machars. But as if in reaction to the specificity of *Wigtown Ploughman* and what it entailed, the tale of the Kyles – traveller folk – told in *No Resting Place* is not directly pinned to any place or map. The trained eye and ear acquainted also with a knowledge of Machars family names – such as Craig and Kyle – might none the less realise from the book alone that it too belongs in and to Wigtownshire, and not at all to Ireland and Co. Wicklow, where it was made into a remarkable film by Paul Rotha, with a cast of Abbey and Gate Theatre players.

John McNeillie might have rejected his first novel. It is an author's privilege to do so. There is no reason why we should. On the contrary there is every reason for taking it seriously as did the world it entered, in terms of social commentary and actual politics, as well as from a literary point of view. An almost exhaustive collection of the numerous reviews devoted to this debut novel is provided in an appendix here. So are the deliberations of the committee established in its wake to investigate the state of rural housing in the area, together with reports on the controversy and letters to the press.

In literary historical terms we must acknowledge the example, already alluded to, of Lewis Grassic Gibbon – James Leslie Mitchell. He had died in February 1935 (our author was then eighteen). Although McNeillie did not aspire to Grassic Gibbon's mythological and poetically heightened approach, he knew and revered *Sunset Song*. As may be seen, several reviewers compared the two works, and *Wigtown Ploughman* didn't always come off second best. Given the standing of the competition, it stood its ground well.

One or two chose to detect and lament the legacy in McNeillie's book of *The House with the Green Shutters* (1901) by George Douglas Brown. But this seems to me a more tenuous matter not attuned to the wild and poetic spirit of the later book. By the strangest of coincidences *Wigtown Ploughman* was published in the same year as James Barke's epic – set in the Rhinns of Galloway – *The Land of the Leal*. The two books might not share scale but they occupy neighbouring and related terrains and have much in common as to the depiction of agricultural life and its associated hardships in southwest Scotland, in the first half of the twentieth century. Together with these books, and in its different Melvillean manner, also *Gillespie* (1914) by J. MacDougall Hay, *Wigtown Ploughman* makes an important contribution to our understanding of Scottish regional life in the period before the Second World War. Such novels by Neil M. Gunn as *The Grey Coast* (1926) and *Highland River* (1937) belong powerfully in this picture too. A wider context might also include the work of Thomas Hardy (whose mapping of Wessex is also worth bearing in mind). Like Andy Walker, Hardy's characters Tess and Jude are never allowed to escape their inheritance. It is hard not to sense Thomas Hardy's presence somewhere in the wings here. The Irish poet Patrick Kavanagh is a different case. But he comes forcefully to mind as a figure haunting ahead, at the headland towards which Andy Walker ploughs his furrow. The author of 'The Great Hunger' shared with John McNeillie a deep suspicion, illuminating to consider, of romantic notions about the real, laborious nature of life on the land. The world of the Welsh poet R. S. Thomas's Iago Prytherch – a direct literary cousin of Kavanagh's Maguire – also comes to mind here. A step further and we are in the world of Seamus Heaney and the mythical groundedness of Mossbawn. The very Irishness of the Machars and its presence in *Wigtown Ploughman* gives added, revelatory force to such allusion. So does Heaney's idea of 'local work'. It would be hard for a novel to be more locally attached than this one and empowered by being so.

This new edition uses on its cover the image commissioned from Robin Darwin for the original dust jacket. Darwin was a figure well-established in the art world, a principal of the Royal College of Art (as well as a great-grandson of Charles Darwin). He would produce the jacket artwork for McNeillie's next two books. Although it is nowhere stated the image here clearly alludes to one or other version of the Biblical text: 'No man having put his hand to the plough, and looking back, is fit for the Kingdom of God' (Luke 9: 62). So the cover with its ploughman looking over his shoulder passes oblique judgement on Andy Walker as deliberately the book itself does not. There is a further interesting aspect to Darwin's illustration. It seems to acknowledge Max Beerbohm's caricature of 1904: 'Robert Burns, having set his hand to the plough, looks back at Highland Mary'. In this instance the equivalent of 'Highland Mary' is just round the corner, on the spine of the book.

Putnam's blurb on this same dust jacket compares the book not with a Scottish example but a Welsh one. This was well before McNeillie settled in North Wales, where he would live for most of his adult life and write the great majority of his books, his mind set directly due north across the Irish Sea to the Machars. Putnam saw the novel as one 'describing a remote part of the British Isles with the truth and strength of Caradoc Evans's *My People*'. Evans's book came out in 1915. It scourged the Welsh in a series of stories of brutal peasant life and hypocrisy and earned him the title 'the best-hated man in Wales'. There is no doubt that for a while at least McNeillie was very well hated by some people in Scotland. But the comparison is misleading. As we know, McNeillie does not preside in judgement over his characters. He offers in his own words 'something of the best and the worst in them'. We might question the proportionality here but in true 'realist' spirit, John McNeilllie leaves it to his readers to come to whatever conclusions they wish. Which is now open for you to do.

ANDREW MCNEILLIE
March 2012

NOTE ON THE TEXT

The present edition has been keyed and proofed from the original, itself a remarkably clean setting from a typescript that does not differ substantively from the surviving nineteen manuscript chapters. A very few typos in the Putnam version have been silently corrected. The occurrence on p. 139 in the original edition of 'whisky' and 'whiskey', apparently from the same bottle, has been left to stand as a happy accident reflecting the cultural and racial mix of the Machars (see p. 87). Both spellings occur across the published book and in the surviving typescript. I have left as given in the original map the misspellings: 'Garieston' for Garlieston and 'Monrieth' for Monreith.

ACKNOWLEDGEMENTS

I owe great debts of gratitude to Professor Alan Riach of Glasgow University and to Dr John Brannigan of University College Dublin for their enthusiasm for this project and invaluable conversations about the novel and my brief introduction to it. Similarly I am grateful to Professor Fiona Stafford of Oxford University for her support and for the inspiration within her landmark study *Local Attachments: The Province of Poetry* (OUP, 2010). I thank warmly Tom McCreath of Home Farm, Garlieston, retired farmer and noted local historian for help with key information; similarly I am grateful to my cousin and memory-woman Jean Rennie of Kirkinner. Thanks also to: Gillian Campbell of Newton Stewart; Linda Galloway of Whauphill; John and Mary McNeillie, and Janette McNeillie, and Alan McNeillie, of High Balcray; Madge Vance of Whithorn; and last but far from least my wife Diana McNeillie.

Jean Rose provided remarkable hospitality and help with the Putnam and Heinemann publishing files in the University of Reading Library and Archive. She unearthed the Libel Report published in the appendices here and brought it to my attention. For permission to reprint the Report I am grateful to the University of Reading Library and Archive, and to The Random House Group Limited for their co-operation. Sally Harrower of the National Library of Scotland, where the John McNeillie papers are now housed, generously performed some last-minute checks.

Above all I must thank Adrian Turpin of the Wigtown Literary Festival for suggesting such an edition and Hugh Andrew of Birlinn for backing the idea at once, with great enthusiasm. I also thank warmly my editor Andrew Simmons; Liz Short of the production department; and Tom Johnstone.

WIGTOWN PLOUGHMAN

Set in the Machars of Wigtownshire, Scotland, and particularly in the locality of Malzie school, the Malzie farms and the district bounded by Wigtown, Kirkcowan, Mochrum, Portwilliam and Sorbie, this is the story of part of the life of a ploughman, son of a cotman. Cotfolk are the dwellers in the small stone cottages which house the agricultural workers of the north. Part of the life of a simple man of the soil, this story refers to no particular ploughman, for all are not great fighters, poachers, drunkards or wife-beaters. This story is an attempt to portray something of the best and the worst in them.

Only those who live near the soil can see true beauty; few can know beauty when it is before their eyes. I make no ambitious attempt to give a conception of hidden beauty, but offer a humble story of the things that the eyes of thousands have seen in the country, and, I fear, their minds have forgotten.

The text will clarify the dialect, which has been written phonetically as far as possible. Geographical detail is more or less preserved, although, for the sake of the story, farm names and names of characters have been invented to suit what is purely fiction. No reference is made or intended to any living person. As for the harshness of this tale . . . there is no need to invent truth. Would you have me tell you a fairy story?

CHAPTER I

CORMORANTS stand on the rocks of the Portwilliam shore of
Luce Bay. Long-necked, ungainly black birds, they stand there
while the incoming tide creeps up the shore and mist drifts across the
bay and up the glen to the Alticry lodge. When the rocks are awash,
the birds rise and fly slowly, less than three feet from the surface, out
over the water, where they vanish into the mist. The gulls remain
afloat on the swell and great waves crash with thunder on the shore.
The crash echoes up the cliffs and fades into a soft sigh.

When the cormorants come back through the swirl of the mist
they are flying higher. Their arrow formation mounts into the rain;
wings beating fast, then pausing in a glide. They rise above the shore
and the heather slopes that run down to the sea, pass over the fir and
spruce wood that shelters the Alticry road as it falls to the beach, and
fly on over green hills and white-washed cottages nestling beside
stacks of peat.

This stretch of Wigtownshire, the Machars, sticks out like a spear-
head into the sea and is bounded by Luce Bay on one side and
Wigtown Bay on the other. Cormorants fly often across from the Bay
of Wigtown to the Luce Bay, crossing rough moorland, smooth red-
earthed country dotted with quiet farms and small plantations, artificial
coverts for the pheasants. Like black geese, the cormorants seem, only
that they make no sound, flying unheeding of the life of man below.

Running eastward from Alticry, the hard grey road winds by a
lattice-windowed lodge, a stone cothouse, a lonely school, and four
or five farmsteads, before it reaches High Malzie. There is a signpost
at High Malzie pointing the way to Whauphill in the south. Ahead
lies Wigtown, but first the road throws off a branch to Kirkcowan
on the left, and afterwards passes a cluster of houses named Hillhead,
standing up off the roadside on the right. Farther on is Barness farm

overlooking the Bladnoch, which winds away northward to Kirk-cowan. Bounded by stone dykes, the road rises and dips till it drops suddenly to run beside the Bladnoch to the straggling village of Bladnoch itself, where the water streams under a bridge to meander between muddy banks to the sea.

Back along the road, past Hillhead and round the bends to the High Malzie signpost; retracing these steps up the road toward Alticry, can be seen, now on the right hand, the ruins of a cothouse, just past the dwelling of a herd, where the mossland stretches into the distance like the soft brown skin of a deer. Only the walls at either end of the ruin are standing; a monument to the lives of cotmen a hundred, perhaps two hundred, years ago. The stones where once there was a fireplace are blackened with the smoke and heat of fires that fell in dusty embers on bygone winter evenings. The broken remains of slates and glass strew the floor, and weeds grow between the stones of the crumbling walls. The place is desolate and scarce a soul passes it in the course of half a day. The mossland to the north is a barren expanse of peat holes and heather banks, while in the south its tail-end meets the sweep of the hills and woods.

It was in this ruin, on the edge of loneliness and time eternal, that Andy Walker lived with his wife Sarah in 1907, but it was no ruin then. The walls were white, the slates intact, the windows cracked but whole. The shaws of potatoes littered the garden; hens scraped in the furrows, and a lean, half-starved collie slept on a stone flag at the door when it was dry. The garden was fenced with strands of barbed wire, to which clung tufts of sheep's wool; the rails of an old iron bedstead, an ill-built dyke, and three thorntrees.

It was not strange that Andy, a ploughman, should live back there where only shepherd folk or herds lived. He worked at the farm of Drumlin, a hilly place off the Alticry road some three miles from his cothouse. In November 1907 he brought his wife there after their marriage. She had already borne him two sons out of wedlock. One was a strong boy of five and the other was three. It caused little stir that Andy should marry Sarah, for many men did not marry until their intended wives had demonstrated their fertility, intentionally or carelessly, once, twice, or even three or four times.

Sarah was pregnant in the summer of 1907, and in November another son came. With no ironical intent the first legitimate child was blessed with his father's name. They named him Andy Walker. The other two were James and William, although to their father they were Wee Jimmie and Wee Wullie.

Andy Walker, ploughman, was short and thick-set, with black hair. His rugged face was always adorned with a black stubble. Yet the stubble, by virtue of a weekly shaving with a none too sharp razor, never developed into the promised beard. Andy was a good man, a grand worker, not too often drunk, but hard on his wife. Sarah at twenty-five was a great fat wench. She had borne eight children. One had died and five in all had been fathered by Andy. Her lawful husband, as was the custom, forgave her previous follies and stipulated only that the results of her former adventures in love did not eat the food which he worked for or share the roof he provided for her. And was this ungainly baggage his first folly? – there were stories bandied among the gossips of the countryside of three or four women who had mothered his seed; of five children in all that he had sired when the down of youth was still on his chin.

Born in a cothouse near Stranraer, Andy had served many masters before coming down to the Machars. He had since ploughed for the McDowals, Kellys, Pattersons, Littles and Craigs. At twenty-eight, when his indiscretions loomed larger in his mind than ever before, he took Sarah Todd, the redoubtable servant of a farmer near Newton-Stewart, to be his wife. The marriage was celebrated in the style of the cotfolk, with drinking, brawling, arguing, singing, coarse joking and uncouth laughter in the cothouse that the two made their first and only home. Twelve men, eight women, and three or four children crowded the small dwelling.

Some were sick, all, even the pale-faced children, were drunk. There was laughter and ribaldry until the early hours of the morning, and Andy was not sure for a week or two whether his wife had slept her first night with him or one of his bosom cronies. Yet even that, had he been sure of the offence, would scarcely have disturbed him. For better or worse they had taken each other and for

better or worse would they remain together. At least that was his
feeling when they were first married.

The child Andy was born when the ploughing was at a standstill.
At birth he was a yelling red lump of flesh that tore and struggled at
his mother's breast like the overgrown calf at the teat of the cow. No
doctor attended the event. Instead a 'freen' from the Port sat with
Sarah in the dim light of the November afternoon while she
laboured. Andy cut the shaws and lifted turnips on the hill above
Drumlin, for the plough was at the smithy. Sullen in face of the
visitor's knowing looks when he came in at night, he sat down to
untie his sweaty boots with only a word of enquiry as to whether the
thing was a girl or a boy.

With his father asleep on the floor, his two brothers restlessly lying
by his side, Andy the younger first saw the light on a Sunday morning
when the rain lashed the windows and the wind howled round the
four walls of the cothouse. The room stank with the odour of
unwashed bodies, a dirty collie, dungy boots and damp clothes. It was
a wet, cold Sunday when no dinner, scant meal at best, was served;
when the door was only opened as his father went to relieve himself,
or empty a handleless pot that served the sick woman as a commode.

Half the day had passed when Andy drew his damp tweed
trousers over his hairy buttocks and tucked the tails of his grey
flannel shirt between his legs. At once roused out of the stupor of its
sleep, the collie rose and slipped out as Andy opened the door to
heave the contents of the pot over the potato patch. It returned
again with its hair matted with rain and mud when he went for the
third time to perform the same duty. It was into this atmosphere that
Andy, the baby, was born.

Nothing untoward in the type of household in which he first
breathed the humid air of life. From the Isle of Whithorn to
Glenluce, from Loch Ryan to Glen Trool and Creetown, throughout the length and breadth of the Lowlands and Highlands of his
rugged native country, the same cothouses stand as the birthplace of
thousands of humble folk of the soil. The same squalor, the same
one-roomed dwellings with cracked tile, or rough earth floors;
untidy fireplaces, torn clothes, creaking bedsteads, faded willow-

pattern crockery, smoked ceilings of wood, and the same pungent smell of baby napkins.

It is strange how the poor folk of the earth, living on the meanest of life's requirements, seem to thrive and reproduce, coming up again in the next generation stronger than ever before.

His mother, untidy, slovenly, bedraggled creature, was in keeping with her household; one of hundreds of cotwomen. Creatures of toil, cow-like solidarity, placid, unthinking females mated to hairy, wiry men who work under the open sky and ask nothing of life but to be allowed to live. Their toil is wearisome and endless. A battle waged year by year with the wind and the rain. A fight for a good harvest, hoeing in the chill days of spring and working in the broiling heat of midsummer, turning hay and forking sheaves.

None, except the romantic who revels in the work of Robert Burns, would expect the son of such people to be unusually brilliant. The opened eyes of the newly born Andy held no sparkle of promised genius. His head was small, even for a baby; the thin legs kicked feebly from the red flesh that was his body, and the surest indication that the creature was born of higher intelligence than a calf was the ferocity with which its hands clawed at the breast of its mother. Sarah had lost interest in it; it was the result of so much pain and discomfort, nothing more.

It had to be fed, and when it cried she gave it her breast. No such thing as chivalry prompted the father to sleep on the floor for a night or two. Chivalry was far above the finest aspects of his character. The coldness of the floor was preferable to the bed which smelt strangely like the byre at calving time. The groans of his wife from time to time, and her restless shifting about on the torn sheets, would have made sleep impossible.

Unable to lie still on the floor any longer, he rose just before dusk and struggled into his jacket. Half a day lying on his back was irksome to a man whose normal days were spent cleaning stables, wheeling great barrow-loads of dung, ploughing, harrowing and trudging along sodden furrows with his boots weighed down with clinging soil so that they could not have been heavier if they had been lead.

The strong smell of his pipe drifted across the room as he slid his feet into his boots. He did not trouble to tie them but tucked the laces into them and clattered over to the door. The peats in the fire blazed suddenly as the draught rushed in and dust rose from the embers to float in white flecks over the bed. His wife, as she reached down for the milk jug by the bedside, heard him spit even above the roar of the wind. He coughed and cleared his throat with a hollow grunt that might well have been the cough of a sick cow in the byre.

The two boys wailed with hunger, but their mother was too fatigued even to call to them. They prowled round the room and dragged a half-empty jam-pot from the table. It slipped and fell with a crash that made the baby start. They sat down beside the broken pieces, dabbling in the jam with their grubby hands and sucking their fingers. When all was quiet once more, the woman in the bed fell asleep. Her sons finished the jam. The hairs of the dog, picked from the floor with the gooseberry pulp, were sucked down their hungry throats. Then Wee Wullie discovered a hole in a sack of potatoes that stood in the corner. These they gnawed with quantities of the black earth from the bogland in which they had been grown.

There were many such dreary days in November, for it was a cold and wet month. A few days after the birth of Andy, Sarah was on her feet again; not that the cothouse was cleaned, but the fire was brighter; the dog was turned out in the morning; the strong smell of life was dispelled when the freezing blasts of wind were admitted as she opened the door. The ancient clock on the wall ticked again after she had balanced somewhat unsteadily on a chair to wind it; life went on as before. Her husband came home in the dark with horses' hairs clinging to his coat and the smell of their sweat on his hands. He would light his pipe and doze in the firelight with his socks steaming on his feet. The three children were asleep when he returned each night, bringing with him the rain from the fields. It trickled from his leggings and topcoat and formed a pool behind the door where he hung his outer clothes on a nail. His dark face glowed with the cold and his ears stood out red from the sides of his tweed cap.

At the end of the month the weather changed. The swamped land froze solid; the north wind chapped the naked face and hands, and the turnips in the field snapped off when men tried to pull them. Only in the sheltered fields were they able to plough. Andy ploughed under a clear sky. Not a mist or rain came with the wind for weeks. The puddles at the stable door were solid like white marble. On the icy roads horses slipped and skinned their knees, and many a high-stepping trotter that had been the envy of the countryside had to be shot where it fell on the brow of glassy hills. It was the hardest frost in years. Milk in cans froze overnight and there was no water to be had.

Wee Andy was unaware of it all. He lay snug beside his mother's warm body, crying when he was hungry, and wetting the sheets when fed, so that his legs became fired and sore for want of attention.

It was poachers' weather. There were fine moonlight nights when a man could see almost as clearly as in daylight, and the shadows by the fir woods were deep and friendly to those who wandered abroad hunting for game. Andy prowled with his dog and gun in search of rabbits, hares, roosting pheasants, or even a cock from an unlocked fowl-house. Shooting by such bright frosty moonlight was simple, and when the iron pot bubbled at night the tempting flavour of a mixed stew mingled with the other odours of the cot-house. Snare wires hung in a bunch behind the door and a dozen wooden pegs dried in the oven. In a box covered with wire netting were two red-eyed ferrets. Wee Wullie, who was particularly interested in them, was bitten badly for his pains and brought the house down with his screams for an hour afterwards.

Once poaching gets into the blood of the countryman he cannot resist the lure of frosty nights when the moon shines. When he can walk over hard-frozen furrows; steal along the shadow of a hawthorn hedge between one and two in the morning and lay the long nets, whistle the dogs softly, and lift the squirming bundles of furry life from the meshes. With the moon on the windows of his lonely cothouse he lies unsleeping on his bed. He watches the stray clouds that flit across the lime whiteness of the moon. He sits up and gazes longingly across the hoary fields and imagines the bag that awaits him in the quietness of his favourite glen.

Then, if his blood is thick and has a trace of the adventurous spirit of his wild forefathers in it, he will rise, pull on his clothes in the chill shadows of his bedroom, put a string through the collar of his dog, and roll his nets. No one sees him as he opens the door, which through the day creaks and grates along the tiles, yet in the 'wee sma' 'oors' opens with magical silence. His heart beats fast; his hands tremble and his boots clatter for a moment on the stones by the door. Maybe the hens in the nearby shed scold him for disturbing them, with that strange crooning sound that is half a whistle; or a fence will squeal its protest as he straddles it; maybe the iron shod on his heel roots a stone from the grass; but he hurries off into the ghostly moon-light with the night air reviving a sleepy body.

There were nights when Andy lay in his bed but little, when he crawled up ditches and stole along the lonely dykesides. The misty beams followed his dark outline through the marches of Malzie, over the hills of Clutag and into the shadows of Barnbarroch woods. The beams found him in the quiet fields of Sheep Park or by the burn at Capenoch, his collie tripping daintily by his side, the nets hidden by the roadside or amongst the whins, and a heavy bag across his back carrying thirty or forty rabbits to the shed behind the cothouse. Four pheasants roosting close together on the low branch of a fir tree, or a curious hare standing in silhouette on rising ground were marks for his shots.

Who heard the roar of the gun in the wildness of the mosslands, or who cared if their slumber might have been disturbed by the crash of a stone falling from a dyke near at hand? No one heard the excited yelp of the collie as the rabbits ran blindly into the stretch of net, or the whack of the experienced hand as it broke their necks.

A nine-mile cycle ride to Newtown with seed bags full of coupled rabbits was a profitable journey at four o'clock in the morning. Often the bodies were still warm as the bike sped into the sleeping town to a house where the dim light burned and the goods were delivered and purchased. A brief greeting; the emptying of the bags; price quoted; reduced, and accepted; another brief farewell after a pause to light a pipe, and the bike would speed away down the road again. A note or two crinkled in the pocket. There was the exhilaration, the profit, the adventure and the thrill of it all, to urge him to do it again another night.

Andy's days were tiresome, half asleep in the stable at dinner-time, wearily jolting along the furrows behind the plough in the afternoon. In the evening home to bed till the moon rose and then up again and away across the quiet hollows, through drowsing farmsteads bathing in the light of the clear night sky.

CHAPTER II

WHEN Andy was one year old and crawling the floor of the cothouse between attempts to walk, Jimmie, who was five, first went to school holding seven-years-old Wullie's hand. They walked down the quiet road to the signpost at High Malzie and on to the other post pointing the way to Kirkcowan on the left. Down the Kirkcowan road past Low Malzie is the smithy, the bridge over the bubbling Malzie burn and then Malzie school. You could hardly call it a village, that little cluster of grey houses. There is, on the north side of the burn, the schoolhouse and a ploughman's cothouse; on the south side, the smith's cottage. Beside the smith's dwelling is another cottage and across the road from this is the smithy itself, standing on the bank of the burn. They are a dilapidated lot. The smithy has a slate roof and a chimney, but the smoke not only comes from the chimney, but through the chinks in the roof as well.

At the door, which is adorned with carved names, stand red-rusted ploughs and broken reaping machines, bits of grubbers, harrow teeth and irons of cart-wheels, whose owners have died long since. The ploughs are incomplete. Days have been when ploughmen have brought their ploughs in carts for repair, and pieces have been taken from the collection of worn-out ploughs at the door. The reaping machines, too, are minus many parts. The burn, a strong flow of peaty water from the moss all the year round, is, at this point, fairly shallow and on its bed lie horse shoes and scraps of iron, thrown there by idle youngsters, who, on coming to school, spend hours round the smithy doors.

The smith's house has a fence round it and, at the front, bushes and flowers grow so thickly that the windows are obscured. A long potato patch stretches into the wood at the back. The wood stands on both sides of the burn and finishes at the back of the school. The potatoes thrive there in the damp shade of the firs. In every tree-top there is a dark building of sticks and twigs, either an abandoned crow's nest or one in the making. The burn above the wood has been dammed into a wide black pool where eels swim. In a storm once one of the lofty firs fell into the dam. It stretches almost across it, and on quiet summer evenings the boys sit on the tree holding brown eel lines, fishing in sacred silence.

In the early morning you may see the smallest child of three or four throwing a line into the fast-flowing water of the burn or the still depths of the dam. There is a scarcity of grass in the neighbourhood of the smithy, for always the smallest turf has been pulled up as it appeared, when fishermen searched for worms. The smith himself digs his potato patch for bait. Worms are scarce. The fish are not in abundance. There are, however, thousands of young trout for the catching. These are known as 'beardies' and the men throw them back though the boys catch dozens; cooking them and eating them, heads, tails, fins, and all without removing the insides.

Fishing is always the topic. Smiths at Malzie are always anglers, and if they are not when they arrive they soon become anglers. They tell stories, as anglers do, of great fish caught, of salmon hooked and lost, and eels 'twice as long as a man's arm', which they have shovelled from the bed of the burn when the water has been low. Some use a crude fir-wood rod, but a net is the smith's favourite, and though he is usually more of a fisherman than other visitors to the burn, he sometimes walks in the stream striking likely stones with a hammer. It is a useful trick. If a trout or salmon lurks under the stone he is numbed and floats out to be lifted from the water.

About twenty children attend the school across the burn. They come from miles around. Some walk three or four miles. Ragged boys and girls they are, the children of ploughmen and byremen. The elder ones lead the younger ones by hand. The boys explore the hedges for hips and haws and nests of birds, sometimes climbing a dyke to lie face-downwards on the ground with one arm buried in the dark burrow of a rabbit. Wool and dry grass come from the hole, and then young rabbits, often with their eyes unopened and no fur, sometimes furry and large, almost ready to leave their isolated burrow for the banks where the rabbit tribes live in hundreds.

The luckier children often obtain a lift to school from a kind-hearted driver of a milk-dray or cart, and, arriving early, they mostly fish in the burn or play those quaint old-fashioned games peculiar to Scottish country children. The boys ape their fathers in mannerisms and swearing. They talk scandal, gleaned from their mothers' gossiping of doings at such and such a farm, or of whatever young girl that has gotten herself in trouble, as they, oh so frequently, do in this lonely district.

The schoolroom has a fire, and one aged teacher is responsible for the education of the twenty pupils, whose ages range from five to fourteen. They are never very brilliant. It is difficult to teach boys whose minds are on fishing or on fighting; who refuse to be punished, and retaliate, when this is threatened, with oaths which their fathers have unwittingly taught them, and wild kicking with hob-nailed boots.

Wullie was not even the least bit intelligent. In fact he refused even to attempt to learn, and swore profusely when remonstrated with. Jimmie was timid on his first day, but soon he became as all the others, impudent and careless.

Sarah, an unintelligent creature herself, thought it a waste of time to send them to school, but they were out of the way when things not for their eyes to see, or for their tongues to betray, took place in her husband's absence. There were herds who sometimes called when passing the lonely cothouse; a burly grocer gave her provisions, and asked for no money!

When Andy's small black eyes began to take an interest in things in general, and his tongue formed words other than baby talk, he was shut outside the door while his mother entertained her guests. He used to bang on the door and kick in childish impatience on these occasions, and his mother scolded him in muffled tones from the bed. Before Andy was two, a sister was born to him and another before he was four.

Sarah lavished no particular form of love on any of her offspring. At times she almost beat the life from Andy, partly because he irritated her and partly because she was in a bad mood. He was short legged and dark, with a heavy, drooping mouth. His hands were forever grimy, as was his face, and his slovenly mother washed him only on the rarest of occasions.

In spite of the beatings and the cursings, little Andy was astoundingly unperturbed by the outbursts of his mother. He was unafraid of her anger. Though he yelled like hell when she beat him, it was only to bring the discomfort of the ordeal to a close as quickly as possible. The first words in his vocabulary were 'bastard', 'bloody', and others of varying degrees of expressiveness. He could lisp 'Goddamit to hell' in the most convincing manner and say 'Christ' with profanity equal to his father's.

Jimmie and Wullie were at school all day. They left at eight in the morning with a piece of bread and butter for dinner, and returned in the evening after five. When Sarah was not out in the fields working with her man, she had plenty of time to spare for amusement. She lay in bed till past midday after the boys had left, and in the afternoon too, sometimes with Andy, who was a lazy child, sometimes with whoever of her men friends happened to pay a call. Some of them were reluctant to leave even as it drew near to five o'clock. They quarrelled too, and often Jimmie and Wullie came in to find their mother looking more bedraggled and coarse than when they had left in the morning.

When Andy was very young, Sarah allowed him to remain in bed with her and her latest lover. He lay and cried at the foot of the bed, and was usually silenced with a kick or two. Once he had been badly burnt when playing on the floor; he slipped and his hands grasped the bars of the grate. Sarah had been too slow to disentangle herself from a fond embrace, and the marks remained on his hands all his life.

It was on one of these occasions when Sarah was busy, and Andy was shut outside the door, carrying on his usual methodical kicking, that his father came home. A plough had broken at Drumlin and he had taken it to the smithy to be called for the next morning. The rest of the day was his and he came home. It was cold, and young Andy was weary of waiting outside the door, so he was kicking hard and continuously for admittance. It was not locked, but he could not have reached the handle had he been a foot taller. His father came through the gate.

'Come on, Andy boy,' he said, and lifted him as he opened the door.

It was a surprise for Sarah, who was sprawled across the bed half naked. It was an unpleasant shock for the herd who was with her. Both lay still for a minute. At the second of her husband's entry, Sarah had been unaware that it was he. She thought that perhaps Wee Andy had forced the door open, and though neither of them was much concerned about what Wee Andy saw, Sarah struggled with the man, who, without turning his head, fought to overcome this strange reversal of mood.

Wee Andy was set on his feet, and the closing of the door made the herd glance over his shoulder. Sarah drew her clothes about her as her husband advanced towards them.

'Come oot o' there, ye bastard,' he yelled, 'an' tak' whut's comin' tae ye.'

Wee Andy began to cry, but no one paid any heed to him. Sarah tried to run past Andy, but he knocked her to the floor with a blow on the mouth. The man sought to get clear of the bed before Andy was on him. He was tall, but thin and had a soft, stupid-looking face.

'Lae me alane,' he whimpered. 'Dinna hit me. It's no ma faut.'

But Andy scowled the more and clenched and unclenched his hairy hands.

'B'Jesus,' he cursed, 'A'll brek yer bloody back. Come oot o' that, ye bastard, ye.'

The thin devil was not so soft as he looked.

Suddenly he rushed and Andy went down. He scrambled past him for the door. Wee Andy, squealing with fear, rushed to get out of his way. The frightened man tripped over him before he reached the door. The child lay howling as his father rose like a tiger and leapt upon the fallen man. The thin man was weak; herds rarely do strenuous work. Andy smashed his head again and again on the floor, forced him over towards the fireplace and seized the poker to batter him. He became unconscious. Blood trickled over the floor.

Sarah, fascinated, had watched too long. Before she could escape, Andy grabbed her; bent her arm and drove a powerful fist into her face. She wailed and screamed with pain until he opened the door and, grasping her in his arms, threw her out on to the potato patch. She lay, scarcely breathing, where she had fallen, while he went back inside and lifted the limp body of the herd, carried him through the door, out of the gate and on to the road. If the man had been near to coming round, the force of striking the road as Andy pitched him from his shoulder would have been enough to have knocked him senseless once more.

The two small boys, Jimmie and Wullie, saw him lying groaning in the wet grass as they came in. Sarah, with her bruised and bleeding face, kept out of their sight, sliding round the corner as they came up to the door.

'Whaur's ma mither?' asked Wullie of his father as they entered.

When he repeated the question, he was paid for his inquisitiveness with a clout on the head that made the room black and tiny sparks fly before his eyes. Terrified, Jimmie kept his mouth shut, and went and sat down on the hob stool. Sarah came in when Andy, wearing his topcoat, strode off down the road. She sat down by the fire and sobbed as she tenderly felt her lacerated face.

The tall thin herd, walking ahead of Andy, began to run drunkenly when he saw him coming. The latter made no effort to pursue him, but walked steadily on, turning at High Malzie to take the road to Whauphill. The exhilarating feeling of having battered both his wife and the herd made the whole countryside seem smaller to him. He walked with a springy step; and a strange prickly sensation at the back of his neck reminded him of a dog fight he had once witnessed. He strode on into the gloom; past Cape-noch, Sheep Park, and Barnbarroch, until he came to the homely little public house that stands at the cross-roads at Whauphill. He felt cold when he reached it and called for a whisky to warm him.

There were others there. Feeling savage and strong, he told them of his afternoon's experience. They sympathized and agreed with him, but stood back from him when he drank more and more. They spoke warily to him, for he was known to be a strong man and he was in a funny mood.

Later, when he became quarrelsome, he was too drunk to fight, but his temper was bad and he sat and slobbered and cursed. When the place closed, he left after a deal of cautious persuasion on the part of both customers and landlord. For the best part of half an hour he yelled his head off outside, and then, swaying and muttering, he took himself off down the road. Twice he fell into the frozen grass, and when a man passed him on a pedal cycle he lurched away in the belief that it was going to hit him. He fell again, and struck his head on the road.

It was a while before the world stood still enough to let him rise to his feet. Even then a nearby wood persisted in drifting towards him and receding suddenly into the darkness. He stopped and relieved himself in the middle of the road, and began to recite a passage of Burns' most popular work. He ranted on, reeling off the adventures of 'Tam o' Shanter'. The words were hopelessly muddled. He kept trying to remember them, but his throbbing head refused to recall the exact version. A woman on a bike came towards him. The light of the carbide lamp almost blinded him. She was a servant girl, from a farm not far away.

'Comere,' he mumbled and staggered over as if to catch at her. She screamed and rode past him with a crazy wobble of her handle-bars. Had he been a little more sober, he might have caught her. As it was, he rushed drunkenly into a thorn tree which scratched his hands and face. He stood yelling curses after her until she had vanished into the shadows. The echo of his voice came back to him from the surrounding woods.

Sarah had put the boys to bed and washed her aching face before joining them. A floorbrush balanced against the door would warn her by falling on the floor when her husband came in. She lay awake listening for him for a long time, but finally fell soundly asleep. There was a wooden box near the door in which slept four-months-old Jess, the sister of wee Andy. A coat covered the box; part of it hung over the side and lay on the floor. The brush fell silently on to the coat as Andy opened the door and Sarah slept unknowingly. He was sober enough to pick his way across the floor, and his hands were on her before she knew that he had come in. She screamed and the boys awoke too.

'Come on, get oot o' there. A'm gan tae gie ye a hell o' a hemmerin,' he slobbered.

The bedclothes were dragged on to the floor. He punched and battered her, but she made no attempt to rise. Wee Andy and Wullie began to cry. The dark eyes of Jimmie watched his father in terror as he pulled her off the torn mattress.

'Lae me alane, Andy,' she pleaded.

He went on hitting her, and kicked her in the back till he lost his balance and fell. When he made no movement to get up she crept back to bed, lifting the blankets off the floor as she did so. After a while he was violently sick and, rising, he shut the door and began to take off his outer garments.

As he climbed into bed beside her she sobbed, 'Dinna hit me ony mair, Andy.'

He pushed her over roughly and muttered, 'Shut yer bloody mooth.'

He had forgotten to take his cloth cap off. In the flickering light of the fire she noticed it pulled down on his brow, but she let it stay for fear of rousing his temper again.

There were many times when Sarah and her man quarrelled; many times when he beat her, justly and unjustly. He never found her with another man. She was much too careful for that, but when his suspicions were aroused he made a rule of beating her until she could hardly stand. Invariably, although he did not know it, she mended her ways for a week or two. She never entertained the same herd again. He was much too terrified of Andy, who met him one afternoon on the moss and felled him with a blow in the face. There was still the grocer with his gifts and one or two others, though the story of the fight frightened some of them.

When Jimmie was nine, he took Andy to school with him. Andy sat by him in class and talked out loud when the rest were quiet, so that they laughed and the teacher told Jimmie to 'Make him be quiet, James.' But Wee Andy would not be quiet.

A loud 'Whut?' was all the satisfaction he gave Jimmie when he urged, 'Had yer tongue, man.'

The 'man' still said 'Eh?' and 'Whut dae ye say, Jimmie?' and 'Whut daes the oul' wuman want stanin' there, Jimmie?' He said it so loudly that the whole class heard him and laughed louder than ever. A few were brought out and given the strap. Wullie was among them.

The leather hurts the hand, and Wullie returned to his seat bending double with his palm across his stomach to relieve the stinging pain. The hard-faced old dame came up and shook Wee Andy till he whimpered.

'Be quiet, do you hear?' she stormed.

He was quiet for a while, and then when Jimmie whispered something to him he burst out with another loud 'Whut?' that set the giggling girls and foolish boys tittering once more.

Somehow Wee Andy could not understand the golden virtues of silence. It was some weeks before he could control his tongue or speak in a whisper like the others. Even then he could often lapse into childish observations that all might hear. Such comments about the few pictures that hung on the wall, or the colour of the teacher's dress, the adventures of a blue fly that buzzed on the window pane, the things he could see in the fire, and the flight of crows passing the open door, earned him many a shaking.

He had an unusual ability for discovering beetles and other insects crawling on the floor, and it was not long before the whole of the small school knew of the existence of the particular earwig and, until the teacher could rush to him, they were kept well posted with its course and actions.

He talked too much for his own good. Soon he was being treated with the strap in the same way as the rest. On the first occasion he protested when dragged to the front.

'Och, lae me alane,' he yelled and struggled valiantly.

Later he learned better, but the 'goings-on' around him never ceased to hold him interested, and perhaps his education suffered more than that of the others in the class.

CHAPTER III

T H E war broke out soon after Andy went to school, and its effects were felt even in that quiet countryside. Every boy was killing imaginary Germans in his spare time. The tramps that passed the school became objects to strike terror into the hearts of the boys and send the girls running in to the teacher. Every particularly ragged tramp was a German, and the enemy took the place of the 'Deil' and the 'bad man', who was used as the chief threat to frighten the mischievous children. Although food was rationed in the towns and cities, the cotters did not want; at least they were no more hungry than usual.

There were always fields where rabbits could be poached and turnips stolen. In the woods twice a week patriotic women and aged men shot pigeons for the hospitals and in some places sawmills were set up to utilize the timber. There was a smell of pine wood and resin in many lonely plantations, and the dark green swaying firs toppled day after day, while the great saws whirred and whined in the echoes that told the infrequent passers-by of the work of the woodmen. Woods that had stood in silence since the day they were first planted, save for the occasional roar of a poacher's gun, knew for the first time the hubbub that goes with the life of man. Pheasants left the shelter of the trees and roamed the ditches and bare fields.

Sarah's sister Meg was left alone when her husband enlisted in the

Borderers. All her children had died at birth so she came to live with the Walker family for a while. Sarah, Andy, Meg, and the latest-born baby, Mary, slept in the same bed. Things went well for a time, but after a week or two, there was a great uproar. Wee Andy watched it all from his bed on the floor. Sarah began the quarrel after they were all settled for the night. It was Andy's fault. He wanted to sleep with Meg beside him. Sarah fought and struggled in the bed till he rose and pulled her across the floor, opened the door, and threw her out. She was only half dressed. She screamed and battered on the door, but he replaced the bar and went back to bed with Meg. After all was quiet and his father lay still, Wullie rose and let his mother in. She said nothing, but made her bed on the floor with the boys.

When Andy went to work Sarah made his breakfast for him. He sat eating it without a word and drank his tea with a loud sucking noise from his saucer. He had left half an hour before Sarah roused Meg, who lay in the bed nervously looking at her sister.

'Come on, get yer things on an' get oot,' stormed Sarah, 'ye great dirty bitch. Ye'll no' lie anither nicht wi' my man. Get oot, dae ye hear?'

Meg rose and pulled on her black darned stockings, shamelessly displaying herself to young Wullie, who did not conceal his interest in the female form. She stood up naked and pulled her dress over her head, smiling at the boy as she did so.

Sarah bundled her things together and threw them at her feet.

'Get oot!' she ordered.

Meg was slow. She had lost some of her fear of Sarah, who sat and waited for her to leave, pulling at the horsehair which protruded from the old chair. Her anger mounted to an uncontrollable fury. She jumped up and seized Meg, raining blows on her thin dark face. Meg cried as Sarah lifted her bundle of clothes and threw them out into the road.

After she had gone Sarah poked the fire viciously and clouted Wullie, who cursed and swore the while. Wee Andy was soon on his way to school. Jimmie, who was not so lively, got a crack over the head with the brush for no reason at all.

The boys soon forgot the fight on their way to school. Wullie was more thoughtful than usual, and made sundry observations on his Aunt Meg's body, but these were interrupted when a Kelly boy began to pelt him with haws. The haws were hard, old and black berries pulled from a sheltered tree that the birds had not raided. They stung Wullie's face, so when the Kelly tyke came near he grabbed him. They rolled over the frozen road, tearing and punching at each other. It was a great fight. Wullie cut his head on a sharp stone. The Kelly rose and ran while the three Walkers sent a thick hail of stones after him. One bled his ear and he howled all the way to the school gate. The teacher gave them both the strap, but Wullie only swore and refused to cry.

Wee Andy had his first fight that day too. A short fat boy called M'Clelland pushed him down outside the school door, and when he had regained his feet he punched him till he cried. M'Clelland's brother clouted Andy's ear for him and the clan spirit in Wullie and Jimmie led them to hammer M'Clelland, the elder, until his nose bled and he ran in to the teacher. They both got the strap for that.

Jimmie imitated Wullie and cursed and swore, but would not cry. She punished him again and as she did so Wullie ran up behind her and kicked her on the leg. The class was in uproar for a while. The grey-haired old dame beat them both across the face with the black strip of leather, but neither stopped swearing and Wullie still wouldn't cry.

When dinner-time came Wullie was tired of school and took Jimmie and Wee Andy up the burn. They pulled pieces of twig from the water till they found three hooks lost by some other fishers. Wullie had some line and they sneaked into the smith's garden to dig for worms. The teacher sent a boy to look for them in the afternoon. Wullie pushed him into the burn because he refused to report that he could not find them.

He ran back to the school drenched and cold, crying, 'A'll tell,' 'A'll tell.' They all moved up the burn and hid until the teacher, standing on the bridge, had tired calling for them. She was short-sighted and could not have seen them anyhow. Wee Andy got his feet wet and shivered. They caught nothing and decided to go home. Arriving back on the road, they found that school was out. Wullie chased the Kelly boy up the road to the signpost. Jimmie joined in and threw stones at him. Andy was wet and miserable and was left far behind: a short solitary figure on a lonely road.

'Whaur's Meg?' asked Andy of his wife when he came in.

'She's awa' hame,' answered Sarah sharply.

'An' wha sent her hame?' he demanded.

'Naebody sent her, she jist took her things and gaed this mornin'. No' lang efter ye did.'

'Ye're a bloody liar! Ye flung her oot. Ye flung yer ain sister oot!' retorted Andy.

'Sister!' she spat. 'The dirty bitch! an' afore a' yer weans ye laid wi' her last nicht, an' me on the flair lik' a dog. Ye rotten bastard.'

Andy struck her across the mouth and she lifted the poker from the hearth to strike back. He turned and lifted his coat from the back of the chair.

'Whaur ir ye gan noo?' she demanded. He made no reply and she asked again.

'A'm aff tae the toon tae enlist.'

Sarah laughed harshly.

'Mair like ye're awa tae look fur her ahin' a hedge.'

He ignored the remark. In fact he did go to Wigtown, and after getting hopelessly drunk, and lying a night by the roadside, he enlisted in the Borderers. He was in France a few months later. Maybe he was killed, for he never came back to Wigtownshire. No one informed his 'sorrowing' widow, and little she cared one way or the other.

Wee Andy was the most fortunate of the three brothers. His mother vented her anger on Jimmie and Wullie. The latter fought back and kicked, so that usually she dealt with him with the poker or the brush. She cursed their father day after day. Later she got a job at Drumlin where they were short of milkers, for there were few men left in the countryside. Through the spring she hoed turnips and weeded, and in the summer she worked at the hay and corn harvest. In the spring, Andy, Jimmie and Wullie were kept off school to hoe. If anything, they were better off than when their father worked for them. The hay found Jimmie and Wullie still working, but Andy, who was as yet unable to be of real use, was sent back to school again. Some days he really did go, but mostly he looked for nests or stole eggs from Low Malzie's deserted steading. The little fat M'Clelland boy, who was in much the same position, with his brother at the hay, went with him. They fished for hours and explored the hedges together every afternoon. Sometimes Andy was not home before six in the evening.

At seven years of age Andy was a short thick-set sturdy boy with his father's dark hair and black eyes. He was almost as broad as he was long, and his legs were strong and bony. He had his mother's crazy temper, a foolish, flaring, childish temper that spurred him to fight with any adversary, no matter how big or formidable. He lost his first front teeth fighting the same big Kelly boy who had often been the object of Wullie's anger.

The old black collie and Andy were firm friends. The dog ran through the fields in search of rabbits at his instruction. Neither Jimmie nor Wullie was attached to the dog. Wullie was only fond of kicking it and Sarah battered it out of doors with the brush whenever she found it in the house. Andy's interest was not confined to the dog.

He was unusually attracted by all animals and soon accumulated a pair of rabbits and a hedgehog, although the latter did not lend itself to petting. He fed his collection – the rabbits soon bred – on porridge, oatmeal and tea-leaves. They lived in two boxes, wired up by Wullie, which had been placed on an empty barrel behind the house. Andy added an injured thrush and a young hedge-sparrow sparrow to his menagerie later, but neither lived. The hedgehog, a young one, became quite tame and no longer contracted into a prickly ball when stroked. The rabbits grew tremendously fat on the great heaps of clover he gathered for them every morning before he went to school. He cleaned them often too, and was happy till a rat, or perhaps a stoat, killed two of them. In the end he took them to school, four in all, and 'swopped' them for a bright-eyed jackdaw, which had, in accordance with an ancient belief, a slit tongue, which was supposed to ensure that it would one day talk. Its feathers were scant, and Andy had really got the worst of the deal, for it was an old bird. It was much prized and was kept, while Andy gave it a course of 'taming', in the rabbit box.

After some persuasion Sarah allowed him to bring it into the house to live. It used to sit on a nail high on the wall and croak, or huddle by the side of the fire. Wullie often kicked it out of his way, but the bird knew when to flutter over the floor. It lived for four or five months till the collie, in a boisterous mood, raced after it round the room and accidentally nipped it too hard. Andy tended it, and, wrapping it in a piece of rag, laid it in the oven, but it died.

He buried it with ceremony and sorrow in the potato patch. The collie unearthed the body the following week and made a meal of its decaying flesh.

When he actually went to school, on such days as it rained, or there was some minor attraction to lure him there, Andy was quite happy. He revelled, in fact, in arrogance and impudence. For his age he was the most unruly, stubborn boy the hard-faced old dame had ever had to handle. The strap now held little terror for him. Often, when he was discovered at some wrong, such as kicking his neighbour under the desk, he refused to come out of his place to receive the punishment. The old dame would waddle on her none too steady legs up the passage to drag him out. The strap would be held ready and her thin lips would be pursed in determination. Without fail Andy took his cue as she advanced. He would pull his legs clear of the desk, step on top of it, and spend perhaps ten minutes dodging the enraged old woman round the classroom. He amused himself further in the meantime by kicking his enemies as he raced across their desks. His dirty boots soiled papers, cracked writing-slates and bruised fingers as he ran noisily to and fro.

If the dame caught him, as she rarely did, he would kick her thin legs till she ceased to beat him round the head with the strap, and then, seizing his opportunity, bite her on the hand and run for the door. On one occasion, after the usual game of chasing over the desk tops, he made for the door with the panting woman at his heels. He had just time to pass through before she arrived, and then his imp of mischief prompted him to grasp the handle and hold against her. He felt her tug at it in her anger, then with all his childish strength he threw it open in her face so that she reeled back with a bruised nose and collapsed among the desks.

Her fury was intense, and after calling her threats after him she hurried down to the smithy and urged the smith to pursue him. Andy could run and did, and the smith, who was not flushed with anger as was the old dame, had not the same urge to chase him far; besides he had work to do.

For six weeks Andy made no appearance at the schoolhouse. When he did the old dame eyed him threateningly, but for once he took his place and sat silent all morning. Continual misbehaviour would have terminated Andy's school-days early had there been no limit to his mischievousness, but such amusements as kicking his neighbours, pulling the long hair of the girls, spilling ink, and swearing at the teacher grew tiresome. It was an exhausting and dangerous pastime dodging the strap.

Once in a while, when he was not just sitting quietly dreaming, he paid attention to the lesson. Usually he listened when all other subjects, such as fishing and bird-nesting, had passed through his mind. He would dream of rabbits and piles of clover, of tame mice, rats, hedgehogs, pigeons, birds and dogs. Everything, in fact, of interest to a country boy. Then he would spend an hour gazing round the class; watching the faces of the boys and girls; the dame; studying the pictures on the wall; trying to get a glimpse of what was going on outside.

If this was his mood in the morning, then by afternoon he was tired of thinking of things, and either he leapt to life in pulling the hair of the pupil in front of him, or sat listening to the teacher. Alternatively he was noisy and quiet. On his quiet days he learned something of the alphabet, although he never could recite it through. In a slow, dull-witted fashion he learned to count, but most of all he listened to the history of Scotland and the stories which were read out at the end of the afternoon. He liked the innocent little stories of fairies and magic that came from a fat book written by Grimm. All the children shared the same liking for these simple tales, for they had inherited, many of them, the superstition and belief in mystics from their fathers and grandfathers.

When he was alone, walking along the road home to the cothouse, Andy imagined elves and fairies stepping out from behind briar bushes. He waited for the old black collie to speak to him when they wandered on the moss together, and would not have been surprised had the toothless hound sat up and addressed him. Often he was more surprised and sorry that it did not, and pleaded with it to talk with him.

There was the story of Robinson Crusoe, too, which had a strong appeal for him, and the Swiss Family Robinson. He was slow to welcome this last book, for the dame issued a small red-covered copy to each child of his age and began teaching them something harder than 'I am it' and 'I am up'. The simple sentences of the first reading books had held no interest for Andy. He hardly took the trouble to follow as the rest of the class chanted, 'Dan is a man', 'I saw a cat' and 'I can run'. When the Swiss Family's adventures became the topic of the class he was suddenly eager to read the story for himself. Each day he struggled to read his sentence as the dame went round the class.

The lesson was brief and the tale was slow in unfolding. Perhaps his eagerness to know the end of the tale was the main factor in his learning to read, but with counting he never progressed far. In reading, big words were too much of a setback for him to tackle anything more than a newspaper, although the opportunity of securing one was rare.

So he learned to read and he learned to count. Neither very well, but he was no worse than his brothers or the sons of other ploughmen and labourers. He excelled both his mother and his late father in reading and writing. Laborious hours writing, 'Andrew Walker, Malzie School, Wigtownshire' and the like, on a slate with a sharpened slate-pencil, that scratched and squealed to put his teeth on edge, made him proficient enough. There were boys who were much cleverer. One, the twelve-years-old son of a struggling farmer, had ideas far beyond the wildest dreams of his fellows. He promised to become a 'vet' or a doctor, though the means of his father would never have permitted it, and the lad's brightness at the one-roomed school would have diminished to almost backwardness anywhere else.

When Andy was nine there were changes at the cothouse. His father had not come back from the war. Indeed Sarah would not for a moment have expected him to, even if she had heard that he was back in the shire. Andy and Jimmie, who was almost ready for work, were introduced to their new 'faither'. Neither of them cared much.

He was a byreman from a farm near Alticry and he had often been round the cothouse since their legal parent left. Once or twice he had shared the bed with Sarah. One night she had stayed out with him after getting hopelessly drunk at the cattle show at Portwilliam. His name was Tam Brock and he was a slovenly, lazy man who sat by the fire most of the time. He chewed tobacco and groused at times, but Sarah had chosen her new mate well. It was she who gave the orders and he obeyed. She scolded and he was silent.

When he was sober, very infrequently, he talked to Andy. The boy liked him well enough. There was something dog-like in his weather-beaten face and his ragged whiskers. The habit he had of squirting the yellow tobacco juice from the corner of his mouth intrigued Andy. His laugh, when he showed his blackened teeth, was loud and hearty, and tears often stood in the wrinkles of his eyes.

There had been no more trouble than usual when Tam – Andy called him 'Tam' with the easy familiarity of his kind – moved his bundle of clothes into the untidy cothouse. Sarah nagged just as much as ever. The easy-going Tam smoked or chewed by the fireside with the regularity of a bullock chewing in a field. When her temper was bad, Sarah stormed and cursed him, but he sat in silence and the torrent of abuse passed over his head. Sometimes he laughed and impudent Andy joined him, though Tam's laugh was free and genial, while Andy's was more in scorn at his mother's stupid outbursts. Tam often made feeble protest when Sarah seized the laughing Andy and hammered him for his impudence.

On such occasions Andy defended himself with as much ability as he fought the old dame at school. He kicked hard and cleverly with his hob-nailed boots and punched and wriggled while she held him.

As he grew older, Sarah became a little afraid of his impudence and temper, even as had the dame, who was careful when she reprimanded him and rarely threatened the strap, for Andy was the spirit of antagonism and ferocity. He had a temper that burst into flame at scarce a moment's notice.

CHAPTER IV

WEARING the cutdown clothes of both Jimmie and Wullie, Andy, though not acutely conscious of his appearance, was at times uncomfortable. It was not that often his shirt stuck out through a hole in the seat of his trousers, or that his jersey had ragged sleeves, but more that the sleeves of his jacket had to be rolled back to let him use his hands. The shoulders of his jacket, too, made him conspicuous, for they drooped and showed that the garment had been bought for one perhaps twice his size. Baggy-legged trousers that hung below his knees, and boots that were too long for his feet, made him a laughable sight. The other boys themselves were not too well-dressed. All had patched clothes and ragged elbows, but they found something specially funny in Andy's appearance.

At first he was shy to defend himself against their ridicule. He pretended, though he went red at the ears, that he had not heard their remarks or the great bursts of laughter that greeted him when he chanced to stumble in his over-large boots. When fighting his sleeves would fall down and his ferocity become comical. He dealt great swinging blows with the ragged sleeves flapping in the air. Although his opponent was careful to keep a straight face, the onlookers could not conceal their amusement. They called him 'The wee man in his faither's oul' claithes', and the description almost broke his heart.

If determined to fight, Andy generally removed his jacket; often, while his intended victim fled, he would sit on the roadside and take off his big boots before beginning. When so prepared he met with no jeers or laughs. The smaller boys, taking advantage of the fact that he was fighting, would throw the dusty boots and tattered jacket over a hedge or into a ditch. Once his boots were off Andy was dangerous. He could run like a hare on his stockinged soles along the hard road, and his onslaughts were terrific and unmerciful. The boy who had jeered at him a moment before would race fear-stricken to escape. With his neat little fists clenched, Andy would attack and there would be blood flowing and yells of pain before he stopped, often only to attack another of his tormentors. With dour, malicious temper he would remember those who had escaped him and seek them out another day.

The fated one would often have forgotten the incident when next he met Andy. At times such an offender, knowing nothing of Andy's grievance of the previous day, would come offering him an apple or a sweet, not out of fear but as a simple friendly gesture. Whether he accepted the gift or not Andy never overlooked his wrong. The innocent giver would be paid with a punch in the mouth and a brutal attack that would bring tears to his eyes before he could defend himself. Although he fought for his boyish rights and dealt unmercifully with his enemies, Andy was nothing of a bully. It was only that his temper was quick, and what a more placid nature would have taken as a joke he regarded as an insult or a threat.

Once he was leaving school in the evening to fish in the burn, and, to enable him to move with greater ease, he removed his big boots, laying them beside a stone at the bridge. There was a Milroy boy who had a reason for disliking Andy. One day he had received a kick on the face when Andy was enjoying himself in a race over the desk tops. Milroy was not plucky enough to face Andy and fight the matter out, but he saw the boots beside the stone and, lifting them, he threw them into the burn. Andy was fishing under the bridge, and after getting drenched in rescuing the hated boots he raced to the road and made after the fleeing Milroy. Milroy lived in a cothouse two miles along the Kirkcowan road and he ran like blazes for home, turning at every bend to see if Andy had grown tired of the chase.

Andy had not. Gritting his teeth and swearing between gasps for breath, the short black-headed youngster became the more furious as he ran. They passed three silent cothouses before Andy began to gain. The thin white-faced Milroy gradually became exhausted and stumbled along sobbing with fear as Andy drew nearer. Andy's feet were bleeding. He had removed his stockings to fish. When he was within a few yards of him the Milroy boy turned to meet Andy. He was weary and breathless, but a certain determination dominated his lanky form as he groped in the grass for a stone. He had not found one when Andy raced down upon him, knocking him on his back and dropping to the road with him as he punched and battered him with savage satisfaction.

The strength of the beaten Milroy was short-lived. His forehead was grazed and his lip split as he limped home. Andy, sitting by the roadside to regain his breath, rose to his feet after a moment to throw stones after him. He did not notice the hardness of the road as he walked back to the smithy. The blood had congealed in the cuts on his feet. He sought his boots and stockings and, putting them on, made for home. He was not unaware that the skinny Milroy had a brother, a long spiteful boy with little strength, yet just big enough to hammer a boy of Andy's age.

Not only did the Milroy boy whine his story to the teacher, who made a futile attempt to punish Andy, but he threatened darkly, 'Wait till the nicht, Walker. Ma brither'll be ootside waitin' fur ye.'

Andy was not by any means frightened; he was just a bit uncomfortable the whole day, and nervously watched the clock throughout the afternoon. Half the school knew what was coming to him that night.

He took pains to assure them whenever they mentioned it, 'Och, A'm no feert o' Milroy, or his brither. A'm no' feert o' onybody.'

His tone was not boastful, nor was it to console his own fear. For a boy of his age he was remarkably stoical. True enough, he was not entirely comfortable, but the nervousness that he alone was aware of was merely the nervousness of anticipation. Shortly before four o'clock one of the boys 'asked for leave'. The 'boys' closet' was a small wooden box down by the burn and the request was made in

order that he might see if the big Milroy was really waiting for
Andy. He came back with the news that Cha Milroy, or Charles
Milroy, to give him his correct name, was leaning over the bridge
with a scowl on his face, waiting for the school to come out.

Andy removed his boots and quietly shrugged himself out of his
big jacket. His hands were shaking and he could hardly keep still.
There was a pregnant silence as the dame said, in her clipped
accents, 'You may go.' He rose and gathered up his boots and
jacket. The smaller Milroy hastened out of school ahead of him to
point him out to his avenging brother. Andy stepped gingerly over
the cinders in the playground, laid down his boots and jacket at the
gate and waited.

The big Milroy straightened from his leaning position when his
younger brother ran to him and pointed out Andy's black head. He
scowled in his most manly style and strode slowly up the road with
the rest of the school at his heels. He wore a pair of long grey
trousers. They were of tweed and were tight-fitting round the
knees. There were patches of earth on them through his kneeling at
the hoeing.

'You're Walker, ir ye, ye bastard, ye?' he asked Andy, who stood
with his hands clenched by the gate.

'A im,' said Andy, 'whut aboot it?'

'Weel, yer mither'll no ken ye whun ye gae hame the nicht,'
promised the 'growing man' as he grabbed Andy's braces.

Milroy had been counting too much on Andy's fear, for he
released the braces and staggered back as Andy drove his fist into his
face. A tooth was loosened and blood trickled from the corner of his
mouth. None of the boys standing round said anything, for when
Milroy was through with Andy he would perhaps treat some of
them the same way if they had dared to take Andy's side. Swearing
through bleeding lips Milroy rushed at Andy and dealt him a
swinging blow on the head that knocked him down.

Once his victim was on the ground he proceeded to kick him.
Andy held back his tears and seized the swinging leg. Milroy tried to
shake himself free as Andy pulled him to the road. He struck his
head on the stones and began to whimper. Andy lifted a chip of

stone as a weapon and punched his adversary with it till the blood ran among his hair. The 'big man' was a small boy in a short time. He began to cry, although there was no doubt he could have overcome Andy had he been given a moment's grace, but Andy followed blow after blow with no mercy.

Then, satisfied that he could beat his man, he stood up and urged, 'Come on, Milroy; get up, ye bastard. A'll show ye wha's gan tae dae the hemmerin' '.

But Milroy had had enough. He scrambled to his feet, and, avoiding Andy's rush, made off up the road as his brother had already done. Andy considered pursuit unwise. Calmly he picked up his boots and jacket and put them on. The other boys praised him. To the biggest of them there was not one with the courage to face Andy's ferocity. He was not popular, but they respected his fighting ability.

'Ye fairly gie'd him a hemmerin',' they said.

Andy allowed himself to boast, 'Och aye, A kent A could batter yon docken, an' if there's onybody else here that wants a fecht noo's the time.'

There were no offers.

He went home scowling at the girls, who glanced shyly at such a clever fighter. He cursed and swore and knocked against the other boys to show them all how unafraid he was.

When he reached home he banged into the cothouse, strode to the table, and, for once, he kicked the old collie. For no reason at all he swore at Sarah and scowled at Jimmie. He felt a most accomplished fighter, and when Tam came in he spent the night describing the fight to him, repeating all the oaths, and telling of each stage of the combat with due exaggeration. Tam was a good listener, and slapped his thigh and laughed as Andy told him.

When it was all over he offered him a sup from his whisky bottle. Andy took a long draught that made his throat burn, and spent half an hour holding his chest, which seemed to be on fire, and coughing. Tam was more delighted than ever. He offered him the bottle again and again during the evening. The two of them sang and laughed like fools while Sarah muttered and scolded to herself, but she was afraid of the boy though he was only twelve.

He declined to go to bed. Sarah cautiously asked him twice but he refused, and Tam, thoroughly drunk, was swayed by the boy's boisterousness, so that he, too, defied Sarah. The babies cried; they were the latest additions to the family; but Andy swore at them like a man. He laughed, and, as he had seen the smith do, he pushed at Tam to bring the point home. After staggering about the room, banging into the door and tripping and stumbling, he at last fell and struck his head on the hearth. He was sick and wanted to die. Tam had fallen into a drunken sleep; the peat glow sank until no heat came from the grate. Andy was ill, spots danced before his eyes, the room rushed to him and fell back just as quickly, and a dull throbbing pain kept him from sleeping.

Sarah beat him in the morning when he was too weak to defy her. He lay where he had fallen at night, his eyes were wrong and somehow the room had filled with a milky mist. His stomach heaved and made him writhe, wishing he were dead. At last Sarah put him to bed, and when Tam came home she continued her harangue.

He came over to the bed.

'Come on, Andy,' he said, 'ye're no sae bad. Here, look, tak' a chow o' this. That's whut A aye dae whun ma belly's sair.'

He handed him the stump of his tobacco twist, and Andy felt too ill even to refuse.

In a day or two he was all right again and went to school. When the dame asked him the reason for his absence he proudly replied, 'A wus fou. Drunk as a sojer.'

The boys tittered, but the dame paid no attention. She knew Andy of old as a confirmed liar, and lifted down the tattered register and wrote in it the word 'sick'. Andy saw it and was ashamed. He had wanted the word 'drunk', or even 'fou', but 'sick' . . . He protested,

'Missus, A wusna sick. A wus drunk.'

'Walker,' she snapped, 'get back to your place.'

Regretfully he went. Half the glory of his adventure had gone, but he told the others just how drunk he had been. How he had drunk two bottles unaided. They listened with bulging eyes and mouths agape.

'Ye're tellin' lees, Andy Walker,' said a small girl with freckles. He looked at her with scorn.

'Och awa',' said one sceptic, 'ma fether canna drink ony mair than yin bottle afore he's fou.'

'Then yer fether's an oul' wumin,' retorted Andy. 'Tam an' me can drink a gallon atween us.'

He told the story colourfully of how he and Tam had sung all night and swallowed glass after glass of whisky. Of how poor Tam had fallen down drunk, and he, Andy, had had to put him to bed before he finished the remainder of the whisky. He felt proud and thought himself justified in describing three or four sips as two bottles. He let them smell his breath to prove that he had been drinking. There was certainly an odour of something about it and the credulous were ready to believe that it was whisky.

One envious hearer asked, 'Whut made ye stey aff yesterday an' the day afore, Andy?'

'Och,' he replied, 'ma heid was sair an' A wusna sober till last nicht.'

He felt more of a man than ever that day and swaggered as best he could in his big ungainly boots. He wished he had had a waistcoat to wear so that he could have pulled back his jacket and tucked his thumbs in its armlets as the farmers and horse-dealers did. The fear of being violently sick prevented him from chewing the piece of tobacco that Tam had given him, but he did his best to spit through his teeth and make that fascinating squirting noise that Tam could make. He was a hero by his victory over the Milroy boy and by his fabulous account of getting drunk.

'Av coorse,' he assured them, 'A hae been drunk afore. Och aye, mony a time.'

He was twelve years old and a whale of a liar.

Andy did try Tam's whisky bottle again. He did not sip so greedily or so frequently. Tam, in the fashion of cotmen, could see no wrong in giving the boy a sip of whisky, any more than some mothers of the working class in England see harm in pacifying their babies with a sip of beer while they wait for their husbands with the pram outside the public house. Tam never gave the matter a thought.

Jimmie, too, would have liked a sip from the square-sided bottle, but Tam had never taken much to Jimmie. He was a silent, dull boy who rarely had anything to say for himself. When the bottle was produced Tam tilted it to his own mouth, wiped his whiskers, and said, 'Here Andy.'

After he had drunk, Andy always returned the bottle to Tam, who offered it to Sarah, if she happened to be in a good mood. Andy always awaited Tam's return from the Port or the Whaup with eagerness to sip from the new supply of whisky that was bought each time.

Some days Andy would go to the shore or across the moss for whaup eggs. The whaups would be wheeling and making their weird cry over the black moss that stretched away into the blue mists of the northern horizon. He would wander on, a solitary small figure on the barren sweep of heather and stagnant water-holes. The whaup lays a surprisingly large egg for its size, often only one or two, though sometimes three. They are to be found on the damp mounds of peaty soil. Boots are frequently filled with water in searching for them, for the moss is always sodden with spring rains that fill its hollows and hags. The peewit lays on the bare patches. Their nests are smooth basins in the moss and there are four eggs lying point inwards. Andy wore Tam's tweed cap when on these expeditions. It presented a strange appearance when perched on his head, for it bulged with the eggs of the whaup, peewit or grouse. They are tasty when fried.

At the shore, after a long and tiresome walk down the Alticry road, he would climb the black rocks in search of the hawks' nests, the gulls and rock pigeons. It was precarious, and a pastime of which he often tired after a few minutes on the shore, for it was lonely with only the cry of the seabirds and the sound of the lashing waves.

His return would take him on a wide circuit of the ploughed fields in search of peewits' nests. Later in the spring he would hunt the hedgesides and whins for pheasant and partridge eggs. The partridge was the harder to find, choosing as it does the long grass and bare open fields.

Amongst the fir woods he scaled even the highest tips to rob the magpie, though the disused nest of the wood-pigeon often deceived him into a climb that brought too poor reward. The wood-wren nested in the low branches of the spruce, building a round dainty nest of moss and dry rust-coloured leaves. Such birds as these lured him to the farthest plantations to climb the loneliest trees and wander through the morning mist on a quest that would last all day.

If he went as far on his way to school as the bridge at the burn, the cawing of the rooks in the tall trees behind the smithy tempted him to turn aside and climb in the hope of finding a young bird of the right size and age to tame and keep as a pet. Often he wrecked the nest if his climb was in vain, or worked his way as high into the branches as was safe, so that he could overlook the nests in nearby trees. It was nothing for him to climb a difficult tree and, after returning to the ground for a brief rest, scale several others.

His time went quickly, he was agile and fearless. Often he fell, but not far. His wiry hands gripped the decaying branches in just the right place, and, when he paused to wipe the small pieces of pine dust and bark from his eyes, his grip was sure and his legs well placed. Now and again he came to the ground with a half-feathered rook in the breast of his shirt. His effort to rear them was never wholly successful. They would eat worms day after day, then unexpectedly refuse to take food at all.

Placed in the oven in a piece of rag they failed to revive. The small blue eyelids would close over the bright black eyes; and the head would droop. It was only a matter of hours before they were dead, and he was conducting another funeral on the potato patch. While the rooks nested he was untiring in his efforts to rear one of them, but, like his experiments with young pigeons and yellow-hammers, they were useless.

When the time for mushrooms came, Andy was abroad at sunrise, walking the dewy fields, picking them and eating them. They grew on the knowes and slopes where they were least expected, but Andy could tell without error just where they would be found clustering. When the harvest was nearing its end, he picked blackberries, eating them with unappeasable appetite. They were a palatable delicacy as were the 'fairy taties' which he dug for beside the burns. These fairy potatoes, actually the round fat roots of a grass that grows on wet ground, are strangely sweet and fresh.

Andy's liking for such things as sloes, 'sourocks', and blueberries, was great, and if he fancied a young turnip or a carrot, a handful of ripe oats or crab apples, he had but to seek them and eat his fill. On all of his wanderings he went alone. No one accompanied him to forestall him in finding the whaup's nest, picking the freshest mushrooms or blueberries. He walked alone and talked to himself in sober tones.

He thought aloud and would say to himself often such things as 'A think A'll awa' hame,' 'A wunner whut o'clock it'll be?' or 'Wha'll yon be?'

If he thought of a particular enemy he would address HIM as he walked and swear at HIM. If he met anyone, he fell silent and said nothing till spoken to. If the man or woman spoke he answered, if not he went on his way, stopping to look back after a while to see if they were out of sight.

CHAPTER V

IN the summer of about 1921 Andy left school. It was a fine, cool misty morning when he made the walk for the last time and the shadow of the mountains in the north was a blue ridge in the fleecy white sky. The cocks were crowing their welcome to the rising sun as he passed High Malzie, and the kye were grazing lazily in the fresh green fields. The smell of hay was in his nostrils; the smell of hay and damp earth.

He felt light of foot and his new well-polished hob-nailed boots clattered as he went down the road. He brushed a dewy cobweb from his eyes as he passed under the over-hanging ash trees at the signpost, and went on down towards Low Malzie. He whistled. He was late but careless. He could see the others who attended the school far ahead. They were running and he watched them till they disappeared from his view as he went down a hill.

He stopped to study a fat black snail that clung to a swaying grass by the roadside; he listened to the bleat of the sheep and the chirping of the starlings that descended among them to pick the lice off their backs. At the burn that runs under the road at Low Malzie, he stood by the drinking-pool and threw stones to scare a red-footed water-bird from the rushes on the opposite bank. He pondered as he watched an eel wriggling across the clear bed of the pool, and a linnet that sat on a twig near by twittering its appreciation of the morning.

He was not yet fourteen; little over thirteen and a half in fact; he was leaving school to work at the hay. Then there would be the harvest and the potatoes; by that time he would be nearly fourteen, so what would be the good of going back? Who wanted to go to school anyway? There were the fields, the scented hay, the white-gold corn, the sweet smell of potato blossoms and Swede turnips. There would be warm byres to work in in the winter; frosty mornings when he would plough across the hard earth, horses to clean, sweet tiredness after strenuous days at the sowing and harrowing. All these things would be part of the great adventure that was before him from that day on. He would smoke and chew tobacco, sit in the stable and play the mouth-organ at night. He would kick his heels as he sat on the corn chest, and when he fed his horses, shoulder them over saying, 'Get up, ye oul' bastard,' or 'Come ower, ma lass.' He would wear long trousers and oilskin leggings, and swear and be a man.

As he stood gazing into the water where the green weeds floated, he thought of all these things till an hour had gone and he was later than ever. It seemed hardly worth while to go to school at all, but he had promised the others that he would be there, and that, 'Efter the morn, A'll niver set fit in the place again.' They would expect him. He was sorry that he had no long trousers to wear on his last day, but he strode down the road in his manliest style and chewed a stalk of grass.

With his hands tucked in the tops of his trousers he felt he was a real ploughman, for they always had their hands in those big, deep waist pockets. He stopped again at the smithy with his tattered schoolcap on the back of his head. The smith noticed him and smiled at the attitude. Andy kept his hands in the imaginary pockets and placed his feet astride.

'Weel, Andy?' said the smith.

'It's a gran' day,' observed Andy in his most old-fashioned voice.

The smith smiled and spat a stream of tobacco juice to hide his amusement.

'So it is,' he answered, 'an' whaur ir ye for the day?'

'Och, A'm for the skule the day,' Andy announced importantly, adding with haste, 'but efter the day A'm fenished. A'm leyin' the day. A'm for work noo, ye ken. A'm gan tae be a plooman.'

'Aye,' said the smith, 'ye tell me. Ye'll sine be a man, Andy boy.'

'Och aye, A'll be a man in nae tim',' boasted Andy, and after kicking a sheet of rusted iron that resounded musically, he strode on over the bridge to the school, followed by the amused grin of the smith.

It was only a 'veesitor' who ever knocked at the school door, but on this day of days Andy felt himself a visitor. He knocked loudly and waited, with his feet well apart and his head held high. There was no reply. He could hear the class chanting a lesson, and there was a strange mingling of voices as the older ones recited tables, the younger ones struggled with the alphabet, and the dame read a fairy story to the 'babies'.

He heard her cracked voice admonishing a wrong-doer; it was fun listening to the class, standing in the sunlit doorway with the roar of the swollen burn coming from the direction of the bridge, and the buzz of the bees in the honeysuckle. He knocked again. Louder this time. He could hear a voice telling the old dame that there was someone at the door and the class fell silent. Behind the brown-painted door he felt their eyes gazing to see who would enter. For a moment he was nervous, then the hinges creaked and the dame stood in front of him.

'Good morning,' he said, imitating the school-board man.

She looked at him in amazement, hawk-faced behind her steel-rimmed spectacles.

'Where have you been, Walker?'

Andy walked in.

'A've been comin',' he said stupidly.

She gave him a smack behind the head; someone tittered and he scowled at them as he took his time to deliver his message.

'A'm leyin' the day,' he announced loudly for all to hear, 'an A'll no' be back. A'm gan tae be a plooman. A hae fenished wi' skule.'

'Sit down at once, Walker, and no more of your impudence,' rasped the withered old woman.

'A wull not,' Andy said quite definitely, 'A'm for hame. A hae telt ye. A'm no' comin' back tae skule, an', he added as an after thought, 'if ye hit me again, A'll gie ye a hell o' a hemmerin'.'

She looked at him in surprise. Good sense told her to leave him alone, but dignity demanded punishment. The skin tightened round her jaw bones as she brought the strap across his face with all her might.

'Oh, Christ,' said Andy, 'ye oul' bitch. Tak' that!' and he kicked her viciously on the leg.

'That's the last time ye'll hit me,' and, seizing the strap, he slashed her face with it, repeating the blows before she could cover herself.

The class was a hubbub of sound. The girls cried or screamed and the softer boys said, 'Oh'.

One of the spiteful pupils in a back desk encouraged, 'Gie her yin fur me, Andy. Batter the guts oot o' her.'

But Andy feared to go too far. There were such beings as policemen, two of them, in Wigtown. He hurled the strap into the grate and walked out. The dame sobbed and held her red-marked face, and he kicked her as he went past. Two of the boys crept out with him unnoticed.

He left the school never to return. Since his early days as a pupil there, a backward, unwilling pupil, he had fought the teacher. His wild, aggressive temper had been unable to knuckle to the weak, spiteful tyranny of the old dame. Some she had terrified and dominated, others she had restrained with beatings, but Andy had been untamable. He had fought stubbornly and refused to be cowed. All her puny rage had been levelled at him. To him she seemed a fool to try to withstand his temper or his growing strength, and both were exceptional for a boy of fourteen. There was tenacity in his character; a quality which would suffer no restraint; a spirit that would never be enslaved.

He walked down the road with the two boys and near the bridge picked up a dusty, folded newspaper. They gazed at the brown water of the burn and talked, till the subject was exhausted, on the happenings of the morning. Andy climbed through the fence and sat down by the bank to read. The newspaper, *The Scottish Farmer*, was weeks old. When his interest in binders for sale, artificial manures and calf meal had waned, he threw the paper into the water and watched it drift down stream, round the bends and out of sight. The other two, who were afraid to return to school, stood at the smithy.

When the school bell rang he was beginning to feel hungry and removed his 'piece' from his pocket and ate it. The school was out for an hour and the boys clustered round him; talking about his escapade; about all his previous great deeds; the many times he had disturbed the class; the fights he had had, and the laughs he had raised. He dangled his legs over the bridge and basked in their admiration. He felt sleepy.

Life was great in the warmth of the sun and the sound of the burn. Listening to their praises he almost wished he did not have to leave the grey slate-roofed building that was the school. He wanted to play on the road every day; fish in the burn; sit on the wall and watch the quiet world go by. He had no enemies that day; they all seemed friendly, and he forgot his grudges against those who had laughed at his strange clothes and big boots. He wanted to talk and laugh with them every day in the noon-sun; to run and shout in the frosty mornings of January. They asked him about his 'place' and he told them of all the things he intended to do; where he would work and the rest. The bell rang before all had been told.

He joined the two truants at the smithy door and watched the smith shoe a Clydesdale mare. The smell of the burning nail as the smith held the hot shoe to the foot made him choke; he pumped the bellows and made the coals glow white as the smith turned the shoe in the fire. The clanging of the hammer on the anvil was music to his ears; the smell of the smoke and the horse was sweet to him. When the smith was attending to the mare, he pocketed nails; those long steel polished horse nails that serve so many purposes. They stuck through the pocket and pricked his side, but they were worth the discomfort.

It amused him to shout insults at the smith in the roar of the bellows and hear the smith reply 'Aye' as he paused with his hand on the handle. After a while he grew tired of the heat and the constant pulling on the bellows arm, and offered it to one of the two boys. The breeze was cool and scented as he walked up the road for home, and the freshness of it made him more alive.

McKeown of Drumlin was a hard man to work for, sore on his folks, his son, his two daughters and his wife, who worked under the same task-mastership as his ploughman and byreboy. There were three hundred hilly acres to Drumlin, stony shallow soil that yielded crops only after sweated labour in sun and rain; in the warmth of spring and the frozen air of winter. There were three firwoods on the otherwise bare round hills, and stretches of bog earth in the hollows.

The hard wind-swept slopes had bred in the bones of the McKeown family an equal hardness of nature. The women were thin and bony, yellow-skinned and weather-beaten; the men were tall and rugged. The elder McKeown was bearded and his son had the down of a youthful beard on his face. The farmstead, erected in the dim long-ago, had neither drainage nor sanitation, but when the sun sank in the mists of the west the white walls of the byre and farmhouse were beautiful, set in the blue shadows of the pines that stood beside them. In addition to the byre there was a barn, a straw-house, a turnip-shed, a stable for eight horses, a cartshed and five or six pig-houses. The buildings were old; rain sometimes dripped through the cracks in the slates, and the steading was untidy with broken implements, worn-out horse-shoes, bottomless milk pails and rotting hen-coops. The dung midden was at the byre door. The tang of it was in the air all the year round; it stank as did the pig-sties, which, although they were cleaned frequently, were so old that the smell would have remained even if they had been pulled down and rebuilt. Yet it was a pleasant farm in spite of its untidiness and lonely situation away from the road and the sight of men.

Andy's father had been ploughman to the McKeowns before he left to join the army. The dour devil McKeown knew young Andy by sight and was in need of a boy – a boy that would work hard for next to nothing. So Andy was waged. There was no bargaining as with the waging of a ploughman. McKeown sent his daughter down to tell Sarah that if Andy could leave school there was a job for him. He would be paid five shillings a week and sleep in.

Andy knew the Drumlin land well. He had often wandered through it and climbed in the fir woods in search of nests. He was delighted and rolled his clothes in a bundle ready to go. Tam bought him a suit of heavy serviceable tweed. The day after he left school he walked over to Drumlin. Early in the morning he rose with Tam and had his breakfast. When Tam rose he rose too, picked up his bundle and went out after him. He was wearing the new suit and his new boots. It was a special day. He had never had so many new things before. A new flannel shirt, the suit and boots.

Tam went up the Alticry road and Andy climbed the dyke to cut across to Drumlin. It was half past four in the morning and the grass was wet with dew. A mist hung over the hills and the breeze was chilly. There were five fields to cross before he came to the Drumlin land, then he had a hill to climb and descend before he would come to the steading. Along the side of a ripening cornfield he passed, and through an uncut stretch of rye-grass hay. His new trousers were soaked with dew but his strong boots kept his feet dry. He wanted to dirty the new smelling tweed before he arrived at Drumlin; all the way he chewed a stalk of sweet grass; his step was light and fast and he felt more of a man than ever with his bundle of clothes hanging on a string over his shoulder.

The sun was rising as he climbed the dyke at the Drumlin marches, and pigeons that had been sitting round the cornhill rose and flew across a hollow to a near-by wood. Andy noted the ripeness of the short oats and wondered when they would be ready for cutting. It was an early summer; maybe by the second week of August the greenness would have faded into pale yellow gold and the reaper and binder would whirr round the field. When he reached the top of the hill and looked down towards Drumlin the mist and dark shadows of the hollow hid the steading from his view, but as he descended in the cold breeze, that wafted the turnip leaves and made them dance, he began to make out the white walls.

Soon he saw the farmhouse quite clearly. Smoke curled from its chimney and beyond he could see kye wandering up a rough road from their field. A dog barked; the sound of a man's voice drifted across to him and echoed strangely in the quietness of the morning. The steepness of the hill made him run down it; he dropped his bundle and stood still while it rolled slowly down to him between the turnip drills.

At the foot of the hill he crossed a burn that trickled in a deep cut, overhung by dark green whins and thorny blackberries. A startled pheasant rose from a clump of long grass in front of him and flew away with wildly beating wings. One of its feathers dropped and fluttered at his feet. He picked it up and stuck it in the tweed cap that Tam had given him. Going across the field he straddled the squealing fence to enter the steading. There was no one about, though he could hear a man talking to the kye as he chained them in the byre, so he went up to the house and knocked. A collie dog came and sniffed his leg as he waited. No answer came so he stroked the thin black-and-white dog. It was a friendly creature and rose on its hind legs to lick his face. He staggered a little with the muddy paws on his chest and said, 'Hullo boy.' It whined response and dropped to the ground.

Andy could hear the clatter of boots coming across the tiled floor to open the door. The murmur of voices from within died. A thin woman stood before him, McKeown's eldest daughter.

'A'm the boy,' said Andy, a statement that conveyed all to the woman in the red skirt and man's jacket.

'Oh, ye ir. Weel, come in. The maister'll be doon in a meenit. Hae ye had ony breakfast?'

'A hae had nocht since last nicht,' lied Andy.

She took him in and sat him at a long, bare wooden table.

'Ye're a son o' the Walker we had afore the waur, ir ye no'?' she asked as she spooned porridge into a great white bowl.

'Aye,' said Andy and removed his cap.

A flowered-faced grandfather clock ticked musically by the wall; there was another thin woman sitting over the fire drinking tea from a cracked cup, and an older woman bending down at an armchair laced a pair of dirty boots on her feet. Only the one that had opened the door to him paid any attention to him. When he had finished the porridge, she told him to put his clothes 'up the stair'. There was a wooden loft above the kitchen. A pine ladder led up to it. Andy climbed and entered through the hatch door to lay his bundle on the floor. There were two single beds and a large cupboard in the loft. A byre-lamp stood on a rickety table and the stumps of two candles ornamented the mantel-piece.

The floor was bare; the clothes of the man strewed about it together with the bedclothes which had been thrown aside when he had risen. Andy wondered which bed would be his, for if he was to be byreboy, one of the beds was sure to be his. He tiptoed across the floor so that the woman below would not know that he was taking stock of the room. There was a space between the big cupboard and the slope of the roof which went down almost to the floor level. The space was filled with bits of harness, a manure-sower or 'fiddle,' binder-sheets, and a few rolls of grass-rope, yellow and new. He tiptoed back to the hatch and began the descent of the ladder.

Without his bundle he was able to view the room below with greater ease. There were two dressers, laden with willow-patterned plates and cups; four or five unpainted wooden chairs; a tall glass-funnelled lamp stood on a small round table which was covered with oil-cloth. A great range filled one end of the room, and inside the fender three bleary-eyed cats dosed in the warmth. The women were all sipping tea; not one of them looked towards him, even when his boots slipped on a step.

He reached the floor and walked quietly to a chair by the side of the rosewood dresser. He could see only a bit of the room with a window and a fuschia in a pot when he sat up straight, but he bent over and supported his chin with his elbows on his knees. Now his eyes could wander round the whole of the room once more. From the salted hams hanging on their hooks in the roof, to the shotgun on the rest above the door, his eyes took in all things. He noted the shepherd's crook leaning against the clock, the long binder whip tucked away behind the dresser, and the reaper blades on a string from a nail on the blue distempered wall. He was wondering where old McKeown was when a voice thundered from the depths of the house, 'Jean, Jean, whaur the hell ir ma clean claithes? God dammit, wuman, A hae wurk tae dae the day.'

The youngest of the three women rose hurriedly and clattered down the passage in the direction of the angry voice.

Andy felt less comfortable.

CHAPTER VI

ANDY was surprised when old McKeown walked into the kitchen. He had not heard a sound. The house had fallen quiet when the three women clattered out leaving a bowl of steaming porridge on the round table and a cup of tea with a saucer over it to keep it warm for the 'Da' to come down to. He entered the kitchen silently, walking uncomfortably on his stockinged soles and buttoning his braces as he came. The black beard turned in Andy's direction; the small dark eyes took him in at a glance from under the shaggy eyebrows. The man said nothing, and the boy, too, was silent as he watched him reach under the black leather armchair for a pair of large dirty boots.

The old man, or the 'oul' maun,' as Andy came to call him, supped his porridge noisily. He drank his tea, ate a thick slice of bread and jam, then wiped his beard with the back of his hairy hand. His hands were large and horny, making the coarse teacup look a fragile thing between the enormous fingers.

'Stan up tae A see ye, boy,' he ordered Andy; the voice was deep and strong.

Andy stood up.

'Ye're no' vera big,' he commented, 'dae ye think ye could wheel a barra' o' dung or han'le a hey rake?'

Andy drew himself up to his full four feet three; the thick soles of his boots made him look bigger. 'Aye,' he said, 'A could dae that.'

'Can ye milk, boy?' and the black beard wagged comically.

'No,' admitted Andy, 'bit A could learn. A stribbed a coo yince.'

'Weel ye maun learn they things fast, an' wurk hard, fur A hae nae use fur boys aboot the place that disna want tae wurk hard.'

Andy resented the implication that he might be lazy, and wanted to answer, but the long man straightened out of his chair and bade him 'Come awa', boy.'

Andy almost trotted to keep pace with the great slow strides of his new master. At the byre, which was warm with the smell of the kye, they stopped.

'Tak' aff yer jackit,' he ordered Andy.

'Here, see, gie the boy a stil an' let him in at a coo,' he said to a red-haired man with a red face whose head was buried in the black flank of a cow.

The man rose and, carrying his half-full pail of milk, found a stool for Andy.

Nervously Andy placed his stool at the side of an Ayrshire that chewed and paid no heed to him. He was awkward at first; the stool was too near, so he moved it back a bit; it was too far away, so he brought it nearer, and sat, wobbling slightly, with the pail balanced between his knees. He was uncomfortable; the cow flicked her tail in his eyes and moved from one foot on to the other.

He grabbed the fat teats and began to milk. . . . The milk came easily at first, but his arms and hands became tired. The oul' maun watched him and he was determined to show his worth.

When the pail was half full his arms were heavy and sweat ran from his hair. The cow, too, seemed tired of his laborious efforts and moved more frequently. It was harder work as the pail filled; less and less milk came. He could hear a few of the milked kye being let out; the jingle of their chains and the sound of their feet on the byre walk; the bark of the dog as it hastened them down the road. . . .

Andy went on pulling at the teats till no more milk would come and rose stiffly with his pail and asked, 'Whaur dae A empy this?'

The oul' maun showed him. 'Ye hae din no' sae bad, boy,' he said and then yelled 'Johnnie.'

The red-haired man came hurrying to them. He was shorter than old McKeown by a foot, but had a pleasant friendly face with sandy eyebrows.

'Stribb this coo fur the boy.'

Andy watched the stripping. There was almost half a pail of milk when the man rose from his stool again. Andy was astonished and ashamed.

'Dae twa mair,' the oul' maun ordered, 'an' he'll come back an' stribb them fur ye.'

He sat down at the next cow, a round-sided black Galloway with short blue teats. Her stomach rumbled as he milked. The stiffness in his arms became worse and his hands ached. The oul' maun stalked off up the byre and through the door at the top of the walk. The sandy-eyebrowed man was milking a cow in the opposite stall.

'Whut's yer name?' he called.

'Andy Walker, ma fether wus plooman here a-fore the waur,' said Andy.

'A'm Johnnie Todd.'

'Ma mither wus a Todd.'

'No' frae Whithorn?'

'No,' said Andy, and they ceased conversation.

Andy felt he would like him; the oul' maun too, though he wasn't sure about the two hardfaced daughters or the mistress. He milked on, wondering at everything.

When the last of the kye had been chased down the byre to prevent them soiling the walk, and the gate of the field had been shut upon them, the oul' maun came to watch Andy clean the byre. The barrow was large and heavy; its sides and wheel were caked with dung so that it was difficult for him to wheel it empty. He pushed the long-handled brush and cleaned the walk; carried pails of water and brushed till his face was as red as Johnnie's. He shovelled and swept, and, when the barrow was almost full, he wheeled it, staggering along the slippery plank to tip it on the midden.

The road had to be swept too, and afterwards the pigs had to be fed. It was wearying work, and at half-past nine, as he walked round the pig-houses with arms straining under the weight of the pails of mash, he wished for noon, but the morning wore on with the feeding of hens, sweeping the stable, washing milk-pails, carrying water, and washing the dairy floor.

Johnnie was away to the field with a pair of horse, and from ten o'clock Andy could hear the noise of the reaper going backwards and forwards over a field of hay. All the while old McKeown watched him at his work and led him from one task to another, instructing him in what he expected done every day. With his back and hands aching Andy waited for him to go to the hayfield that he might rest for a minute or two, but he remained at his side.

It was a disappointment for Andy that almost brought tears to his eyes when, instead of going off to the hayfield, the oul' maun stood on the second bar of the gate and gazed over the fields to see how the cutting was getting on. The machine went to and fro without a breakdown. Andy's vexation and fatigue made him bite his lip and swear to himself. He was so tired that he could have lain down on the cool floor of the dairy and rested on his back till mid-day, but as he straightened his legs and dropped the piece of sacking that served as a floor-cloth into the pail, old McKeown marched him off to the barn, where he made him lift corn in a scoop and pour it into bags which he held.

When the bags of corn had been filled he pulled his watch from his pocket – it was fastened to his waistcoat by a bootlace – and grunted, 'Dennertim'.'

He walked to the fence and, putting a whistle to his lips, blew three long blasts. Shortly afterwards, the whirr of the reaper ceased.

'Come on tae the stable, boy, and pit a laddle o' corn in the troughs for the horse.'

Andy staggered after him. The knees of his tweed trousers were baggy and damp; the sleeves of the flannel shirt were wet and, as for the jacket, he had thrown that down somewhere before the whole nightmare began. He was too tired to know just where he had left it. A slow burning rage mounted in his weary body. Did the old bastard think he was made of iron; would there never be a minute for rest again in his whole life? He thought of the freedom of the fields and woods, and glanced across at the hills as he went to the stable. The sun would be hot and stifling on the slopes; the dark shadows by the woods made him think of sweaty discomfort and thousands of flies buzzing round him; the world seemed strangely dull as though he was closer than he had ever been to the earth and seeing for the first time all its harshness and ugliness.

The sun had beaten down on the stable roof till the interior was hot and pungent. He tripped on the cobbled floor and the empty laddle shot from his hands and rattled into a corner.

'Hoots maun,' said the slave-driver, 'can ye no' keep yer feet an' be less hanless?'

Andy scowled darkly at the great broad back as he picked up the laddle. When he had put the corn in the troughs he could hear the jingle of harness chains and the sound of horses' hooves on the stones as they came up from the pump.

'Awa' in fur yer denner,' was the first human comment Andy had heard from the oul' maun for an hour and more.

He hurried across to the farmhouse, and, after scraping his boots at the door, went in.

'Ir ye no' gan tae wesh yer hans, boy?' asked the mistress.

'Aye,' said Andy, 'hae ye a toal an' some sape?'

The cold water from the pump was soothing on his face and arms; he began to feel lighter and tremendously hungry, the carbolic soap nipping his eyes revived his weary senses; he drank a draught of the crystal-clear water from the pump and carried the soap and towel back into the house with him. As he sat down at the long table he noticed that the young McKeown was sitting in the oul' maun's chair. A walking-stick was by the chair and the son's foot was bandaged. The youngest woman fussed round a black pot at the fire, and the other two drank soup with loud sucking noises. Andy brushed back his hair from his eyes and waited in pleasant rest for his dinner. His legs and arms felt weak and every minute was deliciously sweet and comfortable. Jean placed a soup plate before him. It was hare soup, out of season, though Andy was unaware of that, and even if he had been it would not have worried him.

Before he had finished, the boots of Johnnie and the oul' maun grated on the stones outside the door. They were talking about the crop of hay and the oul' maun was giving instructions as to how he wanted the field cut and how much he expected done by night. It was all so strange and interesting, yet so tiring and continuous. Andy felt suddenly a man again; not the same man he had imagined himself when strutting before the boys at school, or talking with the smith, but a tired, muscular, sweating man with blistered hands and weary back.

Johnnie came up the steps from the pump, having washed himself, and he winked and smiled at Andy when he drew in his chair. It was quiet for a while as they ate. Andy forked the steaming potatoes into his hungry mouth and sucked the flesh from the bones of the hare. When he had done he scraped his plate with the point of his knife and sat watching the fuchsia at the window as it swayed in the breeze. After a time the oul' maun spoke from his seat at the other table.

'Andy, ye said yer name wus, did ye no', boy?' he asked.

'Aye,' said Andy.

'Ye'll be a guid worker, boy, if ye're lang wi' me. Ye made a guid han' at learnin' the milkin', an' ye're strong a'tho' ye're wee. We'll sine mak' a maun o' ye. Ye're wullin' an' smert.'

Andy said nothing but he felt a glow of pride in spite of his weariness.

Johnnie paused with his knife on the way to his mouth, looked slyly at him, and winked again. He knew he was taken into Johnnie's confidence, one of the men; a good worker as his father had been; but his heart sank again. Only half the day had gone and he was dead tired. The prospect of the same hours of toil throughout the afternoon made his dinner turn in his stomach. He drank the cup of tea that was placed before him and waited for the rising of Johnnie and the oul' maun.

The grandfather clock, with its redwood case and faded dial, ticked on monotonously. At one o'clock it chimed, a resounding note that was echoed by the scraping of Johnnie's chair and the sound of boots on the floor. The elder of the two daughters began whisking the dirty plates from the table. Andy rose and hurriedly followed Johnnie out.

They sauntered over to the stable. His stomach was full and he was sleepy.

'Ir ye tired, buy?'

Andy liked his voice, he said 'buy' instead of 'boy'.

'Ma erms are a bit sair,' he admitted.

'Ye'll be fur the hayfiel' this efternin,' Johnnie told him. 'The oul' maun taks a rest efter his denner. Ye can ride tae the fiel' on the mare if ye like.'

Andy helped to harness the horses and listened to Johnnie's opinion of the farm, the oul' maun, his son and daughters, the mistress, and the byre-boy who had left. The farm was good, the steading was worn out and done, the old man was a slave-driver; although Andy had long since reached this conclusion; but he was all right if you worked hard. The mistress was a hard 'oul' bitch', her daughters 'withered hags', the son a 'nesty bastard', and the previous byreboy a 'lazy hanless sod'.

Strangely enough, Andy's opinion of it all was much the same. The son, lounging in the armchair with his bandaged foot, had struck him as being a nasty individual who would order him about when he was fit, and maybe cuff his ears and kick him. The daughters were obviously withered virgins who would never marry for the simple reason that no one would ever ask them, and the mistress, with her sulky silence and clattering to and fro, was a bitter, cantankerous woman. Of the oul' maun he had had practical experience and could give his opinions from knowledge, yet the odd comments of praise inclined him to believe that the oul' maun was not so hard to get on with if one could only work his hardest every hour of the day.

Johnnie hoisted him on to the back of the black mare, when they were ready to leave for the field, and he ducked low to pass through the stable door. Johnnie whistled happily as they jogged up the road.

The air was cooler and he could smell the newly cut hay in the breeze that wafted the scent of the whins and the earth to him. It was the most enjoyable moment of the day. He clutched the heavy collar and was careful that the points of the plated hems did not strike his face. They passed through an open gateway and jolted across a stretch of cut hay to where the reaper stood.

His legs were sore and stiff when Johnnie helped him to the ground. He wanted to sit down, but Johnnie's example, though he assured him that it was only because the oul' maun would not sleep till he heard the reaper start, made him hasten to a pile of rakes and forks.

Singling out the lengthiest rake he began to turn the powdered hay that had been cut the day before. Johnnie cursed the horses as he yoked them to the reaper. One, bothered by the buzzing flies, lashed him in the face with her long black tail, and the other, in shifting over to the pole, trod on his foot. Soon the knife was shooting backwards and forwards and the reaper seemed to race round the swaying grass. Andy loosened his shirt and watched Johnnie disappear over a rise in the ground. The chatter of the reaper came like music across the field to him, interspersed with the gruff notes of Johnnie's voice as he urged the horses on. Andy went on turning hay. His rake sped along the sweet-smelling grass till he forgot his blistered hands and was eager only to turn as many rows as he could before five o'clock. The reaper passed him frequently and Johnnie shouted a greeting each time. Andy found himself rushing along the rows at a surprising pace. He even began to watch the sky in fear that rain would come and tried to work out how many rows he had turned and how many there might be when all the field was cut.

The jingle of cups in a basket startled him and he looked round to find Jean at his elbow with a jug of tea. She smiled her approval at his energetic work and he visualized her going home and telling the oul' maun what a hard-working and good boy they had.

'Ye'll be dry, boy,' she said, 'here's yer tea.'

'A im,' agreed Andy and sat down on a soft sward of hay while she poured the tea into his cup and handed a buttered scone and a thick slice of bread and honey.

He took his time to drink the tea and eat. He heard the reaper stop and Johnnie jumped down. Laying his cup on the piece of paper in which his bread had been wrapped, he heard the reaper start again. Johnnie was losing no time, or perhaps he, too, knew that Jean would carry a report of his progress back to the farmhouse. Andy plied the rake with renewed vigour. He was tired in a dull, painless way and his raking had become mechanical. Jean came back and collected his cup.

'Ye'll sleep weel the nicht, boy,' she called to him.

'Aye,' said Andy as though he had hardly time to speak.

A great watery blister rose on his thumb, but he raked on till it burst and then sucked it to ease the pain.

Three blasts on the whistle told them it was 'drappin' tim''. Andy felt that for him it was just about as near dropping time as he would ever be. He sat down at once and undid his boots to tip the hay seeds from them, taking off stockings too, to clean the powder and dust from his feet. The reaper became silent and soon Johnnie came leading the horses across the field. Once again Andy rode the black mare to the stable, helped to remove the sweat-drenched harness, and roll the lines. While the horses were feeding he called the dog, Spot, and went for the kye. Johnnie washed himself and went for his porridge. The dog did the running and Andy shouted and threw stones to hurry the kye up the road to the byre. The three women came out to chain them and he went in to the house. Johnnie was on his way to the byre with a sack apron round his waist and his sleeves rolled high.

The oul' maun was sitting by the fire smoking, for every farm-house in that country had a fire all the year round.

'They tell me ye wur workin' hard this efternin, boy,' he said; 'weel, ye'll hae din the day whun ye hae milked yer kye. It'll no be sae sair on ye the morn'.'

Andy supped his porridge in silence and rose to go to the byre. The milking was the most tiresome job; sore on the hands and arms. It was a precarious business balancing the pail between his knees, but he pulled at the teats grimly; desperately tired and weary, he was determined to finish his day's work. The byre was filled with the sound of chewing kye and milk spurting into pails; the sweat and hair of the cow he was milking stuck to his arms and neck . . . The chains jingled; the kye were let out; the dog barked them down to the field; he emptied his pail and rubbed the hairs from his skin before going in for his supper.

After the meal of cheese and scones, he washed himself again. He had never washed so often in his life before, but it did not remove the dizziness and fatigue that were overcoming him. He sat for a long time in a chair just watching the fire, almost asleep and completely unaware of anything going on around him. Johnnie went across to the stable to let his horses out and he went with him. It was half-past eight and would not be dark for two hours, but Andy wanted to go to bed. When the horses trotted into their field he hung on the gate with Johnnie and surveyed the hills.

'Yin o' thir nichts whun ye're no' sae tired ye can come wi' me an' A'll tak' the gun fur a shot,' suggested Johnnie.

Andy yawned and said 'aye'. On the way back to the house he went in to the byre and found his jacket.

The kitchen was filled with pipe smoke, one of the daughters was darning a pair of men's socks. The mistress talked to the oul' maun and her son. Andy would have been interested to hear the conversation of the son had he not been so tired.

Johnnie showed him up the stair and told him which bed was his; Andy removed his boots and trousers and pulled the blanket over himself. His body seemed one great bruise and his blisters throbbed, but it was pleasant to lie looking at the brown wood of the roof. Dreamily he reviewed the day.

It seemed an age since he had left home in the morning. He had forgotten Tam and his mother; they had become part of a dim past that was yesterday. He heard the hum of voices from below; the tick of the clock; faint squeals from the pig-houses; the lowing of the kye in the boglands. Slowly it all became indistinct. Weariness put him to sleep. He lay as still as a log, breathing deeply and groaning now and then as though he dreamed of the first day in his life's struggle against the soil. He did not hear the voices below as they babbled on till dark; he did not smell the peats that burned in the fire. Johnnie came up to bed and stripped. He did not hear his good-night greeting or the creak of the iron bed-frame as Johnnie laid down. The peats sank in the grate in the room below and the women went to bed.

Old McKeown sat smoking and dozed when the night air became chill. A breeze made the fir trees and pines sigh forlornly and the moon rode above the fields. Andy slept peacefully till the moon had descended once more and a cold grey dawn stole over the heights beyond Wigtown Bay.

CHAPTER VII

THAT first day of Andy's, a Tuesday, seemed the worst. The rest of the week was hard; sore on his hands and back, but the days were not so endless, and never quite the same.

Awaking in the morning in the strange bed, he was stiff, but alive and ready for the new day, even with the tediousness of the first still fresh in his mind. He milked with the blisters aching on his palms and carried pails with the same twinge of tiredness in arm-joints. The milk came from the kye just as reluctantly as the morning and evening before, but he faced it all with the idea that it was a job to be done and not an ordeal of agonising physical effort. He thought of it all in his crude boyish way.

Utterance of his thoughts would have been in no high-sounding adjectives, but strange straight phrases that would have taken hours to make clear. He was less engrossed in milking and consequently did it better; his eyes were not glued in hypnotic stare on the heavy udder of the cow he wrought at; he pulled mechanically and looked round occasionally.

In the field the reaper broke down twice; the hay was not so light and powdery; the night came quicker with the milking of the kye and driving them back to the field. He stood in the warm evening air after supper and listened to a dog barking far away in some small farm behind a hill. He could see a thin streak of smoke curling above the hill and the quiet evening carried the sound of children's voices as they played in the field in the distance. Everything was so still that he could even catch the drowsy cooing of the pigeons in the woods and imagine the sleepy farms in the red mist of the west where the sun was setting. He wandered across to the turnip field and the potato plot in the hollow. Rabbits scuttled into the black earth banks as he approached, and an owl, early on the raid, flew slowly and lightly along the hedgerow in search of food. The shadows of the hollow deepened as the sun sank behind a hill.

He sat on a ramshackle gate and breathed the scent of the mauve and white potato flowers; he was no more lonely than he had ever been at home, but happy in a peaceful tired sort of way. He dreamed of a long warm summer, all dreamy shadowed evenings with the breath of firs and potatoes and damp earth always in the breeze. He wanted to remove his sweat-stiffened shirt and roll in the dew that had fallen; run like a hare across the fields till he dropped in breathless exhaustion; stand all night and think till the white moon rose in the clear sky and its beams caressed the tree-tops.

Weariness made it seem all the more beautiful; he was dumb; an uneducated boy, son of a ploughman, without words to express himself or the mentality to find a method of expression, but he stood and the night stirred his imaginative soul till the tears started in his eyes and his throat became choked with emotion. The soothing beauty of nature overcame him and he was in a trance till the night air chilled his body. When he began to walk back to the farmhouse his legs were stiff. The moon rose higher and lighted his way with a ghostly silver glow.

He revised his opinion of the mistress when he went in, for she said quite pleasantly, 'Andy, boy' – the 'boy' made her seem more friendly and motherly – 'there's a gles o' milk fur ye, an' awa' tae yer bed, fur ye hae tae get up the morn an' ye'll be tired.' He drank the milk in the dark room and removed his boots. The oul' maun smoked as was his custom. Andy could see him in silhouette against the faint light which came through the window by his chair. The dark head, broad high brow and unruly beard. He sat drawing at his pipe. The daughters were in bed, and Johnnie, too, had started snoring. The grandfather clock ticked the minutes away and an ancient cat breathed wheezily under the dresser. Andy went up to bed with the stair creaking under his weight. He smelt Johnnie's earthy clothes, his sweaty socks and the aroma of a hand-rolled cigarette.

Another great day had passed. . . . His head was full of thoughts and he tossed uneasily on the chaff mattress. The old clock below chimed twice before he fell asleep, and the second of many days wore into a third. He dreamed and turned over.

The white-walled farmstead slept; a sow in the pig-house groaned and her litter squealed as she changed her position in the straw; a rat crept along the nest-boxes in the hen-house.

By Saturday, Andy's blistered hands were harder and the stiffness gone from his arms. He was less tired at nights and sat longer in the shadows of the kitchen before going to bed. Johnnie was fond of being early abed, though he was up early enough in the morning. Andy listened to all the oul' maun's stories and the complaints of the injured son. The son was tall and sharp tempered.

Unlike his father's burning rage, there was a weakness about his outbursts that made Andy hate him instinctively. His was the temper of a spiteful weak animal that resorted to a demonstration of rage as a defence. Andy himself would have been unafraid of him physically. His name was David, but they called him Davit or Doit. The two sisters worshipped him as a protection against their father, but he was a weak, grumbling soul. Andy disliked him intensely from the first and he was not slow to realize the intolerance of the oul' maun when he spoke to his son. There was an air of knowledge that was false and assumed about the son and the oul' maun resented the air which was embodied in the tone in which he gave his opinion. Had they not been father and son, Andy felt sure they would have quarrelled and parted, but the women opposed the oul' maun too. He was not afraid of them, resigning himself to their antagonism to prevent a row.

There was a contemptuous insinuation in the son's voice when he criticised his father, and he expressed his own views with the condescending voice of a braggart that hurt even Andy, who felt warmly for the old tyrant. It would have delighted his violent soul to have seen the oul' maun rise and strike him a crushing blow on the mouth or clout him with his great heavy hand. He could imagine the frightened look that would come to the son's face as he cringed before his father's rage.

The oul' maun gave his opinion between long draws at his pipe – in a slow, steady voice he spoke, appealing to none; the voice of experience and conviction, fearless and careless of disagreement and contradiction. It worried Andy, for Davit was in the habit of seeking confirmation from his listeners. Not that he asked Andy, he was too young to be recognized, but if Johnnie or his mother or sisters were present he would turn to them smiling and say, 'Is that no' richt?'

It was hard to know just what to answer. McKeown's was a strange household indeed, with its strained air of antagonism. It had hardly been discernible to Andy at first, but he soon sensed the bitterness that existed and was sorry for the oul' maun in his loneliness. Yet the unreasonable slave-driving fits of him often killed Andy's sympathy and he would feel on the side of the son, the sullen daughters and the silent mistress of the house.

Five days he had been there and all these things he knew. It seemed longer than all his life that had gone before; in fact there had been nothing before he came to Drumlin. His head was full of new things and he had forgotten the cot-house on the Alticry road.

On Sunday Andy went down on the cart to the road end with Johnnie, who took the milk to the lorry from the creamery, which waited every morning for the cans of milk. There was no excuse for lateness, Andy learned. If you happened to be late, there was the long journey to Wigtown taking the milk to the creamery yourself. When he came back he had breakfast, not just a steaming bowl of porridge, but ham and eggs as well. There was no religion at Drumlin. The day was spent, between feeding pigs and hens, in sleeping or sitting by the fire. Johnnie rode home on his bicycle and Andy walked over the hill to the cot-house, but he waited for his dinner at Drumlin before starting.

It was one o'clock and warm when he made his way up the greystone dykeside and over the hill. It was fine, that feeling of freedom from work. He stopped almost half-way home and removed his boots to lie down on a springy patch of grass. The air was warm and hazy; he debated whether to go home or lie on the grass till kye time. A cool breeze from Wigtown Bay drifted across the land; he smelt the freshness of it and walked on. Its soft cool gusts wormed their way through his clothes till his whole body was enlivened by them. There was a buzz of insects in the air and a shimmer over the moss when he crossed the road and came down to the cot-house. A wisp of smoke trailed from the blackened chimney but the place was serenely and silently asleep in the heat of the afternoon.

There was a murmur of voices as his boots disturbed the stones by the gate. He could almost hear them saying, 'Wha'll this be?'

Tam was sitting by the dead fire when he went in, chewing tobacco and spitting on the store of peats.

'How's the boy?' said Tam.

Sarah looked up from the dishevelled bed. 'Oh, it's you, Andy?'

'Aye,' answered Andy, 'it's me. A'm fine, Tam, bit, Christ, A hae been wurkin' helluva hard. Jist look at they hans.'

He held out his damaged hands for Tam and his mother to see. His two sisters looked too, and rubbed the broken skin. Andy was a man; he did not wince. Sarah brushed her rat-tails of hair from her eyes – the fluff of the bed still stuck to her head – and began asking questions. Andy was proud to tell of his work from first day to last. He told Sarah all about the mistress, the daughters and the house; Tam about the oul' maun, his son, Johnnie, and how far they were on with the hay.

Tam was sympathetic and proud of him and gave him a lump of tobacco to cut and roll for cigarettes. Andy put it in the waist pocket of his trousers. There was nothing new-looking about the tweed suit or heavy boots after five days. The boots were scratched and dull; the trousers muddy at the knees, and the jacket dusty with hayseed and pollen from the grass.

Sarah made a cup of tea for them; they sipped it slowly, sitting on three low stools before the smouldering fire that she had coaxed to life for the boiling of the kettle. After a while Andy, who had related every incident he could remember, asked Tam the time.

'Holy Christ, boy, it'll sine be five o'clock,' said Tam, pulling his battered watch from his waistcoat pocket.

'A'll hae tae awa',' said Andy, 'A'll be ower Sunday. Hae ye a box o' matches an' a piece fur me afore A gang?'

Tam provided the matches while Sarah cut a slice of bread and soon he was hurrying back towards the hills of Drumlin, eating the bread and butter as he went. He ate slowly, letting the soft bread lie in his mouth till it made his mouth water, then swallowing it in a sweet wet paste. It was ten past five when he reached the steading. The collie was out looking for him; he whistled to it and went down the road for the kye. Johnnie came pedalling up the road as he brought the milkers in; he waved to him and hurried to get his 'Sunday claithes' off and the sack-cloth apron round his waist ready for work. With the kye all in the byre he went for his tea. It was ready and the three women were scurrying about the kitchen looking for aprons and boots. The oul' maun came down from his bed and looked darkly at the women to signify his annoyance.

All three left the house and clattered over to the byre as the oul' maun groped for his boots under the chair, 'Ye brocht the kye in, boy?'

'Aye,' mumbled Andy, swallowing a piece of cheese.

'It's a guid thing that somebudy gets their wurk din aboot the place. Johnnie, Johnnie, Godsake maun! Ir ye no' at the byre yit? Whut's hinnerin' ye?'

Johnnie muttered, 'A'm comin',' and the stairs creaked loudly as he almost stumbled down them and hastily pulled his boots on at the bottom step.

He made for the door, tying his apron round him without waiting for his tea, but the oul' maun was still not satisfied.

'Haste ye, maun, haste ye,' he thundered after him.

Andy suddenly realized that he was not exempt and gulped down his tea.

'That's the boy,' approved the oul' maun as he raced out in front of him.

Andy sat in at his cow with a feeling of pleasure; he was the only really good man about the farm, all the other folk were lazy. They needed a strong hard-working man like him to keep the work going.

The milking had never been done so quickly, and afterwards he borrowed Johnnie's knife to cut the piece of tobacco that Tam had given him. It took him a long time to cut and roll it all and his pocket was half full when he had finished. He searched for a thin paper to roll a cigarette and Johnnie gave him two cigarette papers and showed him how to roll and hold the paper while he licked the edge. It was all so manly, the cutting and rolling the cigarettes, but the smoking was not so pleasant. Andy had smoked Woodbines before, but never a hand-made cigarette of black twist tobacco. He felt dizzy, though on the whole it was worth it.

After the ordeal he walked out in the open air with his eyes smarting and a bitter taste in his throat. His head began to ache and he would have gone to bed if it had not been for what Johnnie might have thought about him. He was back to normal before the old clock chimed ten, and drank a cold draught from the pump to add to his returning feeling of comfort on going to bed. All the skylights were open to let the smoke out and after he was sure that the air in the loft was fresh again he closed them down. The oul' maun had gone to bed early for once, and Andy could hear the high-pitched titter of the three women who sat round the dying fire and talked.

He remembered something he wanted to tell Johnnie.

'Hey, Johnnie,' he whispered, but Johnnie was soundly asleep.

He leaned over and shook the bed. Still the sleeper breathed deeply. He climbed on to the bed and repeated the words in his ear.

Johnnie woke with a loud 'Whut?' It was so loud that it almost deafened Andy, who was so surprised that he forgot what he had intended to say. The women below were startled by Johnnie's voice and fell silent. Andy gazed down at Johnnie and he smiled.

'Whut did ye want, Andy?' he asked.

'A hae forgot,' confessed Andy.

'Och, get tae yer bed, maun. Wur ye feart or somethin'? Waknin' a falla up for nocht?'

'Bit A had somethin' tae tell ye,' protested the offender, 'only ye shouted that lood whun ye wakned that ye made me furget.'

'A' richt,' said the good-tempered Johnnie, 'mebbe ye'll hae min' in the mornin'.'

'Aye,' said Andy, but he did not remember.

The thing had slipped from his mind completely. The women were talking again as he pulled the clothes up over his chest. Johnnie was breathing deeply.

In a fortnight the hay was ricked. Andy had helped at the ricking; one or two of the small round-topped ricks were his. The oul' maun believed in carting and stacking as soon as possible. He had seen many fine crops of hay ruined by the weather breaking before it could be carted to the stackyard. Andy, being short, was little use for forking, but he built the hay on the carts under the oul' maun's direction. He was learning more every day. In the stackyard he forked the hay from the cart. It was not so hard for he was high up and his lack of inches was no handicap. The stacks were up and thatched before the weather changed as the oul maun had feared.

It was on the morning that Davit came out for the first time without a stick. He hobbled to the stackyard, coming painfully across the court, a long thin figure of a man with a gaunt narrow face and straight sandy hair. He was almost at the stable-door when the expected downpour came. It gave Andy delight to see him drenched as he tugged at the bar of the door to take shelter. The bar was hard to shift. Andy usually struck it back with the handle of the byre shovel, but he stood in the dryness of the barn and watched Davit struggle with it. . . .

For days, until he was weary of the job, Andy sat with Johnnie on the granary floor rolling grass rope in readiness for the harvest. The ropes were taken from the stacks as they were used during the winter and left in a tangled mass that had to be sorted for the next year. They rolled ropes for hours, rising occasionally to see if the rain was likely to clear. When it did they saw that the corn, red ripe, had been beaten to the ground. It was a despairing sight and brought curses from the oul' maun each day that the sun failed to make it rise. It meant a job for the reaper, the binder would be unable to cut the lying oats on the hills, where it was flattened in all directions. The only consolation they had was in looking round at neighbouring farms and finding them as badly stricken. In some cases they had more lying corn. It meant a late harvest, for the cutting would take longer working with the reaper. Then when all was ready for stacking it might even rain once more.

Pessimism descended upon Drumlin. All save Andy, who failed to realize the meaning of the catastrophe, were self-pitying and grumbled. Johnnie spent days mowing out the worst parts and Andy tied the sheaves for him. It became warmer, and after the roads had been cut round the fields and projecting rocks, the three women, Andy, Davit and the oul' maun were in the field to tie sheaves, as Johnnie opened the cutting. Half the morning was through before Jean was allowed to go home to 'see tae the denner, the pigs an' the hens'. The others worked like fiends tying sheaves as the horses tore round the field in front of the whirring knives.

It was the supreme test for Andy. He had never felt so tired, not even on his first day. The greatest battle against the soil and elements was in its final stages. Men had ceased to be human; backs bent and straightened in rhythm; sheaves were tied and tossed aside to be stooked; the reaper rushed round again and again. No sooner had the last sheaf been tied at the end of the row before it came once more and spewed out hundreds more to be tied with a strand pulled from the bunch. In places the sheaves were full of thistles; they stuck in the fingers till the finger-tips seemed nothing but raw flesh. The ends of the oats stung the bare arms and made the skin inflamed; there was no such thing as rest; the same feverish race went on from the first day.

Till the last sheaf had been forked to the stack, and the field was dull brown with rotting stubble, the race went on. Andy slept soundly at night and worked every day of the week till sunset. The three women brought in the kye and milked alone. Andy and the men, there was an Irish harvester working with them, carried on until it was too dark to see, then staggered home to supper and bed with sweat cooling in their shirts.

Sunday, too, found the same unending toil in the heat of the afternoon and the cool breeze of evening; forking sheaves to carts; forking sheaves to stacks; till all three cornfields were bare and raked with the horse-rake for the gleanings. The rushes in the bogs were cut and carted to the stack-yard for thatching. Round the stacks on ladders the men stood laying on thatch, passing ropes round and making the stacks watertight. Andy did his share of passing ropes round and climbing up with sheaves of rushes. He climbed up with a sheaf on a fork, pushed the fork through the sheaf into the stack, and waited till the men needed another.

It was late September before it was all over. Hay and oats stacked; bare fields that the pigeons searched for stray heads of corn; only the green shaws of turnips to contrast the red autumn that had come withering away the green from the potato-patch.

To Andy his few weeks seemed like years. He had found his place among men; he knew what life held for him . . . a back-tiring struggle, against wind and storm, to drag a crop from the soil after months of labour. He had seen the withered yellow-skinned women slaving beside the men all day without a grumble or a pause. He had watched Davit working among them as feverishly as any . . . and it was all over.

A weight had been lifted from his mind, from the minds of all of them. The year's crop was in. It was pleasant working on the damp black earth of the potato field; lifting the crop from behind the spinning prongs of the digger, and carrying the pails of potatoes to the dry earth-smelling bags at the hedgeside. The mists of autumn drifted down the hollows. It was pleasant and cool and gave him a greater love of the soil than ever. There was a great crop of potatoes, mauve ones and white ones in different patches. The women helped again at the lifting and the oul' maun estimated his crop with a stump of pencil on the back of a tattered seed catalogue. The day that the last bag was taken in the rain came in sheets. . . . It was November before it stopped.

Andy spent days in the barn sorting potatoes for seed, for pigs and for sale. When that was over he went in the rain for turnips. The oul' maun bought him a pair of button-on leggings of oilskin and he shawed turnips by Johnnie's side till his birthday came and passed.

Between whiles he fed kye, cleaned the byre, the stables and the pig-houses. The kye were in at nights and the byre was a heavy task. His muscles became big and hard and the oul' maun was pleased with his work. When the dry spell came Johnnie and Davit went to the ploughing. They worked all the hours of daylight; the teams passed to and fro across the hill as they struggled to regain lost time. Andy watched their progress each day as he fed his kye and mucked his byre. The kye stayed in all day, for there was no grass on the hard cold land. Andy foddered them and mixed mash, helped by the oul' maun.

Time flew past. New Year came and, soon after it, sowing time. He worked his first horse before the harrows; sat on a roller and rolled the ground when the oats were sown. . . .

The crop rose in a carpet of green shoots; the grass in the fields grew again. Soon it would be summer, haytime, harvest. . . .

CHAPTER VIII

I T rained every day for three weeks in February. The low fields were submerged in water and the burns grew into torrents. What had been a pleasant sighing murmur of water in the summer and autumn became roaring frothy floods that swept dead wood and rotted grass before it into eddying swirls in the inundated hollows. The soil was sodden and clung in leaden clogs to the soles of boots, and the rain swished across the fields and beat down on skylights night and day. The sound of it became lost to the ears; it seemed part of life.

Day after day it thrashed the dead brackens in the woods, and saturated the mossy earth at the shallow roots of the fir trees till they swayed in the gale and remained leaning drunkenly. The sky was a haze of rain; the Bladnoch overflowed its banks; sheep were drowned; gates, fences and feeding-troughs floated away to the sea, bobbing merrily in the rush. Andy stayed at Drumlin three Sundays for it was impossible to go home. He lay in his bed all day doing nothing after his morning work; he tossed restlessly unable to amuse himself.

The weather seemed to have had a bad influence on the McKeowns for their tongues were sharper than ever and the oul' maun's voice thundered as he raged at them. He, too, was irritated by the constant rain. On the fourth Sunday the sky cleared; it still rained, but it was light showery rain that promised to abate at any minute. Andy decided, from no love of home or family ties, but purely to relieve the monotony of the day, that he would go over to the cot-house.

He wrapped the oilskins round his legs and set out after dinner to climb the hill. There was a coldness in the drizzle that told of a freezing spell to come. A white-coated stoat came racing over the ploughed field after a rabbit. They disappeared over the brow of the hill, the wicked little white slayer gaining every second. A few minutes later Andy heard the rabbit's squeals of fear as the stoat leaped upon it. He tried to run but his boots were heavy with mud and the slope slippery and wet. Perhaps the cunning little killer was watching him as he strode on and climbed the dyke. A stone toppled as he jumped to the ground on the other side. The echo of it ran through the small fir plantation on his right. It was growing colder; he hurried on, his legs weary with the effort.

The cot-house was strangely silent when he lifted the latch and went in. His sisters were nowhere to be seen and Sarah lay on the bed groaning. Tam rose.

'Whut's the metter wi' her?' Andy asked, nodding towards the bed.

'She's hurt her leg,' answered Tam. 'She fell a fortnicht ago an' hisna been able tae walk since. A dinna ken whut she can hae din. It's affa sair an' she keeps groanin' an' greetin'.'

'Whaur ir the lassies?' asked Andy.

'Och, A sent them ower tae ma mither's. She'll look efter them till she's better bit it'll maybe be a lang time A'm thinkin'.'

Andy looked at Sarah.

'Whaur daes it hurt?'

Sarah groaned and turned white-faced towards him.

'Ma knee's affa sair, boy, an' richt up tae ma hip. It's nae better ether than it wus. A canna eat ocht fur the pain o't.'

She went on groaning and breathing heavily.

Tam sat smoking.

After a while they made tea and drank it, then Andy had to start back.

'Och, ye hae jist twisted yersel',' he reassured Sarah as he left, 'ye'll be better in a day or twa.'

Tam smoked in silence.

On the following Wednesday Andy was carrying a basket of turnips to the byre when he saw Tam's long-striding form coming down the hill. He dropped his basket and walked across the field to meet him.

'She's daid,' said Tam sorrowfully as they met.

'A kent it whun A saw ye comin',' said Andy.

There were no tears in his eyes. In fact there was a note of pleasure in his voice that suggested he was proud of his premonition.

'Come ower the nicht an' see her,' said Tam, 'the joiner's sen'in' a box fur her the morn.'

'Whun did she dee?'

'Yisterday efternin. A had tae gang fur the doctor tae her. She was daid afore he got there, an' he gied me a helluva tongue lashin'. He said he should hae been telt whun it happened. A fractur' or somethin'. A wus at the joiner's this mornin'.'

'Ir ye gan tae fetch Jimmie an' Wullie?'

'Aye,' said Tam, 'A'll be gan ower fur them this efternin. The lassies'll be a' richt at ma mither's.'

'Weel, A'll hae tae be back at the byre,' Andy remarked after a pause, 'A'll be ower the nicht efter kye tim'.'

'Richt ye ir,' said Tam, and turning, he went back the way he had come.

The day wore on, and after kye time Andy washed himself and set out for the cot-house. It was dark and windy. The rain blew cold in his face and he felt miserable; the sound of his boots on the soft earth and stones made him only the more nervous; he was shaking and breathless as he walked down the fields towards the flickering light that shone in the cot-house window.

He called, 'It's me, Andy,' when he pushed the door open.

Tam was sitting by the fire, a downcast unshaven figure. The shadows and lights of the room played on his face as the lamp flame danced in the draught. He pulled his pipe from his jaws and looked at Andy.

'Tak' a look at her. She's ower there on the bed.'

Andy lifted the lamp and the shadows frolicked along the walls as he walked over to the bed. Sarah's body was lying on the tattered sheet, uncovered save for a white cloth that Tam had wound round her. The hard lines had not left her face. There was a gipsy-like darkness about her that was increased by the uncombed bedraggled black hair which Tam had hurriedly smoothed back from her brow. Andy looked and the lamp shook in his hands. He felt there was something he was expected to say.

'She's daid a' richt,' he muttered.

'Aye,' said Tam and spat in the fire.

Andy touched her; the flesh was as cold as stone, like frozen butcher-meat. The lamp shook until he was afraid that he would drop it, and the dead face seemed to be moving in a yellow blur as though the dead woman was speaking in whispers. He turned away and laid the lamp back on the mantelpiece. The wind whistled round the cot-house and rattled the loose window frames; the peat smoke came curling back down the chimney and swirled out of the fireplace across the room.

'A dinna ken hoo a broken leg could hae kilt her,' observed Andy.

Tam rose.

'She never said ocht aboot this.' He walked over to the bed with the lamp and pulled the covering off the body. The thigh and hip were a dull blue-green shade. Andy turned his head away. Tam came back to the fireside.

'Jimmie an' Wullie'll be here afore lang,' he remarked. Then, after a pause, 'The perish'll see tae the funeral.'

Andy said nothing, he was wondering what would happen to all the odds and ends of rubbish that the cot-house contained.

As if he had read his thoughts Tam said, 'There's nocht here ye'd be wantin', is there, Andy?'

'Nocht bit the oul' gun o' ma fether's if A can hae't.'

'Ye can tak' it the nicht,' answered Tam, 'an' there's twa three cartridges in the drawer . . . A wus thinkin', if there's nocht that Jimmie or Wullie wants, A micht get the len' o' a kert an' tak the twa three bits o' duds ower tae ma mither's. They'd dae the lassies fine. A hae nae need tae stey on here.'

'Nae need at a',' agreed Andy, 'the place's din onywey. The water's comin' through the roof an' the wa's ir nivir dry.'

The night wore slowly on as they sat one each side of the fire, Tam with his face propped on his hand, Andy with his arms clasped round his knees. The wind died down and after a few minutes they heard the sound of voices; the creak of a bicycle chain close to the door. The sudden click of the latch startled Andy. Jimmie and Wullie came in together.

'Hullo, Tam,' they murmured in unison.

Both went over to the bed and held the light above their heads to look at their dead mother. Andy stood up and went to the drawer of the rickety dresser to find the cartridges Tam had spoken of; he found them, eight grimy cartridges wrapped in a gun-cleaning rag. Wullie and Jimmie squatted beside the fire as Andy lifted the old shot-gun from its corner.

'Whut ir ye dae'n wi' that?' asked Wullie.

'A'm takin' it,' said Andy shortly.

'Ir ye, b'Christ? A wus thinkin' o' takin' it masel'.'

'Weel, ye wur ower late o' thinkin' an' it's mine noo.'

Wullie was a quiet boy.

'A' richt, Andy,' he assured him, 'dinna scraich at me. A'm no' argyin' wi' ye.'

Andy pulled the gun-cleaner out of his pocket and wiped the dust off the barrels. Jimmie pulled the string through as he cleaned it. They sat in silence. Andy poured oil into the triggers and slipped two of the cartridges into the breech. He was glad that the coveted gun was his at last. It had never occurred to him to ask for it before. Wullie handed round his cigarettes and they smoked. Tam threw another peat on the fire.

Jimmie was the only one who seemed uneasy at the proximity of the dead body on the bed. He glanced round nervously, half expecting Sarah to be sitting up or even walking softly across the floor to startle them. Wullie yawned.

'Whaur ir ye gan tae sleep the nicht, Tam?' he asked.

'On the flair,' said Tam. 'A'll be a' richt. A'm no' feart o' yon.'

He thumbed and nodded towards the stiff figure on the bed. Andy caressed the old gun lovingly and sat looking into the peat glow, dreaming of all the things he would do with it. Already he saw himself poaching in the moonlight, slipping through silent woods after pheasants, the thunder of the shot roaring in his ears and echoing across the hills.

Wullie rose, 'Come on, Jimmie, we'll hae tae awa'.'

Tam told them of the funeral arrangements and what he intended to do with the furniture. They had a sip from his whisky bottle before they set out. Andy left a few minutes later and Tam bedded down in front of the fire, having barred the door.

It was dark going up the dykeside towards the hills of Drumlin. The moon shone at times from under a watery black foreboding cloud. There was a slight breeze of frozen air and the earth was already freezing hard. The soil cracked under his feet and the moisture below the surface made him slip and slide as he walked. At first he was content to tramp on and watch how he stepped, but the thought of the gun came back to him with a rush as he entered the unholy shadows of the trees. He was afraid suddenly. The moon had gone again; it was black dark; not a speck of light or a star to be seen. His fear rose steadily till his hands shook. The icy drips from the swaying branches of the ash trees fell on his face and down behind his coat collar. The sighing dead branches seemed to threaten a dark and hellish doom. He would have run, but it was too slippery underfoot. He stopped and fumbled in his pockets for two of the cartridges.

Even the sound of the opening breech startled him as he pushed the cylinders in. Once this was done he felt a new fiendish courage that made the skin on the back of his neck creep, but a sudden cold spatter of rain from the branches and the mournful sighing note in the wind brought the terror on him again. It was slow going. When he reached the edge of the trees he was afraid to leave the friendly darkness that hid him from the nothingness that was haunting him. He stood still, white-faced and shaking. To console himself he pulled back the hammers of the gun and half-crouched over it as he walked forward.

His imagination was playing him tricks. The sound of a horse's hoof striking a stone as it stood in the shelter of a nearby hedge made him jump. He clambered over the dyke; a stone fell with a crash that filled his head with sound. As he crept up the side of the turnip hill his foot caught on a whin branch and he stumbled forward, regaining his balance with difficulty. There was a roar as though all the devils in hell were upon him; he was almost stunned with the explosion and his heart thumped in his chest . . . The raised hammer had fallen and the shot tore through a hedge on his left. Though he could not see it, a wisp of smoke trickled from the barrel of the rusty gun. The echo came back across the hills like the crack of a roadman breaking stones. He began to run, slipping dangerously from side to side. He was too nervous to try to put the other hammer of the gun down, but stumbled on in fear up the hill, over another dyke and down into the black depths that was the hollow of Drumlin. . . .

The farmhouse door was unlocked. He lifted the latch and went in, bolting the door behind him. In the flicker of the dying fire he took off his boots and dried the gun, after gently releasing the hammer. The spent cartridge case made the fire bright for a few seconds, then the shadows rushed in towards him as the small flame sank. He climbed the stairs holding the gun in one trembling hand and his boots in the other. Johnnie was snoring loudly, the noise comforted him and he felt a new sense of security and strength. Hurriedly pulling off his socks and trousers, he got into bed. The rising wind whistled and moaned round the house and boomed in the chimney.

It was hard to sleep and he began to see Sarah's yellow bony face staring at him from the darkness. He could see her bedraggled hair across her cheeks and the holes where her eyes should have been. She must have followed him over the hills . . . he wanted to scream, but his voice had gone. He lay staring into the darkness while the rain swished on the skylight. Sarah grinned at him . . . he turned his neck to peer over the clothes into the depths of the loft. It was an endless tunnel; the mouth of hell with Sarah's head hanging. Even with the clothes over his head the spectre was slow to leave his mind. Once or twice he was tempted to throw them back suddenly and surprise her staring down upon him. An hour passed and he slept.

The dreary days of February wore on, with their wind, rain and frost. In the hot, animal-smelling byre Andy was at home. He loved to hear the kye chewing and the strange intestinal rumbling that came from their round hairy bellies. He fed them and cleaned them, shouldering his way between them with a basket of cut turnips, a pail of mash or an armful of hay. Sarah, Tam, Wullie and Jimmie were soon all forgotten. They had been slipping from his memory since he came from school to Drumlin. They faded as the winter faded into spring.

He never saw Tam again after one Sunday meeting at the Drumlin road end. Andy was turning the milkcart; the milk-lorry was racing away down the road, when a man came pedalling head-down in the driving rain towards him. He looked up as he drew near. It was Tam.

'How's the boy?' he said as he jumped off with a clatter of boots.

'Fine,' said Andy, 'how's yersel'?'

He was pleased to see Tam. The old black horse was eager to be away and tugged and pulled till his arms ached holding it back.

'Hoo did the funeral gang aff?' he enquired after a pause.

'Och fine,' said Tam. 'The place's empy noo, ye ken. A took the bits o' things ower tae ma mither's. The roof's leakin' bad, an' the door blew doon yin nicht in the wun. It's queer, ye ken, the wey a place fa's tae bits whun there's naebudy leevin' in't.'

'It's a peety,' said Andy, but he was not sorry. In fact he would not have cared had the cot-house been blown down altogether one night in the wind.

'A'm fur leyin' this pert o' the country,' ventured Tam after another pause, 'A hae a freen oot bye in Ayrshire that haes a wee place, an' A'm gan tae wurk fur him.'

'Ir ye? A'll miss seein' ye, Tam, bit mebbe ye'll no' be lang afore ye're back.'

'Mebbe no,' agreed Tam.

They stood saying nothing till the rain trickled down their faces.

Tam spat on the toe of his boot, and when the horse almost dragged Andy off his feet again he said, 'Weel, A'll hae tae awa' on, Andy boy. If A dinna see ye afore A gang tae Ayr mebbe A'll see ye whun A come back.'

'So long,' said Andy.

Tam mounted his bike and pedalled on into the wind and rain. The cart jolted up the stony slope and on through the puddles. He turned and stared down the hollow where the road wound into the mist. He could see Tam's struggling figure as he fought his way into the wind.

Tam never came back from Ayrshire and Andy did not see him again. He rode down the misty hollow on his rattling old bicycle and vanished for ever from Andy's sight, a redfaced weather-worn man with a stubble of hair on his chin and a plug of strong tobacco in his cheek. The milkcart swayed and jolted through the mud up to the farm. Andy's heart was low, he felt the passing of a friend, the only man for whom he had ever felt affection, the only being he had ever loved as much as himself. The horse breathed quickly and its breath shot from each nostril in grey puffs of steam.

The frost of the morning formed on Andy's black coat and settled on his eyelashes, so that, when it melted, it seemed as though the forlorn boy was crying. He sat in half-frozen silence, thinking, and oblivious of everything. When the iron-shod wheel passed over a big stone and all the bones in his body were jarred he scarcely noticed it. He sat in such a day-dream that when the old horse stopped at the second gate, waiting for him to dismount and open it, he did not realize it and it was only the lack of motion that brought him back to conscious thought. He jumped down, lifted the rope from round the post and ran back with the tarred gate. The horse went on up the road and he ran after the cart and clambered up on front without stopping the progress.

As the sun dispelled the mist he could see gulls flying over the hills. It was Sunday and there were no plough teams traversing the slopes to turn up worms for them, in fact the ploughing would soon be over. The early weeks of the month had been wet and little harrowing had been done, but if the weather held the next few weeks would see the ploughed land harrowed and the sowing done. These things passed through Andy's mind with a jumble of other thoughts. He noticed the plough lying in the furrow of the last half acre of bogland where the potatoes would go.

Johnnie came riding down the road in his Sunday clothes, a crumpled brown suit under a heavy overcoat. He jumped off to allow the cart to pass, and Andy grinned as the wheel shot mud and water over his trouser legs, which were tied with binder twine for the want of clips. Johnnie swore loudly and roundly, but grinned too, for he was a good-natured man. The road was rougher at the steading, great stones had been laid down to fill the water holes and as the cart passed over them the world danced before Andy's eyes and his inside seemed to turn over. When the horse was back in the stable and fed, and the milk-cans had been washed, he went for his breakfast. The byre had still to be cleaned and the kye fed from the diminished heap of turnips, many of which were already rotting.

It was a slimy, unpleasant task lifting the pulpy turnips from the frozen heap to find the harder and firmer ones, but the kye had to be fed. Cleaning the byre was a nicer-smelling and warmer job than feeding the black Galloways and the half-bred Ayrshires. It was one o'clock before it was all over and he walked up to the stable to take the horse to the pump for a drink. It neighed as it caught sight of the two young colts hanging over the gate.

The day passed, a dark February day that was typical of late winter in the bleak corner of the Machars. The woods were dark and dreary and the boglands hung with mist; the hills were freezing up for what promised to be a hard, dry spell before winter gave up her last hold on the land and a frosty bright spring came to take up the brief lease. It was dark in the byre at nights and lamps swung over the stalls.

Andy and Johnnie liked to sit in an empty stall that was filled with hay, and talk at nights after the milking. The byre was quiet save for the breathing of the kye, many of them nearing calving.

So it was that Andy saw the last of Tam and Wullie, for Wullie recruited in the Borderers and was taken to India, and it was a long time before he met either of his sisters or Jimmie again. Jess had three children and was still unmarried when he saw her at a cattle show with her illegitimate brood years later. She was little more than eighteen, but fat and sluggish, with the looks of a woman of thirty. Like her mother she was an untidy slut with a vicious temper. Her babies were unwashed squawking little creatures. One clambered in her arms while the other two stared stupidly from a worn pram that she pushed down the street before her.

CHAPTER IX

IN THE spring showers Andy worked with Johnnie while the green shoots of oats carpeted the hills, and long lines of growing turnips began to appear up the furrowless, harrowed land. They were quiet, bright days when his heart was happy at the changing of the season, but the McKeown household was not happy. The cares of the sowing were over, it was merely a patient wait to see what crop the summer would bring and what harvest would come at autumn. There was a viciousness in the shade of the sprouting pine spikes, in the sudden bursting into life of the mosslands, and in the farmhouse there was a sympathetic flash of tempers as though the family had tired of its proximity to the winter. The oul' maun stormed and swore as he sat in his chair by the window; the women harangued him and nagged.

His son, who could not have faced his tyrant father alone, was urged by his mother and sisters till he strutted and pruned himself like a cock on a midden. He faced his father and disagreed with all he said insolently and nervously arrogant. Throughout those show-ery days they all remained in the house. Andy, coming across the steading with Johnnie, would hear the thunder of the oul' maun's voice and the high-pitched protests of his son. Andy hated the son as the strong despise the weak and rough men despise fops.

There was a falsely fine look about the oul' maun's son when he closed his mouth and sulked. His rages were hysterical and weak. He moved uneasily as he verbally fought his father and avoided the fierce glare from beneath those bushy eye-brows. Under his fine greying beard, the oul' maun's mouth would be tight and deter-mined, his temper was scornful that anything should oppose his strength of will and body. Something of that stubborn nature that was Andy's, lurked in the oul' maun's defiant face, a quality which refused to be driven and admitted no master. It was a battle against a will of iron, a strength untirable. The women scolded when the oul' maun removed his pipe from between his clenched jaws and spat on the tiled floor.

Where was a man to spit?

They scolded the more because they knew that from a strong man there could be few apologies. The son, having inherited the wish to command from his father, though not the strong body or mind, had long wished to run the farm his own way, to give orders that would be unquestioned whether wrong or right. When his cantankerous mother turned against his father as she had longed to do since the day they were married, he sought from her the support to face the lord and master of the house who sat in his chair cursing the twinges of pain that shot through his rheumatic legs.

Andy had been helping Johnnie to rebuild stretches of dyke that had fallen during the winter. They came in to dinner one day when the row was at its height for the tenth day. The oul' maun, with his boots caked with mud and dung, came across to the table to talk with them. The floor had been newly washed and the women heaped abuse on him. He sat down unheeding and smoked as he talked. After a time his voice became thick as the saliva from smoking formed in his mouth. Andy smiled to himself; he knew what would happen, the oul' maun would turn his head and spit on the floor.

He did . . . carelessly he spat. It was too much for his wife's
flaming temper. She seized a brush and brought it down on his head,
but the brush stopped before it struck the bearded man. His great,
strong hand rose and grasped it before it landed. The face flushed red
under the beard. He rose and snapped the brush as though it had
been matchwood. His wife, blind in her rage, rained blows on his
face till he clouted her well and truly on the side of the head. The
spoon fell from Andy's fingers; he was terrified. Johnnie stopped
eating, but kept his head still, looking out through the window
across the steading. The woman reeled back and fell, dragging down
the small table where her dinner and that of her daughters were laid.
The daughters ran crying to their mother to help her to her feet,
whimpering, 'Oh my God,' 'Oh mither.'

Andy laughed inwardly, for they had no God, and were afraid,
not for their mother, but of their father. The son leaped to his feet in
a fit of Dutch courage and rushed at his father.

'Hit yer faither, wud ye?' thundered the oul' maun. 'Be God, an'
that's a thing ye'll only dae yince.'

As surely as he had staggered his infuriated wife he felled his son.
The gangling youth crashed to the floor without a sound and lay
there while his sisters and mother cried in nervous terror. There was
no more. Andy rose and left with Johnnie. He was half-way to the
stable when the roar of the oul' maun's voice made his heart leap
with fear.

'Come back here, damn ye! An' feenish yer denner.'

They turned as one man and came back. The son lay where he
had fallen; the women had disappeared, but Andy could hear the
sound of crying and self-pitying voices down the passage. The clock
ticked on. The oul' maun served the remainder of the dinner; Andy
and Johnnie sat in reverent silence, although Andy's heart leaped at
the sight of the motionless body on the floor. He wanted to laugh at
it, to see it rise and receive the same treatment again.

When the dinner was over and they were hurrying out once
again, the figure on the tiles groaned and sobbed. The oul' maun sat
smoking by the window and spat at frequent intervals where he
pleased, oblivious of his moaning son. His great hands shook with

the effects of his rage and his teeth bit the stem of his pipe until it cracked. The sobbing still came from down the passage, and the dog slunk out past Andy with its tail between its legs.

Neither of them spoke as they walked until they were past the stable where the rain dripped from the slates into a sizzling vat of lime, for the oul' maun would have noticed their heads come together, that slightly attentive jerk that betrayed men conversing from a distance. When they were hidden by the white walls Johnnie laughed.

'Yon wus a fine to-do,' he said. 'The oul' maun fairly showed them wha wus boss.'

'Christ, did ye see hoo he felled the docken?' asked Andy.

They called the son the docken out of mutual contempt for him, and he was not unlike the swaying dockweeds in the stackyard.

'A wunner whut'll be tae dae noo,' mused Andy. 'Dae ye think they'll gang awa' an' ley'm?'

'No, they're far ower feart, an' they hae nocht. The oul' maun wud gie them nae muny, an' ony-wey, they'll be a'richt in a day or twa. A hae seen them at it afore. They dinna spake tae him fur a while, an' whun he gets angrier they get feart he'll clod them oot. Efter that they start tae forget things a bit, an' at a whiles end the place gaes on as if nocht had happened.'

'A wud like tae see him clod them oot an' pit them aff the place,' laughed Andy. 'Be God an' they'd rin wi' him ragin' ahin' them.'

'A bit he wudna dae that. Oul' tear-arse kens whaur tae stop. Whut wud he dae fur milkers, an' wha wud mak' the denner?'

Andy fell silent and they went up the field to their dykes. Now and then during the afternoon he recalled the scene in the kitchen and began to watch to see if the tea would be coming and who would bring it.

'Ye can be share it'll no' be ony o' the lassies or the docken. He'll bring it up himsel',' Johnnie assured him, but it was exciting for Andy to watch for the coming of the tea.

At length he saw the bearded figure with the stick coming round the end of the stable with a basket swinging in one hand.

He suddenly felt afraid. Would they be due for another swearing, would the oul' maun rage? God, he might even hit him with his stick. Andy began to lay the stones on the broken dyke more hurriedly and kept his eyes on his job till the jingle of the cups in the basket sounded only a few feet away. Johnnie did the same and went on working until the oul' maun stopped to watch.

He said nothing more than 'Here's yer tea, boys.'

Andy placed a slippery moss-covered stone on the dyke and turned for his cup, avoiding the oul' maun's face in fear that the terrible rage would burst upon him. There was nothing about the two jammy scones or the buttered pancake to tell them that the women had not prepared the tea themselves. Andy ate quickly, feeling more uncomfortable as the oul' maun stood watching him. They put their cups back in the basket together and went on with their dyke building.

'If ye hae din afore kye tim' ye can gae doon an' clean the stables the twa o' ye.'

'Aye,' said Johnnie, but Andy said nothing.

The cups rattled in the basket as the oul' maun strode back down the field. The smoke from his pipe streamed over his shoulder as he walked through the damp, still air.

It was an hour before kye-time when the broken dyke was rebuilt and they went down to clean the stable. Andy wheeled the barrow to the midden and Johnnie swept and mucked the stalls whistling 'The Road to the Isles'. Andy laughed for he knew an obscene set of words to the tune. When the stalls and troughs were cleaned Johnnie filled the hecks with hay, but Andy sat on the corn chest and blew discordant notes on a rusty mouth organ, glancing in the direction of the house every now and then to see if the oul' maun was on his way over. Johnnie went in for his supper when he had finished and Andy, who was just as hungry, went for the kye with the dog. He hurried them up the road and began tying them.

No one came to help him and he concluded that the row in the house was still on, but as he went down to the pump to wash the dirt off his hands and arms, the three women went hurrying over to the byre. Their boots were untied and they fastened their aprons as they went splashing through the mud. In the kitchen, where the porridge pot was rumbling as it boiled, the oul' maun was in his chair, but the docken was nowhere to be seen.

Johnnie spooned his porridge rapidly; cats clustered round a plate of milk under the dresser. The milking was over before Andy saw the docken. He came down into the kitchen, and lifting the gun from its rest, plundered in the drawer for cartridges, and went out sulkily into the drizzling rain. The women went to bed early, and Andy sat with the two men, Johnnie and the oul' maun, in the gloom. Before it grew dark they heard a few shots echoing from the hills, and after a while the oul' maun rose, stick in hand.

'Guid nicht, Johnnie; guid nicht, Andy,' he said.

Andy's heart was with him. It seemed pathetic, though the oul' maun made no use of pathos or sought sympathy. They sat in the firelight removing their boots and talking quietly till they heard the docken's steel-shod boots grating on the path outside. He came in with the rain standing in glistening beads on his coat, a pair of rabbits and a hare swung in one hand.

They became silent. Andy lifted his feet to the dying fire to warm them. The docken dried his gun and threw his kill on the round table. The interval of silence grew longer as he took his boots off; his socks left wet tracks on the floor as he went up to bed. Johnnie and Andy sat dreaming for a while, enjoying the quietness of the night. The stairs creaked . . . they stripped and climbed into their re-spective beds.

It was as Johnnie had said. For a while the house was quiet at mealtimes. The women bustled sulkily to and fro, clattering the dishes and scowling at the oul' maun. The docken was never present. Then the air began to clear again and things went on as always. Andy was relieved, for the oul' maun's temper was less dangerous and the house pleasanter. When the hay grew ready for cutting and the sun shone red in the mornings the docken helped with the work and cleaned the reaper in his spare time, sharpening its knives and straightening its rusted dividers.

It was an eventful hay harvest for it saw Johnnie riding down the road with his clothes in a brown paper parcel, never to return. It saw the breaking of tools, the savaging of horses, and tempers aflame again. It was all due to the hay itself.

The ryegrass had grown long, but at the roots there was a growth of fine thick green blades that were damp at sunrise and remained wet till after noon. The thick undergrowth of grass stuck the reaper, pulled at the horses' shoulders, broke the driving rod and made men swear. Johnnie had driven the reaper at haytime and the binder at harvest, as is the usual custom for a ploughman in summer. Johnnie had done this work from the summer he had first come to Drumlin, but the docken sought to change it and mounted the reaper himself for the first cut.

A brute with the horses, he raged and stormed when the machine stuck, so that the great smooth-sided Clydesdales stood with heads high and aquiver with nerves. When they started forward again they pulled sullenly and the machine stuck once more. Had he coaxed them, soothed their nervousness when the machine stuck, spoken quietly and sworn less, they would have pulled steadily and surely, but that was not his way. Johnnie, mowing out the hay from the rocky patches, watched in fury, cursed and laughed when the horses took off without their erratic driver. Had the knife been lifted higher it would have cleared the thick bottom. Johnnie knew this and was silent, for it made him jealous to see the docken working his horses and riding round the hayfield.

Yet in a way, it was Andy's fault too, the affair in the hayfield. An injured rabbit loped painfully before the oncoming reaper and disappeared into the swaying hay. Andy dropped his rake and ran after the rabbit. He fumbled in the grass till the reaper was almost on top of him, then the big sweating Clydesdales stopped and the knife choked in the thick bottom.

Red with anger the docken leaped down from his seat.

'Whut the flamin' hell wur ye daein' in there? God blast ye, ye hae stuck the machine again.'

He was upon Andy in a flash, his fists smashing into the startled dark face. Andy fell, and as he went down he felt under his jacket for a stone, but the docken applied his iron-shod boots to his side.

'Get oot o' there, ye useless bastard.'

He kicked again and again. Johnnie in a murderous rage came lumbering over the swards.

'B'Christ,' he foamed, 'ye'll no' dae that tae the boy while A'm aboot the place.'

Then he was at him. The horses pranced. The reaper pole was broken before anyone knew how it had happened, and they were too mad with rage to care. The harness jangled as the horses galloped off dragging the broken pole behind them. Johnnie's first hit must have smashed the docken's nose, his second rocked him off his heels on to the breadth of his back. There was no more fighting.

'Jesus, Johnnie,' gasped Andy through his tears, 'whut hae ye din? Whut'll they dae tae ye fur this?'

Johnnie, his red hair trailing in his eyes, lifted him to his feet.

'Ye're a' richt, boy?' he asked, 'nivir min' whut they'll dae tae me. They'll hae tae catch me first.'

He was off across the field to the house. Andy looked at the docken, blood trickled from his nose and mouth; he gaped at the sky and a fly walked over his cheek to the congealing blood. The horses were standing by the dykeside in the hollow munching hay. Andy went after them and led them down the road towards the stable; the reaper pole bounced along behind them. The docken lay where he had fallen; he seemed dead. Andy's hands shook with fear at the thought of meeting the oul' maun.

When he reached the stable door he saw Johnnie hurrying down the steps at the pump with his bundle of clothes. His bike leaned against the moss-covered dyke; he turned and looked back.

'So long, boy,' he yelled, 'ye'd better dae the same.'

As he spoke the oul' maun came out.

'Whut's daein'? Whaur ir ye fur?' but Johnnie was in a fiery mood.

He feared no one in his moment of rage and went on tying his parcel to the handle-bars. Then the oul' maun noticed the broken pole behind the horses.

'Come back here,' he roared, but Johnnie was on his bike and pedalling fast.

He looked over his shoulder and yelled, 'Awa' tae hell wi' ye'.

The oul' maun cursed and raved: the women came running out crying, 'O my God', at the sight of the broken pole, and, 'God sake han'.'

Andy was more afraid than ever. The oul' maun came stalking across the court towards him. His hurried steps betrayed his anxiety. Andy wished he had been with Johnnie rushing downhill in the fresh clear air of the summer morning.

'God sake, boy, whut hae ye been daein' tae brek the powl? Whut took Johnnie awa' lik' yon?' he stuttered through his beard. Andy told the story. . . .

'Whut the blazes wur ye daein' rinnin' in afore the reaper?'

'There was a rebbit . . .,' began Andy.

'God curse ye tae hell, dae ye see whut ye hae din?'

He said nothing when Andy told how the docken had been treated. The unharnessed horses were left in the stable, and they went back to the field with tools to take out the stump of the broken pole. The docken was climbing a dyke on the way to the house. The oul' maun shouted abuse after him, but the lean Davit was too bruised and too much concerned with holding his aching head to pay attention. The oul' maun raged as they undid the bolts which held the broken stump of pole in place.

Andy was glad when he was sent back to harness a horse and take a cart to the joiner's for a new pole. As he jolted down to the house the mistress came out with his dinner in two cans with a bowl and a spoon. Andy hoped it would be a long time before the new pole was ready. At least milking time, for the oul' maun would be still raving when he came back.

As he passed the cot-house on the road down to High Malzie he noticed that it was still empty. Weeds filled the potato patch and long grass grew between the stones where he had sat as a baby. The slates were sliding off the roof too, and the windows were all smashed. It seemed more lonely than ever, but Andy whistled as the cart-wheels ground along the white road. The sun shone and there was a breeze swaying the heather and wafting the scents of the moss to him.

He began to eat his dinner at High Malzie and by the time he reached the joiner's spick and span sheds, where the red-painted cart-wheels and dung barrows stood together, it was all finished and he sucked the morsels of sweet rabbit flesh from between his teeth. The hay cutting was held back while the new pole was put in. The women came out and raked, the son, his face a ghastly sight, drove the reaper and the oul' maun looked on.

At the end of the week he advertised and a new man came to take Johnnie's place. He was a tall, thin, grey-headed man with a sour face. He was a master's man, worked hard every minute, asked advice at every turn, and urged Andy on. He always called Andy 'boy', not the friendly word that Johnnie had used, but with an old-fashioned expression that made Andy hate him all the more. Andy laughed when 'stiffy', as he secretly called him, put his hand to his back after bending, or panted when he lifted a corn sack. He laughed inwardly and despised the man all the more, for he was using a subterfuge to cover the growing inefficiency of age.

They saw hay and harvest through together, then 'stiffy' began to feel his rheumatism. He was late to rise for the milking, slow in his work. It might have been called 'age', but the mistress called him lazy. The hardworking tribe at Drumlin had no use for a man who could not, or would not, work. Old or lazy, in either case they deemed him useless and at the term he went, and Andy was glad. He was tired of old sober-sides who slept like a log.

A new man came, small and fat-faced. He was pleasant enough. In fact Andy would have grown fond of him, but he found the oul' maun's fits of temper unbearable and left at the end of a week, silently packing and tramping off while the household slept.

Only Andy knew he was going and sat up and smoked a cigarette with him hours before dawn. Then the door creaked on its hinges; boots clattered down the steps, and he was gone. Andy lied convincingly at the milking when they asked him if he had heard the little man go. Another week passed before a new ploughman was fee'd. The Drumlin hills were in need of ploughing, and the docken was a slow workman.

Then came Paddy O'Hare, dark, with sparkling brown eyes and a devilish carefree smile. He was only twenty-three, thin and sinewy, with black hairy arms and chest. He walked with a conceited swagger, his black curly hair hanging down from under his black felt hat. Every inch an Irishman, though he had been born in the 'shire', and spoke its language. He could work, though his main boast was of the men he had fought and the drink he had had. He laughed loud and recklessly and shook hands with Andy so warmly that tears came to his eyes. Not sentimental tears, but tears of pain at the strength of the grip. The oul' maun could not dominate Paddy, for when he looked at him from under his threatening brows Paddy returned the stare and grinned carelessly. He told the docken to go to hell when he had worked with him but an hour; defied the oul' maun in the heat of his worst rages and laughed at Andy's words of caution or alarm.

The second night he was at Drumlin, Paddy tramped straight across hill and dale to the Whaup and came home drunk, singing all the way to the house door. Then out of consideration, although it was much too late to think of lowering his voice, he became silent and scrambled up the stair laughing at something. He shook Andy, who was already awake, to tell him the joke. Andy could not make out a word of it, but Paddy laughed loud and long and handed Andy his bottle. The neat whisky burned his throat and trickled down to warm his stomach.

There was something about Paddy's happy drunkenness that reminded Andy of Tam. The whiskey, too, made him think of the cot-house, the shaggy collie dog, his sisters and brothers and his dead mother. Paddy crawled into bed, muddy boots, wet clothes, battered hat and all, and slept that way till the morning, when he rose as happy as ever. The oul' maun said nothing, ploughmen, even drunken ploughmen, were scarce.

Andy had found a new friend, a wild reckless companion, who shared his own love of fighting, showed his temper and was afraid of no one. They were to enjoy themselves, man and boy, in the quietness of Drumlin, the lonely roads to the Whaup, the Port, and Bladnoch, fighting, quarrelling, laughing.

CHAPTER X

A ploughing match at Kirkcowan took Andy on his first adventure.
Never before had he spent a whole day away from either the cot-
house in his schooldays, or from Drumlin. He was excited. The
McKeown women stayed at home. Paddy rode off on the cart early
with his plough, his harness polished and the second horse, trimmed
and beribboned, walking behind at the end of a rope. When his byre
was cleaned Andy washed himself at the pump. The water was
almost freezing and his face became as red as the rising sun. The
docken and the oul' maun waited for him and when they were all
ready they climbed into the spring cart and trotted off down the
road. Andy looked round him all the way; at the dry frozen fields,
the weather-beaten thorn trees, the sheep sheltering in the hollows,
the half-ploughed hills and the steady flow of the Bladnoch,
winding its way to the sea through the dormant land, past fir trees
and dead bracken that looked red in the morning light. The smithy
was deserted and the door barred, for the smith was away at the
ploughing match too.

His black-and-white bantams huddled together under the ever-
green hedge by his cot-house windows.

Up over the bridge and the gurgling dark water of the Malzie
burn they went, on past the silent schoolhouse and the cot-house
beyond, farther than Andy had ever prowled in search of birds' nests
in the spring.

The wind came cuttingly chill down the hollow of the Bladnoch,
lashing the willows at the junction of the Malzie burn, and driving
against five wild duck that flapped their way into the north where
the plum-blue hills lowered above the Machars. It was a thrill for
Andy. Now and again they caught up with a man on a bicycle on
the way to the match, then they went downhill towards Kirk-

cowan where there was a field with men of all kinds, farmers, ploughmen, byremen and loungers from the village, watching the competitors ploughing. Teams of horses passed up and down, the field was patched with stretches of turned furrows. The farmers, wrapped in greatcoats, advised their men, the spectators shouted their advice, the ploughmen 'Hupped' and 'Highed', spat on their hands and held steady, treading one foot up and the other down on the edge of the turned earth.

There were long smooth furrows turned as straight as man could ever plough; swarthy broad men with their jackets off in spite of the freezing cold, holding the plough handles with determination, keen eyes watching the horses. Young ploughmen of eighteen or nineteen competed with the same tense faces and steady hands as the veterans. The wildest of them cursed their horses now and then and bit great lumps off their plugs when, sweating manfully, they reached the end of the furrow. Andy went to look for Paddy while the oul' maun and the docken loosed the horse. He passed men who talked of the great ploughers they had been, how they had carried off hundreds of prizes and never been beaten. He smelt whiskey as he passed them. Here and there a bewhiskered man would lift the bottle to his lips to keep the cold from his body.

Paddy was ploughing, but he was drunk. Andy saw him halfway up a furrow, and out of his back pocket stuck a large bottle. He whistled and sang as he staggered up the field behind his horses, but his ploughing was strangely straight and even. Andy was surprised. At the other end he saw him push back his hair under the old felt hat. Then his head went back as he tilted the bottle before setting his horses in. The oul' maun came and stood by Andy.

Another farmer was with him.

'He's plooin' a richt guid fur, McKeown,' he said.

'Aye, no sae bad,' agreed the oul' maun, 'no' sae bad at a'.'

Paddy began to sing again.

'Be God, boy, but yer man's drunk,' said the stranger to the oul' maun.

'Weel, he's makin' a richt guid han' fur a' that,' came the pleased reply.

The oul' maun had nothing to say against a man who could take his whiskey.

'Had on the wey ye're daein',' he advised Paddy, who grinned at him.

'Richt ye ir, oul' fella.'

At the end, the bottle came out again and Paddy handed it to the oul' maun.

'Hae a sup yersel' an' keep it fur me, A hae had enough till A hae din.'

He looked at Andy and added, 'Gie the wee falla a sup tae, he's lookin' cal'.'

Andy's teeth were chattering, he was cold, and he wondered if the oul' maun would give him a sup of the whisky when he had wiped his whiskers with the back of his hand. . . . He did.

'Here boy,' he said, 'that'll waurm ye, bit dinna drink it a'.'

The stranger laughed. Andy took a long drink just to show the man that he could drink whisky. He tried not to choke and handing the bottle back he resumed watching Paddy.

When it was mid-day the oul' maun unyoked Paddy's horses and gave both him and Andy half a crown, saying, 'Awa' fur yer denners, boys.'

Paddy asked for his whiskey bottle and the two of them went down the road to the village. There were dozens of other men going down to the village for dinner. Some were quarrelling loudly about the practice of allowing another man to hold the plough at the opening of the furrow. It is the custom at ploughing matches for older or more experienced men to hold the plough for the competitor along the first few yards of the furrow. There were arguments about how far so and so had held it and other details. Paddy carried his jacket over his arm and his shirt was open to the waist, but Andy shivered with his jacket buttoned to the neck. His ears were red and raw and the cold made his eyes run.

They had broth, potatoes and stew for their dinner and helped it down with sips from the whiskey bottle, which was already almost empty.

'Gran' stuff,' laughed Paddy, 'a gran' day, an' A'm a gran' plooer.'

'Ye can ploo nane,' said a bleary man standing near.

'A seen ye. God, A hae a wee boy at hame that could ploo a better fur ner yon. Ye'll be nae-whaur.'

'B' the holy Jesus,' spluttered Paddy, 'ye red-faced oul' bastard, A can ploo better than ye, or onybudy here, an' if ye'll aff wi' yer jacket A'll show ye wha's the best man.'

The bleary-eyed man spat out his plug and jumped towards him.

'Had on, Jock,' his friends cautioned, 'he'll half-kill ye. Hae ye no' min' whut he did tae Bob Keir?'

Jock did not remember, and if he did he cared not.

'Get oot o' ma bloody road,' he politely ordered his friends.

So addressed they moved with perhaps less regret than they might have shown. Paddy rose too, and laid his jacket on the table.

'Tak' yer hat aff, maun,' suggested a self-appointed second.

'Ma hat steys on,' said Paddy. 'A cud lether'm wi' ma een shut.'

Andy sat trembling with excitement, clenching his fists and waiting. He had not long to wait before the two men were at it and the room was filled with the sound of voices. The bleary-eyed man was big and broad; he swung a great slow punch at Paddy's head, but missed and staggered across the floor before regaining his balance – the onlookers laughed.

Andy's heart raced as Paddy went after him and drove a brutal hairy fist up under his ear. The blow landed with a dull thud. Bleary-eyes shook himself and gaped foolishly as Paddy stepped close to smash blows into his defenceless face till it was a bloody spectacle. The crowd was silent; the landlord ordered the fighters out, but Paddy, with an aptness that he had not shown yet in dealing with bleary-eyes, felled him with a neat quick blow. He lay groaning and unconscious on the floor while Paddy finished his task by lifting a chair and bringing it down on his reeling opponent's head. Then he lifted his coat and left with Andy at his heels. . . . . They had not paid for their dinners.

The men at the door stood aside. There was a wild look on Paddy's face. Those who knew him were silent from experience;

those who did not were frightened by his brutality and ferocity. Andy, walking by his side, shared the awe which met them in the faces of the men they passed. Down the street and up the hill to the ploughing field they went; Paddy's hat still stuck at the jaunty angle and his hands tucked in the waist pockets of his trousers. The drinks of whiskey had made Andy's walk a little unsteady, but his stomach was warm and his heart happy. There was blood on Paddy's shirt from the face of the bleary-eyed man, who lay, a battered heap, on the floor of the public house. And the police? Andy had given them a thought. Would a policeman be down for Paddy and himself before the afternoon was over? He need not have worried, for the policeman was out on his bicycle, and besides, there were many fights at every ploughing match.

At the end of the day Paddy lifted his plough into the cart, a feat which was watched by a large number. One envious man tried to do the same with another plough and dropped it before it was shoulder high. An old farmer gave Paddy a drink for the performance. Andy shrewdly suspected that was the reason for Paddy's display of his wiry strength. At Drumlin he had always asked the aid of the docken or the oul' maun, who also boasted of the feat, when a plough was put in a cart to go to the smithy. Paddy was successful. First prize for his horses, trim and neat they were too, and second prize for ploughing; his furrows after the fight had been slightly uneven, for he had trembled with anger for the rest of the match. Andy rode back in the cart with Paddy.

'Be share ye're back in time fur the milking,' shouted the oul' maun as he trotted past in the spring cart.

'A'll be wantin' ma money the nicht,' Paddy yelled after him.

'A' richt, boy,' came the answer.

There was a reddish glow on the oul' maun's face which showed not only that he was pleased, but that the whiskey had increased his pleasure. They were home by milking time and Paddy was given his share of the prize money, thirty shillings. After supper he and Andy tramped off to the Port, where there was a dance.

'A hae nivir been tae a dance afore,' confessed Andy.

'Och, it's nocht. A canna dance masel',' was Paddy's consolation.

'That disna metter. Mebbe we'll fin' somebudy tae argy wi', an' ye can get fou, jist tae see whut it's like.'

Andy recalled his first effort at getting drunk; the discomfort of it and the sickness that had kept him away from school. He was gloomy as they crossed the frozen fields.

There was a big crowd in the hall at the dance at the Port. Men in heavy boots, some in leggings; women in variously coloured dresses, coarse servant-girls and dairymaids. Few of the men were drunk; it was disappointing, but Paddy dispelled his gloom.

'Ye hae yer half a croon, hae ye no'? Weel, come on an' hae twa three drinks. Ye'll no' be sae bad whun ye're waurmed up.'

Andy followed him out to the public house. Paddy had whiskey. Andy surveyed the possibilities of half a crown and decided to buy beer, it was cheaper. He had never tasted beer before and the sour smell of it was uninviting, but he drank one glass to savour its malty flavour and ordered another. They were quiet folk in the public house; weather-beaten men who eked out a living on the shore, fishing part of the year, and helping at potato lifting and other farm work for the rest. Paddy was the loudest-voiced man in the place, and as he became warmed with drink he began to brag of his ploughing at Kirkcowan.

No one argued. They were all in good mood and laughed at his antics even when he stole his neighbour's whiskey and poured it into Andy's beer. After a while they tired of the mild atmosphere, there were too few strangers to cause trouble, so they left to return to the dance; Andy and Paddy stood in the corner watching the wild performance. Twice Paddy winked at a plump girl who was dancing with a tall raw-boned ploughman and earned a scowl for his pains, but it pleased him and he waited for the couple to come round again.

Andy grinned at an ungainly thin girl who wore a tattered black dress and had visible holes in her stockings. She came over to the corner beside him when the dance finished and stood smoothing the creases from her dress as he watched her.

'Hullo,' he ventured.

'Hullo yersel',' she laughed back, and her untidy hair fell across her cheek.

Paddy stood smiling at the plump girl to the annoyance of the raw-boned man. It seemed that trouble was to come. . . .

'Whaur ir ye frae?' asked Andy of the thin girl.

'A leev at Brachan. A hae seen ye afore.'

He was surprised.

'Hae ye?' he asked doubtfully.

'Aye. Ye're the boy at Drumlin, ir ye no'? A saw ye whun A wus up fur milk yince.'

The band started to play.

'Can ye dance?'

'No,' admitted Andy, 'bit A'll try, if ye like.'

'Come on then,' she said and they joined the milling throng on the floor.

Andy was awkward. He trod on the girl's feet and banged against her, but she just laughed and held him tightly. He looked back over his shoulder. Raw-bones was talking to Paddy; a few seconds later he saw them go out of the door together.

'Had on,' he said, 'there's gan tae be a fight ootside.'

'Is there? Weel A'm comin' wi' ye tae see it.'

She followed him as he threaded his way through the crowd to the door. Paddy and raw-bones were arguing and the plump girl stood looking on.

'Paddy'll murder him if he starts,' he told his companion.

'Whut yin's Paddy?' she questioned.

'That's him wi' the black hair an' hat.'

'He's no' big enough. Ye're wrang. The big falla'll blin' him.'

'Awa' tae hell!' was Andy's retort. 'Ye ken nocht aboot fechtin'. Jesus, ye should hae seen him leyin' aboot him at Kirkcowan the day. He felled twa men an' never even took aff his hat.'

Paddy stopped arguing. It looked as though there would be no fight. Then the girl smiled at Paddy as her escort turned to her. It was enough.

'Look here, ye bastard,' he muttered as he turned, 'A'm . . .'

'Ye're gan tae get a helluva hemmerin' if ye ca' me bastard,' cut in Paddy, and his fists began to fly.

The raw-boned man took the first full in the mouth and

staggered back. A crowd came out of the dance to watch. The long man was not so easily beaten; he rushed in at Paddy and carried him off his feet.

'A telt ye,' said Andy's friend, 'he's gan tae get battered tae bits,' but Andy knew Paddy.

He had faith in him even although he went down hard on the road. The two rolled over amid the yells of encouragement of the men and women alike. Andy found himself pushed to the centre of the ring of people hemming the fighters in. The thin girl put her arm round his neck and squeezed him as the struggle on the ground went on. Suddenly Paddy rose to his knees. There were gasps of amazement, for he balanced his opponent on his outstretched hands like a baby. The strength of his wiry body was surprising. Slowly, despite the struggles, he straightened his legs and held the other above his head. The men nearest to him fought to get out of the way as he swayed and threw the body to the ground. Raw-bones lay as though dead and blood trickled on the stones by his head.

His friends came and lifted him. No one stopped Paddy as he went back into the hall with the plump girl.

The careering round the ill-lit hall went on, to the blare of a trumpet, a drum and piano. Repeated excursions to the public house had made most of the men drunk. Andy and the thin girl set out for home; they walked close together up the road to Brachan; through sleeping Mochrum, the dark little village where the dogs barked. There was a gate to a field just before Brachan and he drew her over to it and kissed her. She was a fiery creature and clung to him. Her whole body pressed against his till he felt the blood coursing through his veins. He fumbled with her dress and his hands sought her warm body.

'Tak' me, Andy,' she whispered, and her breath was hot against his cheek.

He buried his head in her shoulder and tried to control his shaking body.

'A hae nivir din this afore,' he mumbled.

It seemed as though they had clung together for hours and his body was weak. He wanted to lie in the damp grass until his heart stopped racing. Instead he clasped her waist and walked at her side. For a long time he said nothing. He was uncomfortable and wished he had never gone to the Port, but maybe it was just the beer that made his head ache.

When they reached her cot-house door she clung to him, and laughed when he struggled to free himself.

'Whun'll A see ye again?' she asked.

'Och, A'll be ower Sunday efternin,' he said. 'Mebbe . . .'

It was 'maybe'. All he wanted was to get home. He had a dull throbbing ache in his head.

He was glad to kick off his boots and mount the stair when he reached the farmhouse. He did not sleep. In the warmth of his bed he wanted the girl again. Before he had slept what seemed half an hour it was morning. Paddy's bed had not been slept in. He ruffled the clothes and tousled the sheet and made it look as though Paddy had been abed, just in case he came in while the women were getting ready for the milking. He looked at the dial of the alarm clock and went downstairs to put his boots on. As he bent down to tie the laces he heard the fence behind the house squeak and knew that Paddy was back.

'Ye're back then,' he said to Paddy when he came in.

'Aye,' answered Paddy, 'an' b' Christ it's cal'. Is there ony tea in the pot?'

Andy put the kettle on and made tea.

'Hoo did ye get on last nicht?' Paddy grinned, 'A saw ye wi' yon skinny lass frae Brachan. She kens the wey, yon. Watch yersel' or ye'll hae her wi' a wean, an' ye'll no' be the first at that.'

Andy's face went red but he said nothing as they drank their tea. The alarm in the oul' maun's room rang and shortly after the women came rushing downstairs in various stages of dressing. They all went over to the byre together.

On Sunday, Andy hung round the steading till dinner-time. Paddy, who had slept in the hay-shed, came looking for him with the black hat on the back of his head.

'A'm awa' tae Mochrum. Ir ye comin'? A thocht mebbe ye wud be gan tae Brachan.'

Andy pretended lack of enthusiasm, though he had thought about it all day and the day before.

'If ye're comin', come on,' urged Paddy. 'A haena a' day tae wait fur ye.'

As they straddled the fence one of the daughters came out of the house.

'Whaur ir ye awa' tae, Andy?' she called to him.

'Brachan,' he yelled back.

'Be share ye're back in time for the kye then,' she reminded him, but to Paddy she said nothing. A ploughman only milks on Sunday if he wants to, which he rarely does.

Paddy walked fast, whistling and singing at intervals. Andy went down through Brachan with him till they were past the houses.

'Ir ye no' gan back tae the lass then?'

'Aye,' said Andy, blushing, 'A'm gan back noo.'

He turned and went back up the road.

'Watch yersel' noo, Andy,' cautioned Paddy in a voice that reached the other end of the clachan.

As he passed her house the girl came out. She was wearing a man's coat and looked coarser than the night of the dance.

'A thocht ye wur gan tae the kirk,' she teased.

He found it hard to look her in the face.

'There's nae kirk on Sunday efternins,' he said seriously, 'an' if there wus A wudna be there.'

They walked up the road and past the wood.

'Whaur ir ye gan?' he asked suddenly.

'There's a hayshed up the road. A thocht it wud be warmer in there.'

'Aye,' he agreed, and then fell silent.

They reached the shed, a tin-roofed place where a farmer stored hay for bullocks. It was warm and dry inside; a wild-looking cat scampered off the hay as they entered.

'Weel, sit doon,' she invited.

He was standing awkwardly, looking round. He sat down a few inches from her and said nothing for about five minutes. She played with the strands of hay and gave him sidelong glances.

'Hoo auld ir ye?' she asked at length.

'Fifteen,' he said and forgot to ask her the same question.

'A'm aulder than ye then,' she observed, but a question had come to his mind.

'A heard ye had a wean yince?'

'Wha telt ye that?'

'Paddy said ye had,' he replied.

'Aye,' and then, after a pause, 'A had a wean last year, bit it didna leev'.'

'Wha wus the fether o't?' he enquired.

'Ye want tae ken a lot, dae ye no'?'

She laughed and he did not repeat the question, but sat kicking up wisps of hay with the toe of his boot. She pulled herself nearer to him and put her arm round his neck.

'Ye're a funny boy,' she said, and her breath tickled his ear.

She drew his head towards her and whispered something. He kissed her and she responded hotly, locking her arms round him. He began to caress her roughly, feeling so strange that he hardly knew what he was doing.

The wind blew round the roof and made the tin rattle in places. He fell asleep after a while and when he awoke she was going through his pockets.

'Whut ir ye daein' that fur?' he asked sleepily.

'Jist tae see whut ye hae in them.'

He was at ease when he remembered that he had left the last remaining sixpence of his half-crown in the pocket of his jacket, which was in the loft of the farmhouse. It was growing dark quickly, and when he tried to embrace her again she pushed him away.

'Whut'll the time be?' she asked.

'A dinna ken, bit it'll be past fower o'clock. Aye, mebbe we'll better mak' a shift. It'll no' be lang till kye tim'.'

They brushed the hay from each other's clothes and shivered a little as they went out of the shed.

'A'll see ye doon the road tae the hooses first,' he decided.

It began to snow as he went over the fields to Drumlin. He floundered through the boggy hollows and slipped getting over dykes in the gloom. He reached the top of a hill and the snow swept across the land in blinding thickness. Twinkling faintly beneath him he could see the light of the house, and hurried down towards it; breathless and cold. The thorn hedges were draped with snow, which fell and quickly dissolved in the water of the burn.

The kye were lowing in the byre and it was half an hour before milking time when he got in. The black porridge pot was bubbling on the range like a small volcano. . . .

CHAPTER XI

IT was the day before the cattle-show and at night Andy went to Wigtown with a heavy-uddered Galloway to be entered for the milking competition. He led the cow, a placid shaggy black creature, at the end of a short halter, and Paddy walked in front with the big-bellied mare and her foal. At a place near Bladnoch they left their charges. Andy milked his cow and secured fodder for her before beginning the long tramp home. Paddy, in his eagerness 'no' tae be late fur the mornin',' resisted the temptation to have a drink. It was dark and the moon was up as they reached the silent steading of Drumlin.

Andy went round the house before going in, just to see that the hens were shut up. He paused on his way back to look at the moon coming up behind the hills; the silhouette of the curving cornhills; the shadow on the braeface; the gap in the dyke that ran like a black snake up the slope; the bars across the slap; the ghostly shadows of the clouds flitting over the lonely moss in the west.

When he went upstairs he pulled the rusty old gun from its hiding-place at the back of cupboard among the seedbags and grass rope. Paddy came and looked.

'Wha's is that?' he asked.

'It's mine,' said Andy, 'but A had furgot A had it. A'm gan tae hae a shot wi' her yin nicht. A hae some cartridges tae.'

'Hae ye, b'God.'

Paddy was too tired to say any more. He sprawled himself on the bed and fell asleep without taking his boots off. Andy sat fondling the gun, then crept downstairs in search of oil. The fire was out and only the tick of the clock broke the silence. He prowled through the drawers and went upstairs with oil and rag. Paddy slept on as he dismantled the gun and picked the dirt from the hinge of the breech with his knife, oiled it and rubbed the thin layer of rust from the barrels. He pulled the cleaner through and held the gun up to the skylight to see the result. The barrels shone as clean as a new pin. He was sleepy too, so he slipped the gun back behind the cupboard and left the oil on the floor to be taken down in the morning. He had been in bed five minutes when a new thought came to him, so he rose and went down the stair with the oil. The oul' maun's cartridge box was on a shelf under the gun rest. Both guns were twelve bore, so he took five and went back to bed.

The sun was low in the eastern sky and the morning mists rose off the fields in the hollows down by Bladnoch. At mid-day the tar on the dyke which bounded the show field would begin to melt, and the flies hover in thousands over the heads of the stock in the pens. Carts came jolting up the hill to Wigtown with nets over them to keep the restless sheep from jumping out on to the road.

Calves were being led along by boys; men in their best clothes, with flowers in their button-holes, walked ahead of well-groomed mares with foals trotting behind. The birds sang in the hedges and there was an air of rustic excitement on the way to the town where the smoke curled from the chimneys into the peaceful sky. Early many of the men had risen to leave the lonely little steadings in the mosslands, the big white-washed home-farms of the Machars, the crofts in the rough land between Portwilliam and Whauphill.

Women remained milking twice their quota of kye in the byres that the men might be off with the finest stock, which would, before the day was out, be judged in the shaded field on the hill of Wigtown. In the showfield at seven o'clock half the pens were filled. Horses, one-year-olds, two-year-olds, geldings, mares, foals, prize milking cows, thorough-bred Ayrshires, Galloways and Shorthorns, bulls, calves, and sheep, all in their sections. Pails clattered, horses neighed, men whistled and the dew was trampled off the grass till the long green blades were crushed down and gave off a moist, succulent smell.

Setting out from Drumlin with the oul' maun, the docken and Paddy in the spring cart, Andy was looking forward to the cattle-show. His father had gone when he was a child, but that was beyond his memory. He did remember Tam's expeditions to the show and the stories of the pony racing, the fair and a fight or two. The fun of it all appealed to him, even though half his day was to be spent watching his cow and walking with it back to Drumlin. The oul' maun had given him five shillings and told him that he need not milk when he came back, but, if he wished, return to Wigtown at night. There would be hard work on the morrow to make up for it all.

Farmers gave their men cattle-show day, at least those who were not taking cattle, and they were usually glad of the duty for it helped them to spend a day that would have become irksome, waiting for the public houses to open, wandering round the pens looking at exhibits, meeting cronies and relations. Balancing with knees bent on the top bar of the gate of the pen in which the Galloway was tied, Andy watched the men wandering past. He enjoyed the rattle of the sawdust cans, the sight of the men with their sleeves rolled up putting the final touches to their horses; washing withers and fetlocks, combing dishevelled manes, soaping the sides of mares and foals in a pretty but artificial fashion.

Old farmers came past and stopped to look at Andy's charge.

'Whas baste is that, boy?' they would ask.

'Can she gie a guid pailfu'?' 'Whun did she calve, boy?' or 'Ye hae her tied ower close tae the bar, boy.'

Andy answered the questions as best he could and took their advice willingly.

He presented an amusing sight himself, wearing Paddy's old hat, his ragged tweed suit and collarless heavy flannel shirt open at the neck. His black hair hung in curls on his forehead, for the hat was high on his brow, and, because he had never shaved, he had side-whiskers down past his ears, fluffy black adornments to his devilish appearance. When the time came he concentrated on milking his cow. The oul' maun looked on.

'Mak' share ye dae her richt,' he instructed. 'Dinna ley her till ye hae her dry.'

The Galloway milked well, but the Ayrshire in the next stall, milked by a woman, did better, and was, in fact, the winner of the silver tea-service that went with the first prize. Nevertheless it was with pleasure and pride that Andy received the blue ticket for second.

In the afternoon, admiring folk stopped to look at both his and his neighbour's pen. Paddy was not so lucky. The foal was placed third, although Paddy, admitting that its legs were too long, swore that it was better than the second prize winner. The mare had no prize at all. Her belly was heavy and her back hollow. The judges disliked her legs, a disqualifying feature which she had passed on to her off-spring.

Andy led his cow home after the parade and presentation of prizes. Paddy, who had already soothed his chagrin with a drink or two, went with him. They were the first on the road for home. When they came back at six o'clock, or thereabouts, the road was congested with horses and cows being led back to their farms. The men had lost much of their spirit. A hard day in the sun, with the flies, the stink of sheep and manure, the blasting notes of the band and the unaccustomed buzz of voices had harassed their nerves and senses. The sheep bleated, and the bullocks and cows bellowed their discomfort, soiling the road as they dragged along on their halters. The biggest day of the summer was at its close. Women with their children, having lost their husbands in the showfield or public houses, trudged down the road.

The men as they reached the road ends and crossroads called to one another, 'A'll see ye the nicht then,' or 'Wull ye be in tae the dance?'

Andy and Paddy went up the hill and back to the showfield. In the morning men with cattle had had a blue stamp printed on the backs of their hands and on leaving the field or returning they showed the mark as their right of re-admission.

Paddy and Andy showed the backs of their hands to the tired little bespectacled man, who smelt of whiskey, and passed through the gate to see the tug-of-war and the pony racing which usually concluded the day's events. Ragged children, the sons and daughters of cot-men, chased each other to and fro, having long since spent their few pennies and lost interest in the programme.

Some had crawled under the enclosure to get a closer view of the pony racing and were in constant danger of being trampled under the hooves of the horses. Others hung round the ice-cream barrows and made repeated endeavours to steal the delicacy which they had no money left to buy. The bending race and the straight race round the field were the most exciting features of the day. Men roared and cheered their fancy. A few interested farmers betted amongst themselves. The stock in the almost deserted pens was left un-attended while the ploughmen, dairymen and byreboys added their voices to the wild yells of the crowd. The band played jerkily and out of tune, for even the rustic bandsmen, sweltering in their red-braided black suits, could not keep their eyes off the fortunes of the horses.

Andy and Paddy shouldered their way to the enclosure, gripped the wooden rail and yelled themselves hoarse in their excitement; crying, 'Gang on, the wee yin. Pit him oot o' that. Gang on, the wee yin!'

And when the race thundered to a finish, 'Och, bit it was a peety. The wee yin should hae won.' They disagreed or agreed with those round them, and between whiles munched apples which Paddy had bought.

Soon it was all over. The voice-ruining cries for the tug-of-war and the races, and the uproar of the day died. The crowd drifted to the gates. Men hurriedly removed their horses and cows from the pens and led them away. Here and there a solitary cow lowed because her attendant was passing the time in the public house. Byreboys searched in the hay in the pens for their pails. The day was over. Wigtown basked in the setting sun and rooks fluttered to rest in the branches of the trees round the square, as Paddy and Andy went into the Halloway Arms. The place was crowded and noisy with the boom of voices. As they passed through the door a voice hailed Andy. It was the thin dark girl from Brachan. Andy had not seen her all day although he had looked carefully.

He was going back to her, but Paddy called over his shoulder, 'Och, come on, maun. Dinna trail awa back oot there. Ye hae a' nicht tae see her. Come on.'

Andy changed his mind, and the girl, who had hesitated at the door, said, 'A'll see ye at the dance then?'

The door swung to and he made his way to a corner while Paddy brought the drinks. A weedy-looking boy of about his own age sat near him.

'Whaur ir ye frae?' he asked Andy, who looked at him for a moment before replying.

'Drumlin.'

'Whaur's that,' questioned the weedy one. Andy thought him a fool for the vacant way his mouth hung.

'Och, oot by,' he said vaguely.

'Hae ye had ocht at the show?'

'Aye, we took a second and a third.'

'Weel, ye didna dae as weel as us,' came the scornful rejoinder.

Andy refrained from asking who 'us' happened to be. He was in an unfriendly mood. The drink was affecting the weedy youth.

'Can ye fecht?' was the next astonishing question.

Andy made no reply and the stranger evidently thought he was afraid of a challenge for he turned to his companion, kicking Andy's leg as he did so, and said, 'The wee boy here's lost. He's lookin' fur his mither. He's affa feart.'

Andy's temper rose.

'Ye're a helluva big talker. If yer shoulders were as big as yer tongue ye micht grow tae be a maun yet.'

The loose-mouthed youth kicked his leg again, 'Och awa' hame, wee boy. Ye're milk'll be cal.'

Paddy was coming across from the bar as Andy jumped to his feet.

'Richt, big mooth,' he muttered.

'Big mooth' lashed out with his foot once more, but Andy was too close for a damaging blow. He drove his fist into the thin boy's face and was about to do so again when his companion struck him behind the ear. Andy saw dazzling lights, but before his new opponent could repeat the blow Paddy had laid down the beer.

'Had on,' he said grimly and toppled the man right over his seat with a swing that split his lips and broke his teeth.

Andy shook his head and seized his enemy.

'Geordie,' shouted the weed, but 'Geordie' had had enough.

He sat wiping the blood from his face and feeling his mouth.

'Ye're a' talk,' gritted Andy through his teeth. He bent his head, shook off his hat, and drove his skull into the other's face, pulling him towards him as he did so. It was a trick that Paddy taught him, a brutal but most effective measure for taking the spirit out of a fighter. The weed was no fighter and had never had spirit. He lolled back in his seat, tears and blood from his nose trickling down his face.

'Ony mair?' asked Andy.

The eloquence of the stranger had gone. He held his face with both hands, groaning and sobbing alternately. Paddy picked up Andy's hat.

'Ca' canny, Andy. We're no' at the Port noo. There's polis in the toon. They'll be efter ye if he canna get hame wi' the smash ye gied him.'

Andy looked at his adversary. He seemed to have fainted. It was the first fight he had had since leaving school and, although it had been brief and uninteresting in that there had been little retaliation, he had enjoyed it. He sat down rubbing his ear.

'A would like a wallop at yon bastard.' He pointed to the man with the broken teeth.

'He's had plenty aff o' me,' said Paddy. 'Yon was a richt smash in the face we gied the wean, bit for Christ's sake watch yersel' or ye'll hae us baith in the jile.'

It was true enough. The police were only too ready to pick up individual offenders, for there was no telling what it might lead to when the town was crowded on cattle-show night.

The few who had watched the incident turned to their drinks again. A man came across to Paddy.

'This'll be yer brither, Paddy?' he asked, and added, 'he can gie a richt yin jist like yersel'.'

Paddy grinned but did not disillusion the speaker.

'He can that,' he remarked.

There was a striking resemblance in Paddy and Andy, each with his deeply sunken dark eyes, black curly hair and lean frame, although Paddy's face bore signs of recklessness, while Andy's had more of a flashing malicious temper reflected in its determined lines.

They put their hats on and went down to the County Buildings where the dance was on. As they approached they could hear the thump of the tenth-rate jazz band. Paddy paid his money and went in without taking his hat off. Andy followed.

A shapely young man with his hair greased came across to Paddy and said bluntly, 'Tak yer hat off.'

Paddy was smiling at a girl. He turned and caught the sleek individual by the lapel of his coat.

'Whun A'm guid an' ready,' he replied and shook him till his plastered hair came unstuck.

Then he straightened his arms and threw him back against the wall. The youth – he looked like a draper's assistant – for a moment seemed as though he would do something about it, but he felt the pain where Paddy's steely fingers had seized him, and decided to sit down, slightly ruffled, and humiliated, to rub his bruises. Andy grinned at him and he scowled back.

At that moment Paddy looked and grinned too, but when he saw the scowl he made as though to come over to him. The man rose, straightened his tie, and went up to a girl for a dance. His greasy head was lost soon after in the throng. Andy saw him later looking round at Paddy. He seemed to be telling his partner something. He told Paddy.

'Och, he'll come tae, or A'll bring him tae afore the nicht's by,' said Paddy.

They removed their hats and put them under a chair, Andy looked for the girl from Brachan. After a while he saw her in a corner with a freckled-faced red-headed youth. She noticed him and came across to him. The boy with the freckles frowned at Andy.

It looked as though there would be trouble for both Paddy and him, but the deserted swain swallowed his annoyance and went in search of a new companion. Andy danced in his crude way for a time and then excused himself while he went for a drink.

It was near closing time and Paddy was there, well on the way to being fighting drunk again. They came back to the hall and Andy sought his girl. Paddy staggered round the hall with a woman who was almost as drunk as he.

The sleek one, who looked as though he wore stays, must have voiced his dislike too loudly, for Andy saw him dragged away from his partner while the dance was at its height, spun round by Paddy's powerful arm and stretched neatly on his back under a refreshment table. Paddy's friend clung to his arm, but the greased head remained on the floor. The M.C. approached Paddy, but there was a foreboding fiery gleam in his dark eyes, and the man with the yellow rosette, who was less than five feet three, contented himself with lifting the fallen man.

He summoned what appeared to be his committee after the band had stopped. They eyed Paddy from their end of the room as did nearly all the men and women in the place. But Paddy's reputation was widely known and his lithe, alert figure was warning enough. The M.C.'s friends were mostly pale-faced shop assistants and none dared tackle Paddy alone or collectively.

The dark, thin girl voiced her approval of Paddy.

'Jesus, ye wudna think he could knock a maun flat lik' that, wud ye? They're a' feart o' him tae.'

'Aye,' said Andy, and prepared to explain at length the virtues of his hero and champion.

He had not recited a quarter of his hymn of praise when the band began to play. As they danced Andy saw the injured man leave the hall, holding his face as he went. A bruise was already spreading along his jawbone. He must have suffered great loss of dignity and was off home to console himself in bed.

After midnight Andy and the girl set out for home. Paddy had disappeared. The girl wheeled her bike and Andy walked by her side. Many folks on their way home on bikes shouted 'Guid nicht' as they passed. They were coming down through Bladnoch when the boy with the freckles caught up with them.

'Come on, Nan,' he urged, and slowed up.

'Andy's takin' me hame. Awa' on,' she told him.

'Andy's lucky,' he replied and rode on.

They walked over the bridge talking about nothing in particular. The sighing of the water, passing over the stones where the bed was shallow, echoed up the hollow as they passed along the road at the new house. The moon was high and the trees cast shadows on the white way ahead; a hedgehog scuttled along the centre of the highway nervously afraid that they were chasing it.

A car came purring round the bend and its lights dazzled their eyes, Nan's old bike rattled and the bell jingled as they crossed rough stretches of the road where the menders had been at work during the day. A cart with a broken shaft was drawn up at a slap; they mused on how it happened as they walked slowly on; the passers-by became fewer and fewer and the sound of voices and footsteps on the road died away. Now and then the lights of a car going uphill lit the dim horizon.

In a farm on a brae face a cock, tricked by the moonlight into thinking it was day, crowed shrilly three or four times; a dog barked and the night fell silent. The moon rode the cloudless sky and the air was strangely warm.

They rested awhile and Andy drank a cold draught from a watering trough by a hedge. The chill water trickled over his chin and ran down his open shirtneck. . . .

CHAPTER XII

SOME mornings after the show, Andy rose long before the house was awake, when the dim shadows of the night were breaking to reveal the grey of dawn. The fields were heavy with dew and mists hung in the hollows. He pulled on his clothes and peered at the old alarm clock. It was half-past four, an hour before kye time. The gun came silently out of its hiding-place behind the cupboard and he slipped the cartridges into his pocket. Paddy slept undisturbed as he went down the stair into the cold kitchen to put on his boots. Quietly he opened the door and stepped outside; the grandfather clock struck the half-hour as he went across the court and jumped the gate. He avoided the fence, for it would have squealed and the oul' maun might have been lying awake listening for the cockcrow.

Ten minutes later he was up the hollow and over the dyke by the wood, off the Drumlin land with a hill between him and the steading. It was growing lighter and he could see across the fields easily. He began to crouch and walk silently on his toes with his knees bent; up the side of a hedge, peering through gaps, watching for stones that might betray him if his boots struck them. His trousers were drenched and the morning was as cold as any in winter.

Pigeons left the wood for the cornfields. He clutched the gun tighter at the sight of them. There were two cartridges in the breech and the hammers or 'dogs' were back in readiness, but there was nothing. Not a sign of a bird or a rabbit within gunshot. He was tired with his excited rush across the fields and sat for a moment on a boulder dreaming. Then the feeling of wariness, a primitive cunning, came over him and he strained all his senses to watch and listen. As he did so a hare came loping over the hill and on down the brae-face towards him. The gun came to his shoulder as he sat back and took aim. His body became cool and patient while he waited for it to come within range. It pulled up and sat with its ears cocked for a minute; the suspense was agonizing, but he sat as still as the stone beneath him and it came on again, evidently making its way to a hole in the hedge along a regular track.

His eyeballs became cold as he stared . . . a second and it would be within killing distance, careering aimlessly through the wet grass. His cheek met the steel of the gun, it was cold. His eye ran along the barrel to the bright bead at its tip . . . slowly he swung round with the approach of the hare, then pulled the trigger.

The silence was shattered with the blast of the gun; blue smoke wriggled into the air. The hare somersaulted and lay kicking. The echoes came back to his ears in which the blood was beating uncomfortably. He sat for a second watching the smoke from the gun barrel, then raced across the grass to his kill. The hare kicked in its death throes, bespattering his face and hands with blood. He wanted to shriek a savage challenge to the hills; instead he laid the dead hare on a nearby stone and went creeping on with a new lust to kill urging him forward.

His nerves were so disturbed that, had the dockens swayed or a thrush flown from the hedge, he would have fired. He bent his head and licked the congealing blood from the backs of his hands. He was no longer a boy, but a wild creature with the savage thrills that had incited his hairy ancestors to clan massacre and bloody orgies. The stealth and cunning of the primitive man in search of food was in him. He went down on his stomach and crawled slowly, fifteen minutes it must have taken him, over the face of the hill, where, from behind a knowe, he watched three rabbits nibbling grass. He lay flat and propped the gun on a ridge of red earth by a molehill. Again he caressed the sight with his eager eye and lowered the barrel till it dropped on the rabbits. A pause, a murderous space of seconds in which he anticipated the result of the shot, then the gun roared again as he pulled the other trigger.

Luck was with him. It was a long shot, but one rabbit lay dead and another scurried feebly for the burrow. He was on his feet racing after it and caught it a yard or two from the hole-mouth. Back to where his gun lay with them both dangling by the hind-legs in one hand, then over the hill he hurried to collect the hare. On he raced towards Drumlin in a spirit of triumph. He hid the gun in the stable.

The oul' maun was up when he went in, but he had taken precautions; the oul' maun's gun was hidden in a flowering currant bush at the door and he picked it up as he entered.

'A wus up early an' A thocht A'd tak' a shot,' he said boldly, by way of an explanation, as he threw the rabbits and hare on the floor.

There was a secret satisfaction in having used his own gun and having kept the fact from the oul' maun.

'A didna say ye could dae that, boy.' A frown wrinkled the deep brow.

'Hoo mony shots did ye tak' tae get they?'

The oul' maun was a keen sportsman and admired a man that could shoot.

'Jist twa,' said Andy truthfully.

'Boy, o' boy, that's no' sae bad. A'll sae nocht tae ye this tim', but ask me whun ye want a shot again.'

'Aye,' said Andy, beaming with pride.

Paddy came down the stairs, struggling into his jacket on the way.

'Awa' fur the kye noo, boy,' bade the oul' maun.

Andy was disappointed, for he had wanted Paddy's praise, but he went, still elated, to call the dog and bring the kye in.

His elation lasted all morning. After the milking he went in to breakfast. The oul' maun cautioned him.

'If ye're gan tae gang oot wi' the gun, boy, ye'd better watch hoo ye kerry it, or ye'll be shootin' some o' the kye. Aye keep the dogs doon whun ye're walkin' alang an' dinna pit them up till ye're ready tae fire. Nivir shoot ocht bit rabbits, hares an' craws an' pigeons. Ye manna kill a paterick or ocht that's game, or the keeper'll be ower an' hae ye aff tae the jile.'

Andy nodded seriously. The docken, who had come down to breakfast, looked across at him.

'Did ye clean her?'

'Aye,' said Andy.

He knew that the gun was clean for he had not fired it.

'Whaur did ye get them?' asked the docken, for hares were scarce and rabbits too, on the hills of Drumlin.

'A got the rabbits ower by the wud, an' the hare on ma road back. He wus comin' ower the hill,' lied Andy.

'A didna hear a shot at a',' came the docken's surprised comment.

Paddy saved Andy a further lie by lying himself.

'A did,' he said. 'A heard them baith.'

Andy had been for a second afraid that Paddy would, in his eagerness to support him, say that he had heard three shots and damn him as a liar before the oul' maun, but Paddy's brain was keen.

He thought fast, much too fast for the oul' maun or the docken, as he had frequently proved.

The meal went on with the oul' maun beginning to give accounts of the things he had shot . . . a stray deer, once a badger, although Andy doubted this, for badgers were unheard of in that district, pheasants, an otter, wild duck, and on a rare occasion, a goose, on a cold November day when the snow had driven the geese across the mosslands.

'Ye had yer ain oul' gun, A'm thinkin'?' asked Paddy as they went over to the stable later.

'Aye,' said Andy, 'she's lyin' in yin o' the hecks in the hay noo.'

'Ye did weel. We'll hae tae hae a nicht o't in the wunter tim', you an' me,' was Paddy's remark.

Andy agreed eagerly.

Another morning when Andy came down to sneak out for a shot, having had the oul' maun's permission, he found the gun gone from above the door. The docken, in a fit of jealousy, had been down before him and was off to shoot. He was proud of his reputation as a shot, which was not without reason. He could shoot well. Andy resisted the temptation to take his own gun and steal through the fields on to neighbouring land. He climbed the stair and went back to bed. The docken came in at breakfast time with one small rabbit to show for his morning's prowl in the damp fields.

The shooting fever wore off Andy as haytime, and, following it, harvest came on. Long tiring days in the fields left him too worn out at night and too sleepy in the morning to go out with the gun. A warm dry spell hastened the ripening of the corn and brought the hay-making to an early close. A week later, after a rush to prepare the binder and reaper, mending tools, and having horses shod, the harvest was on them. The gold of the oats became almost white in a day. The roads round the first field were opened and the binder whirred round, disgorging sheaves. A fortnight and the cutting was done. The dry spell held, though the oul' maun was still dubious, for what reason Andy could not tell.

The night the binder chickled through the last sward of waving corn he stood smoking and watching the men lifting the last few rows of sheaves.

'A doot, boys, it'll be a while afore we hae this in the stackyerd. There'll be rain the morn,' he said as they came abreast of him.

The hired harvesters grinned and looked at the sky. The horizon was cloudless and rain was the last thing they expected. They were eager to see this harvest over so that they might yet have a chance of doing another in the later parts of the shire before the season was out. Andy looked at the sky too, yet he was silent when the harvesters disagreed, for he knew the oul' maun and his uncanny ability to foretell the weather. Paddy respectfully looked around too when he jumped off the binder.

'Dae ye think sae?' he asked when the oul' maun repeated his remark to him.

Next morning when they rose it was still dry, but the sky was heavy with clouds. Great black blankets of rain came drifting low out of the west. The optimism of the harvesters died suddenly. Before the kye were out of the byre the rain was on. There was no rush to the field with the binder sheet; the oul' maun had acted on his knowledge of the weather and the binder was covered. He sat unsurprised at breakfast and watched the steady downpour.

'Ye wur richt then,' Paddy voiced the thoughts of the rest.

'Aye, boy, A wus richt, bit some o' ye thocht A wus haverin' last nicht. A hae leeved here a' ma life an' ken the wauther better ner ony o' they young fallas that rins aboot in cars an' taks their stuff tae Ayr tae sell.'

In their depression the harvesters could not fail to admire him. He sat smoking and smiling through his beard as though the coming of the rain pleased him in proving his word, rather than gave him fears for the ruination of his crop. Uncomplainingly he watched the rain; the thing that his kind had always fought against. He resorted to no curses, but sat dreaming while the smoke of his pipe rose among the salted hams that hung from the ceiling.

Ten days in the granary winding endless coils of grassrope into neat cones made them resigned to their fate. They smoked continually and talked while the sheaves rotted in the fields to a rich red and fallen ears began to sprout shoots between the blackened stubble. It was a disastrous harvest and might have ruined many a farmer had not a dry spell followed and saved the sheaves from complete rot. On the first day that the rain abated, nothing at all was done in the fields. The sun shone but the sheaves could not be moved to new places for the ground was wet.

Andy went out with the gun at night, through fields where the sheaves were blown down or had collapsed with the rain. Pigeons sat in hundreds stealing the ears which tumbled off the stooks. The sun on the wet land had raised a damp mist that stretched across the Machars to the sea. There was no rustle in the woods for the leaves were sodden and clung to the boots; pheasants ventured far into the open fields in search of better food than they had had in the shelter of whins and hedges. The rain clouds had vanished, but the sky was dimmed by the mist and the setting sun shimmered through it in shades of red and orange.

A brace of sitting pigeons and a rabbit fell to the gun before Andy returned to the farm. It was not yet too dark to see, but the harvesters would be in the stable with their melodion and their songs. He went back, and straight into the stable. The three Irishmen were happy at the new turn in the weather and sang and played while the candle bickered and made ghostly figures dance on the walls. Andy went to bed long before the strains of their music died across the steading. He awoke when they came clattering up the stairs to make their beds on the floor.

The following afternoon the sheaves were moved. The task took four days, and when the oul' maun was satisfied that they would not heat if stacked, the carting began. Neighbouring farmers, in their haste to take advantage of the dry spell, stacked too soon and found the sheaves heating and setting fire to the stacks. The race against time and the breaking up of summer went on.

The potatoes were up too, before the weather broke for good. The harvesters had left and the gloomy days of another long winter set in. There was trouble ahead foreboding in Paddy's growing discontent. Andy could see it, and at the end of the November term it came.

Over the feeding of the horse the oul' maun and Paddy disagreed. They stormed and swore at one another till the women in the house, who could hear their angry voices from the stable, nervously watched at the window. Andy, coming quietly up the byre, heard the last of the quarrel. Paddy's voice was raised in a passionate stream of oaths.

'Weel, ye oul' bastard,' he threw back over his shoulder as he came through the door, 'if ma wey's no guid enough ye can feed yer bloody horses yersel'. A hae din an' A'm wantin' ma money as quick as ye like.'

'God damn ye tae hell. Get doon the road! A hae nae use fur a stubborn maun lik' you aboot the place or workin' wi' ma horse,' spluttered the oul' man.

Paddy went across the court muttering and swearing, threw back the door of the house with a crash as he went in, and glared at the womenfolk. The oul' maun followed to find the money. No more words were spoken. The insurance card and the few pounds were on the table when Paddy came down with his clothes. He picked them up and put them in his hip pocket; shoved his hat back on his head and buttoned on his oil-coat. Andy watched him splashing through the mud on his way down the road.

On the following Sunday afternoon Andy went across to the stable. He smelt smoke as he opened the door. Paddy was there, he knew in a flash, sitting on the cornchest with a hand-rolled cigarette between his thin lips.

'Howdo,' said Paddy and swept off his black hat.

Andy grinned.

'Whut ir ye daein' here?' he enquired.

Paddy came to the point. 'A'm at Balturk,' he said, 'an' they're wantin' a boy there tae. Ir ye comin'?'

Andy was astonished. The thought of working anywhere else had never occurred to him. Paddy urged him to leave, but the thought of facing the oul' maun with the announcement that he wanted to leave frightened him.

'Ye'll hae mair money, an' A'll teach ye tae ploo,' said Paddy by way of encouragement.

'Whun dae they want the boy?'

'Wensday,' replied Paddy. 'Onybudy can ley Wensday, ye ken.'

Andy knew he could leave on the term day if he wished.

'A'richt, tell Balturk A'll be ower Wensday nicht. A'll hae tae tell the oul' maun the day.'

'Richt,' and they went on to talk of ordinary matters.

It was early dark and soon Paddy left. Andy went slowly over to the house. The kitchen was empty save for the oul' maun, who sat smoking. Andy drew up a chair to the fire and tried to screw up his courage to speak, but it was the oul' maun's voice that first broke the silence.

'Weel, Andy, ye'll be wantin' tae ley me on Wensday?'

Andy was startled.

'Ye needna be feart, boy, tae tell me. Yon black-headed devil's at Balturk, A heard, an' A saw him come oot o' the stable wi' ye the noo.'

It was astounding. Andy sat silent.

'Ye hae been a guid workin' boy,' said the oul' maun rather sorrowfully, 'an' A wusna wantin' ye tae gang, bit ye'll hae tae be awa', fur, he'll be ower pesterin' ye till ye dae. Ye're getting aulder an' mebbe a new place would dae ye guid. A hae nocht tae say aboot Paddy. He's a wild devil, bit ye're o' the same kin' yersel'. Ye're faither wus a guid maun at whiles, bit a restless divil tae. Mebbe ye'll be back afore lang. Work hard aye, boy, an' ye'll come tae nae herm.'

He spat into the ash-can and Andy felt uncomfortable.

'He wus askin' me tae gang, bit A didna say A would,' he burst out at last.

'Ye'll hae tae gang,' said the oul' maun, spitting again, 'ye'll be nae mair use tae me noo wi' that falla aye efter ye tae come an' work whaur he is.'

Andy said no more. The ticking of the clock and the sound of the porridge pot boiling seemed unusually loud. The oul' maun sat lost in thought, puffing at his pipe. On the Wednesday Andy gathered his few bits of clothes, wrapped them round the pieces of the gun which he had dismantled, and came downstairs for his money. The mistress gave it to him

'Weel, ye're awa'?' she said.

'Aye,' muttered Andy and was glad the oul' maun was at Wigtown so that he would not have to face him.

'Look efter yersel', boy,' she said as he went out of the house.

'A wull,' he answered. 'So long.'

The sky was clearing, but a light drizzle stung his cheeks. He
turned and looked back at Drumlin steading and the mist-covered
hills. Tears welled in his eyes. A strange feeling of weariness came
over him and he wanted to run back, but instead he went down the
water-logged road till the farm was hidden from sight, till the
highest trees vanished behind the hills at the road end. A heron flew
out of the mist and passed over his head on its way to a boggy
hollow.

Balturk was another hilly farm about the same size as Drumlin. Its
buildings were on a slope that ran into a wide stretch of moss to a
willow copse in the distance. Behind the copse was the wild bog of
the historic Doulton Loch. The farm buildings were even older and
more in need of repair than the Drumlin steading. Pig-houses were
casting their moss-green slates; the byre was ill-drained and smaller,
and the farmhouse itself was weather-worn and damp. A short red-
faced man named Aird was the tenant and ran the place poorly.
Andy met him on his way over from the stable.

'A'm Andy Walker,' he announced.

The short man looked at him. 'Och aye, A hae min' ye're frae
Drumlin.'

'Aye,' said Andy and waited for him to speak again.

'Weel, A'm needin' a boy an' b'the look o' ye A think ye'll dae
me. Ye ken hoo much A'm gan tae gie ye?'

'Aye.'

'Weel, here's half a croon.'

Andy took the fee-money and went over to the house. Paddy
was nowhere about. He knocked at the door and a pleasant, plump
woman answered.

'A'm the new boy,' said Andy, the words he had used when he
had first knocked at the door of Drumlin.

'Come in an' pit yer claithes up the stair.'

She showed him the way.

It was a homelier kitchen than Drumlin, but there was no grandfather clock. Andy missed it. An ancient 'wag at the wa' ticked musically above the dresser, and there was no range but a wide open fireplace with a hook for pots dangling on a chain. A surly black collie growled at him from under the table.

'Dinna be feart o' him, he'll be a' richt whun he gets tae ken ye,' said the mistress of the house.

Andy went up the ladder which led to the loft. It was a darker place than the one he had left; only one skylight to let in the light. The two iron beds were across the room instead of length-wise and a byre lamp, forbidden luxury at Drumlin, hung from the ceiling.

'The near bed'll be yours,' the woman called up.

Andy undid his bundle and looked for a place to hide the gun. Finding none, he placed it under the mattress for the time being, and went down the ladder into the kitchen. The dinner was cooking.

'A'll gang ower an' see the maister,' he said, using the old-fashioned form of address.

'Ye'll hae nocht tae dae the day forbye milk,' said the woman, 'he's gan tae the toon this efternin.'

Andy went out partly because he felt he was expected to seek his new master, and partly because he was looking for Paddy. The boss, as he came to call him, was on his way to the house but did not stop to give any instructions.

'Takin' a look roon, boy?' he asked good naturedly.

Andy was surprised. This surely was a new kind of man to work for.

'Aye,' he replied, and decided to continue on his way as that seemed to be expected of him.

He wandered through the dirty byre. He visited the barn and straw-house, the pig-houses, cartsheds, and lastly the stable. Paddy was in the stable.

'He telt me ye wur here,' he grinned, sitting on an upturned trough.

He appeared to be doing nothing at all but smoke.

'Whut's the wey ye're no daein' ocht?' he asked.

Paddy grinned again, 'Nocht's din aboot this place on term day, he tells me.'

'That's fine,' laughed Andy. 'He gied me half a croon whun he took me.'

'Aye, A had five shillin' aff him whun A come. He's a lazy devil. Ye needna work hard here. A hae hardly din ocht since A come, forbye a bit o' plooin' an milkin',' Paddy told him.

'A like the mistress.'

'She's no' sae bad,' agreed Paddy. 'A richt hefty waurm lump tae hae in bed wi' ye. A heard aff a cot-man that she's wullin' tae keep the plooman waurm at nicht if the boss gets drunk an' disna come hame.'

Andy saw the plump woman in a new light.

They sat talking in the stable till dinner time and then went in for the meal. In the afternoon the boss harnessed his trap and set out for Wigtown. The rest of the day was spent in idleness. Paddy, Andy and the mistress milked the kye and foddered them. It began to rain heavily and a wind came up while they were having their supper.

CHAPTER XIII

PADDY spent most of his evenings cultivating the mistress, who welcomed his efforts when her husband was drinking at the Whaup or another of his favourite haunts. Andy, for the lack of some one to talk to, would often go to bed and lie listening to their voices till he fell asleep. The rain would thrash across the skylight and trickle down the slates to drain into the overflowing water barrel.

Some nights he would doze off and then wake to hear the murmur of conversation in the lull, coming from the room below. Then the wind would rumble in the chimney and sigh through the trees by the byre till their tones were lost in the roar of the winter's night. At times, when the wind dropped and the dark house was silent, he would lie straining his ears for sounds till suddenly he would be startled and his heart beat faster as they began to talk again.

Once he crept out of bed and lay on his stomach peering down the hatch into the kitchen, but they were sitting apart, one each side of the dying fire. The red glow of the peats cast strange lights on Paddy's dark face, and the buxom form of the mistress, with her full face, dark hair and ample breast, became almost pretty. He lay till he became cold and then at last, feeling that by some strange instinct they might be conscious of his intent dark eyes gazing on them from above, he rose silently and went back to bed.

Plundering in the henhouse one afternoon he found a rusted bicycle. It had flat tyres and was in need of oil, but it certainly presented a means of getting about. On Sunday he spent the day in the stable mending punctures and scraping the rust from the frame. His skill as a cyclist depended largely on three or four 'rides' he had had on the bikes of boys at school, but he practised, with many a dangerous wobble and once a fall, in the stony court, before making long excursions. When he told Paddy he met with encouragement at which he had strangely shrewd deductions. The first night he took a run to Wigtown his tyre went down as he entered the town, and he decided to turn back at once. He pumped up the punctured tyre several times and pedalled fast on the way back. His return would have been a surprise to Paddy, but when he went into the kitchen the place was in darkness.

The boss, he knew, was at Wigtown, but Paddy was at home, or had been when he had left. He looked up the stairs for him then recalled the eagerness with which the mistress had seen him off. He opened the door which gave access to 'ben the hoose', but not a sound came to tell him his suspicions were correct. A new thought came to him and he went out across the rain-swept court, walking on the balls of his feet round the end of the byre, where he could hear the kye shifting uneasily, past the rusted turnip cutter to the barn.

From the high barn he looked down through a wide opening in the wall into the straw and chaff-house. A rustle and the faint sound of whispering caught his ear, but it was black dark, and he could see nothing. He lay imagining the voluptuous form of the mistress, half naked in Paddy's arms, till his thoughts were interrupted by the voice of the woman.

'Come on back tae the hoose. He'll mebbe be hame in half an 'oor, an' the boy'll be back b'noo.'

The straw rustled noisily, then a match lit up the scene for a few seconds. Andy saw them. She was lying back in the straw with her clothes dishevelled. He could see, in the brief space of time before the match went out, the flesh of her round thighs, her flushed face and untidy hair. Paddy cupped the match in his hands and raised it to his face to light a cigarette. It seemed to Andy that he looked straight at him. He began the stealthy descent of the barn stairs. The straw rustled again and he hurried on, leaving the barn door unbarred, round the end of the byre, and over to the house. He went in breathless, tugged off his boots, and scrambled up the stairs. A few minutes later the sneck of the door clicked and he heard them come in. The woman was silent.

Paddy had noticed the boots on the floor and called up softly, 'Ir ye abed, Andy?'

He lay holding his breath till he heard him whisper to the woman, 'He's asleep.'

Five minutes after the trap jolted through the near gate. The boss was back. Paddy came up to bed in a hell of a hurry, and Andy pretended to be breathing deeply.

The clock in the room below seemed to have ticked an hour past before the boss came in. He was drunk and his loud voice shattered the silence.

'Weel, Maggie, waitin' fur the oul' fella? Ye micht hae been up the stair waurmin' his bed fur him, bit never min'. Hae ye the supper ready?'

'Aye,' said the mistress quietly, 'ye're late comin' hame, whaur wur ye?'

He mumbled something indistinctly and belched. They went up to bed an hour later without another word. Paddy was already sleeping soundly. It began to rain again as Andy lay awake wondering. The sighing of the trees, those ragged old firs in the plantation, punctuated the roar of the wind. It blasted round the house, then died with the sorrowful swish that whispered through the small wood.

Paddy was unusually quiet all day. Andy went on with his work without any reference to the previous evening. Once he thought of mentioning Paddy's absence when he came home from the town, but decided not to do so. It was amusing to watch the mistress's glances at Paddy, and the steadfast look which he returned; the silent sharing of their secret which Andy shared too, though they were unaware of it. Innocently enough, Andy officially became aware of their love-making. After a run down to the Whaup one night he came into the kitchen silently, expecting nothing unusual, for the boss had been at home when he left. He opened the door and came upon them locked in each other's arms on the broken-down couch before the fire. Paddy jumped up suddenly and the mistress began rearranging her clothes.

'Och, it's you, Andy?' he said in a relieved tone.

'Aye,' answered Andy.

At first he felt inclined to go straight to bed, but an impulse prompted him to stay and watch the woman's discomfort. They sat silent for half an hour and then she asked,

'Ir ye no' gan tae bed, Andy?'

'A'm no' tired.'

'Ye'll be wantin' a bit o' supper then?'

'Aye.'

She began the elaborate preparation of his supper. He noticed that the jam on the scones was unusually thick and the cheese generously sliced for him. It amused him and he foresaw the position becoming much to his advantage. The woman was afraid of him, and though Paddy was careless he trusted him. When they went up to bed as the boss came in he spoke.

'Ye'll be share an' had yer tongue noo, Andy?'

'Christ, aye, ye ken me weel enough, Paddy.'

'Aye. A dae,' he assured him.

They climbed into bed at that. While he was cleaning the byre next morning, the mistress sought him. She stood watching him for a while before saying anything.

'Andy,' she said at last in a persuasive favour-seeking voice, 'ye'll no' tell on us, wull ye?'

He went on brushing the walk. She came closer and put her hand on his arm.

'Dae ye hear?' she whispered. 'A'll be guid tae ye if ye had yer tongue.'

Still he was silent. It gave him a sense of power to have her pleading with him. When he had finished he walked up the byre. She was standing with her back to the door.

'Come on, Andy, here's a kiss fur ye, ye'll say nocht?'

She drew him to her and he kissed the hot, heavy lips. It was intoxicating. He repeated it to show his hold over her and let his hand fall on her breast.

'A'll had ma tongue,' he said, 'if ye're guid tae me.'

Then as an afterthought, 'Ye could gie me half a croon, bit dinna tell Paddy, or if ye dae mebbe A'll change ma min'.'

She smiled at him and stood while he played with the fasteners of her blouse.

All at once she exclaimed, 'There's somebudy comin'.'

He stepped away from her and she was through the door in a second.

No one was coming. He felt cheated, but put his head round the door and called softly after her, 'Dinna furget, be guid tae me, an' A need half a croon.'

'A'richt,' she flung back at him, smiling.

He went on with his work with a new sense of importance and pleasure. His only fear was that she might tell Paddy and he would half-kill him, so he decided to take a safe course and went looking for Paddy in the stable. He was laying out plough chains on the cobbled floor.

'Paddy,' he said.

'Aye?'

'She wus talkin' tae me aboot last nicht.'

'Aye?'

'She's gan tae gie me half a croon, an' look efter me better if A had ma tongue, aff coorse A wudna say ocht onywey, bit A can dae wi' mair meat an' a half croon or twa.'

He added this as an afterthought not to raise Paddy's temper.

'Ye're a dirty bastard, ye ken, Andy,' said Paddy without anger, in fact he grinned, 'bit A canna blame ye fur lookin' efter yersel'. A'm gan tae see whut A can dae fur masel' tae. Like gettin' mair money an' the best o' meat. Ye're richt enough.'

Andy felt as though a great burden had been lifted from his mind; his uneasiness was gone and the day passed quickly. She gave him his money when the kitchen was empty after kye time and he grinned at her:

'Mebbe anither yin afore Saturday wud dae me noo, bit ye're no' tae tak' any o't aff ma wage, ye ken.'

'God, ye're a' there, ir you,' she laughed, 'bit it's no' ma money A'm giein' ye, an' as lang as it's no' ower often A'll no' say ocht.'

'Richt ye ir, Maggie,' he said familiarly.

She let him kiss her before he went out for his bike. It was a cloying, sensuous contact that made him envy Paddy. He whistled in the teeth of the wind as he crossed to the hen-house and pulled the rattling old bike out. He laughed to himself. There would be no stealthy love-making while he was away. The pony had cast a shoe and was lame, which meant that the boss would have to stay at home for a change. He rode with head down, over the bumps of the wet road, past the cot-house at the last gate, then set out for the Port, on his way round to Brachan to see the dark girl again.

It rained, but he was wearing Paddy's oilskins and rode hard to keep warm. At the Port he stopped and had a drink. The place was deserted and heavy seas threw a cloud of foam flecks high in the air. They fell on the road and struck cold on the face as they were wafted over by the wind. At Brachan he propped his bike against the cot-house door and knocked. Nan opened to him.

'Ye're late o' comin',' she remarked.

'Aye, bit there's a helluva wun' blawin',' he apologized.

'Come in, boy,' her father, a dirty bewhiskered man in a ragged suit, called to him.

He went into the warmth and sat down by the fire.

The man rose after a while and murmured, 'A'll jist gang doon tae Mochrum fur a dram.'

When he had gone Nan smiled knowingly.

'He'll no' be back the nicht. Whut wi' a dram or twa an' a saft bed doon at Mrs. M'Cormick's.'

It was Mrs. M'Cormick, she explained, would be her step-mother, when her husband, a ploughman at Whithorn, died.

'Ye can stey a' nicht if ye like,' she invited.

'A'd better no' dae that,' declared Andy, 'A'll hae tae be on ma road back by yin o'clock onywey.'

They went over to the bed and lay down.

It was a quarter to two and blowing a gale when he set out for Balturk. The wind and rain seemed colder after the heat of the house. He was reluctant to go, but there was work to do in the morning and the kye to milk. He breathed hard as he pushed against the wind.

Life continued unchanged in the Balturk household. Andy made increasingly frequent demands for half-crowns to keep his mouth shut, and Maggie paid for his silence with money, occasional kisses, and even accepted more intimate caresses. In the meantime he held his first plough in the hollows where the potatoes were to be planted. The boss guided him and Paddy gave his advice. It was an exciting adventure in his life, and he decided for all time to be a ploughman. The muscles stood out on his arms as he fought against the jerks and twists of the plough when the coulter struck or glided over hidden rocks.

Two docile horses, one aged, with a whiskered mouth and hollow back, and the other a short-winded heavy creature, re-sponded to his 'hupps' and 'highs'; his praise and curses. The furrows he turned were none too straight; in places deep and heavy, and light and wavering in others, but, after a week of staggering up and down the field, he began to improve. There were signs that when the youth became a man, when his back was strong and his arms and eyes steady, he would plough a fair furrow.

A fortnight and the muscles, coaxed into strength in the hayfield, were hard and sinewy. His brief encounters with Paddy, when they tussled in the stable, showed him a new power before undeveloped.

At sixteen he was strong, at nineteen he would possess a strength of arm and grip rarely equalled. The ploughing filled his thoughts day and night. In the morning his byre cleaning became irksome.

He looked forward to feeding his horses, they had become 'his horses'. Paddy often asked him, 'Hae ye fed yer horse?' and the boss had told him to be sure that he looked after his horses. In comparison harrowing was a tame job. He had never felt the same thrill yoking his horse to the harrow as he did tramping up the road to the field leading his pair to the plough, or riding home at dusk, sitting sideways with the other horse trudging behind at the end of a plough-line. It was a sight that made his heart jump, to come through the slap and see the plough, a lonely object, half-way down the furrowed field, waiting for him to come with his horses and set to work.

At nights, as it had been with his early days at byre work and haytime, he slept soundly. The novelty of the gun or the rattling bike shrank to unimportance. He milked, came in and had supper, washed and went to bed, leaving Paddy to his flagrant love-making in the kitchen. He slept so well that the nervous squeals and laughs of Maggie no longer roused him and set him thinking.

For all that, on Sundays he demanded the price of silence, and went off to Mochrum or Brachan, the Port, or the Whaup; wherever his fancy took him. The boss, whose main interests in the farm were his five or six Ayrshire stirks and a coop of speckled bantams, was rarely at home on Sunday, though where he went between the opening hours of the public houses no one knew, save Andy, who kept the secret.

Hay and corn harvests, when the time came, were meagre at Balturk. It was stony, barren land that had been sorely worked with too little manuring for many years. The reaper and binder were obsolete implements and broke over and over again. Unlike the oul' maun at Drumlin, Aird showed no ingenuity when it came to repairs. His first remedy was a wire or rope repair; merely the tying of the broken part, the second was to hoist it into a cart and take it to the smith, who, when he was busy with dozens of urgent harvest repairs, would take a week or more to put the thing right.

In the meantime they mowed. Paddy with a steady rhythmical

swing; Andy haggling with the blunt scythe in his artless fashion. Andy was wise to a secret which the mistress shared with Paddy at harvest time.

Her slightly swollen body did not escape his observant eye, and one evening in the stable he spoke to Paddy about it.

'She's gan tae hae a wean,' he said as he pulled the collar from the sweated neck of the mare.

It might have been the mare he was referring to, for they had not spoken since they left the field, but Paddy knew only too well the meaning of the words.

'Aye.'

'Whut'll ye dae noo?'

There was no need for Andy to ask whether Paddy was sure he was the father of the as yet unborn child.

'Nocht.' Paddy was as careless as ever.

'Bit the boss?'

'Tae hell wi' the boss. He disna ken whether he's the fether or no'. He sleeps wi' her at nicht, A dinna. An' if he does ken, whut can he dae aboot it?'

Andy saw Paddy's reasoning. It was true. The boss could do nothing even if he were sure that the child was Paddy's.

'A'm tired o' her onywey,' added Paddy. 'A'll be lookin' fur a new place at the term. Ye can come wi' me if ye like.'

Andy made no reply to the invitation, but reverted to the mistress again. 'Whun's it comin'?'

'She's no share, bit it'll no' be mair than a month.'

'That's afore the term,' said Andy resignedly.

'Aye, bit afore or efter it's nae metter.'

Andy went in for his supper. The mistress was in the kitchen alone.

'Sae ye're gan tae hae a wean?' he observed.

She scowled at him and said nothing.

'Paddy an' you'll be aff plaised,' he went on insolently.

'Had yer tongue fur yer ain sake,' she threatened.

'Weel, it'll be five or six shillin' A'll be needin' aff ye noo,' he told her.

'Then ye'll gang on needin', ye rotten wee bastard,' was her furious retort, 'ye'll get nae mair aff o' me, bit, A'm tellin' ye, if ye dinna had yer tongue, ye'll hae tae watch yersel'.'

'A'll watch masel', bit it's you that'll hae tae watch,' he answered.

She was stirring the porridge and turned in fury on him, slashing him across the face with the hot spurtle. His crazy temper burst loose in an instant. He wanted to kill this fat bitch for the burning pain on his face. She made to repeat the blow when he struck her on the side of the head. She staggered back and fell over the creepy-stool on the hearth. He made no move to help her rise, but his face blanched for a moment when he saw her clutch her side. She groaned in agony and feebly grasped the edge of the table to pull herself to her feet.

'Ye dirty oul' bitch,' he cursed, 'ye'll no' hit me, or b'Christ A'll murder ye.'

The agonised sobs and groans continued. He dished his porridge and ate it quickly. The boss was coming. As his feet sounded on the doorstep the mistress rested her hand on the mantel and raked the back of the grate. As he rose to go across to the byre Andy could see sweat trickling down her plump cheeks. A red mark burned on his face where she had struck him. He decided not to ask for the half-crown.

A fortnight later Andy woke in the night with the shrieks of the mistress ringing in his ears. At first he imagined the boss had come home drunk and was murdering her. The awful cries came again. Paddy was sitting up listening too.

'She's haein' the wean.'

'Aye,' said Andy.

They heard the sound of the boss's voice.

'Paddy,' he called, 'pit on yer claithes an' rin doon fur the M'Kechnie wuman.'

They knew the child was coming. Paddy scrambled into his clothes.

After a while Andy fell asleep. He did not hear the clatter in the kitchen; the sound of the cotman's wife giving orders; the boiling of pots of water and the commotion that went on until nearly kye time. Paddy was downstairs when Andy rose. The house was silent.

'Did the wean come a'richt?' asked Andy as he pulled on his boots.

'No. It was afore time. It was daid. So's she. Half an oor ago.'

Paddy seemed stricken with grief. A sorrow that Andy could not understand. He had never thought Paddy capable of feeling. He felt uneasy when he thought of how he had struck the dead woman. His hatred for that burn on the side of his face had gone. Strange thoughts chased one another through his mind.

Going for the kye he decided that it was not sorrow, this strange new mood he was in. A woman he had known had died. A being he had known would never breathe the fresh clean air in the morning again; would never hear the swallows twitter in the summer or chill her hands on the frost-covered pump handle in winter; would never hold her face into the rain as she walked for the kye or let the breeze ruffle her hair as he loved to have it do. He wondered if she had ever breathed the old dead smells of autumn as he had done, and his heart was heavy to think of anyone living and dying without ever having the dream-scents of withered potato shaws and stacks of corn in their nostrils; without ever knowing that these were the scents of autumn, as the newly turned earth was the smell of spring, and honeysuckle and peat smoke the scents of summer. For a moment he knew what being alive meant. The only mystery was death.

It was a sad thing death. More sad than the cry of the whaup. But he did not feel sorry. He was not sorry. Death was a thing far too big for sorrow.

CHAPTER XIV

IT WAS the Saturday after the funeral and past kye time. The three of them were sitting round the fire after supper. Andy, straining his eyes reading the 'wanted' column of the 'Gazette', Paddy smoking and the boss to all intents dreaming with his eyes fixed on the ashpan. After drawing slowly on his pipe, Paddy spoke.

'Ye'll be sellin' the stirks as weel?'

The boss nodded, 'Aye, an' a pair o' horse.'

He had told them at dinner of his intention to sell off and had already given notice to the laird. It would be a year before he could leave.

Andy paid no attention, but read on.

'Boy wanted, must be good milker and early riser. Clean byres. Apply . . .'

No, that was no use, Creetown on the other side of the bay, maybe a lonely place in the hills. Nowhere to go, no one he knew, strange folk.

He read each situation slowly. Shepherds, cotmen, married ploughmen, dairymen, milkers, byremen.

Then on to the next column, 'found on the road near Sorbie, black Galloway calf. Marks on ears. . . . apply . . .'

Who would lose a black Galloway calf on the road? Where had it come from? He thought of the road that ran by the burn down to Sorbie creamery; the hill up to the village, the dilapidated house where the jackdaws nested, and the straight white road that seemed to flash through the village when you rode along it on a summer's evening, rising and dipping through a wood on its way to Whithorn. He visualized the lonely little calf trotting nervously by the ditch side, and running in terror as a car came swishing by.

He looked back down the advertisements again. Ploughman, byremen, byreman, milkers, boy wanted. . . .

That was it. 'Boy wanted. Downhall, Mochrum. Must be good milker and willing worker. Apply at once.'

Paddy's voice burst in on his thoughts again. 'Lookin' fur a new place, Andy?' he grinned at his discomfort.

'No, jist readin' the paper,' lied Andy.

'Ye'll be thinkin' o' layin' then?' the boss broke in.

'A dinna ken, mebbe.'

Paddy was leaving, he knew, for he had asked him to come with him, but there was no certainty of a job for him if he did. There might be before term day, but working with Paddy he had less hope of ever becoming a ploughman, for few small farms employed more than one ploughman.

Tomorrow, he decided, he would go to the Downhall place and

see the man. Perhaps at the same time he would tell the boss he was finishing.

Paddy picked up the paper which he had dropped. 'Let me see,' he tormented him, boys wanted. Aye, here we ir. Doonhall, Mochrum. Guid milker, wullin' worker. That's you, Andy. The very place fur ye.'

'Aye,' then after a pause, 'A wus thinkin' o' gan ower there the morn.'

Paddy was surprised. Andy had taken his joke, though he had only meant to make him uncomfortable with the boss sitting listening. He realized the reason for the boldness. Andy had been thinking of that place, had been afraid to suggest leaving until he had been able to break the news through his teasing.

'Wur ye?' both the boss and Paddy exclaimed at once.

'Aye,' he answered, then deciding on retaliation, he betrayed Paddy.

'Ye'll be lookin' fur a new plooman tae afore lang. He's waitin' tae lay.'

Paddy spat into the fire and evaded the enquiring glance of the boss. Andy felt disturbed too. There was no retreating.

'A'll tak' ma money the nicht if ye hae it,' he burst out. Now he had committed himself. Supposing the place at Doonhall was taken, what would he do then? The boss interrupted his thoughts.

'Weel, weel, weel,' he said wearily, 'bit whut aboot the kye?'

'Ye can get somebody else on Monday. A'll dae ma share the morn.' Andy faced him boldly.

The clock stopped ticking. The boss rose to wind it then went to bed.

'Ye're a fine yin,' said Paddy.

'Weel ye should hae kep' yer mooth shut whun ye saw me lookin' fur a place.' Andy's temper began to rise.

'Awa' tae hell, maun. Whut kin o' dirty trick was that? Telling him A wus layin'. B'God an' mebbe he'll hae somebudy else fur the place afore A'm ready tae lay.'

'Ye canna be made tae feenish afore the term. Ye ken that fine. Ye had nae need o' tellin' him whut A wus daein'.'

'Richt ye ir, Andy.' Paddy was offended, his tone was a hurt one. 'Come on tae yer bed an' gie yer tongue a rest.'

'A'll come whun A think tae come. Ye can gang noo if ye like.' There was an ill-tempered rebuke in Andy's voice.

'Guid nicht then,' said Paddy as he climbed the ladder.

Andy said nothing. The fire died down so that he could no longer see by its light to read. He pulled a crumpled packet of cigarettes from his pocket and lit one, nursing his grievance against everything in general as he smoked. He dozed off to sleep. The peats slumped on to the hearth and woke him up with a sudden start. It was too dark to see the clock, so he took off his boots and went up to bed.

Craig of Doonhall looked at Andy. He saw a medium-built youth, with a lean tanned face, black curly hair and thick eyebrows, small eyes, pointed nose and tight-lipped mouth. His jaws had the dark fluff of a youthful beard, his head was held high on a rather long neck, his hands were large and hairy, and though his boots were heavy, there was an impression of lightness about him. The brow was intelligent; in fact, the whole figure of him, from the breadth of the shoulders to the woman's waist and the well-moulded thighs, which bulged in his thread-bare trousers, pleased Craig.

Rather too handsome and quick-witted for a byreboy, he thought; make a fine man for a farm if he could only shape him and sway him to his will, but there was a flash in the dark eyes, a firmness about the mouth that told him it was hopeless. There was a temper, too, in the make-up of him.

Craig smiled, a pleasant worn smile that revealed a friendliness which his eyes and countenance belied.

'Whut ir ye layin' Balturk fur?' he asked.

'Weel,' Andy hesitated, 'A'm needin' a change.'

'Oh, ye ir, an' whut wull A dae if ye fin' ye need anither change efter ye hae been here a week or twa?'

'Then it'll be term again,' Andy's quick wits came to his aid and he grinned.

Craig was in need of a boy and could not afford to consider such things.

'Richt then, bring yer claithes ower the nicht efter kye tim'.'

A woman came and placed tea and scones before him.

'Ye'll hae a caul trek back tae Balturk, boy, here's something tae waurm yersel wi',' she said.

'A wull that, thank ye,' Andy smiled. He felt he would like the friendly folk of Doonhall, the new boss with his penetrating eyes, hard thin face and half-smiling mouth. He was tall and Andy liked tall men.

'Aird's sellin' a loat o' stuff A heard?' he remarked as Andy drank his tea.

'Aye, there's no' very much worth left.'

Then he decided to beard the lion with a question about wages.

'Ye said fourteen shillin', did ye no'?' he asked.

'No.'

He had expected that answer, Aird had only given him eight.

'Bit A'll gie ye eleeven,' the new boss went on, 'an' ye'll hae tae wurk hard fur it tae.'

He was surprised. Fourteen shillings was almost a ploughman's wage, and in fact when he had asked for it he had known the demand to be outrageous, but eleven shillings . . .

'That'll dae then,' he agreed.

Better not to sound too satisfied, and he said the words as unemotionally as his heart would let him, and praised the imp of mischief that had made him say fourteen.

'Ye'll sleep up the stair,' Craig told him as he buttoned his coat.

'Aye,' he said.

Doonhall had two men. A herd who milked as well as looked after the bullocks and stirks, shawed turnips, fed calves and so on, and a ploughman. Andy would be byreboy again, though not for long he promised himself.

'A can ploo, ye ken,' he reminded Craig as he prepared to leave.

'So ye say. A'll let ye hae a haun at the lea plooin'.'

It was something, he felt, even though the promise had not been too enthusiastic or encouraging. He rode back to Balturk. The boss and Paddy were asleep before the fire. No porridge had been made and it was near kye time. Paddy looked up drowsily as he entered.

'Weel, hoo did ye get on?' he enquired.

'Fine,' Andy replied.

The boss awoke.

'He's gi'en me eleeven shillin' an' A'm gan the nicht.'

'Jesus Christ! Eleeven shillin'?' burst out Paddy.

'Eleeven?' echoed the boss.

'Aye,' said Andy watching the effect of his words.

'The maun has mair money than sense.'

'Aye, he'll hae ye half-kilt tae get his money oot o' ye,' added Paddy.

'Weel, A'm no' feart o' hard wurk,' retorted Andy.

'Ye watched ye didna kill yersel' wi' it here,' was the boss's rejoinder.

'Aicht shillin's no' eleeven tho'.' Andy's reply brought silence.

'Och, come on, boys,' Aird changed the subject. 'It's near kye tim'. Get a bite tae eat an' awa' ower tae the byre.'

They drew up to the table. There were no scones, for there was no one to bake them. The boss was tired enough at trying his hand at breakfast and dinner to attempt that. The bread was hard and dry. Andy plastered it with jam and swallowed it with a glass of milk to wash it down.

'Whut aboot the parrich?' he asked as he rose.

'A'll pit them on afore A come ower tae the byre,' the boss assured him.

'Ye'll hae ma money ready, fur A'll want awa',' he shot over his shoulder as they hurried out.

'Aye, aye, bit fast ye, an' get the milkin' din.'

The moon was coming up and shimmered on the frosted slates of the steading as they went across to the byre, Andy swinging the byre-lamp to light their way in the shadows. They were late with the milking. One or two of the kye began to bellow to be milked.

'Had on, ma lassies,' Paddy consoled them as they stepped into the byre, and shut the door.

It was warm and pleasant in the heat and they hurried on with their task. Andy noticed that they had already been foddered. Probably Paddy had done that while he had been away. He pressed his face against the warm hairy side of the cow and the milk spurted into the pail at the pressure of his fingers. Paddy was singing an old song, a rambling story of love and sorrow that he had learned perhaps from his grandmother. When he came to a part where he had forgotten the words he hummed tunelessly.

The sneck of the door clicked and the boss came in.

'Boys, it's hellish caul' the nicht,' he announced as he beat his arms round his body and panted, short of breath.

Andy said nothing, but lifted back his stool and went up the byre to empty his pail. An old white hen sat sleeping on a bag by the edge of the churn. She cackled in fear as the milk spattered over her, and fluttered off under the belly of a cow in the first stall.

'Pit her oot o' that,' Andy urged the collie who sat on the byrewalk. The dog obeyed; rushed after the hen, and was kicked by the startled cow for his pains.

'Bonnie Charlie's noo awa',' sang Paddy discordantly. Andy's head was full of thoughts. Thoughts of days when he would no longer milk in the byre on Sunday nights, or wheel an over-flowing barrow of dung to the midden, but walk behind his plough, whistling, and bring his horses home at night to the stable, feeding them in the semi-darkness.

'Whut aboot a milker fur the morn?' asked Paddy, breaking off in the middle of his song.

'Yon lassie that wus up this efternin's comin',' said the boss, 'an' her brither's comin' the morn's nicht.'

Paddy being satisfied that more than his fair share of the work would not fall upon him, commenced his singing again.

'Bonnie Charlie's noo awa';' the tune would have better fitted the dead march.

Andy stripped his last cow and straightened his stiff legs. Paddy's face was still buried in the side of a black Galloway and his voice droned on indistinctly. The boss was finishing.

'The parrich'll be ready noo,' he called after Andy as he went out of the lower door, 'pit me oot a bowlfu'.'

'An' yin fur me tae,' sang out Paddy, who had lifted his head.

Andy went across to the house. He could see the firelight flickering on the windows and walls of the kitchen. It was a cold cloudless night and the water in the hollows had become sheets of ice. He was glad when he was inside pouring the porridge. He went upstairs while it cooled and gathered his things, packing into the bundle an old fur-lined coat that had been lying around the house for weeks. He had also acquired a set of oilskins from the stable together with a box more than half-full of cartridges. These things and the old bike no one would miss. He tied the bundle up with string and was down before the boss and Paddy came over from the byre.

'Yer money,' the boss reminded himself as he pulled off his coat.

'Aye,' said Andy.

'Less five shillin' in Mey, an' ten afore harvest, ten efter hervest, an' wi' yer insurance and a pair o' bits an' socks an' shirt. That'll be aicht poun'.'

Andy couldn't follow the calculation, but picked up the notes and put them in his pocket. He wished he had had twice as many, but a year at Doonhall would make him rich.

He sat warming himself at the fire for a while before he rose and picked up his bundle.

'Weel, A'll hae tae awa',' he said.

'Guid luck tae ye,' said the boss.

Paddy came out to see him off. 'Ye're fur awa', then,' he said laconically.

'Aye, A'm that,' said Andy brightly, 'A'll mebbe see ye afore lang tho'.'

'Mebbe ye wull,' agreed Paddy.

'A'll be at the cattle-show next year onywey.'

He laughed, 'God kens whut'll happen afore cattle-show day, Andy. That's a helluva lang time yet.'

'Jist the same', said Andy as he tied his clothes to the handle bars of the bike, 'if A'm leevin' A'll be there.'

Paddy laughed again.

They shook hands solemnly enough before Andy jumped on the bike.

'So long, boy,' said Paddy.

'So long, Paddy.'

The broken bell rattled and jingled as he rode down the road. The ice cracked in the puddle holes.

'See ye cattle-show day,' Paddy yelled after him, and Andy could hear his laughter as he turned away.

The moon was bright and he needed no lamp save when he passed through the unholy darkness where a wood swallowed the road. He pedalled fast, half-afraid of the shadows, and eager to be out of the cold.

Doonhall, as it is called locally, was a well-built and well-managed place. Its three hundred acres were a model of tidiness and shrewd farming. No haphazard work satisfied Craig. He was even more exacting than the oul' maun of Drumlin, though Andy found he could face him easier. He was just and listened to a man's excuses, weighing them carefully before he gave his decision. He did not drink himself, and, though he had no objection to the men drinking, Andy had a feeling that if he did come in drunk things would go ill for him.

'Twelve o'clock's the latest ye're tae be oot tae ony time. God kens whut ye'd be wantin' oot tae twelve fur, bit if A catch ye comin' in here efter twelve ye can get yer duds thegether, an' doon the road as fast's ye like,' was his warning and Andy was inclined to respect it.

Work he demanded done thoroughly and willingly.

'Ye wur sayin' ye could ploo, boy?' he remarked one day to Andy, who was scrubbing cans in the dairy.

'Aye.'

'Weel, A'll mak a plooman o' ye. Come awa' tae the stable whun ye hae din. Ye'll tak' the horse tae the fiel' an' A'll see whut ye can dae. Mebbe if ye stey wi' me A'll learn ye an' tak' ye fur a plooman next year. Yon Alec's nae haun at it. A could teach ye tae dae better than yon.'

Andy had never seen how Alec, the ploughman, did plough, but he saw in this his promotion from the byre to the plough, to do a real man's work. He leaned over the cans and made sure that in his haste he had not left one that was not spotlessly clean, and then went off to the stable.

Craig watched him prepare the horses.

'Tak' yer time, boy,' he said, as Andy struggled with the collar over the head of one of his horses. 'Dinna mak' sic' a helluva tear at it. Mak' haste slowly. The maun that taks his time an sees the thing richt'll be there afore the lazy maun that tries tae dae a' things in the yin meenit.'

Andy felt damped. He had imagined Craig standing there approving his eagerness and show of willingness, and instead this was his lot. He took time getting the other horse ready and the boss said nothing.

At length they left for the field. Andy was careful to shut the gates behind them, carry the plough lines so that they did not trail in the mud, and lead the horses through the gates properly. He ploughed three furrows before the boss said a word, then his criticism came thick and fast.

'Dinna let the horses' heads hang doon among their feet. Watch fur big stanes. Dinna had sae deep. Tak' bigger steps or ye'll sin be tired,' and a thousand more instructions that Andy found it difficult to remember.

He ploughed the next furrow trying to do all the things at once. It was a nightmare, but the praise at the end was worth it. 'Maun, ye'll mak' a richt guid plooman afore A hae feenished wi' ye.'

With the boss following him, or standing in turns at the end of the furrow watching his progress, he spent the rest of the morning behind the plough. In the afternoon the boss came with him again for half an hour then left him on his own.

'Jist gan on the wey ye're daein'. A'll be back at a while's end tae see ye,' he said as he went off.

Andy concentrated for the rest of the afternoon on ploughing as he had been instructed. It was a fifteen-acre field, and he hoped that he would be allowed to do it all by himself, though at the rate he was going it would have taken until near harvest time to finish.

He sampled all the joys and hardships of ploughing in the four weeks that followed. At the end of it all his furrows compared well with the work of the ploughman who was passing to and fro over the hill on his right. Through it all, till the boss decided he must spend more time in the byre, he thought of nothing else. He went to bed whenever the milking was over and rose next morning ready for more.

The Craig family were pleasant, happy folk. There was the mistress, a stout hearty woman with a smiling red face and big strong arms; two dark-haired daughters of thirty or so, and a crippled son who smiled pathetically as he hobbled along on a stick. Andy liked the son. His deformed leg was a handicap that made him survey the world in a different light, with more eagerness and simple interest than the average man has time for. They became friends.

Strangely enough, as in the case of his brothers and Tam, Andy never saw Paddy again. The shire is not a large countryside, but men are hidden from each other by its round hills and its lonely farmsteads. They work on its crofts and stony land, separated from one another by a few acres of moss and a ferny firwood or two, and never meet except at show days or sports held at Wigtown, Whithorn, the Port or Stranraer. So it was with Paddy. He became swallowed up in one of the little worlds of grey stone buildings with its sheltering hills and trees, where only the lowing of the kye, the bleating of the sheep, or the shrill crowing of the cock at morning, breaks the silence from the streak of dawn to the dreamy shadows of evening, when the pigeons coo in the woods and the rabbits nibble the short green grass by the hedges and banks.

Perhaps he tramped the quiet roads on his way to the Port and passed the ash trees at the Doonhall road end, even as Andy whistled on his way by the burn, or walked through the silent empty byres on his way from the stable or the barn. They may have passed each other as they trudged home tired from a night on the spree, but they never met.

The spring followed fast on the heels of winter, and the sunny days, when the crows stole the young turnips and left great bare patches in the fields, wore on into another misty summer.

All the while Andy worked like a slave. Not that he was forced to, but a great desire to please Craig and be his ploughman for the coming winter, urged him on. The harvest ripened and was cut, the stubble rotted in the autumn rains, the potatoes were dry in barrels in the barn, and soon it was winter again. Andy's greatest winter. He was a ploughman at last. Craig, though he knew well Andy's limitations, was eager to dispense with the services of a fully paid ploughman and employ Andy at a shilling a week more.

He was a ploughman on his eighteenth birthday; a strong though youthful figure following his team as he turned the red earth. He cajoled and coaxed the powerful brown Clydesdale horses as he worked them; fed them well at nights, and rubbed their cold heads caressingly as he supped his tea from a bowl in the morning and afternoon. He was in a responsible position, and talked to the boss almost as an equal. The boss liked him and the son was proud of his success. He scarcely noticed the frozen winds that came cutting across the ploughed land. The smell of the soil and the warmth of his body, alive with energy, made him happier than he had ever been in his life, as he struggled behind his plough handles; up the hill, over the brow, down into the hollow and back again; day after day till the grey of the dead grass and rotted stubble gave place to the pleasant red-brown earth of a field that was ready for sowing.

CHAPTER XV

MOLLY Docherty was an angel, even though she wore shoes a size too large for her and let her long black hair hang untidily over her eyes. At least to Andy she was an angel, blushing when he looked at her on the way to the dairy, and laughing when he spoke to her. There was no doubt that the lass at Doonhall, as they called the general handymaid and milker, was attractive in a coarse sort of way.

At first, at least from the time that he first took notice of her, for she had been there before he came, she seemed the loveliest girl that ever lived. He thought of her as he worked and often hoped that she would bring the tea in the afternoon. Later, and more in keeping with her untidiness, she descended to the level of mortals, became no longer an angel, but a girl. A girl to be winked at slyly as he supped his porridge with his head bent over his bowl, to be caught and squeezed in the byre and kissed surreptitiously before he scrambled up the ladder to bed.

Her folks lived in a cot-house at the road end and at times she slept at Doonhall, but often, when she wanted to disobey the mistress, for she had fits of laziness, she would return home for the night and arrive back late for the milking in the morning.

Andy was jealous of the nights she was away from the farmhouse, although he did not tell her so, for his love-making had not reached that stage.

The mistress had noticed Andy's attention to the lass, and though she was a friendly soul, she wanted no trouble about the place, so as she went to bed at nights she would say sharply, 'Come awa' tae yer bed noo, Molly,' and Molly would rise and go to her small room down the passage. The mistress, who was an early riser, would see that the door was locked between the kitchen and the rest of the house. Andy laughed to himself at the thought which prompted the mistress to call the girl to bed, and wondered if the gawky Molly knew the reason too.

After a week or two, when their kisses became more frequent and their mood more intimate, the nightly order of the mistress became tiresome to them, till at last Andy persuaded Molly to outwit her. She would go to bed, and, when the house fell silent, open the window of her bedroom and step out. Andy used to let her in at the kitchen door after she had walked on tiptoe round the house. Later he found it more pleasant to walk round the house himself and join her in bed, slipping through the open window into the little dark bedroom.

It was a surprise to the mistress, though it had meant weeks of worry and anxiety to Andy, when Molly stammered through tears and blushes that she was 'gan tae hae a wean'. At first she shielded Andy, then after a week or two, as his interest waned and his concern decreased by application of a rustic fatalism, she denounced him and cried for hours on the friendly bosom of the mistress.

'Ye hae din a fine thing noo,' said the mistress when he came in to dinner.

Andy was silent.

'Whut aboot the pair lass? Ye'll hae tae merry her.'

Andy glanced at the 'pair lass'. She seemed more grotesque than ever in his eyes, with her swollen body and surging blushes, as she pushed her hair back out of her red-rimmed eyes.

'A'm no' gan tae merry her,' he said, with an air of finality, 'A'm no' tae blame fur it a'.'

'God'sake,' said the mistress, 'ye maun dae the richt thing b'the lass.'

Andy picked up his spoon and gulped down his hot soup. The mistress was evidently waiting for a further statement. He scowled at his reflection in the window pane opposite and said savagely, 'A'll pey fur the wean. Ye canna mak' me dae ony mair than that.'

Molly burst out in another torrent of wailing and the mistress went over to soothe her, holding her arm round her shoulders and saying, 'Nivir min', lass, he disna want tae merry ye. Ye wudna want tae merry a maun that didna want ye, wud ye?'

Molly went on sobbing.

'Ye'll be a'richt. A'll see tae it. Ye're no' the first that's had a wean they didna want. Dinna greet.'

Andy made loud sucking noises as he drank his soup, to cover the words of the mistress and the sobs of the girl. It made him angrier and angrier.

Craig spoke to him in the stable as he went for his horses. 'The mistress was tellin' me,' he said.

Andy knew exactly what the mistress had been telling him.

'Aye,' he broke in.

'Weel, ye'll be peyin', A suppose?'

'Aye.'

He splashed his way up the road to the field till the mud came over his bootheads. The horses sensed his temper and pulled the harrows across the field with their ears cocked back in fear as he spoke to them. Like the rest of his lonely fellow men, who worked day in day out in the silent fields, he talked aloud to himself and the horses seemed to listen attentively to his outburst.

'God damn it, whut did A dae it fur? Whut did A dae it fur? It's no' my faut. A'm no' gan tae merry her. Tae hell wi' her. Tae hell wi' her. . . . Blast ye, get oot o' that, Bess!' He broke off to urge the black mare on. 'Holy Jesus Christ. They canna mak' me merry her. A'll rin awa' an' join the ermy. . . . Hoo much wull A hae tae pey? Five shillin' mebbe, or mebbe mair. It's helluva.' He rambled on for the remainder of the afternoon in the same strain, and at night went off to the Port to get drunk and escape the farmhouse kitchen with the folk sitting around waiting for bed-time.

Molly's child came in April.

Andy did not see her, or his son, for it was a boy, but the mistress told him when he came down in the morning. 'The wean cam' last nicht. It's a boy.'

'Aye,' he grunted and lifted the teapot from the hob. Nothing more was said. He sat thinking as he chewed a crust of bread. So he was a father . . . he had a son . . . what would it be like? . . . when would he see it?

It was a long time before he saw the child. Not for two months did Molly come back to the farm. She passed him with an injured look on her face and did not speak. The child was in her arms on one occasion, and though he hesitated as she approached, she paid no heed and clattered past with a sneer on her lips.

'Jesus,' he thought, 'whut hae A din noo? Sharely she could let me see the wean. A'm its faither, am A no'? A'm peyin' fur it tae.'

One night she sat with it in her arms talking to the mistress. Andy was scanning a paper and straining his eyes to see the print in the dying light. After a while the mistress rose. 'Weel, guid nicht then, Molly,' she said, pretending not to notice Andy.

He lifted his eyes for a second from the paper, darted a glance across the room and looked back at the blurred sheets again.

'It's a plan o' hers,' he thought. 'Did A no' see the canny look she gied her.' He went on with a pretence to read.

'Andy,' came Molly's voice, 'dae ye no' want tae see yer wean?'

There was a cajoling tone in her voice. She was resorting to new tactics, he was sure. He scowled and kept his head down while there was a long pause.

'He's a bonny wean, Andy. Jist look at him sleepin' here. Wee black een he has, an' black curly hair.'

He tried to keep up the pretence of reading, but she began to cry.

'Shut yer bloody mooth,' he ordered roughly and bent over to look at the sleeping child.

There was nothing about it that appealed to him. Certainly it had nice hair, but it might have been anyone's child. Molly had stopped crying. He sat staring into the fire.

'Andy,' she half whispered. He did not answer. 'Andy.'

'Whut the blazes ir ye Andyin' me fur?'

Her heavy bottom lip trembled. 'A wus jist thinkin'.'

'Weel?' he asked brutally.

'A . . . weel, A mean mebbe we micht get merrit an' . . .'

'Ye thocht wrang then. A said A wud pey ye. A canna merry ye. A haena enough tae keep a wean an' ye tae. A dinna get enough money fur masel'. A dinna want tae get merrit.'

She began to cry again. It was an hysterical wailing that annoyed him more and more.

'Fur Christ's sake shut yer mooth, ye kent fine A wudna merry ye. Shut yer mooth, dae ye hear? or b'Christ A'll gie ye mair tae greet aboot.'

She smothered her sobs.

'Tak' the thing awa' hame. Awa' an' droon yersel' an' it tae.'

She rose, crying once more. Andy's voice increased to almost a yell.

'Shut yer mooth. Tae hell wi' ye, ye dirty bitch . . .'

The door in the passage clicked and the mistress, with an old coat pulled over her nightgown, came through.

'God'sake, whut's wrang?' she asked.

Andy clattered up to bed while she listened to Molly's sobbing explanation. The mistress tucked the shawl round the child, which had awakened, and saw Molly to the door with her arm around her shoulders in a motherly fashion. The door closed and the mistress came back into the kitchen.

'God' sake. Tae gan on lik' that tae the pair lass . . . She's weel aff withoot ye. Ye hae brok' her heart,' she called up the ladder after him.

'Awa' tae hell,' Andy muttered as he climbed into bed.

'Whut?' she called. She had not heard anything but the faint rumble of his voice.

He said nothing, and after waiting a few minutes for him to speak, she went off to bed. Andy felt savage.

The boy in the next bed had been lying awake. 'Whut wus a' the carry-on aboot?' he whispered.

'Nocht tae dae wi' ye. Shut yer mooth an' lie quaite.'

'A'richt,' said the boy in a surly voice.

'B'Christ an' A'll a'richt ye', burst out Andy. He leaped from the bed and tore the clothes from his neighbour.

He lay looking up at him in terror. 'Dinna hit me,' he pleaded.

Andy pulled him from the bed by the leg. His head thudded against the floor. Then as a final act Andy threw the bed-clothes down the open hatch. Back in bed he watched the half-naked youngster retrieving the bed-clothes. Had he spoken again he would have murdered him in his temper. The boy said nothing, but clambered back into the tousled bed in silence. It was hours before Andy was able to sleep.

'Whut wus that helluva noise last nicht?' asked Craig at dinner time.

Andy looked up defiantly.

'It wus her an' the wean. She wus greetin' because A said A wudna merry her.'

'A canna hae sic a yellin' keepin' folks frae sleepin' at nicht,' said the boss.

'She kent fine A said A wudna merry her,' Andy muttered.

'Bella, that lass is no' tae be here anither nicht. There's nae use botherin' the boy. He's no' gan tae merry her. Weel, he'll pey, bit A canna hae the lik' o' yon in the hoose at nicht again.'

'A'richt,' said the mistress quietly.

Andy sat sipping his tea when the meal was over. The house was silent. The whole thing seemed too worrying, yet he did not want to leave Doonhall.

He was back-weeding the late turnips when he saw a man coming across the field. He had no idea who it was. He was a short and thick-set man with a heavy red face. Slowly he stepped across the rows as he came directly towards him.

'It's her faither,' whispered the boy who was weeding at Andy's side.

There was no need to ask what he would be wanting. The stranger stopped a few feet from the kneeling figure. 'Ye'll be Walker?' he asked gruffly.

'Aye,' said Andy and straightened quickly. He was at least two inches taller than the man, whom he had never seen before.

'So ye wudna merry her, eh?' he leered. 'Get a lass wi' a wean an' hae nae mair tae dae wi' her?'

Andy's fists clenched.

'Bit she has a faither that'll no' see her din ill by the like o' ye. Ye'll merry her or b'Christ A'll tak' it oot o' ye.'

Andy could see the bulging muscles on the stranger's forearms, for he wore no jacket.

'A'm no merryin' her. Awa' hame afore ye get hurt. She'll no ken ye whun A hae din wi' ye, if ye lay haun on me,' he taunted.

The red face became almost purple. Spluttering oaths the elder man rushed. Andy's hairy arm shot out and took him squarely in the face. He spat blood and staggered. Andy waited for him to come in again. He had not long to wait. Before Andy could counter he was in and had him round the waist. They staggered and trampled down the turnips.

'Here's the boss,' warned the boy.

Neither of them paid the slightest heed. Andy grunted in the powerful hold that crushed his ribs. Slowly his sinewy hands tightened on his opponent's fat neck. There was a grip of steel in Andy's large hands, and as he increased the pressure, the other's waist grip weakened. As it did so Andy pulled the head towards him and dashed his skull into the red face, but the short man had fought before. Even as Andy used the trick, his knee rose into Andy's groin with agonising force. They fell apart as a result of the dual impact. Andy doubled himself to ease the pain and flew at the short man as he brushed the blood and tears from his eyes. Coming back at him the aggressor of a few moments before fought blindly. Andy dealt mercilessly, returning the groin trick and driving his head again into the battered face.

At last he let go and the short man lurched forward with his head hanging down. With the dexterity of a boxer Andy punched downwards behind the ear and he fell with a groan. The boss had just reached them after a long walk across the slope.

'Get on wi'yer wurk, Jock,' he ordered the gaping boy.

Andy rubbed his face and bent down to resume his weeding.

'Ye hae made a haun o' ma turnips,' said the boss.

They crawled on down the rows.

'Come on, Docherty, get up oot o' that,' Craig urged the groaning man who lay with his head among the young turnips.

At the end of the row Andy looked back up the slope. The boss was carrying Docherty downhill towards the slap. The boy was all excitement.

'Jesus, ye gied him a helluva batterin',' he said admiringly.

Andy's vicious scowl faded and gave way to a smile.

'A thocht he wus stronger than ye.'

'Och, it taks mair than strength tae fecht,' he grinned as he began the next row.

He was shaken with nervous excitement as he worked on his bag-wrapped knees up the hill. A whistle as the kye were being driven up the road by one of the women, told him that it was milking time. They rose and untied the earthy bags, carrying them over their shoulders as they went down towards the steading. Molly's father was sitting on the steps beside the pump, holding his head. The boss came out and gave him a small glass of whiskey to pull him round. Andy lifted the tin basin and went to wash. His head was covered with soapy water when he heard the boy's shout of warning.

'Watch yersel', Andy!'

He dashed the soap from his eyes and turned in time to see Docherty, who was close to him, swing up a rusted plough coulter which he grasped in his right hand. Half dazed as he was, Docherty's blow came down too slowly. Andy's hand seized his wrist.

'Pit it doon!' yelled the boss, who came rushing down the stone steps. There was no need. Andy drove his fist into the crazed man's face and threw him on his back in the road. He made to leap down after him with the light of murder in his eyes but the boss's arm detained him.

'Had on, maun. Fur Christ's sake let him alane. Ye'll kill him. The pair oul bastard's no' in his richt min'.'

Andy turned and went in for his tea. He heard Docherty raving and cursing as he lay in the road. His face was a gruesome sight. One nostril was split and an eye red and bloody.

'A'll murder the bastard,' yelled the demented father. 'Come oot here.'

He struggled to his feet. Andy half rose off his chair, but the mistress pushed him down.

'Sit whaur ye ir. Hae ye no' din enough?'

The boss came and led the yelling man down the road. He sobbed childishly as he was taken home, and before they reached the road end the boss was carrying him. His wife and son came running out of the cot-house at the sound of his cries for vengeance. The mother supported her injured husband into the house, but the son, a boy of about Andy's age, dodged past Craig and went running up the road. Straight to the house he went and strode in without knocking. Andy was surprised and jumped to his feet.

'Come ootside, Walker,' he made a grab at Andy, but his hand fell short.

Andy reached forward and caught him by the breast of the jacket. Holding him at arm's length, he backed him out of the door. He made useless efforts to hit him.

'Whut noo?' gritted the infuriated Andy.

The other struggled like a sheep caught on barbed wire. A terrific swing of Andy's arm and the challenger staggered back and sat down holding his jaw. Tears ran down his face. As he got to his feet Andy swung at him again and he fell back, lying with his mouth open.

The mistress rushed out and tried to lift him. 'Whut hae ye din noo? Ye hae kilt him,' she stuttered.

'He asked fur it,' said Andy.

The boy looked up, seeing things in a dark bloody haze.

'Ony mair?' asked Andy.

There was no reply. Stepping over him, Andy went to the byre. The gaping boy, Jock, followed, gazing at him as though he had been a god. The boss came up and spoke to the boy, who was now swaying dizzily on his feet.

'Ye got a' ye deserved,' he said harshly. 'Tell yer faither A'll no' hae ony mair o' this. The polis'll be the thing here if A hae ony mair o' this kin' o' thing. He has said that he'll pay an' that's the end o't. Get doon the road an' dinna let me see ye aboot the place again.'

The boy walked unsteadily down the road, holding his head as his father had done.

'Noo, look here,' said the boss to Andy in the byre, 'A canna hae ony mair o' the like. If ye canna pit things richt in yer ain time, ye're no' gan tae dae it in mine. Ye'll hae tae fin' a new place if it comes aboot again.'

'Wus it ma faut?' asked Andy sullenly.

'No,' agreed the boss, 'bit A canna be daein' wi't.'

'Richt ye ir,' Andy muttered.

He went to the Port on his bike at night. No one appeared to have noticed him as he passed the cot-house. It was dark when he rode home. The moon kept disappearing behind clouds. He passed the sleeping cot-house again and rode to the gate at the road end. He was putting the chain back over the gatepost when two dark figures rose from the dykeside. They said nothing, but advanced slowly, each had a stick in his hand. One was short and thickset.

'So that's the wey,' murmured Andy.

His next action must have been a monstrous surprise to his two intending attackers. He lifted the old light bike and threw it with a sudden ease full at them. They were unable to avoid it and went down in a heap. As the taller one rose Andy felled him with a stone in his clenched fist. The boy dropped with a strangled groan. The old man found his stick tangled in the wheels of the bike. He tugged at it. Too late he realized the ambush was a complete failure and Andy was on him. The same stone, lifted from the top of the dyke, clipped him behind the ear. He floundered forward drunkenly and

Andy lifted his bike. Riding up the road he felt extremely powerful.

In the morning he told the boss about it. He was for sending for the police, but the mistress urged him not to, and in the end he pulled on his boots and went down to the cot-house. Docherty opened the door to him.

'Ye wur at it again,' charged the boss. 'It's you fur the polis this time.'

Docherty went pale and stood at the door looking after Craig, who strode back to the road end without another word.

While he was supping his porridge in the kitchen, the boss saw Docherty's wife pass the window. She knocked at the door. 'Come in,' he called, and she entered sobbing.

'Ye'll no' hae the polis on us, wull ye, Mister Craig?' she appealed to him.

'Ye heard whut A said tae yer maun, did ye no?' asked the boss roughly.

'Mister Craig, Mister Craig. . . .,' she stammered.

'A'll see,' he answered shortly.

'God bless ye.' She wiped her eyes on the corner of her apron and went hurrying down the road.

Meanwhile the gaping boy listened to Andy's account of what had happened the night before.

'They micht hae kilt ye,' he mused.

'Micht,' was Andy's significant reply.

He was uneasy when he thought of what might have happened had his wits not prompted him to throw the oul' bike at his assailants. Jock's 'micht hae kilt ye' became a disturbing truth. He thought of it all day, but the fear did not deter him from going a run round by Brachan when the milking was over.

'A wud be hame afore dark,' warned the mistress as he pulled his bike out of the shed.

'Watch yersel', Andy,' the crippled son called after him.

He smiled as he thought of it and consoled himself by touching the short-bladed sickle resting in his inside jacket pocket. It was a fearsome weapon, but perhaps next time they would give him no chance to throw his bike at them. They might even leap on him as he rode.

Left. John McNeillie at North Clutag in 1938.

Below. Max Beerbohm: 'Robert Burns, having set his hand to the plough, looks back at Highland Mary' 1904.

Right. Author's dedication to his grandfather.

Below. Opening manuscript pages.

Dear Grandfather — The book at last. May you read it, enjoy & understand it, and if at times, like Robbie Burns, I have taken liberties and shocked the modesty of those who open its pages to read it, I hope they will forgive me.

John.

CHAPTER I

Cormorants stand on the rocks of the PORTWILLIAM shore of Luce Bay. Long-necked ungainly black birds they are, standing there while the incoming tide creeps up the shore and mist drifts across the bay, and up the glen to the Grey Mare's Tail and Altiery. When the black rocks are covered, they rise and fly

(2)

lowly, less than three feet from the surface, out over the water, and vanish into the mist. The gulls remain afloat on the heavy swell and great waves crash with thunder on the shore, the crash echoes up the steep cliffs, and fades into a soft sigh. When the cormorants come back from the swirl of mist they are flying higher, their arrow formation mounts into the

Left. Advertisement in the *Daily Record.*

Below. North Clutag steading from afar.

Ayrshires at North Clutag, 1938.

Old John McNeillie in the fields.

Patiently he made a wide circle before returning. He anticipated another encounter with a frightened thrill and became more wary as he pedalled past the cot-house. Through the gate with a loud jingling of the chain so as to give anyone in wait good warning of his approach. The sickle was held ready in his hand, but he reached the house without as much as a sound to betray an ambush.

The boy was waiting in the kitchen for his return.

'Did ye see ocht o' them?' he asked.

'No,' answered Andy, and grinned at the awe in his face.

'Ye wurna feart tae gan oot?'

'Feart, Jesus Christ, no. Whut's the guid o' bein' feart. A wus ready fur them if they had come oot on me.' He showed him the sickle.

'Holy God! Wud ye hae went fur them w' that?'

'Aye,' said Andy simply.

He went up to bed and spent a restless night thinking of two dark figures creeping up the ladder ready to kill him. He could only visualize them together. Singly he felt himself a match for either of them. It was almost dawn before he slept, and the cocks were beginning to crow in the hen-houses.

CHAPTER XVI

THE Dochertys had long memories, and even if they had been forgetful of a grudge, there was a wailing child in the arms of a sister and a daughter to remind them of a great wrong. As for Andy, being unafraid, he forgot; whistling at his work through the early hay-time till the cattle-show day. Even as he wandered round the showfield in a new suit and with money jingling in his pockets, he placed no significance in the sight of three scowling faces that belonged to Docherty, his brother, and his son. Youthful muscles bulged under Andy's heavy grey tweed suit, he smiled and girls smiled back. The jaunty angle of a black felt hat, a fashion in which he was following a discarded hero, Paddy, and his lean sinewy frame, made him a rakish figure amongst heavier-built men. The day wore on. It was quiet and uneventful. Even the flies seemed tired of the heat.

The dance that followed in the evening irked him and it was early when he decided to go home. Riding on a flat tyre, he found the journey unpleasant save for the cool rush of air that met him as he careered downhill. The moon was slow in coming up from behind the hills and on the straight road to Doonhall road end there was a blurred shadow. He looked across to the Doonhall steading nestled among the trees. The night was silent, but nothing betrayed the Dochertys lying in the peat ditch beside the moss.

Almost too late Andy saw the branch of hawthorn that straggled across the road. He slowed down and swerved with caution to avoid it. The three Dochertys rose out of their damp hiding-place as one man. Andy came over, bicycle as well, into the ditch. He fought like a fiend, struggling to rise under the weight of them.

A groan or two marked the results of his retaliation. He lashed out in all directions with legs and arms, but he was hampered in the narrow ditch with the steel frame of the bike meeting the fury of his punches. One of his attackers belaboured his head with a stick and blood trickled down behind his ears. Without a sound he fought, gripping one of them between his knees and fighting back at the other two as well as the struggles of the third would allow. Slowly he began to realize his limitations. They seemed to be tearing one of his arms from its socket and forcing him face downwards. He made a last mighty effort and rose, throwing two of them down. The scramble up the ditch side and on to the road took less than a second, but they were after him. He ran, though his defiant spirit scorned flight. Then, like a cornered animal, he turned and faced them.

The surprise was complete but useless. Full in the face he struck the nearest one and he fell, but the others were on him together, and even as they attacked the fallen one rose and joined in. The moonlight that had flooded the moss a moment before suddenly disappeared and there was darkness in its place. He felt nothing of the pain as they drummed his defenceless face on the hard road. Even the brutal kick in the ribs that ached for days afterwards brought no response from him. Blood ran over his cheeks and down his shirtfront. The moon shone on. The quietness of the night returned.

Slowly his senses came back. He touched his aching body and stared at the starry sky. At first he failed to realize that he was naked, naked as the day he was born, and lying in the damp peat ditch. He stood up. The dried blood on his face felt strange. Part of his suit strewed the road. Wearily, he went and lifted it. The trousers were in shreds. He pulled them over his trembling legs, feeling like a beggar. Back down the road was his jacket. His head throbbed and his side had a stabbing pain. He was almost too exhausted to go for the jacket. Even farther down the road the old bike peeped up from the ditch and his hat hung on a twig of the hawthorn branch. The effort to remove the bike from the ditch was too much, and he could not find his boots in the gloom. He hobbled painfully towards the road end holding his torn clothes round his shivering body. The Docherty cot-house was in darkness, for, although he did not know it, they had been in bed an hour and more. When he reached the farmhouse, he lay down on the bed and slept till daybreak. Rising was impossible.

'Andy, Andy!' yelled the mistress in the morning.

'A canna get up,' he called weakly.

She muttered something about being too drunk. The boss came to the bottom of the ladder.

'God damn it, maun, get oot o' yer bed. The kye's tae milk.'

'Come up an' gie me a haun',' he said.

The effort of calling made a hundred little lights dance through his bursting head. The boss's boots sounded on the ladder.

'Michty me, whut's happened tae ye, boy?' he asked.

Painfully Andy told him. He raved and swore, then called the mistress. At first it was the doctor they would have, but a while's bathing and wrapping with cheese cloths satisfied them. Andy slept a disturbed sleep till dinner-time. Footsteps on the ladder and the rumble of strange voices made him waken again. A policeman, flat hat in hand, stood by his bedside. With difficulty, he answered questions. Three days later, when he rose from bed to exercise his battered body, he learned that the Docherty men were missing and their women folk would say nothing. Craig told him that they had been turned out of the cot-house.

The affair was soon forgotten by all save Andy. His heart burned for revenge and he waited patiently for sight or sound of the Dochertys, swearing that there would be murder if he ever came across them again. He was riding home from a dance at Whithorn one night in the autumn, when a cyclist going in the other direction stopped him.

'Hae ye a licht?' he asked, for his lamp had gone out.

Silently Andy handed over his box of matches and his heart beat with rage. The match was struck and the stranger's face revealed. He lifted his head as the light flickered out. As he thanked his benefactor, the words died in his throat. A look of diabolical fury contorted Andy's face but the young Docherty recognized him. His glazed eyes were standing bloodshot in their sockets before Andy released his throat. Even then, with his victim unconscious, he smashed blows into his face and completed the attack by dropping a heavy stone through the back wheel of the bike which lay on the grass verge. He rode off trembling with satisfaction. No policeman came for him. The Dochertys were too apprehensive of their own fate in punishment for their murderous attack, as it had been described in the paper, to seek the protection of the law.

The elder Docherty – he never managed to come across the brother – received his punishment at Andy's hands on a ploughing-match day. Andy, ploughing in the boys' class, was at his first match as a competitor in Kirkcowan, when he saw Docherty, the elder. After the morning turn he went for his dinner and bumped into the reeling figure of the half-drunk father of the Docherty clan, who was passing out of the public house. Andy stopped and whirled the man round, satisfied that it really was his enemy, he set about him to the puzzlement of a large audience. He beat the hated face into a gory mess under his hard knuckles and dropped him insensible in a heap against the wall. His encounter did nothing to spoil his steadiness of hand for the rest of the day. It crowned his success when he was awarded second prize, having lost narrowly to a man who, it was doubted, was really in the boys' class. At night in the Doonhall kitchen Andy was a hero, and after all the comments on his performance, he briefly told how he had met the Dochertys and revenged himself on them. The story met with approval. A wrong had been righted and the fact pleased the savage hearts of the Craigs as much as it did Andy. Craig was no mean man. He gave Andy his prize money and a pound besides. Andy felt himself a proved ploughman.

His second winter at Doonhall passed quickly. Soon it was summer once more with the scent of the ling and heather in the air, when the wind came from the west. For a while he avoided the company of women, as though he had learned his lesson from Molly Docherty. He would sit on the steps outside the front door of the farmhouse, breathing the sweetness of the honeysuckle and the cool night air, and gazing across at the hills. Night after night he sat there, dreaming or following the course of the grazing sheep as they journeyed downhill to the shelter of the hollows for the night. But his spirit was restless and the blue shadows of the summer evenings lured him away. He began to make long excursions on the bike, riding round the countryside till after dark. Sometimes he stopped at the Port or the Whaup, and other nights he would ride up to drowsy Wigtown, buy cigarettes and ride home again. There was nothing for him to do. He had no friends. He was lonely at Doonhall and the summer nights were long.

One night he rode down through Elrig and saw Kate Strachan. She was as dark as the lonely Elrig loch, as fresh and shy as the village itself, and there was a peacefulness about her as she wandered up the road that made her beautiful. She was the sweetest thing Andy had ever seen. He visited Elrig every night for a week in the hope of seeing her again, but harvest came and he worked late in the fields with no chance to ride the roads.

The first time that he saw that there was to be a dance at Elrig he resolved to go. He anticipated it for a week, and when the night came, a dark mild autumn night when the harvest was over, he could hardly hurry through the milking quickly enough. When he reached the dance he stood alone in a corner and looked for her. She was not there. He felt like going home, but waited in the hope that she might come late. She did. With his eyes fixed on the door, Andy saw her come in. A deep-chested young man was with her and Andy's heart sank. He looked at her and smiled, but for all the attention she paid him he might have been invisible and she blind. The band began to play and the strong-looking escort danced with her. She gazed up into his eyes and smiled. Andy clenched his fists and scowled. One or two unattached girls gave him glances of invitation, but he paid no heed.

One sidled up to him and said, 'Ye're lookin' kin o' lost. Ir ye no' gan tae dance?'

Slowly the meaning of her words penetrated to the depths of his thoughts. 'Aye,' he said. 'Wull ye dance wi' me?'

They joined the others on the floor. Andy followed Kate with his eyes. Once she met his gaze and looked at him in surprise at the intentness of his stare, but she seemed to forget a moment later when she laughed at something her companion had said. Andy continued to follow her with his eyes.

His partner became jealous. 'Whut's wrang wi' ye. Hae ye nivir seen her afore?' she asked sharply.

'No,' he said.

'Ye needna waste yer time starin' at her lik' a goat, fur she nivir looks at onybudy bit Jimmie. God help ye if he catches ye glarin' at her lik' that.'

Andy said nothing, but measured up Jimmie, noticing the bulky shoulders and the bulging neck that supported his heavy head. He was a brute of a man, capable of murdering so slightly built an opponent as Andy. He was still watching Kate when the music stopped and he went back to his corner. The next dance was announced and Andy decided, with fast-beating heart, that he would ask the elusive Kate for a dance. The couple saw him coming towards them and Jimmie scowled. He was almost within asking distance when Jimmie's heavy shoulder came between him and the girl. They stepped out on to the floor together and left Andy with a sinking heart. He wanted to murder the great ox-like creature who danced with her and regarded her as his exclusive property. He glanced across at them and Kate's eyes met his disdainfully over her partner's shoulder.

The girl Andy had been dancing with came up to him and laughed cruelly.

'Come on an' dance, an' had yer tongue,' he said to her. She laughed again and accepted the invitation. For the rest of the evening Andy felt uncomfortable. The girl, who seemed to have attached herself to him, made his discomfort greater by taunting him and laughing.

At last he could bear it no longer. 'Whaur dae ye leev?' he asked her.

'Jist doon the road.'

'Ir ye comin' hame? A'll see ye doon the road if ye ir.'

She paused and then said 'Aye.'

He waited while she searched for her coat. It was a chilly night.

'Ye wur lookin' kin' o' saft at yon Strachan lass,' she teased as he walked by her side with his bike.

'Och, lay me alane,' he growled, 'can a fella no' look at a lass withoot ye hae tae din it intae his lugs a' nicht?'

She stopped at a little cot-house in the shelter of some trees.

As he kissed her she whispered, 'Ye big wean.'

He knew she was still teasing him about the girl at the dance. His temper rose and he twisted her arm till she yelped with pain.

'A'll show ye,' he muttered. She became limp in his arms and he pulled back her coat and began to caress her roughly.

A dog barking half an hour later seemed to bring her back to her senses. She began to cry.

'Had yer tongue,' he ordered brutally.

'Whut if A hae a wean?' she sobbed.

'Och, it's no' the first time ye hae din it,' he told her.

'Hoo dae ye ken A'll no' hae a wean?'

He said nothing. He had only guessed that she had been intimate with someone before, and as for her having a child he cared nothing.

She sobbed as she went through the gate.

'A'll tell ma faither whut ye hae din.'

He waited no longer, but picked up his bike, jumped on it and rode off. The girl went into the cot-house and closed the door behind her.

Andy was slow to forget his mortification at Elrig. Each time he thought of it he felt angry and humiliated by turns. He avoided Elrig for two reasons. Mainly because he could not have faced the girl who had so openly spurned him, but also in fear that his companion of the evening had made good her threat and told her father. It was a serious thing. He had read about a byreman who had been gaoled for assaulting a girl only a week or so before. He wondered uneasily if that would happen to him. It had been no assault though; she had been unresisting and quiet enough. It had only been afterwards that she had cried. The fear was on him for a week or two, but he soon for got all about it with the preparation for the ploughing again.

Going to the Whaup one day for a cart of coals he caught up with a girl who was walking.

As he came abreast of her he called, 'Can A gie ye a sail?'

The girl looked round. It was Kate Strachan. Andy was surprised and his face coloured suddenly.

She smiled at him and said, 'Aye, A'm tired walkin'.'

He stopped the horse and pulled her up beside him with his hands shaking.

'A hae seen ye afore,' he said as the cart jolted its way through a wood.

'Aye, ye wur at the dance.'

She smiled again and Andy's face went redder as he thought of that night.

'Wha wus yon ye wur wi?' he asked.

'Oh, yon was Jimmie.'

'Jimmie wha?'

'Jimmie Adair.'

There was a long pause in which he avoided her eyes.

'Ye'll be gan tae the Whaup?' was his next stammering remark.

'Aye.'

'Whut wud ye no' dance wi' me fur?' he changed the subject again.

'Jimmie wudna let me.'

His heart missed a beat.

'Oh, A see. Wud ye hae danced wi' me if he hadna been there?'

'A wudna hae been there if Jimmie hadna been wi' me,' she replied.

'Holy God, ye wud think he wus merrit tae ye,' he blurted out.

'We'll be merrit sine,' she laughed.

His elation went. 'A canna gie ye a sail back,' he told her, 'A hae a kert o' coals tae tak' back.'

'A'll hae tae walk then, bit A hae din it often.'

They said no more and the cart jolted into Whauphill with Andy feeling more wretched every minute.

He stopped to let her dismount and called 'So long' as she went across to the store.

'So long,' she called back.

He found he had hardly the energy to shovel the coal into the cart when he reached the station. Life seemed blacker than ever before. She was going to be married. She hadn't paid much attention to him, hadn't even thanked him for the lift. It was a long task heaving the coal into the cart, longer than ever before. He hoped he would not see her on the way back.

As he passed down through the Whaup again, a few pieces of coal fell off the cart on to the road. He looked round but she was nowhere to be seen, but he caught her up half-way home.

'How do?' she said and he repeated her greeting.

For a few minutes he walked the horse at her pace, waiting to see if she had anything to say, then he spoke.

'Weel, A'll hae tae be gettin' on a bit faster then this or A'll be late o' gettin' hame.'

'Ye wull,' she replied as the cart drew ahead of her, and stooped to pick up some of the larger pieces of coal that fell from the top of the load as the horse increased its speed.

Andy whistled as he walked at the horse's head. The wintry sun went down and it was almost dark when he reached Doonhall. He decided, as he fed the horse, to forget Kate Strachan. She had large teeth, now he came to remember, and her paleness was less attractive in the cold air of the afternoon than it had been that summer evening. The romantic memory gradually became less vivid.

Soon, as the winter wore on, Kate Strachan had become only a being to be conjured out of his mind as part of a hazy warm summer when the wild cotton swayed on the moss and the woods were filled with the soft love notes of the cooing pigeons. His interest in the opposite sex waned once more and poaching took its place as a more exciting pastime.

The most profitable method of poaching was with dogs and nets, but Andy, being unable to afford the luxury of net or dog, bought snares instead and used his gun when the occasion arose.

Rabbits brought a good price in the winter. They were worth a run to Wigtown before kye time, even if the night's work left him tired all day. His escapades at night came to the notice of McLeod, the keeper, but Andy was too wary to be caught. His speed of foot, even when carrying three or four pair of rabbits and the gun, was too great for the old man who prowled at nights to protect the game on the estate. Often only the width of a burn saved Andy from his clutches as they stalked each other through the woods and fields. They even came to the farm with their suspicions and taxed the boss with harbouring a poacher, but Craig cared little for the laird and his lease was young. Andy had both gun and snares well hidden. On the whole, the winter was most profitable.

CHAPTER XVII

JEAN COPE was born four years before Andy, in the same kind of tumbled-down cot-house on the Kirkcowan road. Her father, a grubby unshaven individual with shifty eyes, had never done an honest day's work unless at haytime or harvest when he was sore pressed for the price of a few drinks. A few drinks, because one would never have satisfied him. One drink to him was but a spot in the ocean of his thirst, and he was oftener drunk than sober. In fact, when his head did not reel with the effects of whiskey he thought he was ill, and at once sent one of his family to the village for the family doctor . . . the square-sided bottle with the hunted stag on the label. His lack of money and unusual ability to absorb whiskey made him none the less prolific, without, as well as within, the bounds of his marriage. His long-suffering slut of a wife had, at twenty-five, borne him nine children, and the last of a motley brood was Jean.

Five were boys, the puniest specimens of boyhood that attended the village school. One of them was a half-wit, though the others were only distinguishable from him by the fact that they could comprehend a five-word sentence at the third repetition. Jean was the handsomest of the four girls. Two had hare lips, and the other had a strange way of holding her head on the side, a defect inherited from her none too healthy father. Twice Joe Cope had been gaoled for poaching, the only time he had abstained from whiskey in his life.

Once, when he had come near to being caught by a keeper, he had torn his thigh on a barbedwire fence in making his escape. As a result of this adventure, he limped for the rest of his life. He was no beauty, even if one overlooked the rust-coloured broken teeth and grimy complexion above the half-grown beard. His clothes had always hung about him as though they had been the throw-offs of a better-built man, and they were ragged and greasy.

For such a father to beget an attractive smiling child, as Jean was in her early days, was surprising to all who saw her. In fact Joe's cronies, casting amorous eyes at the girl when she was fourteen, chaffed him as to whether he was her father or not. When the drink was on him, and the belief in his wife's infidelity stronger in his mind, he came home and all but murdered both mother and daughter, so that Jean's prettiness was spoilt by a cowering attitude which she could not shake off all through her life. The children went to school at Kirkcowan. The girls were no more brilliant than the boys. At thirteen Jean had known more of sex, in its crude country inter-pretation, than she did of anything in the way of reading or counting. She encouraged the boys of her own age who went to school with her, until, at fourteen, life held no more mysteries for her. Certainly she had learned the principal lesson of her life, and had she been a town girl she would have earned her living as a prostitute.

Her mother was careless of her daughter's moral outlook. In fact she openly encouraged a friendship between Jean at fourteen and a ploughman of twenty-eight. No one was near to intervene on the girl's behalf, and the child came in due course. Fortunately it was born dead, and the fruits of the assault, which had taken place in her mother's own bed, were buried in the plot of ground behind the cot-house, where Mrs. Cope had been wont to bury inconvenient miscarriages. There was no storming and vows of vengeance. Joe was drunk when he heard of it. Had he been sober he would have remained unperturbed, for Nell and Jess, the one with her head cocked permanently on one side, had already shown their fertility in the shape of three children between them. All were alive, but there was no telling how many more had died at birth, or how often the family had followed their animal instincts to the end of having children.

When she was fifteen Jean went to look after her mother's brother who lived in a cot-house on the back road from Kirkcowan to Wigtown. It was a lonely cot-house and the uncle was no more morally perfect than the rest of his relations. He found in Jean, isolated from the few friends she had, an unresisting victim. On the first night that she slept in his house he forced his way into her bed, and when his attempts at persuasion failed he assaulted her. She did not cry or struggle and after a while resigned herself to her fate.

He was a savage individual, and thought nothing of thrashing her and throwing her out half-naked to stand at the door in the wind and rain and plead for re-admission. She stayed, because she had nowhere else to go. To have returned home would have earned her the same treatment from her father, who had no scruples even where incest was concerned. The days that she lived with her uncle held nothing for her save the endless cooking of sparse meals, trailing the blankets off the bed which they now shared and putting them on again. Between whiles she argued with him as he hugged the fireside, fought against his more violent attacks, and rubbed her bruises and sobbed when he left her alone.

Ditch-cleaning and poaching were his pastimes. The one was an aid to the other. Cleaning a ditch he could set an odd snare or two and lift it early the following morning, or merely get the good places mapped out in his mind to return later with net and dog.

It was while he was away on one of these expeditions, that Jean met Alec Brody. He was byreman at a small farm up off the road, and often passed the time of day with her on his way to or from work. At first her uncle said nothing, but the outcome of this new association was that she fought him with a more intense fury, until in the end he threw her out for the last time. Half-naked and bruised, she ran through the darkness to the Derry where Alec worked. She sheltered in the barn for the night, huddling her wet clothes around her, in constant fear of the gleaming-eyed rats that scurried across the floor. A little after dawn she heard Brody whistling in the dairy and ran shamelessly to him.

The bed was not so warm without her, her uncle found, and so he came in search of her with a stout hawthorn stick in his hand. He failed to find her, for Brody had taken her down to his mother's cot-house near Wigtown. Jean's early life had hardened her so that her prettiness became a thin-lipped brazenness that attracted and re-pulsed in one. She laughed harshly when amused and sneered at decency, shyness and modesty, though these virtues were rare among her acquaintances. Alec Brody was for marrying her, but she was stubborn and ungrateful. He was a crude, heavy-boned creature with all the gross faults of his kind, but he was hurt and ashamed at her refusal. She stayed at his mother's and needed no renewal of welcome, for she remained uninvited in the first place, and thankless for what the old woman had done for her.

Although Jean was deaf to the hatchet-faced Mrs. Brody's comments, Alec was for ever aware of them.

'Whut ir ye gan tae dae?' he asked her one night when they were alone.

She looked at him and smiled wryly, knowing his soft heart.

'Whut dae ye think A should dae?'

He looked at her uneasily. 'Weel,' he began, 'mebbe ye micht get a place somewhaur, or mebbe . . .'

'Och, it's yer oul mither that's botherin' ye, is it?' she sneered. 'Richt ye ir. A'll no' stey whaur A'm no wanted.'

'Tae hell, A didna say that. Did A?' burst out Alec, 'A wus thinkin' ye like tae get merrit mebbe or somethin' .'

'Wha wud A merry?' she asked innocently, and smiled at the artless man before her.

'Ye could merry me.' His answer was slow and ponderous.

'An' leeve wi' yon oul' bitch?' Jean's temper flared up.

'A weel then,' he said resignedly.

They said no more about it and a week later, after a furious row with the old woman, Jean found a job as a milker at Drumlin, where Andy had served the McKeowns in his early days.

Yet it was not through Andy's Drumlin association that Jean came to meet him. He was at Wigtown one night in the spring having a drink at the Continental, when he met Alec Brody. Andy was drinking on his own and glowering defiance at the other occupants of the public house. No one seemed to notice his threatening attitude.

It was the sluggish Alec Brody that caused the disturbance. He was arguing truculently with his neighbour when that individual lost his temper and struck him across the face with his open hand. Alec sat back and stared and his slow wits began to collect themselves. In a minute he would have lashed out in his own defence.

Andy saw it all in a haze. Someone had struck someone else. For what reason he could not tell, but the injured one had not retaliated. He needed a defender. He rose and sprang across the room with remarkable agility for his drunkenness. Alec was avenged. His attacker of a moment before slumped to the floor from his seat as Andy struck him. Too late Andy realized that he had stirred up a hornet's nest. The fallen one was a roadman and the place was half full of his fellow workers. They came for him in a body. Alec's drowsy attitude vanished. This man was his friend. He had struck down his enemy. He stood up at Andy's side, grasping a beer bottle from the small window at the side. Retreat would have been wisest. The odds were three to one, and two of the attackers were at least six feet tall. It was one of the big men that received Andy's onslaught.

An iron-shod boot in the groin will bring the biggest man down. He sank to his knees and took the coup de grace from Alec's bottle. Hampered by the smallness of the room, Andy and his companion faced certain defeat, in spite of the fact that the roadmen were hindered by their own numbers. Seizing a chair, Andy swung it above his head and held them off while he retreated to the door. Alec took cover behind him. A bottle came flashing across the room and smashed with a crash on the wall near his head; another followed as Alec gingerly opened the door and stepped out. Andy threw the chair and was out in the street in the same second.

The darkness saved them as they ran down the road together. It was half an hour before the road behind them was silent and they knew that the chase had been given up. Breathing heavily, they pulled up and walked slowly. Andy was considerably sobered.

Brody spoke thickly. 'Whaur ir ye fur?' he asked.

They were walking towards Kirkcowan down the back road.

'A'm gan back in a wee while. A left ma bike ootside the Continental,' said Andy.

'Holy Christ, mine's there tae.'

They halted and turned together.

'A'm Alec Brody. Whut dae they ca' you?' he enquired of Andy, who told him.

'Ye're helluva fond o' a fecht.'

'Aye,' said Andy, 'there's nocht lik' a guid fecht tae pass the time.'

They went back up the hill cautiously and found their bikes where they had left them. Brody insisted on taking the long road round to accompany Andy part of the way home, though it was well after eleven. They stopped and talked at Malzie road end till the hours of the morning slipped past and it was near dawn. Each unfolded his history. The things he had done, where he had worked, where he had been, what he thought of the season, and the various habits of the men he had worked for.

Farmworkers have a love of yarning by the roadside at night, and the later the hour the greater fascination their voices seem to have for each other. They will meet a friend on the way home and stop to talk their hours of rest away. Talking, as men do, of women, work, amusements, scraps of news and scandal, harvests and ploughing, the weather and their respective outlooks on life.

The frost of the morning chilled them before they parted at the signpost.

'A'll see ye Sunday nicht, then,' said Alec as he rode off.

'Aye,' agreed Andy, and rode hard, for he was tired. It would soon be kye time and he was eager to have an hour in bed. The wisps of grey were appearing in the eastern sky when he reached Doonhall. Even a cock crowed. He had been in bed but a short half-hour when the alarm told him that it was milking time. He clambered out of bed, brushed the fluff from his clothes and went downstairs bleary-eyed to put the kettle on for his breakfast.

In the course of numerous excursions with Alec, Andy met several new girls, including the cynical Jean. His friendly remarks were repulsed and sneered at on their first meeting. He had never met a woman he disliked so intensely and his reaction was brutal. Living as she did at Drumlin, Andy accompanied Jean part of the way home, though she told him frankly that she had no desire for his company. On the second occasion, her tyre went flat and he decided to ride on alone, but her taunts and sneers forced him to remain and walk with her. As a reward he forced her to allow him to kiss her.

'Lay me alane,' she told him, 'A dinna want ye sleverin' ower me.'

He struck her across the face and the outburst ceased, but she struggled like a wildcat when he kissed her again and he threw her from him. She stumbled over her bicycle and fell into a ditch behind it. He paid no heed, but mounted and rode off with her curses ringing in his ears. The next time she rode a few yards ahead of him till they arrived at her road end and then ignored his 'Guid nicht, soor face'.

Her very dislike for him began to attract, and he proceeded to pay less attention to her and be more brutal as a means of breaking down her unfriendliness. It was a long process, but Jean, isolated as she was at Drumlin, slowly began to warm to him in spite of his cruelty. At last he accepted her affection and she allowed him to kiss her at the road end. She was no virgin, but her shyness as he lowered his face to hers was that of an innocent schoolgirl. The affair progressed slowly, though they quarrelled frequently and he struck her often. She played him against Alec until he flew into furious rages. Alec was miserable too, for he no longer wanted Jean's affection. He was afraid of Andy and often no longer appeared at the appointed place on a Sunday night, to avoid further disturbances.

In the end, Jean's surrender was complete. Andy's anger had had its way one night as she went home to Drumlin. He had beaten her until she cried out in pain, and she sobbed all the way to the road end. It took him half the night, in a fit of regret which secretly upset him, to console her, and in the end she lay back on the grass bank and responded to his kisses with a greater warmth than ever. He forgot his experience with the Docherty girl, and she, if she remembered her treatment in the past from the various men with whom she had associated, was careless in her capitulation. Mutually they agreed not to meet Alec as they had planned for the following Sunday evening, but walked through the fields together.

Andy was gloriously happy. No other girl, in spite of her cruel nature, had ever thrilled him as had Jean Cope. He had never in the others seen such turns of character, so many different moods and aspects. He wanted to protect her when she cowered away from him in his temper; to look after her, and even avenge her for the brutalities she had suffered at the hands of her father and others.

As for Jean, she was attracted by his flashing temper, his vicious-ness, his self-confidence which so often proved well-merited, and his fearless brutal strength. She was in love with the flash of his dark eyes, the cruel line of his mouth, the breadth of his shoulders, the bulging muscles of his arms, and the jaunty air of recklessness about him; things which she knew she would tire of in a short time; things which she would live to hate and watch with terror.

He was no weak pampering lover, but a head-strong commanding young brute who gave the lead and expected the woman to court him. She worshipped his domineering attitude and was weak and affectionate before him. Andy prided himself on the complete conquest he had made. He had forced this girl, who had hated him, to love him. He had brought her to her knees, until she loved him in spite of herself. He soothed his injured dignity and pride with the thought of it, and in these moods was more cruel to her than ever.

The blow came in September when the harvest was over. He met her early on a Sunday evening.

'Andy,' she confided fearfully, 'A'm gan tae hae a wean.'

All the unpleasant memories of the Docherty girl came rushing back to him. Temper flashed from under his black brows, but she stood clutching his arm and staring at the ground so pathetically that he forgot the vivid confidences she had made to him of her chequered past.

'Holy Christ,' he muttered and put his arm round her.

They sat down together and she rested her head on his shoulder. The thought of a past agony in having a child was terrifying to her and she was dazed at the prospect.

'Whun'll it be?' he asked.

'A'm no' share. A thocht it last month. A'm share A'll hae a wean noo. Mebbe it'll be April. Mebbe afore that.'

Andy was stunned. 'Then we'll hae tae be merrit,' he announced quietly.

She looked up at him in surprise, and her eyes were misty with threatened tears.

'Ye'll merry me, Andy?'

She had never expected it. Andy was something entirely different from Brody. Alec was affectionate in a collie-dog fashion, but all she had seen in Andy had been cruelty and hardness; nothing of love or sympathy.

'Aye,' he assured her, 'we'll hae tae get merrit. Ye'll merry me, wull ye no', Jean?' he asked.

'Aye, Andy,' she whispered.

He kissed her hotly and stood up. 'A'll hae tae see aboot it. Mebbe we'll get a place b'the term.'

They parted. She returned to Drumlin in a state of dazed happiness, and he to Doonhall with a mixed feeling of regret and pleasure.

The following day he told Craig. 'A'm gan tae get merrit sine,' he said, 'dae ye think A could hae the cot-house at the fit o' the road?'

The boss looked at him in astonishment. 'Jesus, ye're helluva young tae be daein' that. A suppose ye hae anither lass wi' a wean?'

Andy made no reply.

'Weel, mebbe ye could hae the place, bit the slates'll hae tae be sorted, and the broken wunda boarded up. Whun's the wean comin'?'

'No' fur a while,' said Andy at last.

'Hae ye ony money?' asked the boss.

'Jist twa or three poun'.'

'Weel, A'll tak somethin' aff yer money fur the rent tae the laird, an' gie ye twa oul' chairs an' the iron bed oot o' the grenery tae start wi'. Then there's an' oul' table ye micht hae, bit ye'll hae tae get yersel' some bedclaithes, an' dishes an' they kin' o' things.'

Andy was amazed at his generous offer. The cot-house at the foot of the road had stood empty since the Dochertys had left. It was in need of slight repairs as the boss had said, but it was as nice a little place as any by the roadside. He saw himself planting his own potatoes, rearing a few chickens and sitting at the door on the warm Sunday afternoons. Somehow, and it disturbed him, Jean did not fit into that dream. He was uneasy when he thought of the future when perhaps he would begin to tire of her. The sharpness of her voice; her nasty tongue scolding him; fits of rage when he would have to beat the temper out of her. He dismissed the thought from his mind with the fatalistic assurance that the thing was done now. He had said he would marry her; he had done more, he had arranged to take the cot-house.

Alec Brody was warm in his congratulation.

'Holy God, Andy,' he said, 'A would never hae thocht it. Hae ye min' the wey ye used tae curse an' sweer at her? She would hae murdered ye as sine as lookt at ye.'

'Aye.'

'Whut's the wey?' asked Alec, who saw a reason for it.

'She's gan tae hae a wean.'

'Oh, A see.' Alec fell silent.

Andy's last remark had been all-signifying. It was enough. The remark explained practically every ploughman's marriage.

Andy met the oul' maun when he was up at Drumlin to see Jean. He came out to the door and spoke to him.

'Wee, Andy, ye'll be fur merryin' the lass we hae here, A heard?'

'Aye,' he agreed.

'Deed boy, an' it's a peety. Ye're young an' able, whut dae ye want merryin' yet fur?'

The voice was warm and sincere. Andy felt no irritation. He looked up to that old man; laid more store by his advice than any man he had met. He was, in his eyes, all that a boss, and a clever farmer should be.

'Weel, there it is,' he replied, 'A hae got her wi' a wean. A hae said A'll merry her an' A'll dae it.'

'Aye, ye wull, boy. Ye hae din a silly thing, bit mony a maun has din it afore. She'll no' mak' the best o' wives fur ye. She's a dour soul wi' a helluva temper. Ye'll be a helluva pair.'

The oul' maun gave his opinion in all seriousness. It brought the whole matter before Andy in a clearer light. It confirmed his fears that life might not be quite so pleasant in the future as it had been in the past.

Jean's pleasure and excitement when he told her how he had managed to get the cot-house and the other arrangements he had made, soon dispelled his feeling of depression. They decided to be married before the term. It left them a little over a month to make their final plans. They had decided, too, that they would visit her father and mother the day before to put the matter in a better light. Andy, at twenty, was embarking on married life.

CHAPTER XVIII

T H E fire was piled high with blazing wood. It was raining heavily outside, but the cot-house was pleasant and warm. Andy could feel no change in being married. The girl with the hard laugh and tousled hair was his wife, yet there was no secret way in which he could be sure of it. There was nothing electric or deep-meaning in the glances they exchanged. In fact, any other of the four women who laughed and talked round the old table could have been his wife. Alec Brody was there to celebrate the wedding, with two men Andy had never met before, though they seemed as happy at his marriage as he was. They slapped him on the shoulder and shook hands with him heartily, spoke of him as 'oul' Andy here', and all after less than an hour's acquaintanceship.

The cot-house had been made ready. There were the few chairs, the iron bed, with a new set of blankets and a chaff mattress, the table, an old clock Jean had acquired at Drumlin, a few pots and pans, a sack of potatoes from Doonhall, and an oil lamp as a present from Alec, though Andy had a shrewd notion that the present had cost nothing, but that one corner of the Derry, where he worked, would shine less brightly for the lamp's absence.

Andy's extra clothes, such as they were, hung on a nail behind the door, the cracked windows had curtains of washed and ironed white flour bags, and a few boxes held the meal, tea, and other odds and ends. It was no palace, but comfortable with its wide fireplace and red-and-black tiles. True, the tiles were broken here and there, and the wind blew gusts of smoke into the room at intervals, but it was a place where he could sit and smoke at nights with the storm raging round the four walls and the rain lashing on the windows. He sat for a while thinking, undisturbed by the hubbub of the chattering women or the laughter of the men.

Twelve of them in such a small place was uncomfortable, but Andy was near to the fire with a glass of whiskey to cheer him. They had eaten a heap of fancy stuff that Jean had brought from Wigtown, and drank more than enough beer, sang and laughed till darkness came and the firelight flickered and showed their faces pleasantly red in the shadows. Andy was tired; he began to wish that they would go and let him get to bed. Jean, too, seemed weary. . . . He looked at the clock . . . it was past one . . . and still their boisterous visitors remained to provide their own entertainment, with drunken songs and jokes and idiotic laughter at nothing at all.

Alec Brody was lying on the floor asleep and the women were responding to the crude advances of the men who pulled their chairs closer to them. Andy kicked at the wood on the fire. It blazed up for a few seconds, then the flames died, the shadows deepened, and the room was almost in complete darkness. Still no one seemed to prepare to leave.

'Weel,' he said, 'A'm awa' tae ma bed.'

No one took the hint.

'Jean's waitin' fur ye tae tak her tae bed. Awa' on wi't. We're a'richt,' a woman tittered.

There was nothing else for it. Andy looked at Jean and reached forward to damp the fire. They undressed in the darkness. The small back bedroom was silent, save for the sound of an occasional murmur or a snore from one of the men or women behind the door. Andy soon fell asleep. He was awakened an hour or so later by Alec roughly shaking him.

'Weel, we're awa'. We hae tae work in the mornin'.'

He heard the door slam behind them, and their voices as they went down the road.

When he rose at dawn, he found one of the men and a woman sleeping on the floor. The woman's arms were round the man's neck.

'Come on maun,' he urged him, 'ye'll hae tae awa' hame.'

The man awoke and looked up blearily. 'Whut time is't?' he asked.

Andy told him. The woman slept on as he disentangled his arms from her, rose, put his hat on, and went out.

'So long,' he called back.

'So long,' said Andy, and began to shake the woman on the floor.

She looked up drowsily and put her arms round his neck, but he shook them off. 'Ir ye no' gan hame?'

Jean appeared at the door. 'Och, lay her alane, Andy,' she said, 'A'll mak' her a cup o' tea.'

The sleepy woman began to adjust her under-clothes shamelessly. Andy reset the fire and hung the kettle on its hook. It was still half-dark outside but the rain had ceased. It was a hazy red dawn that greeted his first morning of married life. The air was silent but for the faint sound of water dripping from the slates. The cocks up at Doonhall began to crow, and the dog, bringing in the kye from the field behind the cot-house, barked continuously.

The listless debauched woman raised herself from the floor, brushed back her untidy hair and yawned.

'Wull ye hae a cup o' tae?' Jean asked her.

'No,' she answered, 'A'll hae tae awa' on. Whun did that bastard lay?'

She was referring to her companion of the night.

'Half an 'oor ago,' volunteered Andy.

She lifted her coat from the nail and struggled to get her arms into the sleeves. Jean assisted her and saw her out. Andy was putting on his boots when she came back.

'Weel?' she smiled.

'Weel,' was his meaningless reply.

She held his jacket for him.

'Ye'd better get me a bite o' breakfast,' he told her.

'Aye,' she said and lifted a pot from the fireside.

'There's nae time fur parrich.'

'Jist a wee drap o' tea?' she suggested.

'Aye, bit there'll hae tae be parrich the morn,' he reminded her.

'Och aye, this is jist the first mornin'. A'll hae yer parrich ready fur ye the morn.'

He wondered, as he sipped his tea, whether she would really have his porridge ready for him every morning. The whiteness of her face and the tired look of untidiness about her displeased him . . .

perhaps tomorrow she would strike him as worse looking. It was a fine start; already, on his first day, he had secret regrets.

'Yer faither didna come then?' he remarked.

'No, A dinna ken whut kep' him awa'. Mebbe he got fou.'

Andy was rather glad that her seedy old father had not been amongst the tiresome visitors of the day before.

'They made a terrible haun,' said Jean; looking round at the muddied tiles, 'A'll hae a guid bit o' cleanin' tae dae'.

Andy looked at the floor as he went out.

'Weel, fur Christ's sake, dinna furget ma denner wi' a' the cleanin'.'

She looked hurt and half annoyed, and began to clatter the rickety chairs back to the wall.

He turned as he went up the road to the farm and looked back just to see the smoke coming from the chimney of his own house. She was walking down through the wet grass of the field to the spring, with a pail in her hand. The first step towards washing the floor. He waved to her and she waved back.

'Ye're no' sae late efter a', then,' said Craig.

'No,' he admitted.

'A thocht mebbe ye wud fin' it hard tae rise on the first mornin'.'

Andy coloured. 'Och no.' He grinned uneasily, and went over to the stable. The boy eyed him strangely. Did they expect a vast difference in a man after he had spent the first night abed with his wife? He was annoyed.

'Whut the hell's botherin' ye?' he asked him. The boy smiled.

'Oot o' bed on the wrang side, Andy?'

His first inclination was to burst out in a torrent of oaths, but he changed his mind and smiled back.

'Awa' tae yer byre, Arse an' Pooches.'

The boy hated the allusion to his lack of inches; he stammered out some feeble inaudible retort and vanished round the stable door on the way to his byre. Andy curried his horses and brushed them till their sides shone. There was nothing much to do but cart dung, for the ploughs were at the smithy. He whistled as he led his horses out and yoked them to the dung carts; then down to the midden and on with the job of forking dung. In spite of the unsavoury odours, the carting of dung, with the vigorous swinging of the fork to fill the carts, greatly stimulates the appetite. The boss called him when it seemed he had only been at it an hour.

'That'll dae the noo, Andy. Awa' fur yer denner, it's past twelve.'

He watered the horses and led them back to the stable.

Going down the road he watched the smoke from the chimney again; smoke from his fire, heating his dinner. He began to whistle again and admire the watery blur of the sun in the south. Jean was waiting for him at the door.

'The denner's been ready this last half 'oor,' she told him.

'Fine,' he smiled, 'A'm hungry, helluva hungry.'

She poured out a bowl of broth with carrots and leeks floating thick in it. He decided she was a really good cook. Potatoes and butter and a small piece of salt meat followed, washed down with a cup of butter milk. He brushed his mouth with the back of his hand when the meal was over and fumbled in his waistcoat pocket for a cigarette end.

'Ye ken whut a maun likes,' he praised her.

She smiled back. 'A ken whut a boy likes,' she teased.

He grinned again and lit the crumpled stump of cigarette.

'It's no' sae bad efter a',' he mused.

'Whut's no' sae bad?' she asked.

He looked at the fire and spoke slowly. 'Och, A thocht mebbe it wudna be sae gran' gettin' merrit. A wusna share aboot it aforehaun. A wus mebbe kin' o' feart ye wudna hae ma denner ready, or ma breakfast. An' mebbe ye wud want tae lie in bed a' day. A wus nearly gan tae ask ye if ye could dae a' they things afore we wur merrit.'

She looked at him with his curly black hair falling across his tanned brows as he gazed into the fire.

'We'll be a'richt,' she assured him, 'if ye dinna get flamin' mad an' start yer helluva kerry on. A can wurk weel enough.'

He thought of his temper, his fits of crazy rage. He thought of her too, in her unreasonable nagging moods as he had already seen her, and he was not assured in face of it all. This was only the beginning; the first day. When the newness of working for him in her own little cot-house wore off, what would happen? He spat the burned-out end of his cigarette from his lips and lifted his hat.

'Weel, A'll hae tae awa' back.'

She came over and kissed him.

'Ye stink o' dung.'

'It's a guid clean smell,' he laughed.

They found each other's company pleasant enough for a week or two. It was Andy, and not Jean, who began to cause the trouble. In the morning he found her talkativeness irksome and told her often to shut her mouth. Then she would sulk for the rest of the day and her very silence would make him angrier. She never answered him when he raged, but banged pots by the fireside and clattered the few dishes together.

He bought a collie pup for company, and for poaching when it grew old enough, but he found that no sooner had he gone up the road than the miserable pup would be swept out of doors with the brush and come yelping up the road after him. The fact annoyed him. She began to grumble about the pup trailing in mud and dampness to mark her floor; the one thing in which she seemed to take a special pride.

Andy was fond of the pup; he had always been fond of dogs. The pathetic look in its blue-black eyes when it ran to him with its tail between its legs made his heart sore. He had trained it to sit up and receive tit-bits from his plate, to know him, and swing its wiry little body to and fro as it wagged its tail at his approach. It was full of fun and life and he could not bear to think of her battering it out of doors into the rain when he was at work in the field. When he came home and found it sidling up to the door, its long black hair bedraggled with rain, he would pick it up and console it, and go in to Jean with a look of fury on his face. Her child was coming and she was irritable. She listened to his outbursts with growing annoyance and more continual sullenness.

The climax came one day when he took the plough to the smithy for some repairs. As he left in the morning, he knew that she had hustled the dog outside. It was a bitterly cold day with sleet and snow falling. When he passed on his way to the smithy, the dog was crouched in the shelter of the doorway whimpering. He resisted the impulse to go in and beat her for it, but rode on with his temper growing all the way. It seemed that the morning at the smithy was spent waiting for the return, so that he could see if the pup was still lying out in the wet. He urged the horse on, all the way back. It was past one o' clock and a freezing wind cut through his clothes.

When the cot-house came in sight, he watched eagerly as he approached. The dog was still at the door. His temper had the better of him. All the morning it had been seething and steadily rising. The pup lifted its head as he went past and wagged its tail feebly at the sight of him. Its dejected air was the match to the tinder of his temper. He shook with fury as he unyoked the horse and stabled him. Down the road he strode, twice as fast as usual, clenching his hands and drawing his face into the distorted features of a madman. Reaching the door, he picked the dog up in his arms. It licked his face as he lifted the latch and burst in. Jean saw in a flash that his temper was beyond control. Beyond anything she had ever seen in him before. She stood behind the table clutching her dress round her swollen body and watching him with dilated eyes. He threw the door shut with a crash that made the mortar rattle on the slates as it rolled from the apex of the roof.

Neither of them spoke as he laid the dog before the fire. After rubbing it dry and talking to it like a child, he turned on her.

'A hae telt ye aboot this afore. Ye batter the dog oot o' the hoose the meenit A'm awa'. As share as ye leev, A'll murder ye if ye ever dae it again.' He came round the table after her.

'Dinna, Andy! Dinna hit me!' she pleaded.

He caught her by the shoulder.

'Come here, ye bitch.'

'A'll no' dae it again. A'll no' dae it again, Andy.' There was terror in her face.

'B'Christ, ye'll no'.' He swung her round so that she staggered, and forced her to the door.

'Dinna throw me oot, Andy.'

He pulled back the door and sent her stumbling into the rain. 'See hoo ye like it yersel', ye bitch!' he flung after her as he barred the door.

The dinner was ready, and after he had dried the dog with a piece of sacking he placed it on a chair beside him. It licked his hands and wagged its tail. Jean hammered at the door as he took his dinner.

'Andy! Andy!' she pleaded, 'let me in. Ye'll kill me oot here. The wean'll be born dead!'

He paid no heed but shared his dinner with the dog, and wiped his plate with a piece of scone when he had done. A glance at the clock told him that it was time he was back at the farm, so he pulled on his topcoat, lifted his hat and opened the door. Jean was standing before him, wet and shivering, with tears rolling down her cheeks.

'Come in,' he ordered, 'if ye iver dae that again wi' the dog A'll kill ye. It's a young dog an' no' fit tae stey oot in the caul wauther. Noo min' whut A say. A'll kill ye if ye iver dae it again.'

She looked at the cruel line of his mouth and flash of his eyes and was cowed.

'Get yersel' dried,' he said as he closed the door.

She sat down before the fire and stifled her sobs, trembling with nervousness. The dog was never left out in the rain again. She was careful how she treated it. Andy would sit at his meals watching her out of the corner of his eye to see if she would abuse the pup, but she was aware of his sly threatening look and the dog was allowed to lie dozing where he pleased. Its training went on. A dry Sunday morning found him teaching it in the field, or when it was wet he would teach it to obey his commands in the house, and brush and comb it with the same pride and careful attention that he gave his horses.

The incident was soon forgotten so far as he was concerned, but Jean was in constant fear of his anger and there was a strained atmosphere between them that only decreased as her time drew nearer.

Listening to her heavy breathing as she lay in bed beside him, her faint groans during the night, and the sound of her fast-beating heart, Andy's sympathy grew. He began to change in his feelings towards her. She became to him as the mare at the farm, a beast that was restless and uneasy, carrying not a foal, but a child.

He thought of how he had rubbed the old mare's head and said,

'Dinna worry, oul' lass, it'll no' be lang noo.' The mare seemed to have sensed his sympathy.

He wanted to console Jean, to treat her more tenderly. He saw her more and more as a great suffering animal, a beast that was patiently bearing a burden. The burden of a foal or a child, what was the difference? Jean found herself sorely worn, more and more each day. Her antagonism towards him vanished. She began to smile pathetically at his crude efforts to please her. She saw him again as the strangely moody dark-haired boy she had married less than a year before. Crazy with rage one minute, and again as tender as he had been violent. He made no fuss about telling her to stay in bed in the mornings. 'Lie still,' he would say as he rose. His voice was gruff and unfriendly, but she knew that it was only because he was ashamed of his tender moments. 'Dinna be liftin' ocht noo,' he told her, 'or ye'll be hurtin' yersel', mebbe kill yersel' lik' Mrs. McKey.'

She smiled; she was feeling well enough, although the child was almost due to come.

'A think it'll no' be lang noo,' said Andy to Mrs. Craig, 'wud ye gang doon an' see her fur me?'

The warm-hearted mistress wasted no time, but went straight down the road to the sweating woman who lay on the bed in the cot-house.

'Ye're gan tae hae a sair time,' she told her, 'ye'll need a doctor.'

Jean looked up vacantly. 'Aye,' she almost whispered.

The mistress prepared Andy's dinner up at the house and the doctor was sent for. Andy went down to see his wife before beginning work in the afternoon.

'Ir ye a'richt?' he asked her, leaning over the bed.

She feebly raised her hand and clutched his arm desperately.

'God, the pain, Andy, the pain,' she said thickly.

He looked down at her awkwardly till the mistress hustled him out.

'A doot there's somethin' no' richt,' she said as she handed him his hat.

He went back to his weeding feeling worried. The doctor's car came at two. An hour later, when he was half-way up a furrow,

Jean's shrieks came to him, making his body shake and sweat. It was worse for a woman than for a mare then! He rose and lumbered down the field as fast as he could with the mud clinging inches thick to the soles of his boots. The door was barred. Jean's shrieks went on. He hammered on the door. 'Let me in, let me in.'

'Get awa' back tae yer wurk,' the mistress urged him nervously.

He went on hammering on the door till after the shrieks had died down and the doctor came and told him to go back to the field. She was all right.

'Ye haena kilt her?' he asked.

The lean grey-haired man smiled.

'No, your wife has been in great pain, but she was in no danger of dying. She's a strong woman.'

He was at ease. If she was not dying, what was all the yelling for? He forgot to ask whether it was a boy or a girl. The mistress came up the road and called across to him from the dykeside.

'Ye hae a fine wee son, Andy.'

Somehow he had not expected anything else than a son. He would have been surprised and disappointed had it been a girl. He could not see himself fathering a girl.

He went down after kye-time to see Jean. The mistress was at the bedside. Jean gazed up at him weakly and said, 'Hullo Andy.'

'Hullo,' he said and seemed to become tongue-tied.

The mistress lifted back the clothes for a brief second and showed him the baby. It was a strange little red bundle with no hair. Hardly what he had expected, but he had never seen a newly born child before.

He had his meals each day at the farmhouse. It seemed that the mistress was always in the cot-house doing something. Craig told him he would pay for the doctor and Andy was grateful. It was three weeks before Jean could rise. She was shaky and weak, and sat with a shawl round her, feeding the baby at her breast. Andy was glad to be back in his own house again, in spite of the discomfort and the wailing of the child, for he had been neglecting his pup.

CHAPTER XIX

BEING infused with the wildness of his kind, that restless spirit which seems for ever taunted by the silence of the hills, the immobility of the dykes, the passive grazing of the cattle, Andy began to tire of the novelty of married life; the squalor that revealed itself when his eyes became accustomed to the cot-house with Jean fussing and cleaning one minute and storming when her work was undone by the child, Andy's muddy boots, the dog with his wet feet and the wind that frolicked round the room with a cloud of smoke and peat dust. The squalor was natural – there could never have been anything else and he was used to it, but the houses of farmers are cleaner. His wife had turned out to be all he had feared; sullen and by fits quick-tempered and sharp-tongued.

Perhaps it was because it was winter again and she was pregnant with her second child that she cursed him and grumbled from morn until night. He was tired of her and more tired of her tongue. She had been born a creature of gall and if their affection for each other had ever been as fresh and sweet as the ripening apple on the tree, it had died and rotted like the same apple hidden for months in the pocket of an old coat. As her months of pregnancy passed he sought new company. There was a girl at Whauphill and another at the Port who liked his looks and the healthy strength of his love-making. The news travelled with the breeze. She heard and hated him all the more. They ate together and slept side by side without exchanging a word.

It was hoeing time when she took to bed to bring their second offspring into the world. He was working in the field with the boy when her labour began. They were too far away for him to hear whether she shrieked or not. He had less sympathy for her than he had for the foaling mare. She was no longer his wife. His wife was either at the Port or at the Whauphill, whereever his fancy took him at nights. They were warm women who were eager for his embrace. But she, Jean, had ceased to smile from the month she found herself pregnant. Her tongue had become silent all at once. He had tired of it as she had raved above his head at dinner-time and over his shoulder at night. She had mumbled and muttered endlessly, and at last become suddenly silent as though she had tired of her own voice and the lack of any impression she might have hoped to have made on her husband.

Only once while he hoed did he look in the direction of the cot-house, and that was when the doctor's car came purring up the road and stopped at the cot-house door. Mrs. Craig had insisted on the doctor again.

The boy looked too and said, 'That's the doctor's car.'

Andy made no reply. He was unperturbed and went on hoeing without so much as a frown or even a look of interest.

At night, for the child was born in the afternoon, he went down to the cot-house. She was lying staring at the roof. Her face was pale and she looked weak. Without turning her eyes towards him she spoke, and her voice was bitter and sneering.

'So ye hae come to see yer wean?' she asked.

He regarded her steadily. 'Hoo ir ye?'

She sneered again, and he wondered why he had asked her. They had had nothing to say to each other for weeks.

'Whut the hell dae ye care hoo A am?'

A flush darkened his cheeks, not because he was ashamed, but because she had made him a fool for asking her.

Her face twitched as she looked at him. She seemed to be summoning breath to blast him with her tongue.

'Whut the hell dae ye care hoo yer wean is? Ye hae had a wheen o' ither dirty bitches in the last week or twa, an' mebbe ye'll be peyin' fur anither bastard wean afore lang.'

He leaned over her. 'Ye dirty great lump, ye. Had yer tongue an' dinna meddle wi' whut A dae, or b'Christ A'll be the daith o'ye.'

From then on they were constantly at cross purposes. The children were uncared for. There was no more cleaning. She hated Andy with all her being and she hated his dog. The children were a noisy acquisition to the home. In the quietness of the night they kept him awake, and through the day they were a butt for his wife's crazy fits of temper. Things became worse as months passed. Though he had no more use for her than that of cooking his meals, he had a strange kind of jealousy. A man who had no use for his wife might chase other women, but for the wife to take other men to her bed was a disgrace and an insult, and though she was no longer his wife, his real mate, he was afraid that she would disgrace him in his own bed and the farm workers of the locality would laugh at him behind his back. For this reason he thrashed her frequently, often when she sat scowling and watching his every action, as he prepared to go out alone. When it was not to seek the company of his new loves, he forced her to accompany him, whether it was to set snares, sneak a pheasant from a quiet wood, or wander along the road to the Port or the Whaup for a drink.

On such occasions she protested, and agreed to go with him when he threatened her with a sinister cunning ferocity. She would have to follow him across the wet grass of the fields, over dykes, and crawling through whins and brackens to his orders as he poached. Her fear of him was as great as her hatred. She felt that, when she broke the silence of the twilight by kicking a stone with her loose-fitting shoes, he might, with little provocation, seize her by the throat and strangle the life out of her; holding her in those lean hairy hands and gazing at her with madness in his look.

His viciousness and brutality were increasing as that strange mood of personal jealousy grew on him. There was something childish about it, like the schoolboy who cuts himself a stick, whets it a while and throws it away, only to fight his companion who retrieves it and wants to keep it for himself. He had no use for his wife, but no one else should have her, even though he saw his freedom vanishing in a marriage of sullenness and his life one long torment with the wailing of children for ever in his ears. He felt tired of it all, and had it not been for his more frequent escapes into the night for a meeting on some quiet roadside near the Whaup or the Port, the brightness would have gone from his life completely.

He was not like other men. He had nothing of their placid

tolerance, and the small things spun in his mind till his head ached and he longed to clear up for all time the obscure muddle that existed in his imagination. In others, it would have been a failure to adapt themselves to a new life. If simple minds can be bored it was boredom. To Andy, it was the regularity of eating off the same table with a morose wife; wondering if folks were laughing at him behind his back because she was carrying on while he was away; watching her dip her finger into the jam-pot and letting the dirty-faced children lick the jam; and knowing just as surely as the sun rose, that she was getting near confinement with a third child.

She had not told him. Scowling over the porridge pot, with her body swollen and ugly, she avoided his eye when he asked her and made no reply, not because she had been unfaithful, but because she was afraid to tell him. The thought that he had been made a fool of came to him suddenly. She had been carrying on.

'It's no' mine!' he raved. 'Ye dirty bitch. The wean's no' mine. Christ, A'll kill ye!'

The wooden spoon fell from her hand as she turned and looked at him. A crazy fear blanched thin lips.

'Andy! Andy!' She seemed to be trying to call him back to sanity, to penetrate his fit of madness.

His eyes were staring and his hands opened and closed threat-eningly. As he advanced on her, the two children on the floor began to cry. She stumbled round the table to avoid him. He followed, treading on the hand of the younger child as he did so. The child screamed as his fingers were crushed.

'It's yours, Andy. It's yours,' she panted.

'Ye dirty bitch!' His lips hardly moved as he spoke.

The kettle on the hob boiled its contents on to the fire. There were four or five seconds of frightening silence, as he followed her round the table. She made no sound when his hand closed on the bread-knife, but kept her eyes on his unshaven face. He stumbled over a broken chair and in that second she sprang for the door, fumbled for the catch and was out before he rose. He went after her, saliva trickling from his mouth and his body bent like a strong steel spring.

There was no sound on the road. She was near; where he did not know. He walked slowly round the cot-house. There was no moon and the night was cold. Twice he circled the house and heard no sound, then he clambered over the dyke and crept down the road. Still no sound of her. His hands were cold and a shiver ran through him as the wind puffed out his flannel shirt like a balloon.

Jean, lying in the ditch beside the hedge at the back of the house, could feel the life stirring within her body. The grass was damp and the moisture penetrated her thin clothing. She could not rise for the whole of her body was shaking and her legs were weak. She heard him go over the dyke, waited, and then began to crawl out of the wet grass. At first she felt like running away, then she remembered the two children in the house.

'Mither,' sobbed the elder one, when she opened the door.

The baby, with jam smudges on his face and hands, plodded across the floor to her and held out his arms to be lifted. Her legs began to tremble again. She could hear his boots on the road; he was returning. With one child clutching her skirt and the other in her arms, she ran round the house and back to the ditch.

He stood at the door and yelled, 'Come back, ye bitch. A'm gan' tae kill the weans.'

His voice echoed back to him from the hills, and sent the woman crawling up the ditch in a palsy of fear. He stood at the door for a minute to listen for her coming back, then went in to the house. The place was empty. Even the dog had gone. He looked under the table, stumbled over the floor and searched the shadows by the dresser and stood gazing at the wall; wondering at the strange feeling below his scalp. The skin seemed to lift off his head. His temples ached and a small muscle behind his ears twitched. There were streaks of red and white dancing in his vision; he could neither see the fire nor hear the monotonous tick of the clock.

Instinctively, he reached for the gun above the door and began fumbling in his jacket for cartridges. He left the door wide open and the wind blew the ashes from under the bars of the fire round the room and over the floor.

He went lumbering down the road, laughing and swearing and muttering half aloud, 'A hae ye noo, ye bitch. A hae ye noo.'

He ran almost a mile and then turned and came back up the road; a wild-eyed beast with his hair fallen over his face and his teeth bared in a grin. The safety valve of his temper blown, he entered the cot-house, not even looking to see if Jean and the weans had returned and lay down before the dying fire with the gun by his side. The door was unbarred and the room full of smoke.

In the morning he awoke stiff and tired. They had not come back. It was too late to make the porridge, so he put on his boots and opened the door. The dog was lying on the step. It wagged its tail and padded into the room. The wind entered too, and stirred up the carpet of ash that covered the floor. When he reached the stable, he saw the boss was unaware of anything amiss. He tended his horses as though nothing had happened.

When she had heard the door close again, Jean rose from the ditch and struggled across to the dyke. She had a pain under her heart and the children were shivering with cold. There was nothing for it but to walk to Kirkcowan. She could go to her own folks again. He might kill her if she returned. They went down past the cot-house, walking on the grass in case he should hear them. The boy tripped and fell. When he began to cry, she smothered his face in her skirt and dragged him after her. About an hour later, they came to Malzie and slept in a straw shed, rising at daybreak before the milkers were about.

At the smithy, she told her story to a woman who gave her a cup of tea.

'A'd gan' tae the polis an' hae him put in the asylum,' counselled the woman.

'Mebbe A wull,' answered Jean.

She was still too frightened and tired to feel one way or the other about it. After warming themselves at the fire they went on. The boy complained that his boots were hurting. He was very young to be wearing boots at all, but she understood his baby talk and attempted to carry him. Afterwards she turned a deaf ear to his whimpering and made him walk. The sun came out before noon and made their damp clothes steam. The child in her arms slept.

At dinner-time Andy came in from the fields. 'Mistress,' he said, 'could ye gie me some denner?'

She looked at him for a moment, then answered slowly, 'Aye. She'll be takin' tae her bed then?'

He remained silent.

After the meal, as he was crossing to the steading, the boss asked, 'Wull ye be wantin' the doctor tae her the day?'

'No,' grunted Andy. 'A put her oot last nicht.'

'God'sake, whut did ye dae that fur?'

He scowled and muttered, 'The wean's no' mine'.

The boss looked at him strangely as he led the horse out. The boy was inquisitive too, and earned only curses for his pains. They worked in silence throughout the afternoon and in the evening Andy went down the road without milking.

A week passed, and he ceased to expect her back. He did not miss her. He was much happier alone, and the place was quieter without the sound of children crying and her scolding them to show her spite. He fed the dog every morning and now and then shovelled the ashes out of the fire; the same plate did for breakfast and supper.

At odd times when the grocer called, he would leave his work and go across the field to buy the things he needed; matches, oatmeal, tea, salt and cigarettes. Sometimes the mistress bought them for him, but he was too afraid to face her often, with her expression of open contempt and dislike. Perhaps she remembered the Docherty girl. At least she could not forgive him for forcing his wife out into the freezing night, and her with a child coming. He thought no more until a policeman cycled up to the steading one afternoon as he came back from re-sowing a crop of oats.

At first, he supposed the policeman had called to see about sheep-dipping papers, but, as he was unharnessing his horse from the cart, the boss called him over.

'He wants tae see ye, Andy.'

Making a painfully slow job of taking the horse into the stable, he tried to think of something to say. The horse was feeding from the trough contentedly, but still he stood by, shirking the meeting, till at last he could find no other good reason for waiting longer and walked across to the policeman, who was admiring young pigs on the midden.

'Your name Walker?' asked the officer.

'Aye,' said Andy, 'bit . . .'

The policeman fumbled in his inside pocket and withdrew a paper.

'A have to serve you with this summons.'

'Whut fur?' asked Andy.

'Wife and family left chargeable to the parish,' answered the policeman, and went on to explain the whole rigmarole to Andy, who failed hopelessly to understand more than a word of it.

The policeman mounted his cycle and left him standing with the paper in his hand.

'Bit she left me,' he said to the boss.

'Oh no, ye pit her oot.'

'Aye, bit A didna lock the door, she could hae come back.'

'Ye'll see when ye get tae the coort,' said the boss.

Andy pushed the paper into his pocket and went down to the pump to wash for the milking.

The following day he appeared at court, offered a few shillings, and asked for Jean to return. She refused and said he only wanted her back to save paying the money. In the end, an order was made against him. A total of ten shillings a week and five shillings to be paid when the third child was born. In addition, he was required to pay off his debt to the parish. It left him with no money. During the hearing he stood bewildered, puzzling at the words of the bailie and overawed by the officials of the court. He looked for Jean outside. She was nowhere to be seen, but after a drink he met her at the public-house door.

'Ye hae din a fine thing tae me,' he said.

She cowered away from him and muttered, 'Ye wur gan' tae kill me. Lay me alane. A can keep the weans masel'.'

He would have struck her but a policeman came down the street on his cycle.

'Mebbe A'll kill ye yet,' he murmured and pushed past her.

She stood watching him go up to the sweetshop where he had left his bike. When she saw him ride away she went into the public house where it was warmer and more friendly.

The first week Andy sent his money to the court, posting it at Whauphill. He found his would be a bare existence. When the order was increased he would have only enough to buy food and a cigarette or two. There would be nothing with which to buy boots or leggings, overalls or shirts. He was afraid to withhold the payments. Then notice came that the third child was born.

The struggle through the summer was bad enough. At the end of harvest he found he was needing boots, socks and shirts. Five or six rabbits at a night's poaching were not enough. He had to pay his wife as well as live, so he repaired his nets and snares and went out at nights to get the lie of the land much farther afield than Doonhall and Drumlin; places where there were far more pheasants and rabbits, the prospect of a better bag and a quick means of raising money for the few meagre luxuries of life. He went about it calmly, with a definite object in view all the time. His wife had to have fifteen shillings of his wages and besides he had to have clothes and food. Poaching had at one time been the greatest attraction in his life. It was a joy and a thrill and now it was to become a task: a means of life.

The first two or three nights, followed by trips to Newton Stewart in the early hours of the morning, were successful beyond all hopes. There was more than enough to pay Jean. Forty and fifty pairs of rabbits he lifted off quiet hillsides and hollows that had never been worked with dog, net or snare before. He learned from experience the tricks and points of the art and often had more rabbits than he could carry on his bike on two journeys. It was exciting too. All the fun of his days as a byreboy returned. He poached because he needed the money, but just as much because he liked it.

He grew clever at setting snares so that even the keeper could not spot them, they were hidden so cunningly in patches of grass; he knew just where a bag would escape the keen nose of the keeper's spaniel until he could call for it the following evening, and ride off with it to his dealer. He and the collie spent the best hours of many nights prowling the quiet backwoods of the countryside, netting, snaring, shooting on rare occasions.

The boss became aware of it and not only did he know that Andy was at work at nights, but he knew why. Craig knew his man to be a fine ploughman, a good milker and a willing worker, so he closed his eyes to the night-prowling, though his suspicions fell short by three-quarters of the extent of Andy's bag. There were some, however, who became uneasy at the scarcity of rabbits; the absence of pheasants from the best thickets. McRory, the keeper of Leigh-milns, was worried. He knew that poachers were at work. Three shooting parties had remarked the absence of game. He decided that a watch would have to be kept.

CHAPTER XX

MC RORY worked under Milligan, who was head keeper on the Leighmilns land, a quiet little wooded estate on the north bank of the Bladnoch. It was evident from the November of that winter that the scarcity of game was not merely due to the coldness of the weather alone. The watch for the poacher brought small measure of success on the first night. They heard gunshots and found a pair of rabbits and a snare, but the night was in favour of their quarry. The moon hid too often behind great rainclouds that threw the hills into complete darkness, and the wind was high, singing in the ears so that a listener could hear nothing, except in the infrequent lulls.

So it was that Andy moved at the height of the wind, and when the moon dived into the heart of the blankets of rain and mist. He followed the line of the hedges and dykes and avoided the hills, for, when the moon would burst through the clouds again, a wave of light would come flooding across a mile of fields and sweep the shadows from the virgin sides of ploughed hills. Such a night was ideal for the long net, which was difficult for one man to handle. With a fine bag, he went home sheltering in the black depths of hollows and woods. McRory and Milligan waited in vain till the dawn, hoping for a clearer sky and a falling wind. Encouraged by the rabbits and the snare, they deceived themselves into believing that they would hear the report of a gun again before daylight.

Andy worked on the assumption that always a keeper was watching somewhere. He worked without fear nevertheless, and with a deliberateness of purpose that left him calm and ready for any emergency. His mind was constantly on the alert and his eyes on the watch. Working silently and quickly, he escaped on the first night that they watched for him, but on the second the sky was clear and the wind of the night before had gone.

He chose for safety a hollow bounded by steep hills. Working in its shadows, he was able to watch the four surrounding slopes. It was a hollow that had never been ploughed, hard stony land that was infested with rabbits, though far from the ideal spot for the long net. There were too many stones and out-field burrows where the rabbits would escape both dog and net. There was a disadvantage, too, in the fact that the hills left no cover and escaping with a heavy sack and a net would be a slow progress.

While he was running out his net for the first time, McRory and Milligan were separating to begin their patrol of the likely spots. The younger man crossed the slope running down into the hollow, where Andy was making his first catch. He had already dismissed the hollow as a sensible scene of operation, when the squeal of a dying rabbit came faintly up to him as he was cupping his hands to light his pipe. So startled that the match burned his fingers, he stood and gazed down into the half-darkness wondering. Ferrets or a long net? His mind was made up – a long net – that meant almost surely two of them and he would need Milligan's help.

Andy surveyed the hillside a moment after the keeper had reached its summit and, being satisfied, continued with his task, while McRory hurried to a stunted thorn tree on the other side to wait for Milligan.

Andy's single-handed use of the long net entailed strenuous work lifting rabbits and killing them one after another as they plumped into the net. The frequency with which they came tumbling in kept him running to and fro deftly breaking necks with a cunning swing of the arm, and tossing the bodies out in a row a yard or so behind the net. When the second catch was complete, he waited for the dog. There was no sound of its approach. He called softly to it as he rolled the net, and the two men crawling down the slope in the shelter of the dyke heard him and were convinced that two men were at work.

They parted where the dyke branched and McRory began the slow job of circling the hollow on his knees.

When he had paired and lifted the last of the rabbits into the sack, Andy called the dog again and walked quietly across the hollow in search of it. Half way he found it, perfectly trained collie mongrel that it was it stood without a whimper with its foreleg in an old snare. It had jumped and struggled until the wire had cut into the flesh and hair was matted with blood. The job of releasing it was a painful one. The snare stick was frozen into the ground, and after fumbling for his knife Andy cut the string which held the wire. He was attempting to remove the wire when he heard the sound of the steel shod of a boot striking a stone. Feverishly, he untied the noose from the leg and rose.

There was a dark shape where he left his sack and net. He turned and made for the opposite dyke. McRory rose to meet him as he leaped it followed by the limping dog. They fell together and rolled over among the bracken shoots. Stones clattered from the dyke and came crashing down upon them. The keeper was determined to hold him at all costs, but Andy was fighting a slowly winning battle. With monotonous regularity, he drove his fist into his opponent's unprotected face to break the grip round his waist that held his other arm pinned to his side. Three times he managed to release himself by using his knee, only to find the keeper clinging to his legs.

Finally, struggling to his feet in a state of exhaustion, he seized the keeper's head in his hands, forced it back till he shrieked in agony, and battered it brutally till the grip slackened on his legs and the body fell back limp.

At that moment, Milligan came panting to the dykeside. Andy saw the gun raised to his shoulder and ran.

'Had on!' yelled Milligan. He was shaking with fear and excitement.

Andy continued to run.

The man with the gun hesitated for a second then fired. The shot struck the grass at Andy's feet. He ran a few steps more and felt a numbness at his knees. He fell and could not scramble back to his feet.

Milligan came running towards him and Andy's quick wits came to his aid. He dropped his head into the wet grass and waited for him to bend over him. Milligan went down on one knee and attempted to turn the body over. Andy's hand closed quickly over a stone under his chest and swung it full into the keeper's face. Unconscious, Milligan fell back and rolled slowly down the hill.

An hour later Andy's tenth attempt to regain the use of his legs failed. He could not bear to bend them or try to crawl, and the blood had soaked through his trousers. He was shivering and the damp dew on the grass became a frost. Down the slope he could see the motionless figure of Milligan, but it was too dark by the dykeside for him to see McRory, though he strained his eyes to do so. In fact, McRory had crawled along the edge of the field ten minutes before and eventually managed to pull himself to his feet. After that he had slowly climbed the hill and gone off in the direction of Leighmilns.

Andy's head was aching strangely and his legs seemed dead. He looked up the hill and saw them coming. The dog which had kept him company instinctively slunk off down the hill and over the dyke. Four men came to him.

'Lift him up,' one ordered, and Andy was lifted none too gently and carried by two of them.

The other two followed supporting Milligan. One of the men carrying Andy cursed the blood on his legs and Andy groaned with pain when they jerked his now stiff legs. The journey to Leighmilns, where the shotwounds in his calf and knees were washed, was followed by the journey to Wigtown in the car to see the doctor and the police.

Two days later, Andy was sentenced to six months in gaol for assaulting two gamekeepers and poaching. Craig, who saw him later, told him that he need not come back. His possessions would be sold and the money sent to him on his release. Andy knew that had Craig been anything but a tenant farmer, he might still have had work to come out to. The laird would not allow a tenant to employ a convicted poacher.

The days that followed were long and dreary ones in which he wondered how the dog was faring and whether his belongings had been sold as Craig had intimated. He lost count of the days and wondered what kind of harvest it had been. Sometimes he laughed to himself as he thought of Jean. She wouldn't be receiving her pound a week now. The thought became a great consolation to him as the days wore on. He thought hopefully, too, of the money he would receive for the sale of the contents of the cot-house till to have the money in his hands became almost an obsession with him.

When he was released the first thing he did was to walk out to Doonhall to see Craig. It was late in the day when he reached the farm.

'Jean cam' an' selt the things,' Craig told.

'Whut did ye let her dae that fur?' asked Andy in a daze.

'She had a coort order.'

Andy nodded his head slowly. There was a rumbling noise in his ears, and a black wave rose before his eyes. Mechanically he took the wages due to him and went down the road again. It was dark and chilly, but he had lost all sense of feeling. She had stolen his money, the bitch. He burst out into a torrent of incoherent words and began looking wildly round him for someone to vent his rage upon. He wandered all through the night, going slowly, and from side to side.

Something had happened to him. He had forgotten why he wanted to kill Jean, he knew only that he would kill her. As the sun came over the hills, he climbed a dyke and lay down behind it. He slept till the afternoon was all but gone, and rose and went on his way to Wigtown, looking as he went for Jean. The light of stark insanity was standing in his eyes.

At Wigtown he went in for a drink and sat silently watching the people going in and out. After a while Alec Brody came in. He stood at the bar for a time before he noticed Andy in the corner. When he did, he came over and sat down beside him.

'Hullo, Andy,' he said, 'A heard they let ye oot the day. Ye'll be lookin' fur a job till the term?'

Andy remained silent and Alec looked at him with a puzzled expression on his face.

'Can A buy ye a drink?' he asked.

Andy stared fixedly before him his eyes on the door, and Brody lapsed into silence again, but kept glancing at him now and then. A stranger to Andy came over and began to talk, and Brody rose without a word and went across to the bar with him.

'A dinna ken whut haes come on Walker since he cam' oot o' the jile,' he observed. 'Looks tae me kin' o' aff his haid. He didna ken me whun a spok' tae him the noo. The jile daes queer things tae a budy. Walker's no richt onywey.'

'Aye,' agreed the man behind the bar, 'A had a kisin that went tae the war an' the Germans took him an' put him awa' an' whun he cam' back he wusna richt in the haid.'

'Mebbe A'm rang,' remarked Brody after a moment's thought, 'fur he wusna very lang in the jile. Nae mair than fower or five months.'

'That shouldna pit a man oot o' his wuts,' said the bar tender, 'bit ye can nivir tell. It disna tak' a lot tae pit the brain oot o' oarder. A kent o' a falla that gaed clean mad whun a horse kicked him an' oul' Mirren gaed aff his haid whun his wife deed.'

Brody looked over at Andy again and nervously spluttered with beer in his throat, 'Mebbe he's jist a wee bit sleepy. Hey, Andy, come on ower an' hae a drink!'

It had occurred to Brody that sleeplessness might be the cause of Andy's lack of life, and he was half-afraid that he might rise in one of his frequent tempers and make him do more than swallow his words. But Andy, if he had heard their remarks, had not understood or paid no heed. He rose and stood at the door.

A customer sitting in the draught endured it for a few minutes then shouted, 'Hey shut that door, wull ye?'

When Andy made no move to obey the man jumped to his feet and came over to him.

'Oot or in?' he demanded.

Andy ignored him and remained looking out into the darkness.

'Oot then!' said the man, and seized Andy by the shoulder.

His fingers slipped from the jacket as Andy turned on him and looked at him with wide eyes.

'Christ!'

The man backed away in terror and Andy followed him slowly as he retreated from the door to the bar. Everyone in the house was on their feet.

'Stop him, he's aff his haid!' whispered someone at the back of the room.

No one attempted to stop him as he struck the man in the face and knocked him unconscious. The man sagged against the bar and Andy went on striking the defenceless face.

'He'll kill him!' whispered the same frightened voice.

'Rin fur the polis,' said another, but no one ventured to go.

At last the unconscious body slipped and fell to the floor. Andy remained standing over it.

The silence was broken when Brody stepped forward and caught his arm.

'Come awa', Andy, noo,' he persuaded, 'come awa', ye gin him whut he asked fur.'

When he tried to lead him to the door Andy shook the hand from his arm. Brody saw madness in the glare of his dark eyes. Of his own will, Andy walked to the door. Two frightened customers stumbled over each other in their eagerness to get out of his way. While he stood at the door no one attempted to go out.

The man at the bar said to one of the customers, 'Gang fur the polis, Wullie.'

'Gang fur them yersel',' said Wullie, and glanced at the figure in the doorway.

'Somebody'll hae tae gang fur the polis,' mumbled the man at the bar, 'that man'll dae somebody herm afore the nicht's by.'

The room fell into an uneasy silence again, with all eyes on the door.

'A kent him weel afore he went tae the jile,' began Brody, but decided to leave the remark unfinished.

Jean was in the public house down the street drinking a glass of whiskey with Tam Feeney. Tam had his arm round her and pinched her ample hip now and then.

'Och, lae me alane,' she said when it hurt too much.

They sat down on a form in a corner and he began to become more amorous, playing with the fasteners of her dress and sidling up to her, till she almost fell off the seat. A woman entered and came over to them.

'Dae ye ken wha A saw up the street the nicht?' she enquired of Jean.

Without waiting for a reply she went on, 'Andy Walker! and he looked affa queer.'

Jean pushed Tam's hands away and got up.

'A'm fur hame. Ir ye comin', Tam?'

'Och, had on a wee,' pleaded Tam, 'A'll come in twa three meenits.'

He caught her by the arm and pulled her back down on to the seat. Pacified for a moment, she allowed him to cuddle her again.

When the door of the house swung shut behind Andy, the man at the bar sighed, 'Thank the Lord fur that.'

A hubbub of talking broke out once more and they clustered round the injured man, who was groaning on the floor.

'A think the polis should be telt he's no richt,' said someone.

'A'd hae nocht tae dae wi' it,' cautioned another.

'A wunner whaur he's awa' tae,' said Brody, and went to the door to look up and down the street.

He was just in time to see Andy enter the public house down the street.

'Hoo muny drinks did he hae while he wus here?' he called to the barman.

'Only the yin,' that individual answered, 'he nivir got drunk here.'

Jean looked up as Andy came in.

When he saw her she screamed, 'The coort said A cud tak' the muney!'

He strode over to her and grasped her shoulders in his hands. When her companion tried to release her, he struck him in the mouth and knocked him to the floor. She began to scream, loud piercing screams that could be heard out in the street. At first he just shook her, then feeling some one pulling at him from behind, for the place was in an uproar, he let her go and turned on the man trying to restrain him. The rescuer met two sudden blows in the throat and collapsed. Someone ran for the police and two other men stepped forward and faced him.

In the meantime, Jean slipped out past them. Like an infuriated bull, Andy smashed his way through his two attackers and burst into the street after her. Everyone in the room followed him, women screamed and five or six men ran after him down the street. He caught up with her, threw her to the ground and seized her by the throat. Four of them failed to drag him off her at the first attempt.

His hands loosened when they bent his fingers back. Someone struck him over the head with a bottle and all went black. They lifted Jean; her face was a dark purple, but she breathed, though very faintly. Two of the bystanders produced a rope and undertook to tie Andy up till the arrival of the police. There was a large crowd in the street. Brody was among them.

He addressed the world at large. 'He's aff his haid,' he said, 'A kent he wud gang rang someday. Aye gan half-mad wi' temper. Christ, if ye had seen him in the Continental the nicht. He was fur murdering a falla that asked him tae shut the door after him. He haes been queer since he cam' oot o' the jile. He nearly kilt twa keepers afore he gaed tae the jile tae. He wus aye queer.'

'Whut's his name an' whut did he dae?' someone else asked.

Brody explained in a loud voice.

Jean regained consciousness and sat up and the police arrived.

CHAPTER XXI

THEY had to untie his legs to let him walk down the street, and the crowd stood back when he rose. The knots that had been loosened from his feet had left the rope slack on his shoulders, and in the dim light his first struggles to free himself were unnoticed. The policeman that held him was left with the rope in his hands as Andy broke away. The crowd was on his heels in a second, stumbling and falling over each other, yelling like a pack of excited dogs. The dim light of the street was against them. The policeman sought to break through on their bicycles, but were held back while the runners thinned out. Andy, his head clear again, ran like a deer downhill till he left the houses behind and the fields bounded the road.

His pursuers were a hundred yards behind and he jumped the dyke to take to the fields a few moments before the police came speeding down the hill on their cycles. Only the more enthusiastic of his hunters followed him over the dyke. They were losing energy and breath, and their quarry was a madman whom none of them had the courage to capture. Only the police were eager to continue the chase, and they were well behind the leaders.

Jumping clean over both a hedge and a wide ditch, Andy shook off more than half of those who had followed him over the dyke, and a backward glance told him that only four, two of them policemen, remained on his trail. The full width of a field was between them when he doubled down a hedge side as the moonlight faded and the frosted grass was darkened. He could hear them calling to each other in their confusion as he increased the distance between them by more than two hundred yards. Their cries died away, and he knew that they had taken the wrong track. Without a pause for breath he continued at the same pace till his legs ached and he could run no more. He was at least five miles from Wigtown. There were hills, hedges and woods between him and those in search of him, and feeling safer he began to walk.

Tomorrow the police would spend the day scouring the countryside for him, and he would have to hide himself well. There would be no sleep for him for hours if he was to escape. He passed through the Leighmilns land and went on towards the bridge over the Bladnoch near Kirkcowan. He was puzzled to know what had happened to him when he had left Doonhall; his mind had only seemed to come back to life when he had come round to find himself tied with the policeman standing over him. The people near had been saying, 'He's mad, dinna tak' the rope aff him.'

It had dawned on him that they meant to take him back to gaol, or maybe even to the asylum. He had forgotten Jean completely; he remembered leaving the gaol and walking out to Doonhall to see Craig for his money, though what had become of the money he did not know. A pound note and a few shillings was all that he had in his pocket, and he was sure there should have been more.

So they thought he was mad. He'd show them whether he was mad or not. Maybe they would think differently when they couldn't catch him for a week or two. Where he would go he did not know, but he would hide from them till they had forgotten all about him. Then he might find a job again.

A cold rain was falling when he crossed the bridge and took the fork that ran away from Kirkcowan towards Malzie and the smithy. The mist drifted in front of him and had he been sure of his direction he would have left the road and taken to the fields again. It was impossible to see if anything was coming up towards him, though he felt that the police would long since have given up the search at least till morning. When he began to recognize the landmarks again, he climbed the dyke and struck out into the friendly shadows of the fields, with a flock of sheep running in fright before him.

The dawn was slow in coming, although a faint greyness hung over the hills and helped him to see his way. Black shadows on the right of him told him he was nearing the mossland and he stopped for a while to uproot and peel two turnips from the field he was passing through.

There was a wood on the edge of the moss across the Malzie burn and he put a turnip in each pocket to eat when he reached it. Over on the left, where the greyness in the sky was broadening, he saw the white outline of a farm steading and farther, over the tops of trees, the hollow where the smithy stood and the schoolhouse. He thought of the smith's hen-house and decided that it was too near the smith's rising hour to try to steal a chicken. The whole roost would set up a cackling that would wake the smith, the school-mistress, and the folk in the cot-house up the road. Then he remembered the smith's garden with the potato pit sheltered by a heap of straw as it had been when he had been a boy at school.

Crossing the burn made his feet wet and he shivered in his misery. Wiping the cobwebs from his eyes he walked quietly through the trees into the open garden. A great stack of straw betrayed the potato pit, and his hands dragged the covering off as he went down on his knees and began to dig with a stick. As he did so he noticed a wooden box on an old table beside the wall of he house. Though it was still dark he marked the wire netting that covered it. There were rabbits in the box, and when the task of unearthing potatoes was over he carried them to the box and dropped them in among the rabbits.

Searching a cycle-shed he found a sickle and a pair of snares which he also deposited in the box wrapped in a torn sack. The sound of movement in the cot-house told him it was time to go. A man cleared his throat and spat noisily; a boot scraped across the floor as though its owner was preparing to dress. Listening at the wall Andy thought of the smith sitting on the edge of a warm bed, his shirt tail dangling over his knees; his face rough, sleepy and unshaven; the blankets trailing off the mattress and on to the floor. He pulled his damp jacket tighter round him and picked up the box. As he passed the hen-house at the end of the garden a bantam cock crowed although daylight was an hour and more away. He longed for a place to rest as he went up the misty little glen through which the burn ran.

By and by he sat down on a dyke and rubbed the pain from his arm, for the rough edges of the box had grazed it and left it numb. But daylight was coming faster than he had bargained for and the wood was still half a mile away over sodden ground into which his boots would sink. The last stages of the journey were slow and at every step he wanted to lie down and sleep, he was so weary with plodding through the half-frozen bog-land. It seemed that the wood had no sheltered spot where he could lay down his load and rest; he stumbled farther through the trees till he found a fallen fir with the leaves still green on its branches. Crawling into the centre of the foliage he dragged the box after him and lay down on the sack. In spite of the damp that penetrated to his skin, he managed to fall asleep as the sun came up, a red ball of fire in the east.

The police were out on the roads early in search of him, stopping ploughmen on their way to work, to ask for news of a thick-set man with black hair and the eyes of a madman. By mid-day, half the countryside knew of the happenings of the night before. Many were of the opinion that the madman had drowned himself in the Bladnoch, for not a soul had seen him since he had made his escape. The smith was too slow-witted to connect the loss of his rabbits with the story when it was told him by the grocer on his rounds. The tale had improved with the telling by the time that the smith heard it.

'Aye,' said the grocer, 'it took twelve o' them tae hold him an' he knocked them a' ower, chased the police wi' a great big knife an' would have kilt somebody if he had not heard they were away fur a gun tae shoot him. Then he took to his heels an' ran so fast that they couldna' catch him though they ran doon hill in a car after him.'

The smith grinned his disbelief and the grocer was spurred to enlarge on the story to make it convincing.

'Of course,' he added, speaking as he always did, in imitation of the maids at a mansion he was proud to serve, 'they were slow in gettin' the car started, but when they did he jumped clean ower a sevin-foot hedge an' made off lik' a hare. They say he was yin o' them queer folk that could see in the dark and the police couldna' get him fur he kenned whaur tae run an' they kept fa'in' in water holes an' the like.'

The smith's grin was wider and the teller of the tale fell silent.

'It's likely,' said the smith, 'that he fell intae the Blednach an' got drooned.'

'Aye,' said the grocer somewhat encouraged, 'they'll be watchin' the water fur him the day and the morn.' The postman came cycling up and they called to him.

'Ye heard aboot the fun in Wigtown las' nicht?' he asked before he dismounted, and the tale was retold and discussed again.

Meanwhile, the police had farmers in the neighbourhood of Wigtown searching their barns and out-houses, and almost everyone could recall unusual noises in the night, dog barks, disturbed hens, or the slamming of doors. The supposed trail led in a hundred different directions; grew warm where a cotman on the road to

Newton had seen a stranger cross the field behind his house at dawn, and led to a dead end when a boatman discovered footprints on the sand in Wigtown bay.

The prints led to the mouth of the Bladnoch and vanished in the water. They puzzled the hunters, but they turned out to be those of a well-known shore scavenger who was down in a pair of thigh-boots for a shot at the wild duck.

As the tale was spread by the butchers, grocers, and postmen who visited the outlying farms, Andy slept in the wood off the Alticry road, shivering in the cold light of the afternoon sun. Before nightfall he rose and collected wood for a fire which he lighted in a sheltered hollow once it was dark, to cook a meal of potatoes.

When it came to the killing of the first rabbit on the day following, he spent an hour bolstering up his courage. They were not like the wild rabbits he was accustomed to lifting from snare and net and breaking their necks without a single qualm. They were black-and-white tame rabbits like those he had often coveted when a small boy. He lifted the doe out of the box. She did not struggle, but sat quietly on his knees; her sensitive nose quivering and her body trembling beneath its thick covering of fur. Instead of dangling her by her back legs and delivering the death-blow behind the head he smoothed her fur and stroked her.

She sniffed his clothes nervously and tried to hide in the folds of his jacket. For a moment he was sure that he could never do it, yet what would become of them? If he released them the hungry stoats would find them, and taking them back would be difficult and dangerous. In fact, the wily smith might have some alarm set up as he often had had in his school days when young carrots had been the irresistible attraction. They had to be killed.

He caught the back legs and swung his arm quickly. The black-and-white body twitched and was still. It was easier to skin than he had expected, and it was not long until he had rigged up a crude spit with forked sticks hammered into the ground. The building of the fire in a circle of stones carried from the dyke was a slow business, for really dry wood was hard to find and a constant heat was needed for the cooking. When the process was well under way he slipped his potatoes into the fire and lay watching the steam rising from his clothes as he turned the spit. It was cold, a few feet away there was frost on the trees and when he turned his face away from the fire his breath was a jet of steam before his face.

Wigtown folk had almost ceased to talk about the incident, and the police, though they still hoped to capture Andy, without being quite sure as to the charge they would bring against him, had decided that the search was hopeless. They were of the opinion that the wanted man had either fallen into the Bladnoch or had, in some mysterious way, managed to leave the countryside. On the third day they no longer troubled to look for him.

Jean was in terror. She alone was sure that Andy was still waiting for her and would appear on the road one night to seize her and strangle the life from her. She was living in her father's old cot-house on the Kirkcowan road and every night she barred the door and barricaded it with odds and ends of furniture. The door was never opened till well after sunrise and when she went out at night she made sure that she had company right back to the house. Not infrequently she had company in her bed too, for Feeney was more than a little fond of her. Had she been unwilling to accommodate him in her bed, he would have thought nothing of forcing his company on her, but Jean was sore in need of comforting, apart from the fact that she had never been troubled with moral scruples. So Feeney shared her bed on the nights that it suited his mood though the woman had an uneasy feeling that another child would come of it. The fear that Andy would find her was with her from morning, when she rose, until night, when Feeney arrived, either to make coarse love to her or to take her into the village to the public house. By day, she took care not to venture far from the cot-house, and when the grocer called she glanced up and down the road before going out to his van to make her few purchases. The tradesman brought her the latest news each day but the story was old by now and the telling wearisome.

'Hae ye heard if they hae catched him yet?' she would ask when he pulled up to gossip with her each day on his way out of Kirkcowan.

'Ye ken, Mr Blair,' she would say, 'A'm affa feart o' that man comin' an' murderin' me.'

The grocer, who was a bit of a wit, assured her on each of these occasions that Andy would only do it once, but the frightened woman could no more than summon a faint smile at his gruesome humour.

Andy was tired of his existence in the wood. The second rabbit had been killed and cooked and the snares he had set had brought no results. The fever which had followed his fit of insanity had gone. He only knew that he was cold and miserable, that his clothes were permanently damp and the nights were becoming colder. In the greyness, before a watery dawn, he left the wood and headed back across the moss in the direction of the Kirkcowan road. After a mile of slow progress he went on to the road and walked faster by the grass verge.

Half-way to Kirkcowan a man with a cart overtook him and offered a lift. Andy sat up on the front of the cart with him, swinging his feet.

'Hoo far ir ye gan?' he enquired.

Andy thought for a second. 'Tae Kirkcone,' he replied, 'A'm gan tae a place up here.'

'Term day is no' till the morn.'

This was a surprise to Andy for he had lost all count of time. 'The folks are gan oot o' the place A was at,' he explained, 'an' A didna want tae stey.'

The man appeared to be satisfied with this and they went on to discuss ploughing and turniplifting. Andy found himself at a loss, for he had no idea of the turnip crop, being less than a week out of gaol. He was relieved when the cart reached the road end of the farm it was bound for.

The man on the cart turned his head and gazed after Andy as he went up the road. It seemed strange to him that his passenger had had no clothes with him and almost a beard on his face. More like a tramp he thought. Andy was troubled by the strong growth that covered his chin and neck. There had been no chance to shave; nothing to shave with. He decided that he was growing a beard if anyone asked him because he suffered from a sore throat. At a cot-house on the right side of the road, a child stood and watched him pass; timorously peeping over the dyke that surrounded the garden. It had black curly hair and his own dark eyes, but he did not see it as he walked with his head in the air inhaling the damp wintery smell of the earth and the dying leaves in the ditch.

In spite of the discomfort of wet clothes, he began to whistle 'The Wearing o' The Green', and kicked a stone before him. The woman in the cot-house was wiping out the porridge pot after clearing away the remains of Feeney's breakfast. Faintly, the sound of the tune came to her. It was strangely familiar. The cloth dropped from her fingers and she ran to the door. The child was staring after the man, the top of whose head was still just visible over a rise in the road.

Jean stared up the road too. Her hands were shaking, but slowly as the sound of the whistling died away she convinced herself that it could not be he; that he would not dare to show himself on the road in broad daylight. More than half assured she caught the child by the hand and led him back into the house. The door was barred for the rest of the morning.

The young policeman from Wigtown, making a tour of the district, came cycling down the hill past Andy, who went on boldly whistling. The policeman looked at him puzzled for a moment, as his machine rushed by. He had too much speed to turn and look back, but the realization that the tramp might be Walker was upsetting. At the cot-house he dismounted and turned back. The going was slow and the figure ahead might suddenly take to the fields. That was if he was Walker. But Andy kept going at the same steady pace. He knew that the policeman was coming back without looking round. He was unconcerned. At some time or other, he was bound to meet a policeman again. Much better to meet this one now; allay his suspicions if he were doubtful and face him if he recognized him. Puffing with the effort, the policeman came slowly up behind. Andy waited till he could hear the rattle of the gear-wheel and then turned.

'Howdo,' he greeted him, 'it's a hard pull up that hill.'

'It is,' said the officer and dismounted.

Then cautiously he asked, 'Where are you making for?'

'Lookin' fur a job up here aboot Kirkcone,' Andy answered.

The man scrutinised him carefully. He had only had a brief glimpse of him on that night in Wigtown and he wasn't sure. No, he concluded, it can't be Walker, he wouldn't be out on the road in the broad daylight.

'What's your name?' he demanded.

Without a second of hesitation Andy answered, 'M'Courtney' – he pronounced it 'M'Coortny'.

'Wullie M'Coortny,' he repeated.

The young policeman was an imported specimen from Glasgow, and knew nothing of the local families. He could not have asked where Andy had been born, or who his father was, and been sure of the answer, as his sergeant would have done.

He was satisfied for the time being, and when they had crossed the brow of the hill he jumped on his machine again with the backward cry of 'So long.'

'So long,' said Andy, and began to hum to himself.

CHAPTER XXII

BEFORE buying a copy of the latest issue of the *Galloway Gazette* when he reached Kirkcowan, Andy surveyed the village street for the policeman. There was no sign of him. He had taken the turning for Wigtown evidently, and dismissed from his mind his suspicions of the hatless figure he had met on the road. Purchasing a cheap shaving set, at the same time, Andy went on up the street munching biscuits from a packet in his pocket. He was thankful that he met no one that would recognize him as he passed the last of the houses. Further up the road, he crossed a field and shaved himself by the side of a burn.

Afterwards, having washed and tidied himself, he opened the paper and scanned the situations. There were three or four places open in the Kirkcowan district and he studied them. The most likely was a place for a ploughman advertised by Yates of Blackrigs. On the road again, he stopped a boy on a bicycle and asked the way to Blackrigs.

'Yon'er,' pointed the boy.

Andy followed the direction of the grimy finger and saw a small white farmstead on the side of a hill. It was sheltered by trees, but there seemed to be only two outbuildings besides a tarred hen-house. He thanked the boy and went up the narrow winding cart track to Blackrigs.

When he was in sight of the court, a big brown collie began to bark warningly and advanced down the slope to meet him.

'Hullo boy,' said Andy, but the dog growled and showed its teeth.

Looking up, Andy saw a woman's head peering over the curtains of the window at him. The collie continued to growl as he knocked on the door. There was no answer and he knocked again, louder this time. When he tried the catch he found the door was bolted.

'Is there onybody in?' he called, and listening he heard the slither of a pair of loose slippers coming across the floor.

'Is there onybody in?' he called once more.

The bolt on the door squeaked as it was pulled back and the door was opened about two inches for him to catch a glimpse of the corner of a blue dress.

Part of the woman's head appeared at the opening and a soft voice said, 'Whut dae ye want?'

'Is the maister at hame?'

'Whut dae ye want?' The question was repeated.

'A come tae see aboot the place,' said Andy.

The door opened a fraction wider, but the woman was still mistrustful. 'He'll no be back till this efternin,' she told him.

'A'll wait,' he replied, but the door was firmly closed.

Sitting on an empty hen-coop, he made friends with the dog and shared his biscuits with him, watching the house the while. Twice he saw the curtains shake and the tip of a head vanish below them, but the door remained shut. When the biscuits had been eaten, he began to feel really hungry. The watery outline of the sun told him it was after noon.

He was gazing down the road when he heard the door close and there was a plate of broth on the step.

As he lifted it, the voice from the other side of the door said, 'Wull ye no' gang awa'?'

'A'm no' a tramp,' he assured her, 'A'm a plooman an' A'm efter the place.'

Once more he heard the slippered feet coming to the door. It opened wide enough to allow a plate of potatoes and salt beef to pass through.

'Here,' said the woman.

He took the plate and laid it down on the step with his eye threateningly on the dog. At about half-past three, he saw a pony and trap draw up at the gate in the hollow and a man alighted to lead the horse through. The woman had seen it too.

She opened the door and said, 'Gie me the plates.'

Andy saw a plump red-headed figure of a woman of about his own age. Her face was handsome, and she had shy brown eyes like a frightened animal. She looked at the plate instead of at his face and blushed scarlet.

The man halted his horse near the door and said, 'What dae ye want?'

'A hae come aboot the place,' Andy answered.

'Oh ye hae, hae ye?' and he walked on up the road leading the horse by the head.

Andy was undecided what to do, for the man and the trap went on past the end of the buildings, following the track over the hill. After hesitating for a moment Andy went after them, having made up his mind that this was Yates and not some one on his way to a farm on the other side of the hill.

Catching up with them, the man and the horse, Andy walked at their side till they came to the remainder of the steading, nestling in a small wood at the back of the hill. Yates appeared to be unconscious of his presence.

'Here,' he said at length as he unyoked the horse, 'lead him intae the stable there.'

Andy did as he was told, and once inside the small stable he began to take the harness off. Yates came in when he had wheeled the machine into the shed opposite.

'Hae ye been waitin' lang?' he asked.

'An hour or twa.'

'Did she gie ye ocht tae eat?'

'Aye, she gied me ma denner,' said Andy, wondering what she was to him.

From the look of him, his daughter probably, but you could never tell; she might be his wife. What a wife for such a poor-looking man, thought Andy. They left the stable and went back over the hill.

'Whaur wur ye afore?' Yates enquired.

'A haena had a place since hervest. A wus up in Kir'coobry. A wee place at New Gallowa'. A wus there fur twa year.'

'Whut ir ye ca'd?'

'Hanlon,' decided Andy, 'Pat Hanlon, ma fether wus Irish, bit A wus born up by Stranraer. Ma mither wus a M'Guigan.'

'A bad lot o' folks they M'Guigans,' observed Yates.

Andy grinned. 'Ma fether aye said that.'

'Whut hae ye been daein' since hervest?'

He had been expecting the question. 'A had a while at the taties, an' A hae been on the roads since, up aboot Creetown.'

'A canna' pey a lot tae a plooman, whut wud ye be askin'?'

Andy decided to be moderate in his demands, 'Sixteen shillin'.'

'Ye'll milk tae?' bargained Yates.

'Aye,' agreed Andy.

They were at the house.

'Bring in yer things.'

Andy smiled, 'A hae nae things,' he confessed.

Yates seemed not to have heard; seated at the table he ordered, 'Ma denner, Molly, an' gie the man here a cup o' tea.'

The woman laid a steaming plate of potatoes before him, and went to the dresser for a cup. Andy warmed himself at the fire and watched her. Once she caught his eye upon her and blushed again. Without a word she placed the cup in his hand and poured the tea into it. When the man at the table had finished his meal, she carried the teapot over to his elbow and lifted away the plate.

'Ye'll gie us a han' wi' the milkin' the nicht,' suggested Yates.

'Richt ye ir,' said Andy, still with his eyes on the woman, who had not as much as smiled since the moment he had first seen her.

'There's twa hun'er acres tae this place,' remarked the man at the table, evidently being more disposed to talk after eating, 'an' there's a lot o' work fur twa men. If the place wusna ma ain, A wud hae a man or anither boy tae help me, bit there's nae money in the place even withoot rent tae pey. Whun her mither deed' – he pointed to the woman – 'A thocht o' sellin', bit naebody wanted tae buy, so here A am.'

So she's his daughter, thought Andy, in spite of the red hair. The woman saw he was looking at her again and bowed her head over the pot she was cleaning. Andy could not take his eyes off her. Yates was so sunk in the telling of his story that he did not notice.

It was dark outside.

At length Yates rose. 'We'll hae tae be ower tae the milkin' in a wee while. Hae ye the hens locked up, Molly?'

Molly threw her coat over her shoulders and went out.

'Can A hae a drap water tae wesh ma han's?' asked Andy.

'The water can's in the corner and the basin's on the table,' Yates told him.

Drying his hands, he heard the woman's hobnailed boots across the court.

Yates pulled his coat on. 'She'll be awa' ower,' he said.

Andy turned up the collar of his jacket and followed him out. The big dog stretched himself on guard in front of the fire. Both men bent their heads into the wind and splashed through the mud on their way over the hill. Yates turned once and said something but the wind carried it away.

'Aye,' agreed Andy, from force of habit.

They came to the dimly lit byre and searched the shadows for milking-stools. Molly was already seated with her face buried in the flank of a quiet Ayrshire. The milk spurted melodiously into her pail. 'Start at the bottom,' muttered Yates. There were only thirty-six cows in the byre. He counted them as he walked down. One stall on either side was empty. His hands were unaccustomed to milking and the cow was restless at the touch of a stranger.

He was last to lift his pail and go up the walk to the dairy at the finish. Molly went up the road while they washed the pails.

'Ye'll start whaur A left aff in the fiel' in the hollow the morn,' said his new master.

Andy felt thrilled at being back at the plough again. The horse in the stable had to be fed and the ploughing pair, who stood with their heads over the gate, were led in out of the darkness ready for the following day's work.

'A should hae had them in afore this, but A forgot,' Yates explained.

'You'll be wantin' twa three bits o' claithes,' said Yates.

He had been at Blackrigs a fortnight and the boss was making ready to go to Wigtown.

'Aye,' replied Andy, 'A could dae wi' a tap coat an' a pair o' bits. Anither shirt an' a pair o' troosers tae.'

He was wheeling out the trap and the horse was standing unattended in the court. When all was ready they rode over the hill. At the house, Andy got down and Yates went down the road.

'Yer denner's on the table,' Molly called to him.

He scraped his boots at the door and went in out of the fine rain that was falling. Cleaning his plate, he looked up as the woman came in.

'Ye ken,' he said as she sat down, 'I thocht he wus yer fether.'

She had mastered the habit of blushing when he spoke to her.

'Did ye? Ma mither wus his hoosekeeper,' she told him; 'whun she deed, A took her place.'

There was a pause.

'Did she sleep wi' him tae?' he asked.

'Aye, but he's no ma fether. Ma fether wus plooman here, bit he gaed awa' whun she started tae carry on wi' him. Whun she deed, hae just said ye'll sleep doon the stair the nicht. A had nae whaur else tae gang. He used tae chase me roon the place afore she deed, bit ma mither aye watched him ower much.'

'Whut did the last man ley fur?'

This time she blushed.

'There wus ower much cerry-on at the hervest.'

'A see,' said Andy.

He rose. 'Hae ye an oul' oil-coat?'

'There's nae need tae gang back tae the fiel' fur a while,' she told him.

She was plump and warm, he thought, and friendly too, but the last man had had to go. He could not afford to be on the road again looking for a job; maybe the police still had him in mind.

'No,' he said, 'A think A'll gang doon an' get a bit mair din. There's a hell o' a plooin' tae be din afore new'rs day.'

She was crestfallen as she went for the oil-coat.

In the days that followed he realized that she was more than fond of him, but Yates seemed to ignore the evidence before his eyes.

'Ye nivir gang onywhaur,' she remarked one evening.

Andy grinned, 'Whaur wud A gang?'

'Doon tae Kirkcone fur a drink,' she suggested.

'Och A cudna' be bothered.'

Yates looked up from his paper, 'There's nae need tae be galivantin' the roads in this wauther,' he observed, 'an' ye can gie him a dram oot o' the bottle doon the hoose.'

Molly brought the whiskey and poured him a glassful.

'Dae ye want yin?' she asked Yates.

'A'm gan tae ma bed,' he said.

She filled Andy's glass again when he had gone and poured one for herself. She sat on the stool opposite him and drew her skirt up round her thighs as if to warm her legs before the fire. He knew that that was far from being her idea. Draining his glass, he looked at her. She was surprisingly brazen for a woman who could blush so easily.

'Had on a meenit,' she murmured and leaned across with the bottle in her hand.

She balanced herself with her other hand on his knee and the neck of her dress drooped.

'Hae anither,' she invited.

For a moment he was ready to lay down his glass and take her, but the sound of the boss's voice brought him back to earth.

'Ir ye comin' tae yer bed, Molly?' he yelled from the backroom.

She straightened up without pouring the whiskey and called,

'A'll be ben in a wee while.'

They heard him muttering to himself. She crossed her legs and uncrossed them again for his benefit and allowed her skirt to roll farther back on her thighs, but it was lost on him now.

'Ye're a cool yin,' she laughed as she stood up and took the bottle with her.

He pretended not to hear. At the door she stopped and looked back at him.

'Guid nicht,' she cried.

He grunted in reply, and stooped to take his boots off as she closed the door.

She carried the cans for him while he did the sowing. Yates was in his bed with the cold, a cold that had come as a surprise to him when he tried to rise for the milking in the morning. She sat closer to him at dinner-time and followed him about the steading like the collie. When he went in to the stable for the horse to take the sacks of oats down to the field, she pushed her way up the stall and pretended to help him on with the harness. She blocked his path when he went to go out. He slapped her on the hip playfully, and waited for her to retreat. Instead, she stood her ground, and he could feel her plump body pressing against him.

He was still nervous of Yates becoming suspicious.

'Come on, Molly,' he pleaded.

'Surely ye're strong enough tae clear the wey fur yersel',' and she laughed in his face.

'Is it a kiss ye're wantin'?' he asked her.

'Mebbe.' She put her arm up round his neck and he embraced her.

The kiss sent tremors running through his body. It was a long time since he had kissed a woman, and none had ever responded quite so passionately as Molly.

'Hey let me go,' he murmured into her hair.

There was unusual strength in those plump arms. He struggled with her and the horse became restless. Still she clung to his neck even when he forced her out of the stall by sheer force.

'Now come on, hae feneshed, Molly,' but she only held him tighter. 'A'll hae tae hurt ye if ye daena' let go. Ye nivir ken he micht be ower the hill an' catch us.'

'So ye're feart,' she muttered, and it looked as though she was about to cry.

He stood and watched her helplessly as she sat down on a pile of hay in the next stall.

'Dinna greet, Molly,' he said, 'there's nocht tae greet fur.'

She buried her face in her apron and sobbed.

'Och tae hell, wumin,' he stammered, and went up the stall. She kept her head down while he leaned over her; but when he put his arm round her shoulders, she turned and caught him round the waist. They rolled over in the hay. Her skirt was rumpled round her hips and he saw that she wore nothing underneath.

'Ir ye no feart ye'll hae a wean?' he asked.

'Ir ye feart?'

The horse stamped the floor and a hen in search of a nesting-place picked her way daintily over the hay past them. He sat up after a while, and brushed the hay from his clothes. She straightened her disarranged skirt and lay watching him as he led the horse out.

Hay was still dangling from her when she came out and climbed on to the cart without a word. He glanced at her as he heaved the last bag into the bottom of the cart. Her eyes were big and dreamy. Half-asleep, he thought. At the field, she threw her arms round his neck as he passed the front of the cart and slid to the ground.

'Tae hell wi' ye, we hae work tae dae. Get somethin' din, ye lazy bitch.'

He was cool and irritable. The hurt look on her face meant nothing to him. Dropping the bags at intervals along the field, he turned the horse when he had finished and jogged up the road to the stable. She stood looking after him with a whipped-dog look on her face. She was still standing fumbling with the same bag when he entered the field again. With the sowing fiddle in his hand, he approached her.

'Come on, Molly. Dinna tak' the huff at me. We hae work tae dae an' we hae wasted enough time a'ready.'

She bent her head over the sack and was silent.

'Dae ye hear me, Molly?' he cajoled.

'Aye,' she said softly.

'Come on then, an' let me get started, or we'll no' hae din the nicht.'

She wiped her eyes with the end of her apron and poured the can of seed into the fiddle.

In the evening, they struggled through the milking without the help of the boss. Andy was secretly pleased, for Molly seemed to have lost her senses. She followed him out and in the byre, and pushed herself against him every time he came near her. He said nothing, but hurried through the milking, and refused her help when it came to washing the pails. Nevertheless, she stayed in the dairy, watching him work, and when he had done she walked by his side over the hill. In the house, he escaped her for a moment by going up to his room and changing his shirt. First she called to him, and then, when he failed to answer, she mounted the stair after him.

'Whut dae ye want?' he asked, buttoning the shirt and tucking it into his trousers.

She sat down on the bed before him.

'A think A'll sleep here the nicht,' she smiled.

'Come on, get doon the stair an' get ma tea ready,' he pleaded, and caught her arm.

She pulled him suddenly on to the bed with her and threw her arms round him.

'A'm affa fond o' ye, Pat,' she whispered.

He felt the blood throbbing in his ears. The pressure of her body on his. She kissed his hairy chin with her big wet lips. He realized that in another second he would take her again, and that would be madness with Yates downstairs in bed, perhaps puzzling at the unusual silence.

He pushed her away and stood up. Almost savagely he threw her back on the bed when she reached up to embrace him.

'A think A hear him gettin' up,' he told her.

She rose and stood listening for a moment, then went hastily down the rickety stairs. He waited a while, then followed. She was preparing the supper when he entered the room again. Sitting down on the stool by the fireside, he warmed his hands. A moment later, he heard Yates fumbling with the loose doorhandle. He came into the room with his braces dangling in two loops round his hips.

'Hullo boy,' he said.

He was grinning like an imbecile, and his eyes were bloodshot.

'Ye hae been at the whiskey while A wus awa',' said Molly, and went over to him when he swayed unsteadily, and all but fell.

'A bottle an' a half,' he stuttered, and it was all she could do to stagger across the floor with him.

Once in front of the fire, he began to sing silly little confused snatches of old songs. While Andy ate his meal he recited Burns and fell off his chair on to the floor. Molly asked Andy to help her lift him. Hardly had he settled back in the chair once more, than he fell asleep and snored so loudly that the collie cocked his head on the side in wonderment.

'Gi'e me a han' tae pit him tae bed,' said Molly.

Yates slept soundly as they half-carried him between them into the bedroom. Molly laid him out on the bed and threw the blankets over him.

'He'll lie lik' a daid man till efter denner-tim' the morn,' she said, 'bit A'm no' keepin' him company the nicht. A'm comin' up the stair wi' you.'

Andy looked at the sleeping man on the bed and blew out the light. Molly laughed and came after him. When the fire went low in the grate, she followed him up to bed. Her clothes were off and she was under the blankets before him.

In the room below, Yates lay with his mouth open and snored; moonlight, glinting through the window, fell on his upturned face. He was in need of shaving and feathers from the pillow were sticking in his tousled hair. He slept soundly till long after daybreak.

Molly brought him in a bowl of gruel. He had no idea that she had not slept with him.

'Whut kin' o' day is't?' he asked, squinting to keep the light from his eyes.

'The sun's oot,' she told him, 'bit there's a cal' wun' bla'in.'

CHAPTER XXIII

THEY were working at the hay. It was early July. Andy was first to get to the field and it was a while before Molly and Yates followed. He was raking in the rows round the edge of the bracken patch in the hollow. He looked up and saw them coming down the hill together. Molly was lagging behind Yates. They were almost up to the gate when he saw her fall. She's tripped, he thought, but when Yates bent over her, he knew that something was wrong.

'Whut is it?' he yelled, but Yates paid no heed.

He lifted the woman and carried her up the track towards the farm. Andy saw him staggering under his burden, and followed him with his eyes till the buildings hid him from view. There was nothing for it but to get on with the work. After about an hour, he saw Yates coming back to the field; he was walking quickly. Andy stopped working and waited till he was within hailing distance.

'Whut was wrang?' he shouted.

Yates did not reply until he was close to Andy. He was scowling.

'She's gan tae hae a wean,' he said.

Andy began to rake again.

Yates followed him and caught him by the arm. 'Hae ye been wi' her?' he demanded.

Andy shook the hand off his arm and returned the scowl.

'Aff coorse A haena,' he answered, 'ye ken bloody fine A haena.'

He pushed his face close to the shorter man's and glowered threateningly.

Yates turned and picked up a rake and they worked silently side by side. Molly came down to the field with the tea an hour later. She looked pale and she had a bruise on her cheek. She was strangely quiet as she handed out the cups. Andy lifted his share and carried it over to the bracken patch. Yates was supping his tea from his bowl with a dour look on his face. Molly sat staring vacantly at the blue mist that hung over the hills in the north.

'It's no' mine!' Yates burst out suddenly, 'it's yon bastard that gied ye it.'

Andy pretended not to hear.

'It's yon bastard that had ye whun A was oot o' the road.'

Yates leaped to his feet and threw the bowl of tea at her.

Andy stiffened and slowly balanced his tea on a pile of hay. Yates came running across to him, seizing a hayfork that was sticking in the ground between them. Molly began to run up the field towards the steading.

'A'll fenesh ye, ye dirty bastard,' yelled Yates, and Andy levered himself off the brackens to rise.

'Had on,' he cautioned as he got to his feet, 'ye're an alder man ner me an' A wudna lik' tae lay han' on ye.'

Yates, still running, lunged at him with the fork. Andy reached forward and caught it by the prongs. They struggled for a second and then Andy pulled it from his hands.

'Ye wud kill me, wud ye?' he gritted through his teeth as he advanced on him.

Yate's look of fury gave place to fear. He retreated before the fork which Andy was pointing at his stomach. Then he stumbled backwards on a heap of hay and fell full length. Andy stood over him and jabbed the fork into him.

'Ye're the oul' bastard that was gan tae kill me. A hae a min' tae plant this in yer belly an' let ye lie for the maucks tae feed on.'

Yates made no move to get up.

'So A got her wi' a wean? Whut happens whun ye sleep wi' her? Ye ken fine the wean's yours. A haena been near the wumin. Dae ye hear me?' He bent down and caught him by the collar.

Yates was silent.

'Dae ye hear?' He shook him and dragged him to his feet. Still the scowling little man made no reply.

'Dae ye hear noo?' said Andy and smashed him to the ground with a blow in the face.

Yates made no effort to rise, so he lifted him to his feet again.

'Whut dae ye say tae it noo?' Andy asked once more. He struck the defenceless face with all his strength and prevented the body from falling.

With blood trickling from the corner of his mouth Yates muttered, 'A was wrang.'

Andy released his hold on the jacket, and he fell back onto the hay. Turning, Andy went up the field and through the steading on his way to the house.

The door was locked and he shook it. There was no answer to his knocking.

'Let me in,' he called.

'Is that you, Pat?'

'Aye,' he assured her.

The bar was slipped back and he went in.

'Ye're gan tae hae a wean then?'

'Aye,' she avoided his eye.

'Wha's the fether o' it?'

'Ye'll be the fether o' it,' she told him after a pause.

'Whut aboot him?'

'Weel,' she said softly, 'A hae been sleepin' wi' him for three year an' nivir had a wean afore.'

'It could be his for a' that,' he argued.

She stood up when she heard Yates at the door. He came in.

'Ir ye comin' back tae the fiel' tae gie me a han'?' he addressed Andy, who noticed that he had wiped the blood from his mouth.

'A'richt,' he said, and picked up his battered hat from the form behind the table. They worked on till milking-time without exchanging a word.

Andy was late in getting over to the house for his supper, after letting the kye out. When he pushed through the door, Yates was waiting for him; sitting on a chair in the corner with his gun across his knees.

'Ye were a big man whun ye leathered an oul' man this efternin',' he said, holding the gun higher.

Molly watched him with wide eyes from the passage door.

'A should hae kilt ye,' said Andy recklessly.

The hands clutching the gun shook.

'Gie him his claithes, Molly.'

She obeyed the order by tossing Andy's clothes in a bundle at his feet.

'Noo, get doon the road an' nivir show face here again!'

'Ma money,' insisted Andy.

'Gae ben the hoose', he told Molly, 'an' bring me the money.'

She came back and placed a leather bag in his hand. He opened it and extracted ten pounds.

'Gie him that.'

Andy counted the money and stood hesitating for a moment.

'Whut ir ye waitin' for?' Yates asked.

He finished his slow mental calculation and turned without replying. Yates followed him to the door and watched him go down the road. He turned in the shelter of a thorn tree and looked back through its branches to see if Yates was still watching him. When he saw that he had gone back into the house, he sat down on the bank and examined his clothes. The sun went down, and when he thought it dark enough he went quietly back up the road. As he neared the house, he walked more carefully. The dog was still on the step and he could hear the man's voice as he raged at the woman.

He was just about over the hill when he heard the door open. He stopped and looked back. In the dusk he could make out the figure of Yates. He was standing on the doorstep gazing down the road. Andy sank down into the shadow of the dyke and watched him. After a glance at the sky to gauge the weather, Yates called the dog and closed the door. Andy pulled himself to his feet and went over the hill.

For the first few hours Andy bedded in the stable, but towards morning he rose and watched the dawn. Dodging round the steading, he waited until they had the kye in and started to milk. Then he went quickly up the road and over to the house. The key was in its usual place under the stone by the door. He lifted it and entered the house, locking the door behind him. During the night, he had thought it all out. At first he had decided to fire the outhouses, and finally he had thought of stealing the money while they were at the milking. He searched the back rooms carefully until he found the leather bag. There were thirty pounds in it. He counted them slowly, knowing that the milking would not be done for at least another hour. A last look round brought him a fat gold watch and three half-sovereigns. Back in the kitchen he resisted the porridge on the table, but cut himself a generous helping of salt meat, which he packed between two slices of bread. A cut off the big cheese went into his pocket with three floury scones from a cupboard. He was back out in the road and the key in its place within half an hour.

It was much later that Yates came hurrying over for his porridge. By that time he was well on his way to Glenluce whistling, 'The Wearin' o' the Green' through his teeth.

With more than forty pounds in his pocket, he thought it safer to walk than take the train. After walking till he was tired, and taking the train at Glenluce, he reached Stranraer late at night.

In a public house, he asked a man where he could sleep the night. 'A can pey,' he added.

'Come hame wi' me an' the wife'll fin a place for ye,' said the stranger.

Andy went with him to a small cottage near the water's edge.

'A freen o' ma mither's deed a month ago an' left me twa three poun',' he explained as the woman of the house made up a bed for him on a battered old couch.

'A haena much o' it left, bit whun it's din A'll fin a place.'

He was careful to see that the money was well hidden before he went to sleep.

In the morning he walked through the town. It was unusually crowded for its size, for there was a cattle-show in progress. After paying to go into the show, he wandered round a fair in the next field. The fair was quiet because the men were still interested in the cattle, but in the afternoon, having bought his dinner in the show-field, he went back and spent a few coppers throwing at the coco-nuts.

At the next booth a small man in a bowler hat was yelling himself hoarse. 'Who'll challenge the Battlin' Tinsmith for a purse of five pounds?' he yelled.

The Tinsmith stood on the platform glowering at the crowd. He was beetle-browed and unshaven, with a close-cropped head and bulging muscles. Andy paid and went in after a red-faced youngster had challenged the Tinsmith. There were two other exhibition fights, and Andy, who had never seen a boxing match or a boxing glove before, stretched his neck so as to miss nothing. When the Tinsmith's fight took place, the referee announced that the five pounds would be paid to the challenger if he could face the Tinsmith for three rounds. The red-faced boy, stripped to the waist, came out of his corner with his gloves raised; swayed to avoid a fast left and was knocked down with a vicious right. He failed to rise at the count of ten and was carried to his corner.

The referee repeated the challenge and leaned over the ropes. 'What about you?' he pointed at Andy.

'Gang on,' urged the man at Andy's elbow.

He was pushed through the crowd towards the ring.

'A'richt,' he said, and the referee helped him to clamber through the ropes.

The crowd worried him at first. When he had the gloves tied on they called, 'Murder him, Darkie.'

He smiled back at them and when the bell rang he walked lightly in his stocking feet across the ring to meet the Tinsmith. When the left that had fooled his predecessor came swinging at his head, Andy met it with his broad forearm. The right which naturally followed staggered him slightly, but he shook his head and held against the rain of blows that met him. Then, seeing the Tinsmith's face clear as he was hammered about the head, Andy straightened his thick hairy arm and sent his opponent reeling on his heels.

The crowd yelled with delight. 'Knock the guts oot o' him, Darkie,' they shouted, as he covered his face with one hand and stepped in after the Tinsmith. A left that would have done credit to a veteran put the Tinsmith on his back. Andy wanted to hit the referee when he rushed in and pushed him back. The crowd was standing up and shouting its head off. Andy saw the Tinsmith look at the referee and shake his head. The counting began. At nine the counter paused, but the man on the floor remained where he was.

The referee came across and raised Andy's hand.

'Pat Hanlon, the winner,' he said, and counted out the five pounds.

The spectators had lost interest and were drifting from the booth.

'Just a minute,' said the referee, as Andy prepared to follow them. He turned and at the same moment pushed the money deeper into his pocket. The referee grinned.

'Ever boxed before?' he enquired.

'No,' said Andy.

'How'd you like to fight again to-night?'

'Hoo much dae A get fur it?'

'Thirty shillings, and you lose to Joe here.'

Andy thought for a second.

'Richt,' he said.

'Come back at seven o'clock,' the referee told him.

The crowd outside the booth in the evening was bigger. Andy went up to the man at the door.

'A'm Hanlon,' he said, and he was shown in.

'You'll stand up to Joe for two rounds and then be knocked out half-way through the third when I come between you for holding,' the referee, whose name he learned was Meakin, told him.

The crowd filed into the booth rapidly. After another pair of exhibition bouts, Meakin announced, 'A return fight between Pat Hanlon and the Battling Tinsmith. This afternoon, these two men fought and Hanlon won on a knock-out. The Tinsmith has challenged him to a return contest tonight for a purse of ten pounds.'

Andy grunted. That was the game. The bell went and he went out to meet the Tinsmith.

At the end of a quiet round, he told the man who waved a towel over his face, 'Tell Meakin A'm no' gan tae dae it.'

In the next round he fought back strongly and forced the Tinsmith to retreat to his own corner. The first round had been nothing but pretence, but now, using his brawny forearms to take the blows, and sinking his head into the muscles of his shoulders, Andy shuffled after his opponent in deadly earnest. At the end of the round, having taken sore punishment on the face, Andy went back to his corner. Meakin came over to him and said, 'It's a dirty trick, but you'll no' get away with the money.'

'We'll see,' said Andy.

The Tinsmith came at him like a madman when the round opened. He defended his face clumsily, taking more blows in the mouth than in the previous round. The Tinsmith tried to butt him in the stomach, and he struck him a hard blow in the neck. They were out in the centre of the ring; Andy, by sheer strength, forced back his opponent's arms and dropped him with a hefty punch between the eyes. As the uproar died, Meakin slowly counted Joe out, and at the end he held up Andy's arm, but there was no handing over of money.

'Gi'e him his ten poun',' shouted some one in the audience, but Meakin ignored the demand.

Andy struggled into his shirt and jacket and went across to Meakin.

'Gi'e me the ten poun',' he said.

Meakin shook his head. 'A tell you what I'll do,' he said, 'A'll give you thirty shillings a week if you'll come with us to Ayr and box on Saturday.'

Andy thought for a moment; twice as much as he could get a week on a farm.

'Richt,' he said.

Meakin handed him his thirty shillings for the evening's fight and he took it with a smile.

'You can sleep in the trailer with Joe,' offered Meakin.

'A'll get ma things,' replied Andy, and went out.

The fair was closing when he came back and all the people had gone. One by one the lights guttered out. He went round the side of the booth to the trailer. Meakin stepped down and took his things. The trailer smelt of cooking and sweaty clothes. It was some time before he could get to sleep and his bedmate snored.

In the morning he wandered round watching the fair folk packing away their stalls and booths. A girl who had danced snakelike, supposedly Indian dances in a neighbouring tent the night before, was washing a baby on the steps of a motor caravan. She was as white as he was and not half so handsome as she had looked when she had danced a few times outside the tent to lure the men inside. She looked up and saw him watching her and smiled. He smiled at her and went over to the caravan.

'Hallow,' she said.

Some kind of foreigner, he thought.

'Hallow,' he answered.

'You ain't bin wiv Meakin long, 'ave yer?' she asked.

She was a foreigner, he decided, and yet he could understand something of what she was saying.

'Aye,' he said, after a pause, 'A'm wi' Meakin.'

'Course yer know,' she went on, 'you'll soon git ter like it. It ain't so bad. Nah my ole man, he fought 'e'd never stick it, bit terdey there ain't nobody wot likes the life more'n 'e do.'

He nodded vaguely, not understanding a word she had said. A short man in plus-fours came out of the caravan. He grinned at Andy and slapped the girl on the behind.

' 'Ere,' she said, 'I ain't got nuthin' on underneaf.'

She lifted her skirt and displayed her naked hip. There was a red mark where he had slapped her. Her husband laughed and tickled the baby's feet. The girl smiled at Andy again and lifted the child. He turned and walked on.

A very small man was loading a van with crates of cheap china and delft ware. 'Gi'e me a han', wull ye?' he appealed to Andy.

They loaded the crates together. Andy did the lion's share of the work.

'Ye're workin' wi' Meakin then?' he said when they had finished. 'He's no' a bad man tae work for, they tell me, bit did ye ever fight afore?'

'Och aye,' said Andy.

'A mean did ye ever fight for a leevin afore?'

'No,' he admitted.

The small man looked serious. 'Weel boy,' he said kindly, 'A wud jist awa' back tae the farm. If ye stey here ye'll sterve in the winter whun there's nae need o' shows. Ye're strong, bit there'll be times whun ye'll meet better men an' tak' a sair batterin' for yer money. Awa' back tae yer ploo an' yer byre afore it's too late, boy. This is nae life for ye.'

Andy looked at the small man. He was a strange little stunted being with good-natured wrinkles at the corners of his eyes.

'Think ye're wrang. . . .' He broke off at the thought of the fields he had ploughed in the crisp November mornings; the warmth of the stable when the horses were in to feed in the winter; the yellow gold of the oat crop; the smell of the potato blossom and peats. He thought of them without realizing that they meant all that was beautiful in his life. Those things and the friendly shadows of firwoods; the sweep of the bare brown land in the autumn; the holy quietness of mild spring mornings, when you could hear cart-wheels on roads miles away and the crowing of cocks from hidden farms so that it seemed that the hen-roost was just behind the first knowe. They were part of a past that had been, in spite of his poaching and fighting, a gloriously contented and peaceful life.

'So ye think A'm wrang, boy, dae ye?' said the old man. He smiled ruefully, 'Ye'll be throwin' awa' the best o' yer life, boy. Yer heart'll be broke, an' ye'll sit often an' greet sair for yer fiels, yer cot-hoose an' yer ain folk.'

'A hae nae folk o' ma ain,' answered Andy. He was beginning to resent this old man who had the power to make his heart ache for the things that had always been his unexciting lot; and then, as if to apologize, he added, 'A can aye come back. There'll aye be byres tae muck here, an' fiels tae ploo.' He wanted to hurt the old man for making him feel sorry to go. 'Did ye ever work in a wet hervest, lift rotten turnips that were frozen, get wet tae the skin an' hae yer face an' hans hacked wi' the cal'?'

The old man put his hand on his arm. 'There's nae finer place,

boy, than working in the fiels. There's jist you an' the Lord God and
the green grass. Nocht metters. Folks in the toons haes tae work bi'
the clock, bit in the fiels there's nae clock bit the sun. There's aye
anither day tae work; there's the hills and the dykes like' they wur
whun yer granfether wus a boy. Bit ye gang tae the toon an' ye're
aye wonnerin' whut time o' day it is. Every man is lik' the next.
Everybody eats an' sleeps at the same time. They ken nocht aboot
the fiels an' the wee birds, the snigger o' a horse, whaur the fairy
tatties grow or whaur the hare beds in the holla.'

They were the things that he had noticed as a boy. They were
part of his knowledge of life. These things were all he knew about.
Somehow no one had ever drawn his attention to them; even if they
had asked him why he loved to be alive, he could not have told
them. Yet these things were his reason for being. Once he had been
happy without this urge for money that was forcing him away from
the only life there could ever be for him.

The old man's voice droned on sorrowfully, telling the story of a
thwarted soul in the simple tongue of the farm folk. Had he been a
poet, the old man could not have found Andy's sentimental heart
quicker. He talked with a sob in his throat and the bead of a tear in
the corner of each eye. 'God, boy, there's nae place lik' the fiels an'
hills ye hae kent since the day ye first could walk; lik' the woodsides
an' burns o' yer ain wee bit. Tae ken every turn o' the lonely road
hame; tae ken the road ends as ye come tae them; tae ken tae look
fur chimney-pots abin the hill or amang the trees an' the very twists
o' the dykes that rin awa' on baith sides o' the road.'

He felt the ancient's worn hand clasping his and looked at his
boots. When he looked up again, the old man had turned and was
walking away. He seemed to have shrunk farther into his ragged suit
and his white hair hung over his collar.

CHAPTER XXIV

ANDY'S heart ached. He could not tell Meakin and have him laugh in his face, nor could he slip away, for they were already calling him to come across to the caravan. He turned and walked to them. The caravan was pulling out of the mud into which it had sunk. Meakin and two of his helpers were in the car in front and Meakin was driving.

'Climb up behind with Joe,' he called as they trundled past.

Andy obeyed and clambered into the caravan.

As they left the field he stood looking back, swaying to the bumps. At the gate, they passed the little old man whom he had helped with the crates of china. They looked at each other until the caravan turned the bend. There was misery on both their faces.

It was past mid-day. He went back into the smell of cooking and stale clothes and sat down beside Joe, who was reading a brightly coloured love novel.

Joe put down the book and regarded him for a moment or two.

'Y'know,' he said at length, 'A wouldn't start this game if A could live again. There's nuthin' in ut but movin' from place to place an' gettin' yer face smashed up for a bob or two. Y're good for nuthin' ut the end of ut, an' y'can't fight when y're old.'

'Mebbe A'd be better if A didna start?' suggested Andy.

Joe looked happier.

'Y'would,' he replied.

Andy stood at the door again and watched the white road come racing out from the tail of the caravan. For an hour he stood with his heart sinking as the farms, bathed in the afternoon sun, slipped by on either side. Then the car in front began to labour up a hill with its speed slackening at every yard. He stepped back and lifted his clothes off the bunk. Joe stood aside to let him pass. Another small white farm, with red and spreckled hens scraping in its court, fell away behind them as they mounted the hill.

They were picking up speed again slowly. He swung a leg over the back of the caravan.

'So long, Joe,' he said, and let himself drop on to the hard road.

Joe grinned and waved a friendly hand.

'So long,' he called, and the blue caravan sped over the hill.

Andy picked himself up and smiled. There was something pleasant in the pain of the bruises on his hip. It was fine to be going down the hill, with his clothes in a bundle under his arm; down to the farm on the face of the hill, where the hens sought their food in the tidy courtyard. It was fine to be sure that he would never leave this countryside with its fir woods stretching along the tops of hills like the mane on a horse's neck; with its quiet sleepy farms basking in the sun; its cool breezes and nodding fields of oats.

He walked briskly to the farm.

The hens scattered from his path as he went up and knocked on the weather-beaten door. It was half-open, and through it he could see an old woman coming to answer his knock. A clock ticked merrily from the room. A cat stole past him, and he could smell a girdle of floury scones that hung over the fire.

A dark-skinned old woman stood before him. Her contented wrinkled face smiled and he forgot everything.

'Ma name's Andy Walker,' he said and smiled back at her, 'A wunner if ye'll be needin' onybody for the hervest?'

'Gang doon an' see the master,' she told him, 'he's in the fiel in the holla. They're openin' the roads there.'

He smiled at her again and turned. As he passed the byre he inhaled the cool clean breath of a healthy cow-house. The hens hurried after him in the hope that he had come out to feed them. He squeezed through the gate and remembered the money he had stolen from Yates. It was still in the inside of his jacket. Perhaps it would be all right if he sent it back. He stuck one hand in the waist pocket of his trousers and began to whistle 'The Wearin' o' the Green'. . . .

APPENDICES

NOTE ON NAMING

As stated in the introduction, and indeed in the Libel Report below, there are a number of actual places – farms and so on, rather than towns, villages and roads – named in the novel. Their then owners or tenants or other occupants, at the book's date of publication in 1939, may still be identified from living memory, among the surviving older generation. All will otherwise be erased in the next. The information here is intended to provide further local context for the society described in the book and to suggest its real-life intimacy. It combines oral history, chiefly supplied by Jean Rennie (McNeillie on her mother's side) who grew up at Capenoch farm. Documents including Valuation Rolls have provided (un-nuanced) verification. In some instances information has been expanded by Barnbarroch Estate records in the possession of Jamie Vans. In geographical terms the area and places concerned are all within a short distance of North Clutag farm. The list is not exhaustive.

Barnbarroch: Home and Estate of the Vans Agnews of Sheucan in the Parish of Kirkinner, an association going back to the 1580s. In 1939 (and indeed in Andy Walker's heyday too), the Laird was Lt. Colonel John Vans Agnew. He lived at Barnbarroch House, built in 1780. The house, not far from Kirkinner and Whauphill, was destroyed by fire in 1941, tragically claiming the life of Mrs (Ada) Agnew. The following were the Estate's farms: Barlae, Barnbarroch Mains, Little Tahall, Newton Hill, North Clutag, Sheep Park – the last two, as well as the estate itself, being named in the novel.

Barness: High Barness stands by the Bladnoch to Alticry road, just before Hillhead and North Clutag road end, above the River Blad-noch. Its proprietors in 1939 were Madge (Margaret) and Mary Young, spinsters, related to the McNeillies by the marriage of their sister Jean to Jim McNeillie. Jim McNeillie farmed at High Balcray, near Whithorn. It is his wife Jean who is said to have thrown a copy of *Wigtown Ploughman* into the fire. Low Barness was farmed by a Thomas Wright.

Capenoch: as distinguished from 'Wee Capenoch' stands off the road from Culmalzie to Whauphill. It was farmed by James and Jean (*née*

McNeillie) McQuaker. 'Wee Capenoch' – nearer the road and nearer Culmalzie (High Malzie) – was farmed by Peter McNeillie, a brother of Old John McNeillie of North Clutag.

Clutag: North Clutag, where the author spent his early childhood. A record survives to show that in 1922 the lease was renewed, expiring Martimas 1930, at £120.00 a year, plus 9s. 1d. insurance, in the name of John McNeillie, tenant since before the Great War. South Clutag stood just over the hill, beyond North Clutag's high march wall, by the road to Whauphill, on the opposite side to Capenoch. South Clutag steading has long been derelict. The place was farmed by J. & R. McQuaid of Barvernochan. In 1471 the Exchequer Rental shows the lands of Knockan and Clutag to have been owned by a family of harpers associated with the MacBhreatnaich (Galbraith) and MacShennoig (McShannon) families, at a time when Galloway was part of the Gaelic-speaking world. A parliamentary reference to the land of 'Clutarche', in the parish of 'Kirkkynner, and serefdome of Wigtoun', is cited in the correspondence of Sir Patrick Waus, 1594-97. The word derives from the Gaelic 'clúdach' meaning meadow or cover.

Doulton Loch: a bogland about two miles west of Sorbie village, produced when in 1863 Sir William Maxwell of Monreith drained the loch, revealing, according to the antiquarian C. H. Dick, 'the first discovery of lacustrine dwellings' – that is, crannogs or timber-built islands, in Scotland.

High Malzie (properly Culmalzie): was farmed by a David Morrison. The cothouse there, described in the book as 'still empty', was in 1939 occupied by one James Marshall, his wife and two children.

Hillhead: two houses, standing just by North Clutag road end, one occupied by the joiner David Leitch.

Low Malzie: stands just below Culmalzie on a by-road that leads north towards Kirkcowan. Its proprietors were David McKenna and Marion McKenna, spinster. The steading is described in the novel as 'deserted', and so in this period it was. The land was farmed by Colin and William Christison of Barglass, near Kirkinner.

Malzie School: stood just beyond Low Malzie and all but adjacent to the smithy. The schoolmistress there in Andy Walker's and his creator's day (c.1920) was a Miss Annie G. G. Menzies. By 1939 her place had been taken by a Jessie N. Browne.

Malzie Smithy: The smith was Willie Adair. His sons Bob and John followed him in the trade. When Willie moved to Sandhead it was John succeeded him at Malzie. He was not formally qualified, hence it seems Old John McNeillie's interventions described in the essay 'My Grandfather'.

Sheep Park: farmed by Samuel McQuaid.

unnamed: The book's exactitude is such that it would have been possible for contemporary readers to identify numerous unnamed locations from its pages. For example, the 'new house' on the hill out of Bladnoch as passed by Andy and Nan (p.108) would at once have been recognised as the Creamery Manager's accommodation, new in the 1920s – its then occupant a Mr McGaw. The attractive property is still to be seen, just before the fork in the road that winds on to Glenluce, past North Clutag road end. Even the watering trough from which a little further on Andy takes a drink can be identified as one standing at the roadside beween Kirwaugh farm and Kirwaugh cottage.

WIGTOWN PLOUGHMAN AND LIBEL

The following report dated 17 January 1939 and recently brought to light comes from the publisher's files. It appears to have been dictated and not subsequently corrected. To make matters easier for the reader, some minor adjustment has been made, but not so as to alter the sense of the original.

Before going into any detail with reference to the characters in this book, it may be generally stated that many parts of this book if identifiable with living persons would be of a defamatory nature which it would be dangerous to justify.

If the Author of the book has written a book with entirely fictitious characters but identifying real places, he could hardly be protected by the decision of Canning –v– Collins 1938 in which case it was held, speaking very briefly, that a fictional novel written as such, is in certain circumstances safe from libel proceedings, although a character may be identified with a living person. This protection would exist where the author or authoress has never heard of the persons or was unaware of their existence even if he or she identified himself or herself as the person referred to in the book.

In this book although isolated paragraphs may not be sufficient to identify any person, yet the cumulative effect of many parts of the book might be sufficient to identify the characters referred to therein with living persons.

Dealing now in detail: Page 3, Page 4. The reference to Alticry Lodge, High Malzie, and the school and on page 5 the date 1907 might be a series of facts sufficient to identify Andy Walker and his wife Sarah. Also the reference on page 7 to the place of birth and reference to 'Machars'. With [adjacent (left) margin: 'uninhabited 30 years'] regard to this it seems that a change of date could alleviate any possibility of identification. It is noticed in the foreword to the book that the Author states that farm names and names of characters have been concocted to suit what is purely fiction. In our opinion the foreword ought to be made quite clear stating that the characters are entirely fictitious. [*handwritten*: although this is not a conclusive protection]

Identification of places as on page 17 and other pages clearly defines parts about which the Author is writing and if anyone could identify themselves with a character mentioned in the book, in such a way that reasonable people would think the Claimant the person referred to, there is little doubt that that person would succeed in a libel action. Reference to the War on page 31 again defines the period about which the author writes. Again reference on page 42 to Andrew Walker, Malzie School, Wigtownshire, together with other preceding facts might sufficiently identify a living person with the Andy Walker referred to in the book. Reference to a certain McKeown as on Drumlin, and having a son, two daughters and a wife and other facts, might identify some family with the family as referred to in the book. On page 111 there is reference to someone dying as a result of a broken leg, Sarah (and his mother). This is quite an unusual occurrence and together with other facts might lead to identification. The reference on page 122 to Andy's brother being recruited in the Borderers and taken to India, might be a very isolated occurrence in the part of Scotland about which the book is written and sufficient again to lead to a claim of identification. There is a possibility that Paddy O'Hare might, by a sequence of events in the book, be identified with a living person. On page 186 a man by name of Aird is referred to and a description of the situation and locality of the farmhouse is given, and the references on page 217 to a farm of some two or three hundred acres might identify the locality and lead later to identification of persons referred to. For instance the reference to the Craig family on page 220. Reference on page 245 to a murderous attack being published in some newspaper should be gone into, in case there is any truth in this assertion. Reference on page 255 to a Jean Cope being born four years before Andy at a cot-house on the Kirkcowan road, and the reference to ten children about some of which defamatory paragraphs are written. The reference on page 322 to the police and farmers searching the barns and out-houses might identify a definite period. Reference to the fight on page 357 might lead to identification of certain persons subsequently referred to in a defamatory manner.

Taking into consideration the foregoing, in our opinion the Author ought to be asked: -

1. Whether he knows people, or people know him in this part written about, as this would be material as to the question of identification. If the author has met certain persons who might identify themselves with the characters referred to in the book under another name, the fact that he has met these persons would very much assist in their proving their case.

2. It appears that much of the work referring to places makes no attempt at fiction and as to many of the actual place names enquiry ought to be made of the author as to what names may have been substituted as being fiction.

3. It is not clear from the foreword or from the book whether the author is actually describing living people under a fictional name or whether his characters are purely imaginary. This of course [adjacent (left) margin: 'imaginary'] makes a considerable difference, and if it is merely a case of substituting fictional names, greater care ought to be taken to cover up the possibility of identification.

4. In our opinion if it will not affect the value of the book the dates ought to be changed as this would serve far greater protection.

Our general opinion on this book, assuming that the place names are real and the characters are entirely fictitious, is that it is a 'fair risk' and it would be in order to publish. As a matter of protection though we assume that the Author has signed the standard indemnity Contract.

REVIEWS AND RESPONSES

The following notices, reviews and broadcasts provide an almost exhaustive selection from the author's first 'Cuttings Book', into which he pasted reviews of Wigtown Ploughman. *As is clear the book was reviewed widely, within and outwith Scotland, including to the ends of Empire.*

Bulletin and Scots Pictorial 16 March 1939
'Power and Promise in a Scots Novel' by G. M. Little

An interesting Scottish first novel which holds considerable promise as well as achievement is John M'Neillie's *Wigtown Ploughman*. It's a tale primarily of primitive agricultural living, its scene always the Machars, its people chiefly the local 'cotmen' and their women. For central figure there is Andy Walker, cotman's child, who grows up to be scarcely less earthy and animal than his father, and whose progress from infancy to first manhood we follow in this book.

Andy becomes a good ploughman and ultimately attains the recognition, inarticulate enough, that between him and the soil there is a bond he cannot break – except at the price of his own dimly apprehended happiness. This skill in labour and this intuition are almost the only things which lift him to the level of ordinarily rational humanity; in most of the other activities which fill his existence – his matings, his fights, his rages – he is chiefly animal. Mr M'Neillie has set these things down with merciless force; the book has power to match its harshness, and is impressive accordingly. But the essential sameness of its hero's recurring labours, lusts, and furies ultimately tends to weaken its interest – a flaw which is, after all, understandable in a first novel in this particular vein.

Glasgow Herald 16 March 1939
'New Novels: Experiment and Tradition'
[unsigned review of the following: *The Wild Palms* by William Faulkner; *Wigtown Ploughman* by John M'Neillie; *The Saga of Frank Dover* by Johannes Bucholtz; *The Brandons* by Angela Thirkell; *Malignant Star* by Margaret D'Arcy]

Elemental Man

A nearness to the soil and to the more elemental in the life of man links the first novel of Mr John M'Neillie, *Wigtown Ploughman*, with that of Mr Faulkner, in spirit if not in theme or execution. Its scene is laid in that great triangular part of Wigtownshire that juts into the Solway east of Luce Bay, and it presents an unlovely picture of the cottars who supply the farms with ploughmen and shepherds; a race, wiry, gnarled, primitive in their loves and hates, and through the experience of generations knit to the soil and animals they tend. A pagan satisfaction with the earth and with the lives of those who toil on it is felt in Mr M'Neillie's writing, which has the merit of avoiding any pretence at the poetic in the style of *Sunset Song*.

Andy, the ploughman whose career from infancy to manhood provides the book with its story, has some understanding too of that satisfaction, though it is largely inarticulate; indeed, as the story proceeds and ends it is the one core of integrity in the rough, rude animal life he lives – the stubborn pride in doing a hard job well. For the most part, after a childhood spent in an overcrowded and incestuous home – such as changed social conditions must have very materially lessened in number – and schooldays of somewhat unbelievable violence, his life consists, in incident, in moving from one farm to another, but its background is thickly peopled with men, dumb and voluble, brutal and gay, sly and domineering, evil and generous.

The love incidents are many, usually lecherous, and more mechanical than dramatic in the telling; the book's moments of most vivid life are those in which volcanic outbursts of temper occur, scenes that open the abysses in human nature. Mr M'Neillie writes with obvious knowledge of the life he describes, and his book is a most interesting addition to Scottish regional novels.

Evening Telegraph and Post 18 March 1939
'Among the Latest Books – *A Realistic Scottish Novel*'
[unsigned]

The disappearance of the kailyard novel into the limbo of disfavour caused a swing of the pendulum to the other extreme; realism took the place of sentimentalism.

No one can cavil at this accent on country life in the raw as treated by a writer of the genius of Lewis Grassic Gibbon in his interpretation of Mearns life, but realism of itself – without the spark of poetry – is a dull enough thing.

The lack of this vital spark is the reason why John M'Neillie's *Wigtown Ploughman*, which might have been a great novel, is at times drab and uninteresting.

His hero is a ploughman, a wife-beater, adulterer, a drunkard guilty of almost every sin in the calendar, but he is still a lay figure without the breath of life.

Mr M'Neillie spent his early years on a farm in the district in which he sets this first novel, and his knowledge of the sordid existence of the cotmen is manifest. But though he tells his story well, reports incidents thrillingly, yet he never achieves that 'sibness' with the earth, which once achieved, gives the writer the power to make vital literature of the lives of its workers.

Sunday Observer 19 March 1939
'New Novels – Right Proportions' by Frank Swinnerton
[review of *The Wild Palms* by William Faulkner; *At Swim-Two-Birds* by Flann O'Brien; *The Unbroken Heart* by Robert Speaight; *Tay John* by Howard O'Hagan; *Wigtown Ploughman* by John McNeillie]

. . . They, rather than the character of Tay John, make the book a living picture; but the man himself is there as well.

So is the hero of *Wigtown Ploughman*, although he is a brutal fellow whose savageries begin early and continue through many scenes. Mr McNeillie knows the peasants of Wigtownshire at first hand, writes without sentiment and follows no literary fashion. His writing is plain and good.

Aberdeen Press and Journal 23 March 1939
[unsigned]

From the kailyard to the byre has been the journey of the Scottish novel, with exceptions, the most notable of whom is Neil M. Gunn. Mr M'Neillie is a follower of George Douglas of *The House with the Green Shutters* and Lewis Grassic Gibbon, but Douglas would have avoided the one-sidedness of Mr M'Neillie's work and Mr M'Neillie avoids the exotic style of Gibbon.

Wigtown Ploughman is a novel of strength and interest, written by one who quite evidently knows his milieu and his county, but it lacks variation. One cannot believe that all cottars in that delectable county are like those whom this author depicts. Surely there are some cottar houses that are neat and clean and are not inhabited by men and women who are devoid of morals and who are not savages.

It is the insistence of the sordid, the sensual, and the utterly amoral aspect of rural life that takes away from the value of the novel that, with some balance, would have been a more notable contribution to Scottish literature than it is. But that it is a contribution cannot be denied, in spite of the defects mentioned.

Mr M'Neillie has caught not only the life of the folk, but he has given them their background of country and town that makes one look forward to his next work with keen anticipation.

Apart from their constant concern with the grosser aspects of rural life, his characters have a Theocritan setting and activity that is fresh and attractive. Truth and beauty are here, only balance, light and shade are wanted. Undoubtedly a new and potentially important Scottish novelist has swum into our ken, a Scottish Eekhoud, but his next novel, in a variety of ways, will be more important still.

Weekly Review 23 March 1939 by Michael Burt

This first novel deals with life among the cotfolk in the Machars of Wigtownshire, a locality in which, we are told, the author himself was reared. Whether or not Wigtownshire will be pleased with this return for its hospitality remains to be seen. I should say not, for it is quite the most squalid and unpleasant book that I have read for many a day.

If we are to believe Mr McNeillie these Wigtown farmhands are a vicious, brutish, sub-human breed, unlovable and unloving, whose energies after working hours are given over to drunkenness, fighting, lechery, wife-beating, and comparable pastimes; while their women are sluttish, over-sexed drabs who ask for all they get. Now this may or may not be sound ethnography, but its makes singularly repellent fiction. It is possible to make out a case for salacity in fiction, always assuming that it is also amusing or stimulating: but there is neither amusement nor stimulation in this book. There is not even true salacity, but only a kind of crude bestiality. I found the too frequently recurring rondo of drunken pugnacity, seduction by invitation, and illegitimate child-bearing ineffably monotonous; and all the more so since the writing lacks the distinction necessary to develop such themes into a tolerably attractive whole.

Andy Walker, the central character, simply cannot be assessed by normal human standards, for he is more brute than man. I am sorry, but I could raise no enthusiasm for Andy himself, his exploits, his misfortunes, or for the other sub-humans with whom he worked, drank, or fornicated. With a journalist's addiction to over-emphasis Mr

McNeillie has allowed his characters no redeeming features, with the result that their story is unappetizing and inconclusive. However, the jacket design by Mr Robert [sic] Darwin is delightful, and the book itself is more than adequately produced.

John O'London's Weekly 24 March 1939 by Richard Church

When an author, writing a preface to his first novel, says that 'only those who live near the soil can see true beauty', he makes me suspect that he is a sentimentalist, or a simpleton. Putting aside this initial prejudice, I have read *Wigtown Ploughman*, by John McNeillie. It is the authentic kailyard stuff, with a bairn born on a crofting, and a mother who gets her groceries free during her husband's absence, and all the brutality and blasphemy that Burns and Hugh Macdiarmid have made us soft southerners familiar with.

We are given the first twenty-five years of Andy's life. Before he is fourteen he is helping to keep things going by getting a job behind the plough. He knows the facts of life by reason of his acute proximity to his wanton mother and his sodden father. In spite of that siring, he has a grand physique, which he proceeds quickly to put to its fullest use. Wine, women, and song is perhaps a little too refined a definition of his activities. But he supplies a very basic and solid substitute. As the blurb says on the jacket of the book, 'One feels very close to nature in these surroundings.'

Liverpool Daily Post 28 March 1939
'Books of the Day – Notable Novels' by Pamela Hansford Johnson [review of *The Thibaults* by Roger Martin Du Gard; *Merlin Bay* by Richmal Crompton; *Wigtown Ploughman* by John McNeillie; *Children of the Foam* by Merle Eyles]

Wigtown Ploughman is the absorbing, meaty story of a young ploughboy in the wilds of Scotland, a strong, belligerent, unbalanced and fascinating lad whose further adventures might well be held over to a second volume. Andy is a tartar, and one cannot help feeling that one day, beyond the covers of the present story, he will meet a fighter who can down him and a woman who can give him as good as he gave. There is a lovely sense of space in this book, a sense of light and fresh air. It is one of the best first novels for a long while back.

Western Morning News 29 March 1939
'Books of Today'
[signed 'D']

Many will agree that to portray the life of a ploughboy as the basis of a first novel is a venture that demands the best from the author who hopes to soar to higher literary planes.

In *Wigtown Ploughman* Mr John McNeillie does not disappoint. He radiates Scotland with emphasis on its pastoral life. Those Scots who have gone furth of Scotland and discover this book will enjoy it because of its vignettes of the pure simple life handled in charming manner by this young Scots author, as distinct from the delicately-etched atmosphere of crude existence and illicit love that emanate from novels.

This corner of Scotland, like other sectors of the United Kingdom, has its terrible blemishes and [they] give scope to the social reformers and shock the 'unco guid'. Young McNeillie does not camouflage the low moral standards of some in the colonies of the cotmen, where the environment and weaknesses of the social system tend to contaminate and stifle development of the finer character in people.

Andy, the hero, is described from his birth to the age of about 25. Son of a drunken ne'er-do-well farm labourer, he is the principal character in this novel, and focuses on men, women, and parochial affairs in this remote part of the British Isles. Scots readers will applaud the work as veritas, well presented, and even cynics who take his case to avizandum will no doubt readily admit it is enlightening and entertaining.

Border Standard 25 March 1939
'Books for Border Readers suggested by J. H. C. Laker'
[the same notice was reprinted in the *Campbeltown Courier* 1 April, and the *Perthshire Constitutional* 7 April 1939]

'Wigtown Ploughman'

Life among the cotfolk of Wigtownshire is the theme of a really magnificent first novel from the pen of John McNeillie. In *Wigtown Ploughman*, for that is the title, the hero, Andy, is described from his birth to the age of twenty-five. He is the son of a cotman, and from the day he obtains a job on a farm at fourteen years of age he becomes a true Wigtown character, strong, impetuous, and with great love of life. The author was born in Dumbartonshire and his family have been farmers for generations in Wigtownshire, where he has spent most of his life. It is obvious that he is gifted with unusual powers of observation so brilliantly does he portray life in this remote part of the British Isles.

Times Literary Supplement 8 April 1939
'Three First Novels – Fighting Ploughman'
[unsigned]

The first novel deals with the life of its hero up to the age of twenty-five. Andy Walker is one of the children of a Wigtownshire farm hand whose disreputable existence flickers out into oblivion during the War. Ultimately Andy is left without any family ties, a strong and violent lad who leads a life apparently scarcely raised above the level of animal existence. No outlaw could be more remote from common social life where bells knoll to church and good men give feasts. Ploughman by day, poacher by night, drunken, sensual, and pugilistic, he passes from one farm to another with the bundle of clothes which is all his property. Fighting plays a great part in his life, and parts of the story simply resound with the smashing of heads and the thud of falling bodies. At length, having deserted his wife and children, Andy nearly accepts a proposal to turn boxer and travel the country; but the magic of life on the land, compounded of sight and scents which his inarticulate mind has enjoyed for years, forces him to refuse and to be off to seek another job as a ploughman.

There are passages in the book which might have been horrible in their savagery but are redeemed by this pervading suggestion of the impersonal beauty of the pastoral landscape. The night pieces, when poaching is the theme, are particularly well rendered, and the account of Andy's first days at work is memorable for its powerful suggestion of the boy's crushing fatigue. Considering the squalor of the hero's successive environments, one appreciates the skill with which the author has avoided making squalor merely repulsive, and the sensitiveness of his descriptions of the countryside.

Rand Daily Mail (South Africa) 8 April 1939
'Among the New Novels – The Harshness of the Soil'
[unsigned review of *Wigtown Ploughman* by John McNeillie; *Thorn in Her Flesh* by Eden Phillpotts; *Malignant Star* by Margaret D'Arcy; *Jack of All Hearts* by Annabel Lee; *Trail Mates* by Ney N. Geer]

Mr McNeillie author of *Wigtown Ploughman*, a first novel, observes in his foreword that 'Only those who live near the soil can see true beauty.' Later on, in the same foreword, he remarks: 'As for the harshness of this tale, there is no need to invent truth. Would you have me tell you a fairy story?'

The novel is indeed of the stern stuff of realism, and the characters of the tale who live near the soil appear to have little time for the appreciation of beauty. The soil to them is simply the soil – something out of which to wrest a living, and the pictorial aspect of their surroundings hardly concerns or occurs to them. The Machars of Wigtownshire is the setting, and the ploughman-hero, Andy Walker, moves from district to district as the story proceeds.

The people of the Machars, like the people of many rural parts, have their own elastic code of morals, and the young men do not marry until 'their intended wives have demonstrated their fertility, intentionally or carelessly, once, twice, or even four times'. Andy of the story was the third but first legitimate child of his parents. His mother, Sarah, was a hard-working though morally undependable woman, and the boy witnesses many violent scenes during his childhood. When he finally left home to seek his own livelihood he carried with him few recollections of a pleasant kind, and he proceeded to blunder along in the unreasoning way of his antecedents. The first woman he seduces he stubbornly refuses to marry, but the second succeeds in luring him to the altar and to a more or less stable existence. Not for long, however, do the domestic conditions endure peaceably. And so to fresh pastures, other women. The coarseness and ignorance of the rustics are well conveyed, and the author obviously intends to continue the story into another volume.

Daily Mail (Scottish Edition) 9 April 1939
'Life in the Raw'
[signed J. P.]

In *Wigtown Ploughman* Mr John McNeillie has written a first novel of unusual interest. Many readers will think the lives of the farm labourers, 'cotmen', in the Machars of Wigtownshire abnormal, but the author insists that he has drawn the ordinary everyday folk of these parts of Scotland.

The story tells of the first 28 years of the life of 'Andy Walker'. Born and raised in unspeakable squalor and shame, he is an indifferent witness to the lusts and brutalities of his parents. He leaves home when 13 to become 'byre boy' on a neighbouring farm, and early in life achieves his childhood's ambition to become a ploughman.

His life is made up of working, fighting, lovemaking. Only the author uses a stronger – perhaps more appropriate – word.

Mr McNeillie writes with sincerity, and at times with an almost savage power. From the queer hero, who at times was 'no longer a boy but a wild creature with the savage thrills that had incited his hairy ancestors to clan massacre and bloody orgies' to the farmers, villagers, and children, every character lives.

But it is not a book for the squeamish.

News Chronicle 12 April 1939
'The People in Novels' by Audrey Lucas
[review of *Wigtown Ploughman* by John McNeillie; *October Day* by Frank Griffin; *The House of Travelinck* by Jo van Ammers-Kuller]

Two novels on this list, the first two, tell stories of the 'people'. Mr Griffin writes about Londoners; Mr McNeillie about Scotsmen.

Wigtown Ploughman may best be described as a vigorous counter-blast to Robert Burns's 'The Cottar's Saturday Night'. A promise, found on the blurb, of 'work, fighting and fornication', is by no means made of pie-crust.

Andy Walker's first day as a farmer's boy is so vividly recorded that, when I had finished the chapter, my own muscles ached in sympathy with his; illegitimate 'weans', bashed and bleeding faces recur all through the book with a regularity which would be maddening but for the fact that Mr McNeillie writes so noticeably well, and, more essential still, that he so thoroughly understands the people of whom he is writing.

Wigtown Ploughman is a remarkable first novel. It has no message. And this is restful. Andy, the ploughman, who, over-enjoying two of those occupations mentioned on the blurb, goes steadily from bad to worse and yet contrives to remain slightly likeable, is the inevitable product of his appalling parentage and environment. Mr McNeillie, however, does not say so. He merely tells his story and creates his characters. He also, most superbly, creates a countryside.

BBC 8.5–8.25pm, 13 April 1939
'New Books in Scotland' by Edwin Muir
[titles of the works discussed are not listed with the transcript]

The books I have to talk about tonight are mostly novels and novels of Scottish life. Three of them deal with contemporary Scotland, the Scotland we know or are supposed to know; the fourth is about the Jacobite rising, the Forty-Five, when people evidently spoke like this:

'Blood and destruction, and the tears of women, and the fired thatch. Are not these what follow when the foot of rebellion treads on ordered soil? I would not that they befall Scotland.' I hope we would all say Amen to that, but I think we would agree at the same time that that is not how Scots people carry on a conversation, or ever have done. But what struck me most was the very different pictures of Scotland given in the three novels describing present-day Scottish life. They represent roughly three schools of Scottish fiction: the farm-yard, the back-yard, and the kail-yard. A visitor from Mars, almost the only neutral territory that is left now, would be very puzzled by these three pictures of Scotland. Which is the real Scotland? he would ask. And I'm sure I couldn't tell him, for I can't recognize any of the three pictures from my own experience of Scotland. The farm-yard story, to take it first, is an account of Scottish country life. According to it the Scottish farming community, the ploughmen in particular, spend most of their spare time in fighting and drinking and poaching and promiscuous love-making; all the women are potential or actual sluts; and the proportion of illegitimate children seems to be at least ninety-nine percent. Now I was brought up in the country, but I can't recognize this picture of it. The backyard - in this case it is a back-yard in a mining town – is more credible. It is drab, but the people who move about it are recognizably human, poor people making the best of things; and going on strike when things become too bad even for them. But they are all a little like people out of a book, not people one has met and known. The kail-yard story is about country life, like the farm-yard story; but with a difference. Not a single illegitimate child; not a single broken nose; and a few harmless drinks; one or two idyllic love affairs; a party and a dance conducted in the most respectable style and ending without an incident. Is this rural Scotland, or is it the farm-yard rural Scotland? I can't believe in either of them; if either were true, there wouldn't be much hope for Scotland, for it would be a country of savages, or of small-minded, self-complacent, genteel bodies. I don't believe it is either; it couldn't get about its business if it were.

I had better take the farm-yard story first. It is a first novel by John McNeillie, a young writer, and it is called *Wigtown Ploughman*. It tells the story of Andy Walker, the son of a farm servant, up to the age of twenty-five. Andy is brought up in a cothouse in squalor. His father of course beats his mother; his mother carries on with other men; both father and mother drink a great deal; the mother beats Andy, and Andy kicks her. His teacher when he goes to school, beats him too; he kicks her as well, and fights the other boys; and after that he kicks and fights his way through life, with few interruptions caused by love-making, until he gets married. Thereupon he begins to beat his wife, and ends by trying to murder her; but she luckily escapes him. He is sent to prison for six months, and when he comes out tries to murder her again, but as this happens in the middle of a street he is overcome by force of numbers. After this he moves to another neighbourhood for fear of the police; has another bout of love-making, followed by a terrific fight with the farmer he had been working for, followed by a theft of thirty pounds. On this Andy clears out for Stranraer, goes to a boxing-booth there – the most natural thing in the world for him to do – knocks out the man who challenges all-comers, and is taken on by the manager of the outfit for thirty shillings a week. But as the caravan trundles on to the next fair Andy, looking at all the neat farms sliding past, finds the pull of his old life too much for him and jumps down. 'It was fine,' I quote from the story here, 'to be sure that he would never leave this countryside with its fir woods stretching along the tops of hills like the mane on a horse's neck; with its quiet sleepy farms basking in the sun; its cool breezes and nodding fields of oats.' That's all very well as an end-piece, but we know that no farm would be quiet and sleepy for long with Andy on it.

This is a first novel and it shows a distinct literary talent, especially in its description of natural scenes. The thing that makes it bad as a description of life is not so much the amount of fighting and debauchery as the idealisation of the poor pathetic fool Andy, whom Mr McNeillie seems to see as a sort of hero. A psychologist would set down Andy as a very neurotic type; he is a sadist, a thief and a blackmailer when he has the chance, and a megalomaniac from an early age. But Mr McNeillie represents him as a fine old example of the stout Scottish peasant, and that is really going too far. We have too much mystical glorification of violence as it is; it is something we have to get over, not something we have to encourage. But Mr McNeillie has certainly some talent as a writer, and some sense of beauty, and he may yet give us a novel sometime in which they are used reasonably.

The Montrose Review 14 April 1939
[unsigned]

A first novel of exceptional promise comes from the pen of a young Scottish journalist John McNeillie. It is *Wigtown Ploughman*, a story of the cotfolk of Wigtownshire and, more particularly, of the Machars of

Wigtown. It is the story of 'a simple man of the soil', by name Andy
Walker. He is the son of a drunken ne'er-do-well, some of whose
characteristics he inherits, and after a mis-spent childhood – he was the
terror of the school and tasted liquor before he was 14 – he goes to work
on a farm for a slave-driver of an employer, there beginning his 'life's
struggle against the soil'. His life is made up of working, fighting,
drinking, swearing, fornication, wife-beating and poaching, and
although the author says he has 'attempted to portray something of
the best and the worst' in the ploughman of Wigtown, there is little that
is good in Andy Walker, but his life, from birth to about 25, is told with
gripping realism. There is coarseness and brutality in the book, but there
is also beauty for, as Mr McNeillie says, 'only those who live near the soil
can see true beauty', and reading the story of Andy Walker one feels very
close to the soil. The writing is extremely vivid, and the author makes a
splendid bid to win the mantle of the late Lewis Grassic Gibbon.

Country Life 15 April 1939
[signed V. H. F.]

Small Scottish farmers, their ploughmen, byre-boys and dairymaids provide the human material for Mr John McNeillie's novel. He himself comes
from the lonely north of which he writes, and we recognize in his scenes
and characters the authentic note of personal knowledge. But *Wigtown
Ploughman* is a first novel, and first novels are apt to have one or two defects.
'Would you have me tell you a fairy story?' asks the author scornfully in his
Preface. We would not; but already from that question, we guess what the
alternative will be: Mr McNeillie makes the harshness and coarseness of his
characters too universal, too unrelieved. There is hardly a redeeming
quality in any man or woman in the book. Brutality reigns and is admired
by all, women as well as men. Andy, the young ploughman who is the chief
character, has not a single trait to make him likeable, although our
sympathy seems to be expected for him. The author claims to have
portrayed 'something of the best and the worst' in his characters; but the
best is too rare, even if the worst is not too black. The book's ending,
however, is good, and gives promise for the author's future.

Dunfermline Press 15 April 1939
'Book Reviews – Rough Shod'
[unsigned]

This book, which has outstanding qualities, deals with the life of small
farmers and ploughmen, and up to a point it is not only manifestly a

faithful but a convincing record. The long hours of toil, the restricted interests, the satisfaction of hard physical work followed by refreshing sleep, the delights which the country affords to the eye and ear of the most hardened rustic – all these are forcibly portrayed in this tale. And more. We come face to face with powerfully drawn characters, and with one especially, Andy, who is astonishingly alive. Long after you lay this book down he will haunt your memory. Mr McNeillie's feat is the more impressive because on balance Andy is an unpleasant fellow. Indeed he is largely animal. He is powerful physically but mental or spiritual adventures would be ludicrously unthinkable in him. His joys in life are four – work, women, fighting, and drinking. He commits acts not once but often which earn our contempt and our anger, and yet these become passing blemishes which cannot obscure a certain nobleness. The portrait is tragic – both of Andy himself and as a representative of a class that is of great importance to Scotland, her peasantry. On the whole, the tragedy is stimulating not enervating. What gives Mr McNeillie's work the real, almost haunting, power which it exercises is his insight which strips the commonplace to reveal its stimulating, abiding essence. And the language he uses is restrained but pointed. He can turn a fine sentence and he has an observant eye – 'the peewit . . . lays four eggs *pointing inwards*'. (Italics mine.)

Superficially this is a gloomy book, but to the discerning the grim succession of happenings which overtakes a rather bewildered Andy merely accentuates the underlying triumph of the good earth with her perpetual offer of healing and restoration. In the end Andy turns his back on a good deal which dire experience has taught him to yield poor dividends. Life has bruised his limited spirit a-plenty, but the land, the leal land, will set all things right. Will it though? The man Andy in his fibre was carnal, fierce-tempered, and quarrelsome, and these would go on wrecking his life whether in town or country. The leal land can bring the anodyne of work and sleep in satisfying cycle, but still Andy would remain his own sair enemy. The life of this Andy is going to be turmoil until age weakens the animal in him. His virility makes the book; he is like a hurricane, cruel, awesomely elemental. You are impressed but you do not like the man. He is destined to go up 'the long, bare staircase of life' defiantly alone. You certainly like him well enough to be desperately sorry for him.

Surely the account of drunken fights and sexual laxity is exaggerated? That both obtain in Scotland is undeniable, but to give them a precise location and to present them as the rule rather than as the exception is an error of taste as well as an inaccuracy. The reviewer has lived in close contact with Glasgow hooligans, and he has more than a passing knowledge of rural central Scotland, and neither of these backgrounds enables him to endorse either the fiercest features of the drunken fights nor the frequency of sexual delinquency. But all in all this is an outstanding novel, with its gallery of unforgettable Scottish peasants, amongst who, incidentally, the elderly men stand out, portrayed as they are with marvellous balance and vigour, as, for example, McKeown, who 'refused to be driven and admitted no master', and Craig, mature, shrewd, strong, gentle. You have the countryman's day epitomised in less than a score of words – 'a back-tiring struggle against wind and storm, to drag a crop from the soil after months of labour'. He falters, however, in making Andy set out in summer for the school two or three miles off when 'the cocks were crowing their welcome to the rising sun'.

A word of praise to the publishers, who have produced a volume which is pleasing to the eye and having paper which is sheer pleasure to the touch.

The Sunday Times 16 April 1939
'From Hovel to Hotel – A Distinguished First Novel' by Ralph Straus [review of *Wigtown Ploughman* by John McNeillie; *Marching to Zion* by Kenneth Saville; *Sister-in-Charge* by H. L. Montgomerie; *A Great Adventure* by Muriel Hine; *Phoebe's Guesthouse* by Horace Annesley Vachell]

Let pride of place be given to a first novel, even though it may not be to everybody's taste. As you imagine from its title *Wigtown Ploughman* is of the earth, distinctly and in places almost alarmingly earthy. Yet to my mind one of the book's chief attractions is to be found in the fact that for all its squalor and violence, it is essentially clean. You may be shocked at this or that episode, but you are never disgusted. The young ploughman himself, moreover, may be a violent brute who cares for neither God nor man, a lusty and lustful ignoramus who batters his way through life; but he is alive and (literally) kicking: not a fellow to claim your particular sympathy, but, on the other hand, no monster to rouse your indignation.

'He never has much of a chance.' Perhaps not. Andy Walker's home-life in the wretchedest of hovels is dreadful enough: a drunken father and a blowsy mother who takes lovers whenever she can. But at fourteen he is away from them for all time; hard at work on the land,

and well able to take care of himself. Unluckily for him he passes from farm to farm without meeting with anything like gentleness. Always, it seems, there must be family brawls, sometimes of the most pitiful kind. Soon enough, too, he is fighting himself. Even when he is more or less forced into marriage his fortunes do not mend. Speedily he has had enough of his slatternly wife, and the children who come to mean nothing to him. Worse, the courts demand money when he has turned them out, and there comes a day when he is obliged to fly from police. For a while he plays with the idea of turning professional fighter, but he is a first-rate ploughman, and the land still calls.

A dreary chronicle, you might suppose, but it is very far from being that; for it not only has its excitements (not all of them concerned with Andy's numerous fights), but also its beauties. Andy himself may be little better than an animal, but the land does mean something to him. You begin to understand what a full day's work on those isolated Scottish farms can mean, and just what a clever poacher can find.

Exaggeration? I hardly think so. It is just that Mr McNeillie is not afraid of the truth, however unpalatable it may be. These primitive folk live in a world of their own, and here you see it faithfully mirrored. It is, I consider, a first novel of no little power and distinction.

Daily Record and Mail (Glasgow) 17 April 1939
'Passion & Realism in Rural Life Story'
[unsigned; a slightly shorter version with some rewriting appeared in *Manchester Dispatch* 21 April 1939 under the title 'Novel Inspired by Love of the Land']

It is a pleasure to welcome so strong and promising a first novel as Mr John M'Neillie's *Wigtown Ploughman*.

The setting of the story is in the Machars of Wigtownshire and the countryside is created with impressive power and an authenticity that shuns no detail.

The farm life is described with almost painful truth, showing not only a knowledge of agriculture and its ways but of the people engaged in it.

Andy supped his porridge in silence and rose to go to the byre. The milking was the most tiresome job; sore on the hands and arms. It was a precarious business balancing the pail between his knees, but he pulled at the teats grimly: desperately tired and weary; he was determined to finish his day's work. The byre was filled with the sound of chewing kye and milk spurting into pails; the sweat and hair of the cow he was milking stuck to his arms and neck. . . . The chains jingled, the kye were let out, the dog barked them down to the field; he emptied his pail and rubbed the hairs from his skin before going in for his supper.

The 'hero' of the story is Andy Walker, the ploughman, and the manner in which his life is set forth is as realistic as it is moving. Andy is a violent youth with strong passions and as we follow his peregrinations from farm to farm with the bundle of clothes which is his only worldly possession, we are made to realise what proximity to the soil can be other than poetic and romantic.

There is a good deal of fighting in the book and Andy, after deserting his family, almost accepts an offer to become a boxer and travel about challenging combats. But the pull of the land is too powerful, and he remains a ploughman.

Less sensitively treated, the theme might have been too ugly in its realism, but the author is an artist, and his evocation of the pastoral setting and his sympathetic understanding of the folk about whom he writes are so touched with a sense of beauty that he has produced a memorable piece of work.

Daily Sketch 22 April 1939 by Sir Hugh Walpole

Or take a first novel like *Wigtown Ploughman* by John McNeillie. Here is a difficult book.

It is coarse and violent and crude.

There are more fights in it than I can count, and the young author, in a kind of glorious boastfulness, revels in the details of drunkenness and leachery.

It is not even a good novel as a novel.

And yet it is as authentic, honest a kind of thing as I have met for a long day and it is shot through with beauty. I myself would give a very great deal to have that same authenticity.

But it is a thing that no writer can obtain by prayer, and that no writer bred up in towns, as I was, can ever acquire.

The book reminds me in many ways of D. H. Lawrence's first novel *The White Peacock*, although Mr McNeillie *is* Mr McNeillie.

I doubt if this will ever be a 'sixpenny'. How, then, are we going to keep it alive?

South African Broadcasting Corporation (from Johannesburg) 25 April 1939 [anonymous]

Do you know that ripe far land jutting out into the North Channel just across the sea from Belfast – that rich soil in the Lowland Galloway hills which they call Wigtownshire? A country of yeoman and peasant farmers tanned red as the loam in their valleys, whose speech, whose manners, the stench of whose very clothes reeks with the crude rough tang of the earth and the byres that lie alongside their whitewashed stone houses. Listen to John McNeillie today. 'Up the road to Alticry,' he writes, 'can be seen now on the right hand, the ruins of a cothouse, just past the dwelling of a herd, where the mossland stretches into the distance, like the soft-brown skin of a deer. Only the walls at either end of the ruins are standing; a monument to the lives of cotmen a hundred, perhaps two hundred years ago. The stones where once there was a fireplace are blackened with the smoke and heat of fires that fell in dusty embers on bygone winter evenings. The broken remains of slates and grass strew the floor, and weeds grow between the stones of the crumbling walls. The place is desolate and scarce a soul passes it in the course of half a day. The mossland to the north is a barren expanse of peat holes and heather banks, while in the south its tail end meets the sweep of the hills and woods.'

A lovely, a hard land. Breeding a race of men and women as rough and as vigorous as the heath on which they waged their yearly battle with the wind and the rain. 'A fight for a good harvest, hoeing in the chill days of spring and working in the broiling heat of midsummer, turning hay and forking sheaves.' Into these surroundings, into a room stinking with the odour of unwashed bodies, a dirty collie, dungy boots, and damp clothes, Andy Walker was born, into a life of working, of fighting, of fornicating, from the day when at the age of 14, his drunken father disappeared from the face of Wigtownshire, he got his first job as a boy on a neighbouring farm until, in ruddy manhood, he had risen to be a ploughman.

This tale *Wigtown Ploughman* is crude, it is honest, and it comes closer to Nature than any other tale I've read for years. It may be a story of wife-beaters, poachers, drunkards, and fighters: it is also an epic of the soil. McNeillie's first novel, it bears few traces of literary immaturity – rather does he manage to achieve that vivid and sympathetic naturalness which only a fine writer writing of his own people can achieve. I shall be surprised if every Lowland and North Country reader does not agree with me in my feeling that here is an unusually good story of our people – of the beauty of those narrow hedged lanes, the smoke curling from the crazy chimney pots, and the purple of the heather across the moors. Even though we have grown soft from life in South African towns, *Wigtown Ploughman* will bring back like a gust of swirling mist over the fells, with the smell of beat burning, memories of the rugged spiritedness of our people from the North, like the great horses before their ploughs.

Not only to men of the North do I recommend this book but also to the country folk of South Africa. And there may even be a few soft Southerners, men of the Fens, of Kent, and of the West Country, who are not so refined that they cannot stomach this tale of the earth – which succeeds in catching and keeping the atmosphere of the hill country where the film 'Man of Aran' left us unsatisfied.

Rangoon Times 28 April 1939
[unsigned]

A remote part of Scotland is described in this first novel from the pen of Mr John McNeillie. It deals with the life of the Cotfolk in the Machars of Wigtownshire. It's a life of terrible hardship and discomfort that the Cotfolk live, eking out a bare existence from the earth. Vice seems to be everywhere, and morals of the women appear not to be rigid. Andy, the hero, has a hectic youth. His loves are many and varied. His life is wild. His temper too is unreliable and his right arm is powerful and he never hesitates to use the latter to give force to the former. His is not a gloriously contented and peaceful life. Quite the reverse in fact, as the reader will find out in this rather outspoken book.

Sunday Sun & Guardian Magazine (Sydney NSW) 30 April 1939
'Here is Realism Run Wild'
[signed A.M.]

If Scotland has book censors like those of Australia, Mr John McNeillie for this, his first novel, would be banned with such a blast of indignation that he might be left too paralysed ever to write again. The people in his book are the cotmen, farm servants and ploughmen of Wigtownshire, in Scotland; and these are depicted in a degradation of morals, beside which the peasants of Zola and Balzac, or of the Russian realists, have some air of refinement. As for our Australian 'Redheap', it is in comparison monastic, conventual.

Drunken husbands kick and batter pregnant wives, who themselves are adulterous for a packet of groceries; the farmer's wife or mistress courts the ploughman on the sly; the birth-rate is pullulating with illegitimacy; girls in their teens cohabit promiscuously with boys and men; and the fights among the men are brutal with foul play.

Mr McNeillie was born in Dumbartonshire, which is three Scottish shires north of Wigtown, but he lived in childhood on his grandfather's farm in Wigtownshire, and (says his biographical note) he has spent his yearly holidays from newspaper work in the Wigtown district. He purports, therefore, to give us realism.

Next door to Wigtowshire is Ayrshire, from which the mining boy, Andrew Fisher came to Australia; but Andrew's gentle and chivalrous nature is as far from McNeillie's Scottish peasants as heaven from hell.

Robert Burns wrote: -

The poor inhabitant below
Was quick to learn and wise to know,
And keenly felt the friendly glow
     And softer flame
But thoughtless follies laid him low
     And stained his name!

McNeillie's Lowland Scots, however, are untouched by sentiment or by idealism, whether they are men or women. The author gives you young men with tomcat morals and girls with parallel habits; except that a mother cat has instincts to nurse and to wash her kittens, and no such maternity appears in the women of Wigtownshire.

The whole life of Andy Walker, as the author portrays it, is unlit by any spark of affection. His father is a whisky-sodden wife-beater, his mother is anybody's woman. Andy's love affairs are with girls taken for his satisfaction; his wife is one who has been common property. He bashes a woman as readily as he fights a man; and his only lasting friendship, with the Irishman Paddy O'Hare, is a companionship of boozing, brawling, and woman-hating.

With a slight sneer, Mr McNeillie refers to 'the romantic who revels in the work of Robert Burns'. So we suppose it would 'romantic' and namby-pamby to wish that Mr McNeillie had found, somewhere between Port William and Kirkcowan one labouring man with clean mind and one honest girl. There is, indeed, one girl, Kate Strachan, who does not go with Andy 'amang the rigs o' barley'; but only because she is afraid of her own burly and menacing lover.

Leave Mr McNeillie's book to the judgement of such Scottish Australians as hail from Wigtown and neighbouring shires.

Books of Today
'Reviews' by L. H. Lovegrove
[undated; included in the cuttings book among those for April 1939]

To speak of Scottish ploughmen is, inevitably, to bring to mind Robert Burns and – poetry; and here is no poetry, no romantic youth striving whilst at the plough-handles to acquire literary art and express a philosophy based upon ardent appreciation of the lark singing high over flowery banks and rippling burns. Not at all. *Wigtown Ploughman* opens up an entirely new existence to the reader by means of shading in a most powerful and brutally frank picture in detail of the life of an average bucolic West of Scotland cotman; in truth, the other side of the medal.

The cotman's existence is a struggle, crude and elemental. Eternal and strenuous muscular strain in the work is the basis, varied in the main by fighting, poaching and amorous adventure. The standardised amusements of the machine age have not yet arrived in Wigtownshire. Family ties break easily before hard necessity and human intercourse is free from weak kindness. A normal domestic scene:

> He did . . . carelessly he spat. It was too much for his wife's flaming temper. She seized a brush and brought it down on his head, but the brush stopped before it struck the bearded man. His great, strong hand rose and grasped it before it landed. The face flushed red under the beard. He rose and snapped the brush as though it had been matchwood. His wife, blind in her rage, rained blows on his face till he clouted her well and truly upon the side of the head. The spoon fell from Andy's fingers; he was terrified. Johnnie stopped eating, but kept his head still, looking out through the window across the steading. The woman reeled back and fell, dragging down the small table where her dinner and that of her daughters was laid.

The making of love is equally a matter of sensual necessity expressed with utter frankness; the pendulum swings far from suburban pettiness and prettiness, from fear of what the neighbours may think. Is the book worth while? Very certainly it is. Violent reactions, graphically and naturally interpreted, are always interesting, and the thud-thud of incident in the early life of the dour Andy Walker is a minor saga of great freshness and illustrative power.

Life & Letters May 1939
'Novels' by J. F. Hendry

Comparison will be drawn between this book and *No Mean City*, since it seems to do for the Scottish peasantry what the latter book did for the Scots worker. To some extent the comparison will be justified. In both the action comprises little more than fighting, drinking, and wife-beating; the characters tend to be garish, engines of destruction and victims of determination, rather than human beings. But just how much 'character' modern industrialism leaves a man would be interesting to discover.

Nevertheless *Wigtown Ploughman* is a better piece of literature than *No Mean City*. The prologue to the novel describes it as 'the story of part of the life of a ploughman, son of a cotman. Cotfolk are the dwellers in the small stone cottages which house the agricultural workers of the north', but the story of Andy Walker is not meant to be the story of all ploughmen.

The climax of the book comes when Andy leaves the farm where he works temporarily, to go to Stranraer. He has left his wife because her child was not his; and left his employer because the employer's child *was* his. But these things matter less than the fact that Andy ultimately prefers his country to the town.

Yet the problems of agriculture, like those of the town worker, are still unsolved, and one wishes there were more understanding between the peasant's small nationalism and the townsman's conception of a world system. They are perfectly compatible, though this is not always seen.

In style there is still a lingering influence of *The House with the Green Shutters* and that is a pity. But Mr McNeillie can write well, and together with Daniel MacDougal,[1] he should be a valuable addition to that Scottish literature which lost so much by the death of Lewis Grassic Gibbon; he is equally authentic.

---

1 Daniel MacDougall was the author of *Savage Conflict* (1936) and *Ian of the Burdens* (1937). Described as 'a cripple, who was a cobbler', he was the uncle of James D. MacDougall, one of John MacLean's lieutenants in the Tramp Trust Unlimited. It was his brother John MacDougall who introduced John MacLean to Marx's *Capital*. See Nan Milton, *John MacLean* (1973). I am indebted to John Manson for this information.

Egyptian Gazette 2 May 1939
'A Good First Novel'
[signed E. M. H.]

In this first novel by a young writer one gets back to realities, to the simple things of nature. Set in the rather remote and little known county of Wigtownshire, the story describes the life of Andy Walker from his birth to his early twenties. Andy was the son of a lazy cotman who was a poor example to his children. His education in the scholastic sense was extremely rudimentary, and it was a wonder he was able to read at all. As soon as possible he began to work as a byre boy. He was a good worker for it was his great ambition to become a ploughman – an ambition he quickly realised. His relaxations were women, and the fighting his dealings with them often entailed. His was a life spent close to the earth, and he only discovered he loved this life when he thought to leave it for the more artificial life of the fair ground . . .

> He broke off at the thought of the fields he had ploughed in the crisp November morning: the warmth of the stable when the horses went in to feed in the winter: the yellow gold of the oat crop; the smell of the potato blossom and peats. He thought of them without realising that they meant all that was beautiful in his life. These things and the friendly shadows of the fir woods, the sweep of the bare brown land in the autumn, the holy quietness of mild spring mornings, when you could hear cart wheels on the roads miles away and crowing of cocks from hidden farms so that it seemed that the hen roost was just behind the first knowe. They were part of a past that had been, in spite of his poachings and fighting, a gloriously contented and peaceful life.

Andy is a type one rarely meets in fiction and he is exceedingly interesting to know. The author is master of his subject and writes with conviction. The passage quoted is sufficient to show the beauty of the language. From the great promise and considerable achievement of his first book, John McNeillie is certainly an author to follow.

Sphinx (Egypt) 6 May 1939
'Too Much Realism'
[signed J. H. W.]

This story, set in the Machars of Wigtownshire, tells of the life of Andy Walker until the age of twenty-five. Son of drunken, dissolute parents, who seem more animal than the beasts whom his father tends. Andy is a dullard at the village school with a penchant for violence. He learns what little he does not know of life as a farm-boy. There follows a period of nothing but work, drunken fights and dull, casual amours. Suspicion of his wife drives him crazy until he all but commits murder. He then runs away to find a use for his violent proclivities as a member of a boxing-show until finally he realises that he is bound to the land by ties too strong to break and finds another position as ploughman in a place where he is not known.

If ever was justified the trite criticism of realistic writing, namely, that 'we do not need to hear about these things', it is justified concerning *Wigtown Ploughman*. The seamy side of life can be made significant, but the 'hero's' drunken bouts, his fights, his couplings, are monotonously similar. It gives one the impression of reading the same two or three paragraphs in the *News of the World* over and over again. Hardly the faintest glimmer of a divine spark livens the dull beasts whom the author would have us believe are men and women. They are not capable of thought, of intelligence; they are animals reacting dully and unthinkingly to their environment. We do not need to hear about the things such people do, simply because they are utterly and abysmally boring.

The Mercury (Hobart, Tasmania) 6 May 1939
[unsigned]

A first novel by a new writer, *Wigtown Ploughman* offers promise of good works to follow. It is the simple story of a Scottish ploughman from his boyhood to manhood, and the scenes are laid out in Wigtownshire, a county of which little is heard. Written with deep knowledge of the Scottish labouring type, with keen insight into untrained minds, and with fine perception of life as lived in isolated hamlets and on farms, the story moves with quiet strength. There is no plot, but none is needed. What we see is the bare nature of untutored physical existence, its brutality, and yet its potentiality for greatness in other circumstances. Andy, the chief character represents the kind of person still being manufactured by an educational system that does no more for thousands of girls and boys than sharpen their minds for mischief, and equip them with keener instruments for evil, while failing to impose on them any kind of moral guidance or precept. Youth turned into the jungle of living at the age of 11 years quickly discards the elemental teaching of morality under the pressure of circumstances and before the examples surrounding it.

Andy, son of a drunken, wife-beating father and a loose-living mother, born in a dismal cothouse – a cabin attached to a farm for labourers – becomes a farm boy before the age of 14, armed with nothing more than a village school under a tyrannous, ignorant, and stupid school-mistress, could give him in the way of education. He thus entered on his life a well-grown, pugnacious young savage with respect for no one, fear of little, the ploughman his god and ambition. The author shows him drunk and sober, pursuing girls with brutal success, and fighting Homeric battles, challenging with the fury of animal nature all that dared or opposed him. The prudish mind will be shocked, the moralist will bewail, but in writing this book the author has given a novel that shows the kind of youth being made, and the conditions that help make them.

The Times of India (Bombay) 12 May 1939
'Farming and Fighting'
[signed J. M. C.]

Wigtown Ploughman is a forceful, but humourless first novel about a farm-hand, so grim that it brings to mind Miss Gibbons' preface to *Cold Comfort Farm*. Written in a vernacular which is for fifty pages or so painfully aggressive, it tells the story of Andy Walker in all its crudity. We meet him as a small boy in terror of a brutal father: we leave him as a brutal father and husband whose one redeeming feature is his love for the land he farms. Ploughing and poaching, fighting and womanising account for the best action: the book's appeal depends on the beauty of its background of hills and heather and the little hollows where the sheep graze. There is strength and vitality in the writing: crude and angular though it is, its evident sincerity saves it.

John O'London's Weekly (Scottish Books Supplement) 26 May 1939
'New Scottish Books' by George Blake

Mr John McNeillie's *Wigtown Ploughman* has already had a distinct success of scandal – which is no fault of its author's, indeed. It is, frankly, a brutal book, because its incidents derive from brutal housing and working conditions in the Wigtownshire farmlands. It is simply plot-less. Andy Walker is born in shameful conditions, the unwanted son of a bully and a slut, and we follow him through twenty-five years of fighting, drinking, and love-making of the most primitive kind. In the end, like Mr Corrie's miners, he cannot escape even when the opportunity offers.

The tale suffers, indeed, from monotony – fight after fight, woman after woman betrayed, in a very slow-rising climax of brutality. It is as if Mr McNeillie were more interested in his incidents than in their ultimate meaning. It would be a vast pity, however, if either this, or, on the other hand, the novel's purely sensational values were to obscure his great talents as a writer. He is admitably pithy and detached in his realism. His feeling for nature is exquisite. It will be very interesting to see what this young writer makes of his next novel, for he cannot write another like this.

It is surely the strangest coincidence that *The Land of the Leal* by James Barke, opens in exactly the same setting, the mean, overcrowded cothouses of Galloway, and with much the same sort of people, coarse, fighting peasants and stingy, bullying farmers. It is likewise to the point that this long tale is, like these other two novels, essentially a study of frustration by economic circumstance. The careful reader will find it interesting to make comparisons among the three that would be dangerous in a reviewer!

It can be said at once, however, that Mr Barke aims highest and undoubtedly achieves most on an epic scale. Mr McNeillie is concerned only with the early years of an individual; Mr Barke takes a family of peasant origin through hundred of pages and some eighty years of social experience. [the cutting in John McNeillie's album ends here]

The Auckland Star 27 May 1939
[unsigned]

The setting one of the latest novels, and a first novel, is a farming district in Wigtownshire, not far as the crow flies, from the Mull of Galloway, the most southerly point in Scotland. *Wigtown Ploughman* is the work of John McNeillie, a journalist who has holidayed a good deal in the district. The county has long had an unenviable reputation for the high ratio of illegitimate births that takes place among the class he describes. We are not surprised, therefore, that his 'hero' has for his mother a woman of easy morals. Nor are we surprised that, his pedigree, upbringing and environment being what they were, he should grow up true to type. But the book's realism is too stark and savage. No doubt Mr McNeillie draws on what he has seen and heard as well as on his imagination; but his story contains episodes that can be described only as pornographic. And he could have given us greater variety of character. Every Wigtown ploughman is not an Andy Walker. In his attempt to clarify the dialect spoken, he takes undue liberty with some words. One wonders why he spells whisky with an 'e'? It is not so spelt in Scotland.

Stirling Observer
[unsigned; undated but placed among other reviews in May]

Last week a young Scottish author, John M'Neillie, made his debut. He is the son of an Old Kilpatrick engineer, but his novel deals with the life of a Wigtown ploughman, and derives its title from that fact. It is a powerful but of writing and his pictures of country life have a penetrating vividness; they are as Scottish as peat. He has a tendency, however, surely not to be borne out by the facts, to make sex delinquency the rule rather than the exception. This is hardly fair to a countryside which he manifestly loves. He has the slight, wiry build characteristic of the Lowlander and the defiant, firm mouth that the enemies of auld Scotland have learned to respect. He has a writing future, this young man, when he can deal with the intangible spiritual values with the same unerring power and accuracy that he brings to bear on the more superficial but very real material which in the sum makes up daily life. Only one other living Scottish author has put on paper so excellently the country folks and country scene of his native land. When the writer visited that other author (as far north of the Highland line as Mr M'Neillie's Wigtown is to the south of it) that author deplored the absence of authentic Scottish folk and scenes in modern novels.[2] Mr M'Neillie does not in this fall short; indeed he so excels that we look forward to his next work.

The Countryman (Summer no. 1939)[3]
'New Books: A Short Quarterly Guide'
[unsigned but almost certainly by the editor, William Robertson Scott, whom McNeillie visited and whose visit is reported in the magazine: 'A joyous personality of genius, John Laurie, looked in from his successes at the Shakespeare Memorial Theatre. He was born in Dumfries and was interested in John McNeillie ('Wigtown Ploughman') who had been here a day or two before. McNeillie has youth – he is in his early twenties – candour, charm, humour, fire and poetic feeling. There is no shade of the gloom of his book in his frank and vivid spoken word . . .']

2 This appears to be a reference to Neil M. Gunn (1891-1973).
3 See also from the same issue McNeillie's portrait of 'My Grandfather' in these appendices.

John McNeillie's *Wigtown Ploughman* is a ruthless narrative of illegitimacy, bad housing and low living in cot-house and farm-house in the early nineteen hundreds. It has a basis in fact that few rural writers will face. But, as its author would agree, neither Wigtownshire nor Scotland is all like that. As the first novel of an author of twenty-two it is remarkable. Read with Flora Thompson's *Lark's Rise*, it gives an impression of the price that has been paid by the nation for the maintenance of a supply and demand standard, to the neglect of so much that is vital to moral, mental and physical advancement.

The Northern Whig and Belfast Post 10 July 1939
'A Literary Causerie. Irish Fantasy – A Distressed Island – "The Wigtown Ploughman"'
[unsigned; the wider review not preserved]

There is always a welcome for works of fiction which are obviously sincere renderings of any phase of national life, diligently studied and naturally expressed. Such a work is *Wigtown Ploughman, Part of his Life* by John MacNeillie [sic]. Mr MacNeillie is a new writer, and comes of Scottish farmer stock. The scene of his story is the Machars district of Wigtownshire, where the author's early youth was spent. The hero, Andy Walker, is the son of a ploughman. His bringing up was rough, but he was never subjected to such treatment as the children of city slum-dwellers have to endure. Throughout the whole book the author's aim has evidently been to paint a faithful picture of the land worker's life in this part of Scotland – nothing extenuating, but nothing setting down in malice. Andy has his share of the faults to which imperfectly educated country dwellers are prone, but the brutish side of the peasant is not unduly pressed forward – as it is in Emile Zola's *La Terre*. The over-refined may sneer at the book, which I daresay they will consider 'coarse' and too 'realistic'. But the right stuff is clearly in Mr MacNeillie, and I hope that this book is only the first of many.

Inverness Courier 11 July 1939
'A Terrible Picture'
[unsigned]

Reading a book of this description, one wonders whether life under a democracy for some people is not worse than under a tyranny like the Soviet. That is, of course, if a true picture is given of the life of a ploughman in Wigtown. The book has led to a great deal of controversy, and rightly so, for if such people as the 'cotfolk', the class to which Andy Walker, the ploughman, belongs, are compelled to lead such lives, it is a disgrace to our country, our church and our education. Powerfully written, and leaving no intimate or unpleasant detail to the imagination, it is a most depressing and horrible picture. Andy Walker is born and brought up in the most sordid and filthy surroundings. Through no fault of his own, he has no chance, whatever, of appraising good and evil, and his life is thoroughly degrading. His one redeeming point is his subconscious love of country life, and in the end one is left with a gleam of hope for his future.

THE CONTROVERSY:
REPORTS, LETTERS, ENQUIRIES

The materials that follow here derive from the Sunday Mail *where the novel was serialised over twelve weeks from 30 April to 16 July, with dramatic illustrations (colour for the first three instalments, followed by black-and-white). It is helpful in considering the wider context of the novel's entry into the world not to forget that it was a world on the brink of war. Front page headlines declared: '25 Years Peace Plan. US Call to Dictators'; 'Danzig: Nazi Moves. Poles "No" to Hitler'; 'German Deadlock with Poland'; 'Russia is Joining Up. Paris Predicts Pact Next Week' and so on.*

Sunday Mail 16 April 1939
'Outspoken Attack on Morals of Scottish Farming Communities. Story Creates Sensation'

A controversy which swept the South of Scotland a few years ago has been given fresh impetus by the publication of a sensational exposure of the life of agricultural workers in Wigtownshire.

Following recent strictures by Rev. A. J. R. Shearer, who blamed the housing conditions in Wigtownshire for the immorality that is alleged to be rife in Southern Scotland, the book *Wigtown Ploughman*, has given rise to heated discussions. In fact, it promises to rouse as fierce a controversy in rural areas of Scotland as *No Mean City* did in the cities two years ago.

It may be argued that the story paints too grim a picture, but Rev. G. Paterson Graham, Portpatrick, who startled the people of Wigtownshire, a few years ago, says that the conditions which he described then are, if anything, worse.

Preaching in Portpatrick Church, he said on that occasion that one of the gravest and perplexing problems facing parents was how to safeguard their daughters and sons from the perils of life. He declared:

'No one but knows the district but must be shocked at the low tone of morality which prevails in our midst – a standard of morality that parents and guardians seem to wink at.

'It is a problem so serious that it is becoming a scandal which is damaging the reputation of the place and causing self-respecting people to hide their faces in shame.

'Young girls are allowed to wander aimlessly without supervision or control. Many of the social functions, such as dances got up for amusement or pleasure, are hunting-grounds for the "touts" and "sluts" in our midst, with the result that many of the girls who have an air of respectability disgrace themselves and dishonour their sex by their shameless conduct.

'SENSUAL VULTURES'

'Most of the young fellows are little more than sensual vultures prying about for their next victim, and who, unfortunately, find them all too readily. The moral atmosphere is putrid, hence immorality is rife. The evil is so prevalent, so deep-rooted, that better influences brought to bear upon them are not strong enough to counteract the lax, pernicious and baneful influences of their home life.

'They flaunt their sin before the eyes of the public and even have the audacity to ask for the blessing of religion on the issue of their shame. All that goes to show how low is the moral tone of the community.'

Mr Graham then made an appeal for more control by parents, ministers and teachers. He is of the opinion that conditions have not improved.

Rev. Alan J. R. Shearer, Kirkmaiden, who blames the 'terrible' housing conditions for the immorality, says the shocking and degrading conditions of the large majority of the houses constitute a menace to the well-being of the people, physically and morally.

'Anyone knowing the conditions,' he states, 'would admit that Wigtownshire people are fighting against conditions that make morality if not impossible, as least extremely difficult.'

These housing conditions have been exposed from time to time in the *Sunday Mail* by 'The Judge', and the dramatic story of *Wigtown Ploughman* bears out the truth of his accusations. The author of the story, John M'Neillie, spent his boyhood on his grandfather's farm in Wigtownshire, where the family have been farmers for generations.

The question of immorality in Wigtownshire has been the subject of much debate by ministers in both local Presbyteries, and every endeavour is being made to encourage young people to join the religious organisations. In many cases, however, the response has been so poor that several churches are without facilities for young people.

On Friday, Miss M'Clure, reporting on Girls' Associations in Stranraer Presbytery, stated that there were only five branches of the G.A. within the Presbytery, and attempts that had been made to have more branches had not succeeded so far, though it was hoped they would be more successful this winter.

At Wigtown Presbytery, Rev. Gavin Lawson reported that while every church had a Sunday School, there were four congregations without a Bible Class. In Stranraer Presbytery there are seven congregations without a Bible Class, and Rev. A. G. M. M'Alpine, who drew attention to this fact, said he hoped an improvement would soon be made.

Sunday Mail 23 April 1939
'Let Our Readers Judge. Is "Wigtown Ploughman" an Exaggerated Book?'
[the article is illustrated by a publicity photograph of John McNeillie at North Clutag]

Does the book *Wigtown Ploughman* exaggerate the conditions in Wigtownshire? Is immorality in the County confined to one parish?

These are the questions that are causing a sharp division of opinion in Galloway. The controversy is most fierce in Portpatrick district, but immorality is not confined to the Portpatrick parish, as official figures unfortunately show. Few districts can point the finger of scorn at others in that respect.

Some ministers blame the housing conditions, which no doubt have a considerable bearing on the matter and following the *Sunday Mail* article last week, a committee appointed by Stranraer Presbytery is investigating the housing conditions in the Rhinns district.

Wigtown Ploughman will cause a furore among the farming communities. Already farmers are taking sides in the controversy. The local papers have become the centres for letters; other have taken up the cudgels in the *Sunday Mail*.

Mr John Dalziel, Dunskey Glen, takes the book as an attack on Portpatrick and replies to Rev. G. Paterson Graham from the Scripture point of view. He quotes John Ackworth: - 'Should there be a member of the family who is erring, do the rest proclaim his guilt and magnify it? They realise too well it is something to be hidden, not even to be whispered – they carefully and anxiously conceal it.'

With this point of view many disagree. Foremost among these, of course, is Rev. G. Paterson Graham who feels the matter of illegitimacy should be brought into the light in order that it might be swept away.

FARM ROAD FIGHTS

Wigtown Ploughman has for its scene a portion of the Machars district of Wigtownshire. In the story the author describes a fight in a farm road. Last week at Wigtown Sheriff Court the story of an altercation between a labourer and a motor driver was related. It might have happened in the same road! In the same court a labourer was fined for an assault on an assistant farmer. Again it might have been a page from *Wigtown Ploughman*.

A few years go, the County Medical Officer condemned lack of parental control which resulted in late hours at which even school children went to bed, while a local school-master attacked parents for malnutrition among children caused, he alleged, by lack of proper food.

Had conditions at a certain school in the district been made public not long ago it would have caused as great a sensation as *Wigtown Ploughman* will undoubtedly create.

With regard to low wages, which were blamed for existing conditions, even farmers have agreed wages were poor, but that will be changed with the advent of the Wages Boards. Ministers with Rev. Alan Shearer, Kirkmaiden, at their head, are hoping that as a result of their inquiry into housing conditions, another reason for the immortality that exists in the district, will be removed.

Those who have already read *Wigtown Ploughman* have been forced to acknowledge the ability of the writer to tell, not only a remarkable story but to depict facts with remarkable accuracy.

'What Readers Say'

'Do Something About It'
Sir, – I was much struck and, I may say, shocked by the statements made by the Rev. G. P. Graham in his church in Portpatrick.

One sentence made me go back and read it over again to see if I had got it right. He states that the young women flaunt their sin before the eyes of the public, and even have the audacity to ask for the blessing of religion on the issue of their shame. I am glad he puts it that way, and not, as I presume he means, the sacrament of baptism.

Firstly, I think anyone will agree that people so far lost to all moral decency don't bother about religion either for themselves or for their offspring. Secondly, these little ones are not to blame for the shame connected with their birth, and there was One Who said 'Suffer the children to come unto Me *and forbid them not, for such is the Kingdom of Heaven.*'

Paisley   (Mrs) C. COOK

'Other Counties Challenged'

Sir, – I see that Wigtownshire is again in the news on the score of low living among agricultural workers.

The clergymen concerned, and John M'Neillie in his story, may not be understating the facts. The point I wish to make is: Why single out Wigtownshire?

Is this county any worse off than other parts of rural Scotland? I think not.

I challenge you, for instance, to submit comparative figures for illegitimacy from other parts of the country.

Let me add that it is to the credit of the local clergy that they have given their attention to such an important question. It shows they are alive to the need for reform in housing and other matters.

Clergymen in other districts should be following their example – and I am not excluding our big cities!

Stranraer   J. C. C.

'Kirk Elder Approves'

Sir – Your article on the condition of life in Wigtownshire greatly interested my family, which has very strong ties with the county.

Everything you brought out in the article is unfortunately correct, and my feeling is that Mr M'Neillie has done a public service by exposing the conditions in rural areas.

No doubt much of what happens in Wigtownshire is common to other farming communities, and it is high time national drive for better living conditions for rural workers was instituted.

This is a subject that merits the full glare of public debate.

Perth   KIRK ELDER

'Sweep These Hovels Away!'

Sir – If it does nothing else, I hope *Wigtown Ploughman* will arouse the authorities to a sense of their responsibility for the appalling depths of degradation to which Scotland has sunk in our country areas.

I agree with the Rev. Alan J. R. Shearer when he states that shocking housing conditions are the root cause of evil.

As a commercial traveller, I have visited every town and village of any size in Scotland, and I can honestly say that the blackest spots were those where large families were living in single rooms with no regard to their age or sex.

Sweep those hovels away, and with them will disappear the laxity which is bringing dishonour to rural Scotland.

Dundee   COMMERCIAL

The Sunday Mail *is convinced that the publication of this story should do much towards abolishing the conditions described by Mr M'Neillie, the author, and next week it will begin serialisation of this dramatic story. Don't miss the opening story next Sunday.*

Sunday Mail 30 April 1939
'*Wigtown Ploughman* – They Will Read It To-day'
[the article is accompanied by a red block stamped with 'WIGTOWN PLOUGHMAN' BEGINS TO-DAY]

Wigtownshire people have been looking forward keenly to the publication of the first instalment of *Wigtown Ploughman*, which appears in today's *Sunday Mail*. Seldom if ever has the rural population in Scotland evinced such interest in a novel.

Recent charges of immorality in Wigtownshire have aroused the Gallovidians to fever pitch and every line of the story will be read, by those who defend the county's morals and by those who believe the allegations to be true.

Not even the international situation has aroused more interest and the probability is that as a result of the controversy and the publication of the story in the *Sunday Mail*, impetus will be given to the efforts by ministers and others to remove what are stated to be reasons for immorality – bad housing and lack of proper education.

The disclosures, too, might result in increased interest in youth organisations. Those who have been endeavouring for years to revive interest in church organisations among the young will be assisted by many parents who are already exercising much closer supervision of their children.

If these conditions are improved in Wigtownshire the publication of the book, *Wigtown Ploughman*, in the *Sunday Mail* will be of great service to the district and to other districts where similar conditions exist.

Sunday Mail 7 May 1939
' "Wigtown Ploughman" Brings Housing Move'

Wigtown Ploughman, the first instalment of which appeared in last week's *Sunday Mail*, has added fuel to the fiery controversy that is sweeping Galloway on the suggestion of immorality. But moves are already afoot to remove some of the conditions that are being criticised.

Bad housing has been blamed as the root cause of immorality in Wigtownshire. Rev A. J. R. Shearer says the conditions are such as to make morality, if not impossible, at least very difficult.

Now an early meeting of the County Committee will be held to investigate the whole position of housing. The question of housing figures largely in *Wigtown Ploughman*, and it is significant that, while many public men have stated that the conditions in the book are over-drawn, rapid moves are being made to overhaul the conditions which have been described as worse than any city slums.

Mr Wm Paterson, convener of the Public Health Committee, has said that he hoped it would be noted by the general public that the Council were not losing sight of the problem of housing conditions.

This move by the County Council follows the investigation that is at present being made by members of the Stranraer Presbytery, a special committee of which has been, during the past few weeks, carrying out a tour of inspection of rural housing conditions.

Some people have declared that the publicity being given to the story of country life in the South of Scotland is causing harm to Wigtownshire, but if the recent moves for an attack on the housing conditions are the result of the publication of the book in serial form then a great deal of good is being done.

Last week-end *Wigtown Ploughman* formed the topic of most of the conversations in the district.

'Utter Lie'
Sir – I have just read the first instalment of *Wigtown Ploughman* in the *Sunday Mail*, and to say that the story is 'starkly realistic' is an utter lie.

I have lived in Wigtownshire all my life and am the son of a ploughman and have never seen anything approaching what the author describes.

Decent farmer employ decent servants, and no farmers of my acquaintance would tolerate such conduct in their houses.

These houses are perhaps lacking in sanitation and are anything but roomy, but the majority of them are kept clean and tidy, even if there are two or three illegitimate children in them, which is the exception and by no means the rule.

I only hope someone with more eloquent pen than mine will take up the cudgels on behalf of a very decent, clean, thrifty, hard working people.

High Glenstockadale, Stranraer   R. MCUBBIN

'Parents Blamed'

Sir – I read your article on *Wigtown Ploughman*, also remarks by Rev Shearer and Rev Graham. What they say is all too true, but the fault is not all the young people's: the parents are more to blame. In olden days parents were too strict; now they allow the children too much freedom. The housing conditions are also a lot to blame. With large families in rooms and kitchen, you cannot blame the boys and girls for going out to roam the highways.

The girl who has the misfortune to have a child is not always the bad girl. The bad girl is never burdened with a child, unless she wants to keep hold of the man. Ignorance is often to blame on the girl's part, and parents should take the time and patience to explain to their family the sacredness of marriage.

In a big city like Glasgow much more wrong is done than in the country, and is passed unnoticed. The young fellows may be 'sensual vultures' in the country, but in the cities many more of the sensual vultures are married men preying about for unfortunate women.

How many men at the age of 40 or 45 years can truthfully say they have kept their marriage vows and been faithful to their wives? Perhaps a few but not many. Wives too may forget their marriage vows, but not so often as men.

Until fathers and mothers take their equal share of rearing their children seriously and justly, we will always have wrong-doers.

Glasgow   MARIE FLOWER (A mother)

Sunday Mail 14 May 1939
'Readers' Letters – Were Farm Workers Afraid?'

Sir – The author of the *Wigtown Ploughman* paints a very dismal picture not only of the farm workers in Wigtownshire.

A few years ago, as a representative of the farm works, I was instructed to go round all the cottar houses in my district and make a report on the conditions and get the signature of the householder.

I didn't get one signature, and 75 per cent of the houses should have been condemned.

In one place, there were six cottar houses in a row, and the pigstyes were only a matter of four feet from the living-room windows. The discharge from the pigstyes ran along the side of the footpath in an open channel but not one would complain.

The proprietor was convenor of the County Council, and no Sanitary Inspector came near the place.

'BUT AND BEN'

'A Ploughman's Home'
Sir – I have been very interested in reading about the Wigtown ploughman. But every ploughman and his wife and family do not live like that.

It is the condition of rural housing that lowers the standard of many a respectable family.

I speak from my own experience. I have occupied what was supposed to be a rural worker's cottage, and there was not a decent room to live in. It was rotten with damp, badly ventilated and beds ruined with water, running down the walls.

There was no proper sanitation, and some lacked even a dry lavatory.
Inverness-shire   A RURAL WORKER

'I Am Disgusted'
Sir – I have read the first instalment of the *Wigtown Ploughman* and instead of being interested I am disgusted.

I have been a ploughman all my life in different parts of Scotland, and I never came across anything so repugnant as described by the author.
Robroyston Mains, Bishopbriggs   WILLIAM KELMAN

'True to Life'
Sir – I think the author of *Wigtown Ploughman* describes farm life in Wigtownshire as it really is, and I am sure no person who has travelled round the district as I have done can say otherwise.
Renfrew   DOON HAMER

Sunday Mail 21 May 1939
'Readers' Letters – Ploughman's Wife Writes –'

Sir – I am amazed at some of the statements in *Wigtown Ploughman*.

I was a ploughman's wife from 1910 to 1923, leaving Wigtownshire that year.

As one who lived and worked amongst farm workers I have yet to meet the couple who lived the life of quarrelling and immorality that has been stated.

Certainly, some of the houses were awful and not even fit for pigs to live in. But it is in these where you find (in most cases) cleanliness and thrift.

I knew a cattleman whose wages were 25s weekly with five children, himself and his wife to keep. My husband when he knew of this spoke for a rise for him, and he got £1. 10s. weekly with coal and meal potatoes, but no milk. You should have seen the poor cottar's wife smile when she knew of all these extras. She was so grateful.

Coatbridge   EX-PLOUGHMAN'S WIFE

'Wigtownshire – By a Teacher'

Sir – I was interested to read about Wigtownshire. When I went there in the 1920s to teach in a small school, I had no idea what sort of a world I should find.

But evidence of immorality was soon apparent in the school itself. The illegitimate children outnumbered the others by more than 2 to 1. Families of 3 to 5, with no question of fathers, lived with their mothers who worked in the fields.

Conditions were ideal for immoral 'goings on', I should imagine, with the hard work all day, the long lonely nights and the sparsity of the more of the more civilised villages.

In defence of Wigtownshire, I must say nothing but good of my own stay there. No one's public behaviour ever caused me the slightest misgiving, and I was treated most courteously by all sections of the community.

Grimsby   ELIZABETH SHAW

'Nothing Short of Libel'

Sir – That which inspired our National Bard's immortal work 'The Cottar's Saturday Night', is not yet dead.

Poor in worldly gear he may be, but in morals, refinement and demeanour the Scottish ploughman can take his place amongst the so-called highest in the land.

The writer of your serial should have taken a different route when he wished to gather material for his very modern 'realistic'.

Sugary romanticism does not appeal to us; but 'realism', which is nothing short of libel, only fills us with disgust.

Windsor Crescent, Newtown Stewart E. TAIT

Galloway Gazette, Saturday, 8 April 1939
RURAL HOUSING CONDITIONS IN WIGTOWNSHIRE
STRANRAER PRESBYTERY TO APPOINT INVESTIGATION
COMMITTEE

Rural housing conditions in Wigtownshire were strongly condemned by the Rev. Alan J. R. Shearer, Kirkmaiden, at a meeting of the Stranraer Presbytery, on Tuesday.

Mr Shearer, who was asking the Presbytery to press the Secretary of State for Scotland to speed up the operation of the Rural Workers Housing Act, 1938, said the Act had been five months on the Statute book without meeting with the slightest response.

Anyone knowing the conditions would admit that Wigtownshire people were fighting against conditions which made morality if not impossible at least extremely difficult.

He described the conditions under which many people lived as shocking and degrading and as constituting a menace to the well-being of the people.

'I have worked for years in the slums of Edinburgh,' he stated, 'but have never seen anything comparable to the rural slums of Wigtownshire.

'In some cases the tenants have to wage a perpetual campaign against rats, and in others every drop of water has to be carried several hundred yards.

'We hear a lot of talk about the immorality of Wigtownshire. I venture to suggest that the people of Wigtownshire set a very high moral standard having regard to the conditions under which they have to fight their moral battles.

'We have been told in Wigtownshire that many of these rural houses have been condemned. I challenge that statement for no house is legally condemned until owner and occupier have received official notification from the County Council, and in no case that I know has that been done.'

Mr James Robertson, a member of the County Council, defended the Council, and said the motion should be sent to the landlords.

When Mr James Dunlop, Colmonell, said that many of the rural slums were created by the inhabitants of the houses, Mr Shearer replied: 'If such were true the slums of the cities would never have been touched. How can we blame the inhabitants when the womenfolk have to walk 800 yards for every drop of water required to keep their houses clean?'

Referring to the regulations governing the housing of farm stock, he concluded: 'I hope the day will soon be past when the County Council of Wigtown put a higher value on cows than on human beings.'

Rev. T. Fergusson said the County Council was not composed of criminals, but of miserable sinners. The Presbytery was as much to blame as the Council, and he thought they should approach the Council and work alongside them.

After discussion, Mr Shearer agreed to withdraw his suggestion in favour of a motion by the Rev. J. Brown, Colmonell, that a committee be appointed to investigate rural housing within the Presbytery and report at the next meeting.

Galloway Gazette 10 June 1939
KIRKMAIDEN MINISTER AND HOUSING CONDITIONS

An accusation of insolence, insubordination and disloyalty to the Presbytery because he had raised the question of rural housing conditions in Wigtownshire at the General Assembly was levelled against the Rev. A. J. R. Shearer, at a meeting of the Stranraer Presbytery on Tuesday.

The Presbytery considered for two hours a request by Mr Shearer that Wigtownshire County Council be asked to receive a deputation from the Presbytery with regard to rural housing conditions and that the Housing Committee be asked to expedite matters.

The Rev. G. Paterson Graham, Portpatrick, the Moderator, said he thought the action taken by Mr Shearer in raising the matter before the General Assembly on an addendum to the report of the Church and Nation Committee, was disloyal to the Presbytery, and that, as the Assembly had now the matter in their hands, he did not think the Presbytery should take any further action.

[The Rev. T. Fergusson, Sheuchaun, referring to the motion withdrawn by Rev. Shearer at the meeting reported above, now observed:]

Mr Shearer, however, had seen fit to go to Edinburgh and call the

attention of the Assembly to the rural housing conditions in Wigtownshire, despite the fact that it was *sub judice*. That, he said, was *ultra vires*. It
was insolent and it was insubordination to the Presbytery.

Mr James Robertson, a member of the County Council, said he was
a member of the Presbyterial Committee appointed to investigate rural
housing conditions. In view of Mr Shearer's condemnation of the
County Council he wished to withdraw from membership of that
Committee. The County Council's hands were tied in the matter of
rural housing, owing to the difficulty with regard to farm cot houses,
which were really 'tied'.

Mr Shearer in reply said he had raised the matter as an individual, as
he was perfectly right to do. He was supported by the clerk, the Rev.
Eric M. Nichol, Inch.

[The Moderator referred to Shearer as 'a young man in a hurry' and
Shearer replied:]

'If I am a young man in a hurry, then many of our Church leaders are
in a hurry, because many of them young and old, spoke to me and
supported me at the Assembly with regard to rural housing.'

He went on to submit his report, which shows that 90 per cent of the
houses visited had been in a very bad condition, and that in the majority
of cases no sanitation was provided and people had to walk some
hundred yards for water. He said he had found that in one case four cot
hoses had been built on a farm. These cot houses contained hot and
cold water, bathroom, a large airy living room, a large bedroom, and a
smaller bedroom. If that could be done on one farm, he said, it could be
done on others. It showed that the Acts were not inoperative and that
the County Council could do something in the matter.

The Committee which had visited the houses felt convinced that
these houses were typical and were by no means confined to one parish.
They had wandered from farm to farm, enquiring their way as they
went. They felt their report was a genuine picture of the conditions,
and they asked the Presbytery to consider it. They were putting the
following recommendations before the Presbytery: -

Committee's Recommendations

The committee would recommend that the Presbytery approach the
County Council with a view to obtaining their collaboration in
ascertaining what steps can be taken to improve the conditions of
rural housing. This is desired in view of the following:

(a) A very large percentage of the cot houses within the bounds of the Presbytery are such that they call for immediate replacement or radical overhaul;

(b) The long delay in putting into operation the various Housing Acts has intensified the problem;

(c) That these Acts are not inoperable is evidenced in the fact that in some parishes a proportion of the cothouses have been brought up to reasonable standards;

(d) Our sympathies being with our people who are living under such discouraging and depressing conditions, we should urge the need for immediate action.

We note with interest the question of rural housing is to be considered at a forthcoming meeting of the County Council, and we would appreciate it if the Committee would agree to meet a deputation from the Presbytery.

The Moderator asked Mr Shearer if the committee had the consent of the various factors when they were visiting the houses.

Mr Shearer said he had not. He had approached one factor who said he neither countenanced, approved, nor disapproved. The committee, however, were well aware of their legal rights. Under the Agricultural Wages Act each occupant paid a rent for his house, and was entitled to say who or who should not cross the threshold, not the owner of the house. They had asked permission of the householder and were not refused in one instance.

Mr Robertson said he felt the Committee had selected the worst houses and that these were not representative of conditions in Wigtownshire. There were doing all they could in the matter of rural housing, but, unfortunately, they had to overcome many difficulties. In the towns they could build houses, but they found in the country districts they could not meet the needs of the farming community, a body of decent, hardworking men.

Getting a Raw Deal

They had plenty of trouble at the present time with Sunday serials, and with all this talk of deplorable housing conditions he thought Wigtownshire was getting a raw deal. However, he hoped the general public would follow up the example of Rev. Matthew Stewart, who, when he accepted the addendum, said he not accepting everything that has been said.

They had heard all about the deplorable conditions of farm workers' houses and cothouses, but he had not yet heards a word about the deplorable conditions, or any mention, that cot houses belonging to the Church of Scotland had been found, the conditions of which were as bad as any. He thought the Church of Scotland should put its own house in order before approaching the County Council to have their houses put in order.

Mr Shearer refuted the argument that the houses had been selected and said they were taken at random and members of the committee indeed did not know where they were.

LETTERS FROM NORTH CLUTAG

Old John McNeillie was much taken by his grandson's book and the stir it caused. He wrote to him about it, in pencil, from 'North Clutag Wigtown', generally on a Sunday night, sometimes at length, sometimes with stories for 'that book you are going to right [sic] about me', as many as six pages, sometimes his fingers losing 'the power with the cold', and signed off 'from your Grandfather good night' and 'good night Grandpa'. One short letter enclosed a £1 note as 'a small present owing to you making so clever a job of your book'. The excerpts here are transcribed as written. The other end of the correspondence has regrettably not survived.

your letter to hand today also paper, and by it you seem to be well in favour and a geanues all other papers speaks highly about your book which I now have it all read now and I think it is the very true story of the majority of the coat folks without education or character only lives for day & dily bread and a fight or a quarl after thay have thair bely full and gets thair tail up that is all thay live for and brought up by thair people which knows no better and do not care had you did it more politer than the story was rong and the words Jeasues & Christ and god damit that is all that some of them can learn to here them use it its natural to them but then that is the unwashed ploughmen tribe which is born of Divels imps or poison wasps which is lead by the dvel himself I have shown your book to a few men which have nothing but prase for it and every one that I am talking to wants to know more about it but for my part I fail to find out any thing I could say who it is or who you have selected to be figer to go by the only things the gowing down steps to the pump for water and also the gates & the old walls of the house whare Andies father & mother lived and also altie crie & the roads and signposts & the smithy & the school & the water pool at Low Malzie and the name of the farm Andie went to first but thare was a Ladie rote a noval some time ago used the same name as you do but then it is a field on High Malzie which is a hill and in the corner thare used to be a house that is going past High Malzie up to the foot of the Earlies

roadend with well on the other side of the roand the bend past High
Malzie the pump, steps, gates, rod ends and coathouse is all I can
trace but then I am not shure other places maybe simler whither I can
trace parts the whole thing well done and very interesting, and well
done carry on for the first I must well done. Your phota looks nice in
your paper now John cary on god bliss you . . .

. . . now I give you the news all the people here is divided in
opinion with the story some think why should you select the
ploughman others say it is good and true and happens every day
yet but taken no notice off but thos who has those old tumble down
houses & cant get them repared thinks it good as thay cant get them
made better but now the County Councle has got wakened up and
going to see to it, hope it lasts, after all I do not think when you rote
it you thought that it would caus so much a stir but the book is
eagerly read by every body round here and those that got other
papers changed to the Sunday Mall so the paper man has more than
doubled thair sails still the majority says to me it is good however it is
young yet, todays S Mall the critc is more better but the gilty ones
says most last sundy mail one man a McCubbon rights against it but
than he has a brother which has done the exact same thing his wifes
sister had 2 children to him and than the woman that figered in the
fight with the 2 McLudes that was up at Wiloart had a child to him so
you see the story hits hard on those, as some says the boys name was
not Walker and never lived in Drumlin but in High Barness and his
name was Smith but then thay are rong, but every one is looking at
the story as a great thing to help the G Gazzette says nothing thay did
not put any letters but refused to print them saying it was very like
the cothouses in the district. Mrs Fitzonans my sister from Conmock
was reading the story & hir Daughter wanted hir mother to tell hir
who the J McNeillie was that rote the story as the people in New
Comnock was reading it and newe she was McNeillie the railway
men thare most of them from W Shire was asking who you ware but
thay will know by now as thay ware taken on with it but as your
Uncle peter says the people from W Shire will now be catching over
thair slums of Coathouses. Well cary on you have some parts in the
book which is very good equal with the best of writers so now carry
on John make good and after this washing up give out a good story
which will make up for all the set back you give the ploughman.

Today the talk about your book has aroused a great ado getting it
coted from the pulpits in the churches of port paterick, Kirkmaiden,

and today Wigtown Sorbie Mochrum it is going to be a great ado and everybody making enqurey who you are. One remark I heard was who this John McNeillie was as thay did know him but A Barrett put the crowner on it auch you cen him it was yon boy that used to com his holidays and ran about half naked, well stick in if you do no good to yourself you are shure to do some good to others that is whare you shine in wakening up and showing the publick the houses & condicions people lives in . . .

. . . my word but your book rose a carrieshang got on commissioners to envestigate if you ware right all the houses in the out of the way places was looked into also the old house you said Andy was born in so commishuners returned a verdict only too true so that finished the job that go so many houses as you as you said that thare was no use going further only too true you mad a good hit for your first, last sunday was the last in the sunday male I hope your next one will as good a sucess every body knows it and knows who rote it and your apearns last time helped it grately every body from the one end of the county to the other knows you now the station groom you fairly mismarised him he swares by you carry on do more if you can as thare has been no one yet roused up Wigtownshire that are looking for you to do it if you only roused up the county of Wigtown you would be the white headed boy as all the big ones would like you to do I may give you some information and when you come here again Uncle Charley is going to traill you round

Old John McNeillie was not an uncritical reader, as is already shown, even if he didn't choose to notice the resemblance between himself and the hard taskmaster old McKeown of Drumlin, Andy's first employer, or the savage representation of his son, the author's father, as the 'docken'. . . . Nor were old John's brothers Charles, James and Peter uncritical. But they were none the less 'in thair glea' about *Wigtown Ploughman*. It was the swearing that seemed most to trouble them: 'Uncle peter says if you had cept the swearing out of it, it was better than Crockets'.

But the old man, who 'had it all read over the second time and may I say part of third' found that 'every time it reads better to me and I am fairly taken on with it and as for serten words the first time read looked bad but than second time every word was neaded for the story with out them it would not have shown the story right for that is the coman discourse . . . it could not been beter made up no body ever tried a book of the kind before so that took up the attention go ahead there is always some to criticise'. It stirred him to look forward, on 5 May and on 12 May, to be up at Newton Stewart and Wigtown, to bring back news. He was also ready to give business advice: '. . . you tell me you are getting good offers but I advise you look well into all those offers for mind you a fulish head gives the poor feet much to do think them over your success will come no mater if you ceep a gard on yourself. mind the freedom of our own will is not all that is wanted a man may look and never see until tumbles into <u>what</u>'.

As to the fighting, there were even that week past two cases in Wigtown court that bore out the kind of confrontations that occur in the novel, both over women: '. . . the one about the farm manager was the two McQuade boys and a miligan McQuade one of them got badly laid out with a bad eye he is not washing yet and it was all over a Brigs woman who three of them wanted to go home with when the fight took place on the road past big Capnoch road end so the sunday male makes a point to couple it with your story and says perhaps on the same road well not far apart any how . . .'.

In fact what the *Sunday Mail* of 23 April 1939 reported, under a strapline FARM ROAD FIGHTS, as part of a longer article, was this: '*Wigtown Ploughman* has for its scene a portion of the Machars district of Wigtownshire. In the story the author describes a fight on a farm road. Last week at Wigtown Sheriff Court the story of an altercation between a labourer and a motor driver was related. It might have happened on the same road! In the same court a labourer was fined for an assault on an assistant farmer. Again it might have been a page from *Wigtown Ploughman*.'

MY GRANDFATHER BY
JOHN MCNEILLIE

from The Countryman *July* 1939 Vol. XIX no. 2

Whether you meet him 'at the back of a hill' counting ewes, or bidding at the market, he will be wearing a heavy suit of grey-green tweeds, the material of which has been woven from his own sheep. He is a huge man with an unruly white beard and you must look for him among the oldest farmers in the Machars of Wigtownshire.

Since the days when I slept in an adjoining bedroom and used to call to him, 'Don't let the Germans get me, gran'pa', I have memories of his awakening and arousing the household with a shout of 'Hey-hum-herry'. He greets every morning with the same vocalized yawn, and the sound of it is heard regularly just before the byreman's alarm clock rings in the loft.

He has never been ill a day in his life, but once he was forced to stay in bed because he fell from the spring cart and injured a leg. Even then he was not to be beaten for, with great ingenuity, he rigged up a system of mirrors so that he could see 'ben the hoose', and make sure everyone was hard at work. Because he could not get about he was irritable and, because he is such a giant of a man, it required someone very strong and with more than average patience – for he cursed a lot – to make his bed. After a day or two, when his irritability became more pronounced, he thought out one of his many inventions – a rope and pulley tackle, by means of which he could hoist himself above the bed and remain suspended while the sheets and blankets were changed, hanging on, as he told me afterwards, 'lik' grim daith'.

Apart form the time he 'laid abed' he has always risen early and walked downstairs in his stockinged feet for his porridge, which he sups from a great bowl, spooning into it a bowlful of milk. After seeing the churns 'doon the road' he returns for his breakfast of ham and eggs, and halfway through the morning, giving the ploughman brief respite, he goes back to the house for his cup of tea and heavily-buttered bread. Dinner is at twelve. Two blasts on his whistle announce this to the work-folk, and he then sits down to the broth, chicken, potatoes or 'hash', but never pork, for 'pigs are dirty baistes, boy'. In the afternoon he will work somewhere about the steading, repairing a reaper, patching a henhouse roof, or grinding corn in the barn, which is equipped with a donkey-engine to drive the mill – once one of the many walk-mills in the neighbourhood. Half-way through the afternoon he takes tea again with bread and jam or honey, and at five it is time for a second helping of porridge. The porridge is made during the afternoon. He has a first helping in the evening and the remainder heated up for the following day. When the kye have been milked he has supper and a smoke, and goes to bed to sleep like a top until four or five next morning.

When there are 'veesitors' he will sit and talk, or take a hand of whist, playing cautiously as he has farmed, and sometimes cheating with the pack shuffled and manipulated in his great hands. When he amuses himself in this way he smiles and denies all accusations.

I first realized his strength some four years ago. He was about seventy-four then. During one of his morning jobs, he was building a 'slap' across the front of a shed in which he wished to confine a sow about to 'pig'. I saw him walking from the stack-yard with a full-sized railway sleeper under each arm. Eager to lend a hand, I hurried to him and told him to give me one before he strained his heart. 'Here then, boy', he said, and I put my arms round the sleeper. I couldn't even hold it, and I was eighteen and strong for my age. It fell and badly bruised my toe, and earned me a whimsical smile that made me regret my eagerness. I have seen him push youngsters aside when they have failed to lift enormous sacks of oats. Usually he cursed them and walked off with bag across his shoulders. His shoulders are very broad, for his chest measurement is forty-nine inches, but the most fascinating about him is the size of his hands. They have been broadened, first by the fore-hammer, for he was a blacksmith before he came to the farm, and then by the plough stilts.

He never prides himself on his strength, except to say that when he was an apprentice smith in a certain village, the policeman was a 'pair wee bit body', and the publican used to send for the smith's apprentice to clear his house of fighting Irish harvesters and other wild folk. The one thing he does pride himself on is his ability to foretell the weather, and I have known him give a forecast for forty days ahead, and not be wrong by a day; and he did not merely foretell rain or sunshine. Sometimes, when he is looking at a sunset for a weather sign in the sky, he will survey the horizon and say 'The kerry's risin', boy'. What the 'kerry' is exactly, I have never been able to discover, but invariably he foretells good weather when his mysterious 'kerry' rises, and good weather there is, in spite of what may be said in the weather forecast brought to him by a recently-acquired wireless, which he says 'maistly talks tae itsel'.

When I was three years old, he measured me from the sole of my foot to the knee joint, as they measure horses, I believe, and he said then that I would grow to be six feet tall. I stand five feet eleven and three-quarter inches. He believes in cow dung as a healer, and fortifies his old-fashioned beliefs by first pouring lysol into a cut. Once while playing in a barn, I trod on the rusted prongs of a fork hidden in some straw. The horse-doctor was visiting us at the time, and my grandfather instructed him to remove the rust, and perhaps infected flesh, in order that I might be save from the danger of lockjaw. The horse-doctor did the job with a razor, while I was firmly clamped between my grand-father's knees, and told to keep quiet, or he would 'bumph my backside'. I kept quiet – only a wean would have cried.

My brother, wearing Wellington boots, slipped in the byre and cut his cheek just below the eyelid, so that the wound opened and folded over the eye. He bled badly, but grandfather picked him up, placed him under his 'oxter' and held him under the pump while the pony was harnessed. Finally, he drove the seven miles to town with the child still under his arm, and his fingers folding the wound closed. The doctor managed to stitch it and now the scar is almost invisible.

Besides being a shrewd farmer, my grandfather has a flair for invention. Among many inventions I have heard him claim that of the mousetrap – a story which he tells with a smile in his beard. He did, however, invent a 'scuffler' which brought him a good deal of money. He told me that he actually 'stole the idea' from a gentleman farmer who was 'ower blin' tae see the thing himsel'. The farmer has almost invented the implement, and, according to my grandfather's story, asked him for advice. While grand-father was giving his advice he suddenly saw the solution to the mechanical problem. Subsequently he disclosed that he knew the solution and would reveal it on consideration, 'for it's a nae-use thing wantin' the secret A hae discovered'. The signatures 'o' twa men A kent wudna gie by me' were placed on an agreement with the result that he secured his own smithy and a considerable proportion of the profits. He has told me, with a sly smile, that his contribution to the scuffler in its first crude stages consisted of two milk churns. Being a smith, one of the patentees, and a clever man into the bargain, he made scufflers for farmers in all parts of Scotland, and eventually sold out to a firm of implement makers while the patent was still of considerable value.

Before deserting the anvil for the plough, before the War, my grandfather set about making his own farm tools. He made ploughs, some of them models of his best ploughs which had won ploughing matches time and time again; he made drill and chain harrows, a grubber, drill ploughs and many other things. So he started farming with the best possible equipment – hand-wrought implements. Later he shoed his own horses. He has no use for the electric-milker or 'ony o' they new-fangled contraptions', and he has done as well as, if not better than, most of his neighbours who have forsaken the old methods.

The potato crop presented a problem one year. There was always difficulty in removing the large coatings of earth and sorting the crop for pig-food and market, as well as seed, so, taking a pointer from the winnowing machine, he invented and constructed a wooden potato riddle, driven by a handle like the fanners. Various sized meshes sorted the potatoes from the earth, the small potatoes from the remainder, and marketing potatoes from those from which he selected seed.

One of his ideas which was the talk of his neighbours was a rope-making device. The rope is coiled with two hammer-shaped wooden tools and is made of many strands of binder twine. He initiated his ploughman and byreman into the process, and on wet days they make stack-ropes, plough-lines and so on in the byre. I don't think he buys rope even now.

For a long time he produced bacon of a very fine flavour and puzzled the bacon company. He puzzled the chemist too, because of the large quantities of iodine he bought. He told me that some farmers buy seaweed, but, because the right kind of seaweed is hard to come by, he doctored the pig-mash with iodine, which amounted to the same thing in the end. How he doctors the mash he has never disclosed, but his bacon is always in great demand.

In order that I should have farming instilled into me at an early age, he fitted his binder with an extra seat, and I rode uphill and downhill with him through my first 'working' harvest when I was five years of age. About fifty acres of oats were cut that harvest and I was on the binder through every sheaf of it.

He never struck me, although there must have been times when I sorely tried his patience; but his threat to treat me to the binder-whip – a long cane with even longer leather thing – was more than enough. When I misbehaved he used to fold his 'Scottish Farmer' and wag it at me, and I was silent until bedtime. Most of his workfolks said he was a hard man to work under, but they were always very fond of him, and when he raged, gave him pathetic and offended looks until they were forgiven.

Although he drove his men relentlessly, he worked equally hard himself. Even now he does his bit in the harvest field, and when there is a breakdown, he takes the reaper or the binder, whichever is broken, and drives to the smithy, where he takes off his jacket and gets down to his own job at the forge, in order to get the work done quickly. When the smith meets with a difficulty he walks to the farm with the 'job' over his shoulder, or sends for my grandfather, who points out the right method. If the smith is slow in grasping the idea, grandfather takes the job from him and does it himself. This happens during harvest, at the beginning of ploughing – in fact, all through the year.

Regarded locally as something of a prophet, an inventor, and a wise farmer, he also enjoys the reputation of being a story-teller. Story-telling must run in the family, for he told me that his grandfather was the only man in his neighbourhood who could read, and it was his custom to read books and letters to gatherings of the less gifted. He also told stories by the light of rushes burning in sweet oil.

My grandfather's stories are numerous, and, I swear, could not be bettered, even by his grandfather. That of the cancer-doctor is most interesting.[1]

Grandfather, who believes the story, tells me his predecessor at his first smithy met the cancer-doctor, who offered to remove a growth from his cheek. The smith refused to have the growth taken away, even at the small cost of half a sovereign, and died within a short time. The touch of romance in this story is that, after keeping alive a noble lord, who was a victim of the disease, and refusing a pension and a free house for his services, the cancer-doctor died without divulging his secret, because he had never met the man with the 'right' palm – the sign that the man was a fit person to receive the secret. Grandfather's habit is to tell stories in the twilight, when he sits before a great peat fire. While telling his story he smokes and holds his stick between his knees.

Another story is that of the fidelity and intelligence of his old Irish horse, Bob. Now Bob is 'blind of an eye', black, and extremely cunning. My grandfather frequently lectures him when he finds him dodging work, by just moving enough to keep his trace chains taut while he is yoked in team harness. On these occasions Bob's ears go flat back on his head and he pulls like a youngster. Just before the War Bob was lively and light enough to be put in a trap, and my grandfather drove him to market. One market day grandfather met a few of his cronies and found himself unusually sleepy on the way home. So sleepy

1 See *My Childhood* (2004) for a version of this story.

was he that he had to lie down in the bottom of the trap and allow Bob to take care of them both. Bob knew the long road home well, and when he came to the turning to the farm, he fixed his teeth over the gate chain, opened the gate and successfully steered the trap through. He repeated this performance twice, for there are three gates on the way up to the farm, and finally halted at the steps up to the house, where he waited until grandfather was aroused.

For this and other loyal services, Bob has my grandfather's solemn promise that when he becomes too old to graze in the field to which he has now been retired, he will be shot. I have been present when my grandfather has inspected Bob in the field, and renewed his promise.

Another of his old horses enjoys the same promise. He is Tammy. Tammy was a trotter, at one time known all over the county, for he won every trotting race for which he was entered, except one, in which he finished second because of a bad handicap. Tammy will never be sold or allowed to suffer. One of Tammy's greatest deeds was done when grandfather fell from the spring cart and lay on the frozen road until someone came and lifted him from between the horse's forefeet. Until help came, Tammy licked his master's face, and obeyed his instructions to stand still on the brow of a slippery hill.

Although he has not used a gun for a long time, my grandfather now and then, when I was small, waged war on rabbits. It was his wish that when the time came I should be able to handle a gun in the right way, and therefore, when he hunted, I walked behind at a safe distance, carrying the heavy butt and breach of a converted rifle.

I worshipped my grandfather and today I value his sound countryman's philosophy. Once I stood by his knee to hear worldly advice, and now I receive it in letters. His latest counsel is:

'Never let the next man ken ye, an haud yer tongue till ye are shair ye ha'e somethin' worth the sayin'. Never tak' tae strong drink, for it was the doonfa' o' a' oor folks. They were a' fules when they had the drink in them'.

BIBLIOGRAPHY

This listing of books (and in the case of John McNeillie short stories and some journalism) should be supplemented by reference to: *Country Life* (1953–1993). A complete list of Ian Niall's journalism would be too extensive to entertain here. See also *Ian Niall: Part of his Life* (Clutag Press, 2007) by Andrew McNeillie.

JOHN McNEILLIE

NOVELS
Wigtown Ploughman: Part of his Life (Putnam, March 1939)
Glasgow Keelie (Putnam, April 1940)
Morryham Farm (Putnam, January 1941)

SHORT STORIES
'The Farrowing' *Spectator* 21 April 1939
'The Very Devil's Own Fun' *News Chronicle* 3 May 1939
'Harvest Moon' *Spectator* 17 November 1939
'The Coming of Jim' *Spotlight* 19 December 1947
'The Cadgers' *Spotlight* 16 January 1948
'Boy in the Beanfield' first published in *My Childhood* (2004)
'Tales of the Smith'   ..   ..
'The Cancer Doctor'   ..   ..
'Did you ever hear the like?   ..   ..

MEMOIR
My Childhood (Clutag Press, 2004)

ESSAYS
'Rural Authors – 49. *John Steinbeck by the Author of* Wigtown Plough-
    man *The Countryman*, October 1939 ('In this note a British rural
    realist writes of an American rural realist whose best book has just
    been published in this country.')

' "My Grandfather" by John McNeillie, Author of *Wigtown Ploughman*'
  The Countryman July 1939

IAN NIALL
No Resting Place (Heinemann, 1948) and for Paul Rotha's film of the
  book, BFI
Tune on a Melodeon (Heinemann, 1948)
Foxhollow (Heinemann, 1949)
The Poacher's Handbook (Heinemann, 1950)
The Deluge (Heinemann, 1951)
Fresh Woods (Heinemann, 1951)
Pastures New (Heinemann, 1952)
The Boy who saw Tomorrow (Heinemann, 1952)
A Tiger Walks (Heinemann, 1960)
The New Poacher's Handbook (Heinemann, 1960)
Trout from the Hills (Heinemann, 1961)
The Harmless Albatross (Heinemann, 1961)
Hey Delaney! (Heinemann, 1962)
The Gamekeeper (Heinemann, 1965)
The Way of a Countryman (Heinemann, 1965)
The Country Blacksmith (Heinemann, 1966)
A Galloway Childhood (Heinemann, 1967)
A Fowler's World (Heinemann, 1968)
A Galloway Shepherd (Heinemann, 1970)
The Village Policeman (Heinemann, 1971)
Around My House (Heinemann, 1973)
A London Boyhood (Heinemann, 1974)
One Man and his Dogs (Heinemann, 1975)
To Speed the Plough (Heinemann, 1977)
The Idler's Companion (Heinemann, 1978)
The Forester (Heinemann, 1979)
Portrait of a Country Artist (Gollancz, 1980)
Tunnicliffe's Countryside (Clive Holloway Books, 1983)
Feathered Friends (Chatto, 1984)
Country Matters (Gollancz, 1984)
Ian Niall's Complete Angler (Heinemann, 1986)
Ian Niall's Country Notes (Octopus Books, 1987)
English Country Traditions (V&A, 1990)

Fresh Woods and Pastures New Introduced by Andrew McNeillie (Little Toller Books, 2012)

FOR CHILDREN
Fishing for Trouble (Heinemann, 1969)
The Owlhunters (Heinemann, 1969)
Wildlife of Field and Hedgeside (Heinemann, 1970)
Wildlife of Moor and Mountain (Heinemann, 1970)
Wildlife of River and Marsh (Heinemann, 1971)
Wildlife of Wood and Spinney (Heinemann, 1971)

INTRODUCTIONS AND FOREWORDS
'Introduction', *Tunnicliffe: A Sketchbook of Birds* (Gollancz, 1979)
'Foreword', *Shorelands Summer Diary* (Gollancz, 1985)
'Foreword', BB: *A Fisherman's Bedside Book* (White Lion Books, 1994)
'Introduction', C. J. Munroe: *The Smallholders Guide* (David & Charles, 1979)

AS BY C. J. MUNROE
The Smallholder's Guide (David & Charles, 1979)